FOR THE LOVE
OF EMILY

BY

JOY WOOD

To Allison,
Thankyou so much
for your support
Love & very best wishes
Joy Wood

Published in 2015 by Feedaread.com Publishing – Arts Council funded
    Copyright © Joy Wood
     First Edition

The author has asserted her moral right under the Copyright, Designs and Patents Act, 1988 to be identified as the author of this work.

All characters and events in this publication other than those clearly in the public domain are fictitious and any resemblance to real persons, living or dead, is purely coincidental.

A CIP catalogue record for this title is available from the British Library

To my husband, John.

You have made me laugh, wiped my tears, hugged me tight, watched me succeed, seen me fail, and kept me strong. You promised my mum and dad that you'd take care of me, and you always have done.

Acknowledgements

I could not have written, For the Love of Emily without the assistance of so many. It has been an incredible journey for me, and I am overwhelmed by the support that I have received.

I will be forever grateful to Stephen Kitt and John Allington for their witty inspiration, to Michelle, my stepdaughter for her constant enthusiasm which has spurred me on, and to my stepson James and his fiancé, Veneta, for their input into the amazing book cover.

To Helen, Jackie, Olwyn and Tess, who have had to endure my endless obsession with this book, and never once complained; the drinks are on me! They truly are great friends and I'm lucky to have them.

And last but by no means least, an enormous thank you to my dear friend, Lynette Creswell. Her selfless encouragement and belief in me has helped turn my dream of writing a book, into reality. I will be forever in her debt.

Table of Contents

PART ONE

Kate

PROLOGUE

Where the hell is the anaesthetist?

. . . beep . . .

Do theatre know we're on our way?

. . . beep . . .

Tell them the casualty has been shot twice in the chest.

. . . beep . . .

BP's dropping further, speed up the drip.

. . . beep. . .

Squeeze the Ambu bag and get some oxygen in.

. . . beep . . .

Keep pressure on the wounds.

. . . beep . . .

Have we got a name yet?

. . . beep . . .

Oh God it hurts . . . help me.

. . . beep . . .

I can't move, please stop the pain.

. . . beep . . .

Why is my mother here...she's smiling but she's dead?

. . . beep . . .

It's so dark and cold...please stop the pain.

. . . beep . . .

Are you here?

. . . beep . . .

I never told you I love you.

. . . beep . . .

Can you hear me now?

. . . beep . . .

I love you

Beeeeeeeeeeeeeeeeeeeeeeeeeeeeeeeeeeeeeeeeeeeeeeeee
eeeeeeeeee

In the solitary hospital chapel, Emily closed her eyes and bowed her head. She'd seen the face of death staring back at her and prayed like she'd never prayed before. This time she didn't ask for anything for herself, she just asked God to help as she didn't want anyone to die. The sound of the gunshots still echoed in her ears, and the sight of all the blood had terrified her so much she had thrown up all over the carpet.

A hand touched her shoulder reminding her that she wasn't alone. She turned towards the housekeeper and tearfully mumbled, "I'm frightened."

Dorothy nodded, "I know love, we all are, but we must put our trust in the doctors and nurses."

Emily remembered the hospital programmes she'd watched on television when everything turned out fine in the end, "Like on Casualty?" she hiccupped.

Dorothy reached into her handbag, "Yes, something like that sweetheart," she handed her a tissue, "come on now, blow your nose, we need to get you home."

As she shuffled along the narrow pew, something was still puzzling her, "Dorothy, what is a triangle of passion?" She looked into Dorothy's eyes but saw the familiar look she'd seen in adults so many times. It usually meant they didn't want her to know something.

She watched Dorothy swallow, "Where have you heard that?"

"I heard you say it to the policeman."

"Oh, did I?" Dorothy answered, closing the heavy chapel door behind them, "I'm not sure what I said. I was so shocked at the time, I really can't remember."

"That's what you said, and then you said . . . erm . . . three into two didn't fit and there was always going to be an odd one out." She waited but Dorothy remained silent.

"Please tell me what it means?"

Dorothy shook her head, "Not right now love, maybe tomorrow, but just not right now."

CHAPTER 1

Ezzio was holding a tumbler of fine malt whisky and knocked back the amber nectar, but it was far too slow in hitting the spot. He'd just been informed that there was a problem with the projector, which would delay his presentation for five to ten minutes. His firm warning that it had better not be any longer than that forced the technician into a hasty retreat with a mumbled promise of trying to speed things up.

He was irritated that his speech had been delayed as he'd hoped to be leaving by now. The elaborate function was a celebration event following the merger of his company Marin Enterprises with the Milner Conglomerate. All attending in their finery were employees from both companies. His current lover Ali was working the room charmingly, eager to show all that she had her man. The initial attraction to Ali had waned and if he was truthful the only thing keeping them together was sex, which he liked a lot of without the long-term commitment. Ali, he knew sensed that the relationship was coming to an end and was just clinging on, which made the whole situation twice as bad. The parting would happen soon and he'd be pounds lighter as usual, as he always made provision for each ex because part of him felt guilty that he couldn't commit. Ali would pout and cry and beg him to stay with her, but in the end, she would settle for the pay out and move on to the next guy, they always did.

He tried to analyse why he was so unsettled. Having carved a prosperous life for himself full of discipline, enterprise and sheer graft. He thrived on the challenges of hard work and enjoyed the success of acquiring companies, but did that truly make him happy anymore, he wasn't sure? Following his parents' death in an automobile accident seven years earlier he'd become a loner, and to this day remained so. The caring, loving gene seemed to have passed him by, so marriage and children didn't feature in his life even though that was pretty much the agenda of every female he dated.

Wouldn't it be refreshing to meet a woman who would look at Ezzio Marin and not just see his bank balance? Do such women exist? If they did he'd never met one. With the exception of his mother, of course, who was beautiful inside and out. Memories of his mother and father were faint now, and that cataclysmic day when he was told about their deaths was etched on his mind forever. As if that wasn't enough, there was further misfortune to follow. He had quickly learned that his father had made some poor business investments and had an array of debts, therefore once the estate was settled, there was very little left of an inheritance. At twenty-three not only had he lost his beloved parents and his family home, he was also broke. By twenty-five he'd turned his life around completely.

Circulating the room, he smiled and chatted to each employee and guest, trying not to leave anyone out. Politely they acknowledged him, and inwardly he smirked knowing the stories they would be telling about him. He'd heard them all before, they just became more exaggerated with each new company he acquired, rather like Chinese whispers. The media didn't help either. Pilloried in the press for being ruthless and autocratic, they seemed to relish stories such as him sacking an entire workforce from a newly acquired company, changing the job description and titles, and making the employees reapply for their jobs. The fact that he only appointed thirty percent was the biggest headline, but nobody reported that the unsuccessful applicants all received generous redundancy packages. They didn't stop at his professional life either. Almost daily, utter rubbish was printed about his appetite for the ladies, indeed, according to the gossip columns, his reputation in the bedroom was almost as legendary as in the boardroom.

He placed his empty glass on the tray of a passing waiter and let out a deep sigh, just another hour, and then hopefully he could be on his way. The merger of the two companies had been hard work with months of fierce negotiations, and while he would have preferred full control, his new business partner Darlene was a force to be reckoned with, so he'd have to settle on fifty percent for the time being.

Darlene Milner, a formidable businesswoman whom he disliked intensely. Admired by many for the way in which she had taken over her husband Edward Milner's corporate empire when he succumbed to Alzheimer's disease, she had developed her entrepreneurial skills and became a successful CEO. However, like many other businesses, her empire was hit hard by the recession resulting in the need for additional investment in her company. Her husband resided in a care home, virtually a vegetable, so, if anything she had to be respected for coping with that. The worm in the hole was Darlene's son Piers Milner, who was becoming a liability and, unbeknown to his mother, was selling Milner stock to fund his lavish lifestyle, which Ezzio was purchasing under the anonymity of one of his other companies. Yes, it was just a question of waiting and he would soon have full control, and then he would see the last of Darlene Milner and her overbearing son once and for all.

His eyes swept around the room and he absorbed the glamour of the young dressed to impress, whilst the old, dripping in bling and wearing designer clothes, were trying unsuccessfully to lose the years. Fashionable females were on show like catwalk models displaying zero waistlines and vast amounts of tanned flesh. There were the faithful wives supporting their spouses, and the single folk in their finery trying to grab a catch. Basically, it was the same old routine he'd seen so many times before, just a different venue . . . and then he saw her.

How could a woman be so physically striking? She was absolutely beautiful. His eyes were drawn to her as she engaged in conversation with Darlene's group. She was tall for a female with a sensational figure, which immediately attracted his attention. Being 6ft 4 inches himself, he favoured tall women, and the fact she was also blonde, ticked another box. His interested eyes lingered on her long blonde hair coiled on top of her head displaying a swan-like neck all the way down to her cleavage. The black dress she was wearing clung to her figure as though it had been painted onto her body. He licked his lips, quickly deducing that the dress couldn't be worn with a bra, guessing her achingly touchable breasts had probably been surgically enhanced as they appeared full and pert. He wasn't an expert on women's clothing, but he had paid thousands of pounds in female credit card bills over the years and escorted plenty of women out on dates enough times to recognise designer clothes when he saw them. The cut of the dress emphasised her figure in all the right places, which supported his theory about the label. His mind exploded with curiosity as he felt his male response to her femininity kick in; who was she?

As if aware she was being observed, the woman turned and glanced across at him. For a brief second their eyes locked and then, just as quickly, she turned away. Definitely not one of those lingering 'come and get me' looks, he thought with an inward smile. He continued to stare at her until Ali caught his attention by placing her hand firmly on his lower arm. Glancing down at her long, dark-painted fingernails, he felt a stab of distaste at her touch and without a second thought, brushed her hand away. Ali was becoming high maintenance, another reason he was beginning to tire of her.

Despite numerous waiters circulating with trays of sparkling drinks, Ezzio needed something stronger and headed for the bar. He spotted David his trusted friend sitting on a bar stool and made his way over.

David smiled, "Hi old buddy, great night. Can I get you a drink?"

"Please. I'll have a whisky and a dry white wine for Ali," he said, pulling up a stool while the bartender mixed the drinks.

Ezzio's eyes gestured towards the function area, "There's a female in Darlene's party, mid-twenties, blonde about 5ft 10ish, designer dress, stunning looks, do you know who she is?"

David nodded, "I'd stick to Ali if I was you, mate. That blonde is definitely off limits, even to you." He took a gulp of his drink.

Intrigued, Ezzio pressed further, "Why, is she married, I didn't see a ring?"

David's lips twitched, breaking into a smile, "No, I don't believe she's married."

"Then what's so funny?"

David clamped a hand on Ezzio's shoulder, "The fact that Ezzio Marin is interested in the one woman he can't have."

"Who says I couldn't have her?" Ezzio grinned, enjoying their playful banter, "do you want to bet?"

David shrugged, "Look, much as I love to thrash you on the squash court, on this occasion, although really tempting, I'll not bet with you. There'll only be one outcome and I'm a dead cert to win as I know the odds."

Ezzio rose to the challenge, "How can you be so sure? I'm young, unmarried, and as you know my vast wealth always attracts the ladies, what makes you think this one is so different? She's female, no wedding ring, I'd say worth a go. Shame I'm here with Ali, otherwise, I could get to know her a little better tonight."

David looked thoughtful for a second, and then nodded, "I'll tell you what, when you've made your speech, let's go over and I'll make the introductions. If after meeting her in the flesh you manage to get her phone number, I'll give you . . . ," he paused trying to think of a suitable reward, "a crate of Moet, how about that?"

Ezzio didn't doubt for a second he wouldn't be able to extract her contact details. It wasn't over-confidence, it was years of female heads turning his way once they learned about his incredible wealth.

A male voice interrupted his thoughts, "Excuse me, Mr Marin, we're set up for your speech, whenever you're ready."

"Thank you, I'll come now." Placing his drink on the bar, he stepped down from the stool and winked at David, "Okay, you make the introductions."

Ezzio was used to public speaking and delivered a powerful presentation highlighting the benefits of the merger and underlined it was a shared venture with Darlene Milner. He emphasised the need for change, and while he couldn't rule out redundancies, he didn't envisage any initially, citing early retirement opportunities. At one point he saw the blonde again, standing quietly, looking at the stage area but not really looking at him, and definitely not meeting his eyes. Maybe David was right and this wasn't going to be quite as easy as he thought?

Applause followed him as he left the stage and Darlene stepped up. Normally he would kiss a female on the cheek but he didn't want to kiss her, he absolutely loathed the woman. At the first opportunity, he vowed to be rid of her and had already started the ball rolling, so he just needed to bide his time.

Ali, his ever-faithful girlfriend was waiting as he stepped down, "Oh, darling what an uplifting speech, you had me believing you meant every word."

He stared as if he was seeing her properly for the first time. She had a slight slur in her voice and he hadn't missed the sarcasm. He felt she looked decidedly unattractive in the red dress with matching lipstick. She was a stunning woman there was no doubt about that, but he was seeing her through critical eyes all of a sudden. He knew he was to blame as he became bored quite easily, and like most women he came into contact with, Ali wanted more than he was prepared to commit to.

He took a deep breath in, "I'll have my driver take you home while I finish up here. I have a few more people to speak to then I'll come to you." He ushered her to the cloakroom for her wrap, reluctantly agreeing to call at her apartment when he'd finished, but doubting that he would.

He returned to the bar and found David still looking ridiculously amused, "Is she still here?" he inquired, half thinking he may have missed her.

David nodded, "Yep she's over there talking with Darlene's party."

"Come on then, let's do it," he urged.

They headed to the alcove and Darlene extracted herself from her conversation to greet them both. He knew all in the group except the blonde.

Both David and he politely acknowledged the guests and Ezzio turned smiling to the object of his desire to await a formal introduction. For a second he caught his breath. He'd recognised her physical attributes from a distance but nothing could have prepared him for her stunning features up-close. She was incredibly beautiful with a perfectly symmetrical face and a full mouth defined with the lightest shade of pink. She looked directly at him with the most amazing green eyes. Were they green contact lenses, and those curly long eyelashes, were they false? It was clear that her eyes were enhanced cosmetically, but he knew that even the most expensive makeup palettes would have a naturally beautiful canvas to work with.

Darlene gave him one of the cheesy smiles she seemed to favour and gently touched the blonde's arm, "Ezzio I'd like you to meet Kate Jones, who's a really good friend of mine, Kate, this is Ezzio Marin my new business partner."

He held out his hand which Kate took as etiquette dictated, "It's a pleasure to meet you, Mr Marin." She smiled but he noted that it didn't quite reach her amazing green eyes.

"Please, it's Ezzio, and the pleasure is mine I can assure you." He held onto her hand for a second longer than necessary and she hastily retrieved it, clearly not welcoming his touch. This amused him as he knew he had been gifted with looks and height which appealed to most females, yet evidently not this one.

David took Darlene's arm and moved slightly away which gave him the space he needed to speak to her alone. "I know this is an old cliché and excuse me for saying it but have we met before, your face does seem familiar?" He was genuine; it suddenly felt as if he did know her. Maybe it was because he hadn't been able to keep his eyes off her since he spotted her across the room?

She was quickly dismissive, "No I don't think so. I'm sure I would have remembered if we had, particularly as your name is so distinctive." She smiled but not directly at him, her gaze went to the V at the base of his throat.

He pressed further, "Do you model, maybe I've seen your face on a billboard or something?"

"No, I've never modelled. I've probably just got one of those familiar faces," she shrugged indifferently changing the subject quickly, "It's been a lovely evening, the speeches from yourself and Darlene were inspiring, I'm sure the employees will be reassured by your vision for the future." She smiled again.

He was mesmerised by the lovely diction and tone of her voice; she just oozed sex appeal. He nodded, "Thank you, I hope you're right. There's a high level of anxiety from the staff of both companies, which is precisely the reason for tonight's function." He didn't want to talk about work. He wanted to drag her out of the room to the nearest bed which was so unlike him as he was always so measured in his approach to every aspect of his life, especially sex.

"Would you like to dance?" Not one of his favourite pastimes, but he would be able to touch her legitimately as he felt like a hormonal teenager and if the stirring in his groin was anything to go by, he was behaving like one. No woman had ever made him feel ready quite so quickly.

Her response was a rather swift "No thank you," as her eyes drifted over his shoulder before adding, "It appears my friends are getting ready to leave now."

He didn't imagine the look of relief that crossed her face as she tried to move past him. It aroused his curiosity and he gently touched her arm to halt her immediate progress, "Would you have dinner with me one evening, I really would like to see you again?"

She looked momentarily surprised at his request, and he sensed rejection before it came, "I'm afraid dinner is quite out of the question, now if you will excuse me." Brushing past him, she headed for the cloakroom and his fascinated eyes followed her. He would let her go . . . for now. There was something so elegant about the way she moved, and the dress she wore was cut above her knee and gave him a glimpse of supple legs that appeared to go on forever . . . *I wonder how many men she's wrapped them around?*

Darlene broke his thoughts as she politely wished him goodnight. As he shook her outstretched hand, his mind was elsewhere; there was definitely something familiar about Kate despite her denial that they hadn't met before. *Maybe that's what lust does for you.* He definitely wanted her but clearly, couldn't have her tonight, so he'd call at Ali's on the way home after all.

David coughed, bringing him out of his temporary trance, "Well," he grinned knowingly, "you didn't get her number, did you?"

Ezzio frowned at him, "No, the Marin charm doesn't appear to be working; she definitely wasn't keen to see me again." He was still disgruntled that he hadn't managed to fix up a dinner date.

Amusement was written all over David's face, "I wouldn't take it personally, my friend; it's not your charm that's the problem. You can rest assured she wouldn't be interested in anything you have to offer, even if you were hung like a donkey."

Ezzio couldn't fathom the joke, "What the bloody hell are you going on about, how come you know so much about her anyway?"

"Because, my dear friend," David chuckled, putting his hand playfully on his heart, "it saddens me and every other red-blooded male in the room to have to tell you that the lovely Kate Jones is, in fact, your new business partner's dyke."

CHAPTER 2

As they entered the lift taking them to the penthouse, Darlene looked across at Kate and felt a huge rush of sexual desire. She looked splendid tonight, as always. Her dress showed off her figure to perfection, and her breasts were enticingly close with a cleavage teasingly showing a glimpse of heaven. Kate really was such a stunning woman and she couldn't remember ever being so turned on by another female.

She'd had sexual encounters with women over the years, but none excited her as much as Kate. However, such pleasure came with a price tag. She was a high-class prostitute servicing females only, and she had to pay handsomely for sex with her, but it was an expense she was more than willing to pay as she was addicted to Kate. She recalled Ezzio talking with her earlier and how attractive they'd looked together. "What was Ezzio talking to you about?" Her voice was sharper than she intended.

Kate turned towards her, flicking her tongue casually across her lips, "Your speeches. I was saying that the staff would be reassured by your vision for the future."

Darlene wasn't convinced. "Is that all? I mean, Ezzio didn't come onto you in any way, did he?"

She shook her head, "No of course not, why would he?"

"Because he changes his women like his underwear."

"Well, I wouldn't have thought he'd ever have to pay for sex," Kate laughed lightly, "and if he did, he wouldn't be interested in a gay prostitute, would he?"

"Oh, I don't know. There's many a man that thinks he can convert a lesbian, they think their pricks are irresistible."

The lift opened directly into the hallway of the luxury penthouse suite. Darlene threw her clutch bag on the hall table and turned her eyes hungrily towards Kate.

"I'll make sure he knows you're out of bounds, just in case," she ran her hand up and along her arm, "you are an extremely beautiful woman and I wouldn't want him getting any ideas." She kissed Kate gently, "And just for the record, iron fist Ezzio Marin isn't someone I like at all, so it's best you keep away from him. I know we've gone into business together, but that's as far as it goes."

She watched Kate's eyes narrow and frown, "Iron fist, why do you call him that, he doesn't knock women about, does he?"

Darlene didn't try to control the malice in her voice, "Lord knows what he does. All I do know is that when Ezzio Marin wants something, he can be a real charmer, but I can see straight through him . . . he's just a man with an iron fist in a velvet glove."

For a second neither spoke until she snapped out of her trance-like state and kissed Kate once again, this time for longer and with intent.

"I'm going for a quick shower, darling; these wretched hot flushes are becoming a real nuisance. Put something black and sexy on, would you, and I'll be with you shortly."

Darlene turned the heat on in the power shower and continued to fantasise about Kate. Massaging the shower gel over her body heightened her arousal, and she savoured the sensation of the coarse sponge rubbing across her plump abdomen, heavily scarred from numerous surgical procedures. With scented lather, she caressed her breasts slowly and sensually around her nipples, and then washed her highly sensitive pubic area causing an ache in her lower belly that Kate would take care of.

She'd stopped trying to analyse her craving for Kate, who was like a drug fulfilling every fantasy she'd ever had. Maybe the desire was because she was so successful in business that she subconsciously liked to take a submissive stance, allowing her power in the bedroom. Like now, she needed an orgasm but she knew Kate would prolong the foreplay and make her wait. Never had she felt as sexually aroused as she did around her. As she dried her awakened body with the luxurious Dugi towel, her core throbbed. Quickly, she tied her robe loosely around herself and approached the bedroom, pausing in the doorway.

Kate was sitting at the dresser taking the pins out of her blonde hair and fanning it around her shoulders. Darlene took a moment to observe the stunning sexy vision in front of her. She was holding herself upright like a trained dancer wearing a black basque edged with crimson, tied in corset-fashion down her delightful back. Darlene had a fetish for black, associating it with sex, and was incredibly turned on by it. How could she look so stunning from behind? Her long legs were sheathed in black silk stockings edged at the top with fine lace, and she was still wearing her black stilettos.

Darlene visualised her without the black thong and felt her sex clench. As she stared hungrily at her through the mirror, Kate's green eyes met hers and she gently commanded, "Come here."

Darlene approached the stool with her heart beating excitedly.

Kate swivelled around to face her and instructed, "Take your robe off."

She didn't hesitate, undoing the tie and allowing her robe to drop to the floor.

Kate opened her legs, creating a space, "Kneel down."

She took a step forward, and knelt between her legs staring at her face and beautiful lips, desperate for them to touch hers. Kate took her chin in her hands and gently started kissing her, slowly initially, then increasing the pressure before breaking away. Gently stroking Darlene's cheek with the back of her hand, she whispered, "Who's a hungry lady tonight?"

Darlene nodded and leant forward trying to kiss her again, but she pulled back, "Go and lie on the bed while I finish brushing my hair."

She was being dismissed, only for seconds, but this was part of Kate's foreplay. As Kate turned round to face the mirror, Darlene moved towards the huge ornate bed and impatiently climbed onto it.

Still fiddling about with her hair, Kate seductively commanded, "Bring your knees up and open your legs so I can see all of you."

She was turned on by the visual foreplay, and propped herself up on the endless pillows and opened her legs wide.

Kate met her eyes through the huge glass mirror and asked, "How wet are you, show me?"

Although caressing her own labia excited her, she wouldn't bring herself to a climax; she hated that and was only ever turned on by someone doing it for her.

Kate spun around on the stool to face her, easing her thong off slowly, and opening her legs teasingly to display her female core. She placed her elbow on her thigh, and supporting her chin with her hand, widened her legs provocatively further displaying her neatly waxed mound.

"Okay, kitten, I'm ready to lick every inch of you, if that's what you want?"

Darlene nodded, trembling with anticipation as she watched her kick off her stiletto shoes and walk slowly towards the bed. She loved to be called kitten, and had encouraged Kate to use the endearment during sex as it never failed to enhance her excitement. Hungrily she watched Kate ease herself onto the bed and kneel between her legs. Then she began to feel the glorious sensation of Kate's tongue licking her toes and feet, and slowly working her way up her legs. It was amazing how her knees could be so erogenous. Savouring the stunning vision of her breasts bursting out of the basque and her nipples only just hidden by the material, she groaned, "Don't make me wait . . ."

Kate ignored her, yanking her legs down the bed so she was flat and lay directly on top of her. Their cores rubbed together, and the rough lace material of the basque rubbed on her sensitised skin, enhancing her excitement. As she inhaled Kate's unique smell, she silently acknowledged to herself that every single thing about this woman was an aphrodisiac.

Darlene wriggled as the slow kissing onslaught continued.

"Don't be so impatient," Kate chastised, tasting her nipples and sucking each one slowly. Darlene had always loved sex with females but there was something about this woman that set her above the rest. While she loved every inch of her perfect body, it was her breasts that were such a turn on.

"Show me your tits," she pleaded hungrily.

Kate released her breasts by pulling the basque under them, which gave the impression they were much bigger. Darlene could only stare and marvel at the shape of them as the pink nipples poked tantalisingly at her, "Honey, I really don't want to wait any longer," she begged.

Kate continued kissing her lips and while still massaging her nipples whispered in her ear, "I'm now going to lick you slowly and then when I'm ready I'm going to suck you until you come."

Darlene's speech deserted her as she relished the onslaught on her body, and the gentle kisses to her stomach and groin. She had never had a lover that spent so much time kissing and caressing her tummy, it really was quite wonderful. The anticipation was mind-blowing as she stared down at Kate moving toward her core, and when she felt a finger gently enter her, she clenched her internal muscles around it.

"You're soaking wet, kitten."

Kate gradually moved her head downwards to lick her labia. The sensation was stupefying, stroke after stroke she licked, stopped and licked again. Darlene was in a sexual frenzy with the visual picture of Kate's head pleasuring her. She relished the feeling of her tongue as it moved from her labia, and gently began caressing her clitoris like a butterfly, but she needed more. Lifting her legs onto her shoulders, she pushed her core forward silently begging for release. Kate increased the pressure on her clit pushing hard with her tongue in circular motions. The pleasure was incredible as Kate continued relentlessly, and within seconds pleasure pounded every single nerve ending and she exploded with uncontrollable ecstasy roaring through her body. For a moment, she didn't move wallowing in the feeling of sexual gratification. What was it about this woman that could give such incredible orgasms? Darlene eased her legs down, and pulled her up the bed so that their heads were level and she was back in charge. Kissing Kate gently, she tasted herself on her.

"You really are something; do you know that?"

Kate's gorgeous smile lit up her face as she asked, "Do you want more?"

Tempting as it was, she felt tired, "Not tonight, honey. That was fantastic as always, but I have an early business meeting with Ezzio tomorrow so I need to sleep and be on my toes for that," she yawned, "I've left your money on the dresser. I want you here for seven tomorrow night."

"Okay. I'll be here."

Kate kissed her lightly on the lips and Darlene watched her walk towards the bathroom. Her beautiful body was such a turn on as she craved sexual release on a daily basis at least once, twice if she could get it. Pleasuring herself just didn't do it for her. She needed a woman regularly to meet her needs and she was more than happy to pay. She found great delight in exploring Kate's magnificent body, knowing every inch of it, and her own orgasms were heightened due to the sexuality she oozed. Despite paying for sexual gratification, she had tried to be reciprocal to Kate who played the part well of enjoying being pleasured, but she wasn't totally sure she was satisfied, or if it was all just an act.

She knew little about Kate's life, only that money was her driver and she had to pay handsomely in cash for her, always in cash. While she knew that she had sex with other females for money, it was never with men, thankfully. She hated men with a vengeance.

I'll offer her more money for exclusivity, that's what I'll do, and I'll take her out more. Tonight, was such a turn on having her with me. What is it about this woman that makes me want her so much? For the first time in her forty-five years, she'd met a person she didn't want to live without, nor was prepared to share anymore. Drifting off to sleep completely satisfied, her last thought was that she could never have enough of Kate Jones.

CHAPTER 3

Safe in her bedsit, Kate curled up on the sofa, deep in thought, tightening her towelling dressing gown as if to protect herself. Every last trace of Darlene Milner had been washed from her body. She'd scrubbed her gums until they almost bled, and the bitterness of the mouthwash lingered on her taste buds. Now everything had been erased from the evening, she needed to think.

Ezzio Marin. After all these years, she'd come face to face with him again, but thankfully he didn't recognise her. Disturbingly though, he'd had an inkling they'd met before. Yes, they'd met before all right when she'd been just sixteen and persuaded by her friend to attend the local university ball. Normally, she would never have been allowed to go to such a function at her age, but her beloved mother had died months earlier, and her guardian stepfather was out of his mind on drink, so it was easy to get away.

Smuggling her clothes shoes and makeup in her rucksack, she'd headed for her friend Natalie's house feeling excited. Natalie's parents were away for the weekend and had left Natalie at home with her elder brother who was supposed to keep a watchful eye, but he was too busy in the bedroom with his new girlfriend to care what they were doing.

She had been so excited getting ready at Natalie's house. Aided by cheap wine, they became giddy and girly as they assisted each other with their hair and makeup. The dress she wore was a beautiful sapphire blue which she'd made herself, and it fitted to her body like a glove, clinging in all the right places.

As she looked at her reflection in the mirror, her thoughts drifted to her beloved mother who had been such a clever seamstress and had passed on her skills. She liked nothing better than taking a piece of lifeless material and creating a unique bespoke dress. Mum would have loved this dress. The wine deadened the pain she carried daily about her much loved mother, who she missed so much.

Natalie had managed to style Kate's blonde unruly curls on top of her head with a few tendrils hanging down her neck, which gave her a sophisticated look far older than her sixteen years.

Once ready, she hardly recognised the person staring back at her in the mirror. Whether it was the effects of the wine or just the clever transformation, she didn't know, but for the first time in her young life, she felt beautiful.

Natalie had got tickets to the ball from her brother, so they headed by taxi to the city feeling quite grown up. Once inside the venue, she was mesmerised by so many attractive young people dancing and drinking, she'd never been to such a function before and her heart quickened with anticipation. She and her sister had always been kept on a tight leash by her mother for much of their young lives, unlike Natalie who was much more streetwise.

Natalie had no trouble getting served at the ornate neon-lighted bar. Kate sipped her drink and gazed around the room in awe. It was full of handsome males and females in all their finery, and the atmosphere was electric with the DJ playing hit after hit of catchy music keeping the dance floor busy. She loved dancing, having developed a natural rhythm from an early age due to the endless dance classes her eager mother and made both her and her sister attend. She was so happy when Natalie grabbed her hand and pulled her onto the dance floor. She moved and gyrated her nubile body effortlessly to the music, totally unaware of the seductive figure she posed. Lost in the music, she did wonder if it was the alcohol making everything so wonderful. All she knew was that she wanted the pleasure to go on and on until Natalie broke the spell, dragging her away to speak to some friends of her brothers who were stood in an alcove near the bar.

She first saw him stood with two other males in the group and he was looking directly at her as they approached. As he was head and shoulders above the other guys in height, she immediately thought of the cliché, tall dark and handsome, but it didn't really do him justice. His warm chocolate-coloured eyes met hers, covered by the most amazing dark lashes which seemed to penetrate into her very soul. Her heart began racing and she felt hot and flustered; she'd never experienced anything like it before. Natalie made the introductions until it came to him, who she clearly didn't know. One of the other males in the group, Greg, introduced him as Ezzio Marin, explaining that he was in his fourth year of a university exchange programme as the final part of his degree course. In those first few seconds of meeting Ezzio, the only word that went through her head to describe him was beautiful. Not a word you would associate with a male, but he was just so incredibly handsome.

Ezzio took her hand and gently kissed it, "It's an absolute pleasure to meet you."

The others started sniggering and Greg nudged him, "Ezzio Marin, you really are so full of American bullshit."

She found their easy sparring amusing and watched Ezzio grin at Greg as he continued playfully, "You just don't have any finesse where the ladies are concerned," which brought even more laughter from the group as his fascinating brown eyes turned to her, "Would you like to leave these uncouth friends of mine and join me for a drink and some sensible conversation?"

She looked enquiringly at Natalie, who was quickly becoming engrossed with another male in the group and urged her on, "You go, and we can meet up later."

Ezzio took her hand and led her towards the bar. She really didn't want a drink as she was on a high just looking at him; this must be the love at first sight, she'd read about in novels, or maybe more practically, was it just the alcohol that she certainly wasn't used to? Who cares . . . he was so blinking gorgeous, she was going to enjoy herself.

Their conversation flowed, assisted by the wine they consumed. She was mesmerised by Ezzio as he talked about his family in America and his previous trips to England. His voice and personality were contagious, and each time he asked her a question, she batted it back, because compared to him, her life was simply mundane. He described America so wonderfully with his deep sexy voice. His accent was unusual, not the traditional American drawl which Ezzio explained was because his mother was English and his father an American of Italian descent. He explained his diction must have come from his mother who spoke English beautifully. They discovered they shared the same birthday although she was quick to add two years as she didn't want him to know her real age.

"Shall we?" She had no idea what he was talking about until he gestured with his eyes, to the dance floor. The DJ was urging all the males in the room to grab a lady as he slowed the music down, and although the room was relatively dark, the lights were dimmed even further.

He led her to the dance floor, and once in his arms, she was captured. They gently swayed to the music and she was lost, having never experienced such wonderful pleasure. Not wanting the precious minutes to end, she inhaled his masculine scent and tried to hold onto every second. Was she not the luckiest girl in the room to be dancing with such a handsome man? As she lifted her head slightly to look up at him, he bent his head towards her and their lips met gently. She had been kissed clumsily before, but nothing like this. Ezzio had the most wonderful lips which simply glided along hers. It was such an incredible feeling which seemed to be oh so short as he broke their contact. Unbeknown to her enthralled mind, the music had changed.

His eyes glinted playfully at her, "You really are so lovely." Taking her hand, he guided her off the dance floor just as Greg approached them and told her that Natalie wasn't feeling well. They followed him into the alcove and met a pale-looking Natalie who pleaded, "Can you come with me? I really need the ladies."

Silently she cursed her friend for breaking the magic of her and Ezzio, but Natalie did look a little green round the gills. Almost as if to convince herself, she used a decisive tone as she told Ezzio, "I won't be long," at the same time using her eyes to silently plead with him to wait for her.

As they both made their way towards the cloakroom, her heart was singing. She sat down on one of the stools, staring at her reflection in the mirror. Smiling back at herself, she added some lip gloss, and with her fingertips fluffed her loose tendrils to spring up the curls. Natalie joined her from the toilet cubicle still looking pale,"I've been sick, it must be too much wine on an empty stomach."

"Well, get some water and take a few deep breaths and it'll pass," she chided, before adding firmly, "and don't have any more alcohol to drink for goodness' sake." Some friend she was, but she needed to get back to Ezzio.

As she returned from the cloakroom, her frantic eyes devoured the ballroom looking towards the bar where the alpha males gathered, but she couldn't see him there. She scoured the dance floor but it was mainly females and no one of his height stood out; where was he? Maybe he's in the toilet? Fixing her eyes on the male cloakroom door, she silently pleaded for him to be in there. Now she was starting to feel sick, but for entirely different reasons than Natalie.

She spotted Greg at the bar and dashed towards him. "What happened to Ezzio, do you know?"

Greg shrugged, "Oh, he's long gone; had a better offer to a house party." He must have seen the utter despair in her eyes as he urged, "Hey, don't bother getting hung up on him, he's going back to the States at the weekend, but I'm free and single," he smiled before adding, "and I'm English," as if that made a difference.

He tried to put his arm around her, but she pulled away, staring at him with sad eyes rapidly filling with tears. No words would come. Her youthful sixteen year old heart was broken into tiny little pieces.

So, Ezzio had left the building, never to be seen again until tonight seven years later. Clearly, he didn't realise she was with Darlene and what their relationship entailed, otherwise he wouldn't have asked her to dinner. Darlene had told her she wasn't entirely overt about her sexual preferences due to her husband being in care, but she was sure people knew within the immediate circles she mixed in.

It was still hard to think of herself as a prostitute servicing females. Having to pore over women, mainly overweight rich ones that preferred females, was as disgusting as it was demoralising. As each client's preference was for the female gender, they often subjected her to endless explorations of her own body which she had to endure, and she would satisfy them any way they wanted, usually by delaying their climax which heightened their arousal. Her body was a turn-on and she knew exactly how to use it, but only ever on a one-to-one with a female, she never went near a man or allowed any voyeurism with highly sexed men watching. Females paid highly for her services, but Darlene paid the highest, and although she hadn't known Darlene long, she was becoming needier on the sexual front. It appeared she didn't want anyone else, just Kate. Darlene kept buying her clothes and underwear to dress up in for sex, but they weren't sexy at all, just grossly sluttish, but then again that's what she was, a high class slut. Darlene was turned on by being dominated and paid well for it, so while she did, Kate would continue to oblige.

Staring around her small intimate bedsit, she appreciated its simplicity. It was clean and sterile without any ornaments or pictures donning the walls. It was just beige, beige and more beige. She disliked pretty and fussy, preferring simple and clean. A place to escape from the dreadful level she'd sunk to. Sex was a means to an end which she hated, but she was a good actress and it gave her money, lots of it. So, she used her looks and body to earn as much money as she could to take care of her dear Emily.

Her whole life revolved around Emily, her sweet twin who she loved so much. Physically they were identical, but mentally very different. Although Emily's beautiful body was perfect, her mind was trapped in childhood. Deprived of oxygen at birth, she had been brain damaged and locked in a world of innocence like a delicate bud that hadn't quite flowered.

Their evil stepfather had shaped the life they now lived, even though he was dead. How she hated him. It was because of him she'd been forced to change her identity and escape to London, where there was less chance of being recognised. It had been hard at first, but she was a survivor. She'd tried various menial jobs, but none paid like prostitution, and she needed as much money as she could earn for Emily.

Her thoughts returned to Ezzio, and how attractive he'd been in his early twenties, but now in his thirties, handsome didn't even come close. It wasn't just his brooding chocolate-coloured eyes, or his dark toned physique that was attractive, maturity had afforded him something else . . . power. No wonder women flocked around him as Darlene had implied, he really was simply gorgeous. What was the likelihood of running into him again? Attending functions with Darlene was not something she normally did, so maybe not? Darlene kept her business life separate, and Kate neatly ensconced in the bedroom department, which suited her just fine. Darlene was an extremely successful and rich business woman, but also relatively private, so hopefully, tonight was a one off and she would continue to keep Kate away from the numerous public functions she attended. No, she was unlikely to see Ezzio Marin again, and even if she did, he didn't remember they'd met before, or knew her real name, so she needed to stop worrying. . . she was safe.

CHAPTER 4

Kate felt her phone vibrate and saw Darlene's name for the third time. God, she was so impatient.

"Where the hell are you?" Darlene barked.

She put on her sweetest voice, "I got held up, but I'm in a taxi just five minutes away."

"Well, for God's sake hurry up, I pay you enough to be here when I say."

Darlene cut the call. That's all she needed, Darlene in a techy mood meant that she would have to earn her money tonight. She knew that Darlene would be imagining her with another client. She was becoming more inquisitive, constantly questioning her about other clients which she never fully answered. Why should she? Darlene paid for a service, and that's what she gave her. She wasn't paid to give a step by step account of what she was doing when not with her.

She smiled to herself. As if she'd have another client today, one was quite enough; she was late because she'd been busy completing a bespoke dress for a fashion outlet. Like her mother, she was an excellent seamstress and was paid by Leo, an upmarket clothing retailer, for her dresses. It was such a delight for her to select different materials and create beautiful clothes, and even though she knew that Leo made a handsome profit selling her dresses on, there wasn't anything she could do about that. Having to insist on cash all the time made it impossible to negotiate any better terms, but she was content in the knowledge that the money was to support her sister's care, and she would always stitch a tiny E in each garment as a tribute to her lovely Emily. The enjoyment from sewing was a form of escapism, and she loved to design individual clothing with flair, which seemed popular with large overweight ladies. She selected bold colours, and cleverly stitched discreet panels, which created an overall effect of slimming and somewhat flattering dresses.

Sewing and creating garments was the only pleasure she had, apart from visiting Emily. In another life, she would have studied fashion and daydreamed of being a famous fashion designer, picturing a catwalk show with all the leggy models wearing clothes designed by her. She would sit with her mother and Emily on the front row watching endless models displaying her clever designs, and she would call the range Emily. Afterwards, they would celebrate her triumph eating scrumptious canapés, and toast her success with the finest champagne. Orders from the rich would come rushing in, all wanting her to make clothes for them, and her mother and Emily would be so proud. Lost for a few moments in her fantasy dream, she hadn't realised the car had come to a standstill until the taxi driver jolted her back to reality by requesting his fare.

Darlene was waiting in the hallway as she exited the lift into the penthouse suite, clutching a glass to her breasts. Her eyes were glazed, indicating that it wasn't her first drink of the evening.

"About bloody time," she snapped, "what the hell kept you?"

It was a statement rather than a question. Kate gave her one of her brightest smiles, "I'm so sorry I'm late," she said kissing her gently on her cheek, "but I'm here now." Hoping to distract her, she nodded towards the drink in her hand, "Can I have one of what you're having?" She breathed a sigh of relief that it seemed to have worked as Darlene moved towards the drinks cabinet.

She removed her jacket and followed Darlene into the luxurious lounge area. As she eased herself down onto the welcoming leather sofa, she marvelled again, as she did each time she visited, at the beauty of the penthouse suite. The views over London were quite spectacular.

Darlene returned and sat down next to her, handing her a glass of white wine, as she took a large gulp of her own.

"I've had a pig of an afternoon with that bastard Ezzio Marin; I'm regretting the merger with him already."

Kate looked interested but said nothing. She had developed her listening skills early on when she first became a prostitute as so often after sex, glamorous rich women loved to talk about themselves.

Darlene continued, "He's such a control freak in the boardroom, strutting around and giving out his orders as if I work for him. I was furious with him today and he knew it, but after the meeting he spoke to me as if nothing had happened, asking who my guests will be at the Charity ball he's hosting on Saturday night." She paused and took another large gulp of her wine, "As if he doesn't bloody well know."

Kate already knew that Darlene had purchased a table at the function and had invited selected guests. Darlene leant over and stroked her hair, "You should come, be one of my guests, I'd enjoy having you with me all evening and thinking about when we get home." Reluctance must have shown in her eyes as Darlene quickly added, "I'd pay you, of course."

Although her driver was money, she shook her head, "I don't think it's something that I should be attending, but I could see you afterwards though."

"Why the hell not," Darlene snapped in an irritated voice, "I've invited you and I'll pay for your time?"

"I'm just conscious of the event and the media. I can see the headlines now, Local Prostitute Gives Services to Charity, they'd have an absolute field day."

Darlene drained her glass, "I don't give a shit what anyone writes, I want you there and that's all there is to it. I'll pay you double for the night . . . end of?"

Kate didn't argue further. How could she afford to turn down extra money? She couldn't, she would go to the ball for Emily. She smiled inwardly to herself, oh how Darlene loved getting her own way, money and power always spoke volumes.

"Anyway, enough about that now," Darlene smirked, "I need to relax and for you to help me."

Darlene took her drink out of her hand, placing it on the coffee table and leant towards her, taking her time with a long drawn out kiss. As Darlene broke the kiss, Kate saw the burning desire in her eyes as they focussed on the black sheer blouse she was wearing, which intentionally showed off her best assets encased in a black lace bra.

Darlene reached forward and slowly stroked her breasts, "You're such a bloody turn-on," her eyes twinkled with desire, "I only have to touch you and I'm throbbing."

Kate reached forward and slowly undid the tie of Darlene's light robe, "Well . . . because you are so tense tonight, kitten, we need to do something about that, don't we?" Tilting Darlene's chin, she kissed her lips thrusting her tongue into her receptive mouth. The kiss was long and lingering before Darlene eased away and stood up, quickly removing her wrap and long silk nightgown.

***

Darlene stood naked, boldly displaying her body. For a woman of forty five she didn't look too bad, and as she was paying for sex, what did it matter anyway?

Kate took her hand and led her toward the chaise longue, "Lie on your tummy while I get something to relax you."

She did as instructed, enjoying the cool air caressing her naked back. She waited eagerly until she returned with a bottle of massage oil and a towel from the bathroom, and watched as she pulled up a small stool to sit alongside her. Kate had removed most of her clothes and she stared in awe at her nakedness. She closed her eyes and her sex clenched as she heard the squelch of the lotion being squeezed. As Kate began gently with her feet, she enjoyed the feeling of her clever hands massaging the soles in circular motions, and then proceeding to her calves, kneading the skin and muscles upwards. Kate was using both hands to push on the thigh muscles with her hands spanned outwards making sure her thumbs teased the top of her thighs on the inside.

Darlene opened her legs further to give greater access, but her touch was elusive, ignoring the overt invitation and instead massaged her buttocks. She couldn't get over how wonderful it felt to be touched in this way. While she knew that her backside wasn't her most attractive feature as it was covered in cellulite, the feeling of Kate rubbing and caressing with the full span of her fingers, was completely sensual. It was slow, and she revelled in the sensation . . . this is what I pay her for.

Involuntarily, she cried out at the wonderful sensation of rubbing, kneading and massaging . . . how could your arse be so receptive to massage? Kate's hands efficiently moved onto her spine and followed the contours with gentle pressure generously applying the oil. Darlene became more excited as she knew what was coming next; those dextrous hands would soon begin the slow torture of her breasts. Kate leant forward and started to kiss her neck and ears as she continued to knead and rub her shoulders. She felt the pressure on her erogenous zone, deep in her groin, "Oh God, the things you make me feel."

"Turn over now," Kate commanded. She turned onto her back, excited by her own nakedness. It was a sort of vulnerability that she would never display in business but laid completely exposed, staring at such a perfect woman naked except for pull-up stockings and ridiculously high heels, was so incredibly sexy. She loved her breasts and looked hungrily at them.

Kate smiled knowingly, "Do you want them in your mouth?"

"Yes," she deliriously murmured.

Kate kicked off the shoes and climbed on top of her in a kneeling position and placed her knees on each side of her waist. Leaning forward, Kate thrust a breast towards her face and she grabbed it forcefully sucking hard on the delicate pink nipples that tasted so good. Kate then pulled away and took both of her breasts into her own hands and thrust them in her face, moving them slowly all over her cheeks, nose and forehead. The nipples were taught and felt good. She was in ecstasy as Kate continued to rub her breasts in her face almost smothering her. Breathing in her cleavage was such a bloody turn-on.

"You like that don't you, kitten?" Kate grinned. Straddling Darlene, she thrust her vagina tantalisingly close to her mouth, "Suck me."

Darlene needed no encouragement, she wanted to eat her. Inhaling her sex was an aphrodisiac in itself, even her minge was perfect. She was incredibly excited looking up at Kate naked and so exposed above her, she smelled wonderful, and she grabbed her hips pulling her towards her mouth and licked and sucked her mound. With her tongue, she found her clit and pressed hard backwards and forward, loving her juices on her lips. This woman was sensational.

After a few minutes, Kate moved back to the stool and she felt bereft . . . had she climaxed? She watched her generously rubbing more oil into her hands and then eagerly anticipated the assault on her wanting breasts. Involuntary, she placed her hands above her head to give greater access. Kate rubbed hard and massaged them firmly from under her armpits towards each nipple. Round and round and to a point she rubbed, encouraging her nipples to harden and become erect twizzling them with the ends of her fingers. Darlene moaned at the exquisite pleasure, and could feel her core was hot and soaking wet.

Kate's hands then moved to Darlene's battled-scarred tummy and rubbed upwards, downwards, to the left, to the right, and round her bellybutton. The feeling was so delicate and pleasurable. Kate then used her forefinger and stroked down her navel to her pubic hair extremely slowly, and then repeated it. Tiny little strokes designed to tease before she moved further down to her core. Twizzling her fingers around the opening several times, she then thrust her two inside her moving them as high as she could.

Darlene spread her legs wide, wanting the long fingers to fill her, "Please," she pleaded desperately needing to come. Kate kept her fingers plunging in and out and moved her mouth to her breast sucking hard on the nipple. Darlene gazed down at the beautiful women pleasuring her, relishing the delight of being fingered, and her thumb pressing firmly on her heated nub in circular strokes was magical. Round and round with each stroke the pressure was increasing and bringing her closer, and those wonderful lips sucking hard on her nipples was more pleasure than she could stand. Wanting the sensations to go on but unable holdback, she screamed out loud as waves and waves of pleasure cascaded through her body.

After a short sleep, a fulfilled Darlene sat in the lounge with a drink for each of them. Kate returned from the bathroom and she handed her the glass.

"Sit down; I need to talk to you." Kate sat in the armchair opposite with the coffee table separating them and Darlene continued, "I've got a business proposition for you to consider," she paused, "I want you to give up these other women and be available for just me." She stopped speaking, giving her time to digest the request, but when she didn't answer, she carried on, "I will pay you much more than you can earn servicing other women, you could look upon it as sort of a salary each month."

Kate still looked attentive but said nothing, and Darlene didn't like her silence, "Say something, for Christ's sake."

She appeared deep in thought as she wandered over to the window, "I'll have to think about it, it's a big ask."

Darlene was surprised that she had the audacity to want thinking time, after all, it was a generous offer for a whore.

As she watched, Kate stood with her arms folded staring at the outside vista, Darlene felt the familiar tug of sexual desire again. She looked stunning. Her silk robe was clinging to the contours of her body, while her messy hair was loose around her shoulders and level with her magnificent breasts. She knew that she wore nothing under the robe. What is it about this woman that turns me on so much, I need to see her naked again.

"Think about it later, let's go back to bed."

CHAPTER 5

Ezzio was putting his jacket on to leave the office, when David poked his head around the door, "Ah, I'm glad I've caught you. I just wanted to let you know, Laura and I might be a little late on Saturday."

"You're still coming though?" Ezzio asked as he lifted his briefcase off the desk, "We really need to beat last year's auction total."

"Yes, we're definitely coming. I'd forgotten that it's Amy's end of year prom night and Laura wants us to be there when the limousine arrives to pick her up. Her and five school friends are travelling together to Oak Hall, and Laura wants to see them all dressed in their gowns before we leave."

Ezzio walked towards the door shutting it firmly behind the two of them, "I don't blame her, I'm sure your Amy will look so gorgeous, you'll be fighting the guys off soon."

David took an exaggerated breath in, "I already am," they exchanged a knowing look as he added, "the trouble is, we know what they're after, as we were like it ourselves at their age."

"Hmmm, I remember it well," Ezzio laughed, "the hormones raging, so eager for sex but no idea how to get a girl interested, and when you did get lucky, it was all over in seconds."

David grinned at his sentiments, "Well, I was a bit of a late developer but I'm sure you never had any problems, I bet women have been eating out of your hand since kindergarten."

Ezzio chuckled, "Yeah, I wish."

He valued his friendship with David who he'd met when he'd first started acquiring failing companies. Then, David was a relatively inexperienced lawyer, but conscientiously worked hard, and was extremely dependable, which Ezzio appreciated. David never let him down, and as a result, he trusted him more than anyone in his immediate circle. He was a bright and gifted lawyer, privy to his considerable wealth and business dealings, so he paid him handsomely for his services and loyalty. David was probably the closest thing he had to family.

As they approached the foyer, Ezzio's car was ready for him. It had been driven from the underground car park to the front of the building by one of the security men. Ezzio patted David's upper arm in a farewell gesture, "Right, matey, I'll see you and Laura on Saturday night, hopefully you'll make it in time for the bidding."

"Oh, I'm fairly sure we will," David smiled; "Laura's already got our bids earmarked." As they were about to part, David asked, "Are you bringing Ali?"

He'd cooled things with Ali so inviting her to the ball might not be the best approach, "I'm not sure yet, I'll see."

David didn't press further, "Okay then, see you Saturday."

Ezzio nodded farewell to his lawyer friend and as he watched him walk away, for a fleeting second, he felt a pang of envy. David was going home to his beloved wife Laura, who it was clear for anyone to see, he absolutely adored. David had told him that when he met Laura, she already had a daughter, Amy, but that he had cherished her as if she was his own child. Yes, David was lucky being part of a loving family, which was something he'd been once upon a time, but as each year passed since his parents' death, that memory was becoming much fainter.

He thanked the driver and got into the car. As it was a perfect sunny evening, he opened the car roof and fastened his seat belt, predicting the journey home would take about an hour through the Friday night traffic. He loaded an Eagles CD, and joined the traffic, enjoying the harmonious melody of Hotel California. He mulled over the conversation he'd just had with David. His daughter was growing into a lovely young lady, and he had no doubt she'd look stunning for the prom which would make David and Laura so proud.

His thoughts drifted to an article he'd read about the American import of a prom night, and how popular they were becoming in schools and colleges in England despite the exorbitant costs involved. The ball he'd attended while on the university exchange programme sprang to mind, with the young girls in their pretty dresses, and the boys dressed up in their finery, all eager to make a conquest. He remembered the fit English girl he'd danced with and kissed that night. What a sexy little number she'd been on the dance floor moving her body rhythmically to the music. With a gorgeous slim figure and beautiful blonde hair, by the time he'd met her, his hormones were raging.

While he could vaguely recall her pretty face and luscious blonde hair, it was her stunning green eyes he remembered most vividly. Glistening at him like precious emeralds they had mesmerised him, and his foolish young heart fell a little in love that night until he discovered she was only sixteen. Those eyes had lingered in his mind for months afterwards, and recalling them now, he knew out of all the beautiful women he'd dated, none had eyes that ever matched those penetrating green ones.

His mind went into overdrive . . . penetrating green eyes . . . he'd seen some of those recently at the Marin and Milner function, the girl with Darlene. He delved into the recesses of his brain, she couldn't be the sixteen year old girl he'd met at the university ball all those years ago, could she? Surely not. Her body was fuller and her face a little rounder and she was taller, but yes, it was her alright, he was convinced of it. I knew I'd met her before. Finding out her true age was a shock as he'd thought she was at least eighteen, so he'd left the ball quickly because he didn't want to get involved with a girl so young.

It all fitted together now, and he knew without any shadow of doubt, it was her. However, something had changed, because this woman, recently introduced to him as Kate Jones, was not called that when she was sixteen.

CHAPTER 6

The charity ball was in full swing and the wealthy attending ate a delicious dinner. The food they'd consumed was simply too extravagant for words. Kate wasn't used to such a gourmet diet as food was something she scrimped on to save more money. Looking around at the rich and well-fed, she noted that many of the females had ample figures, and that some of the men had large bellies, all which indicated a decadent lifestyle.

She absorbed the colour and flair of the dresses that the rich wore, filing them away in her mind so that she could try and replicate and sell them to Leo. Every penny counted.

Darlene's table was full of wealthy associates, and she felt certain they must realise what sort of guest she was, especially since Darlene kept staring intensely at her. Kate's dinner companion on her right was Darlene's assistant Henry Carr who was a polite man, but not a great conversationalist, preferring to question rather than answer. This meant they were not an ideal dinner match as talking about herself was always taboo; she was always guarded and never divulged anything personal to anyone. Darlene had told her that Henry had been her husband's assistant and had proved invaluable to her since she had to take over the helm of the company, and she affectionately referred to him as her Man Friday. Despite the strained conversation, Kate preferred to speak with him rather than the gentleman on her left, as he was much younger and fancied his chances regardless of his wife sat the other side of him. Despite being used to men coming on to her, she still hated it.

It was a relief when the Master of Ceremonies took to the stage and the bidding began on the lots on offer. Extravagant sums of money were bid for the prizes, far exceeding their worth. Men tried to purchase gifts for their wives, and females purchased also, but Kate suspected many of them were using their husband's money for the privilege. Despite being cynical about it all, Kate loved the idea that the money went to charity and found she was smiling and enjoying the spectacle.

*****

Ezzio watched her arrive with Darlene and hadn't taken his eyes off her since. As she'd entered the foyer, she looked spectacular in a dress that must have been created for her. It was deep blue, with a choker high neck, but the pièce de résistance was the back of the dress, which was covered with fine sheer lace giving a tantalising glimpse of her gorgeous long backbone. The thought of peeling it off to expose her delightful body, escalated a thrill rushing through his blood. The fine net material at the back of the dress was cut just above her buttocks, which left his imagination working overtime on her rounded derrière. His only criticism of the dress was its length which was mid-calf and covered her amazingly long legs. Had Darlene bought the dress for her? At that moment, he didn't really care, as never in his thirty-two years had he ever felt such an instant attraction to a woman; he wanted her badly.

He kept a watchful eye on her, and bided his time during dinner until he saw her excuse herself from the table and head for the cloakroom. He left the dining area at another exit, knowing that she would came face to face with him in the passageway. It was evident the moment she spotted him approaching as her expression altered. Not through fear, it was more of a, I really don't want to talk to you, look. However, manners dictated that she would stop and speak, so as she moved toward him, he gave her one of his most charming smiles.

"Good evening, how nice to see you again."

***

Courteously, she allowed Ezzio to take her hand, "Good evening, Mr Marin," she spoke almost through gritted teeth and removed her hand quickly. She felt strange when he touched her and couldn't explain why her heart was thumping. What is it about this man?

He shook his head, and smiled, "Oh please, I thought we'd moved past the Mr Marin stage and onto Ezzio?" Not giving her a chance to reply he continued, "You look absolutely stunning tonight. By far you have outshone every lady in the room in that dress, I'm quite sure there will be an abundance of men wanting to dance with you."

Was that sarcasm she heard in his voice, because she was with Darlene? She wasn't sure, but she didn't like it?

Focusing on his dark eyes was her first mistake as his intense scrutiny from under his incredibly long eyelashes made her feel peculiar, almost out of breath, yet she was standing still. Her next mistake was trying to get away from him.

"Well, I'm afraid they'd be wasting their time, since I'm here with Darlene and intend to leave with her." Although his expression didn't change, she knew in that in the split second of looking into those amazing dark eyes, he was aware of the relationship between her and Darlene.

"That is a shame." He widened his eyes, "Does that mean that you're tied to Darlene's hip and not allowed to dance?"

His questioning tone and penetrating look unnerved her; she needed to end the conversation, quickly. Ignoring the inference, she smiled, "It really has been a lovely evening, and so nice to see you again . . . er . . . Ezzio, now if you wouldn't mind excusing me." As she tried to move away, he caught her arm, tightening his grip around her wrist, and as he bridged the gap between them, she felt his masculine thigh brush against her own causing a thrill to run through her. She knew that pulling away from him would only draw attention to them both, which was the last thing she wanted. Her heart was pounding dangerously, and she guessed her eyes would reflect her anxiousness. His hold on her arm was too tight to break, so she had no choice but to listen to him as his face moved close to hers and he asked seductively, "Before you dash off, I'd like us to have dinner together tomorrow evening?"

Why on earth was he asking that again? He really was starting to unnerve her, and she wasn't used to this uncertainty. Again, she tried to move away from his firm hold, but his grasp tightened.

She mustered a firm tone, "I thought I'd made myself clear the last time you asked, I don't want to have dinner with you. That goes for tomorrow night, next week, or any other night in the future."

Instead of looking rebuked, a smug expression passed across his face, "Well, I'd like us to have dinner together, shall we say seven thirty at the Fountains Hotel?" A determined look hardened his eyes as if daring her to say no.

She was furious at his over-confidence, "No we won't," she glared defiantly at him, "What part of no don't you understand?"

He ignored her protest, "I have a business meeting at the hotel until six thirty, but after that I'm all yours." His smile not only oozed charm, but was unwavering also, clearly he was used to getting his own way.

She was really uncomfortable now, Darlene would be noting her absence so she needed to get back, but he persisted, "I'll send my driver to collect you at seven." He raised his eyebrows expectantly for her reply. Did he really think she would just nod and say okay, then, here's my address? He must be joking.

"There would be no point in doing that as I won't be coming." Again, she tried to move away, but he held on. As he moved his face close to hers, her heart accelerated as she thought he might try to kiss her in public. But he didn't. With his hot breath brushing across her cheek, and his penetrating dark eyes never leaving hers, he whispered, "Oh, I think you will definitely be coming, Rebecca."

CHAPTER 7

He'd remembered her. The following afternoon she was still in turmoil, torn between meeting him for dinner and fleeing London. After dropping his bombshell, he'd placed his business card in her hand, requesting that she call his secretary to give details of her address and then, he just casually walked away. He'd called her Rebecca; she hadn't been Rebecca for many years working hard becoming Kate, degrading herself regularly for money. Without directly saying it, he'd implied dinner involved sex. He would think she was fair game and had something to hide so he would no doubt capitalise on that. Was it worth meeting with him, could she earn his silence by having sex with him?

She weighed up the odds, maybe, just maybe, he would have sex with her and then leave her alone. A rich man like him wouldn't linger with a woman like her. With a bit of luck, she would never have to see him again, she could tell Darlene that she was not going to attend any more public functions. Darlene wouldn't care as long as she was getting regular sex, she'd be fine, so unlikely to give her up. Yes, she needed to continue with things the way they were. If she did a moonlight flit now, she would have to start all over again and she couldn't do that. All she needed to do was get through a night with him and things would return to normal.

Sex with him, a man, filled her with absolute horror, but she'd just have to. She'd be able to tolerate it surely, she hadn't come this far to be brought down by a man. No, if Ezzio Marin wanted to take a whore out to dinner then he would get one.

She telephoned his secretary and requested that a message was given to him that she would make her own way to the hotel for seven thirty. The last thing she wanted was for him to have her address.

***

Ezzio was sitting with a whisky at the bar and watching the door, which she came through at 7.30pm, just as he expected she would. An abundance of male heads turned in her direction as she stood in the doorway scanning the room looking for him. The black fitted dress she was wearing left little to the imagination. It was extremely short and there appeared no room for manoeuvre in it, in fact, she would surely have difficulty sitting down. The dress clung to her and was cut so low that her breasts were on display almost in their entirety, one wrong move and the nipples would be on show. Her legs were covered in tacky black tights and the heels on her black stiletto shoes were so high, they could only ever be considered as sex in the bedroom shoes . . . how the hell could she walk in those? The shortness of the dress and the shoes showed off her magnificent legs, and his gaze went from her legs to her head noting her hair pulled back severely and secured in a ponytail exposing her delicate ears which were adorned with huge hoop earrings. Her beautiful face was heavily made up and her eyes enhanced with black kohl eyeliner giving them a dark shadowy appearance. Her kissable lips were painted deep red which matched the coloured talons clutching her handbag. Clearly, she'd set out to look like she was on the game and from where he was sitting, she'd done a pretty good job. What she wouldn't know was the very sight of her, turned him on incredibly regardless of what she was wearing, but dressed as she was, he wanted to fuck her senseless.

She sauntered towards him, and gave him a deliberatively inviting smile, "Good evening Ezzio, how are you?"

His expression didn't change, as he indicated with his head that she should take the seat next to him at the bar. His earlier thought that she wouldn't be able to sit down in the ridiculous dress was confirmed when she remained standing. He took his mobile phone out of his pocket, and his eyes never left hers as he made a call to his driver asking him to come to the front of the hotel.

In a sickly sweet voice, she feigned surprise and asked, "Oh I do hope you're not leaving already?"

"We are, yes," he answered sharply. Leaning toward the barman he requested that the maître d' be informed that they wouldn't be dining in the restaurant after all, but he would need the table the following night at the same time.

He took her upper arm firmly and guided her towards the door. While he knew, she struggled to walk in the outrageously high screw-me stiletto heels regardless, he dragged her along so she had little choice but to keep up with him. As they approached the hotel receptionist, Ezzio saw her give a wink, which infuriated him as he knew the inference would be that he needed hookers for his kicks.

Outside the hotel his driver was waiting, and he ushered her into the back of his specialist Jaguar car telling her to fasten her seat belt. He watched her tugging at the hem of her dress and hoped that now she'd made her statement, she was beginning to regret her actions. Through the divided partition, he gave the driver instructions, and then closed it so they were totally alone. Still he didn't speak as he was so bloody angry with her.

She widened her eyes, as if trying to look innocent, and then asked, "What no dinner? Am I not going to be wined and dined tonight after all?"

He remained expressionless, "As you have clearly made such an effort with your appearance tonight, I thought we'd go somewhere more fitting to your outfit."

The journey continued silently. He watched her looking out of the window, almost as if she was planning what to say next. It didn't take long.

"Don't your dates prefer to be driven by you rather than a driver?"

"You're hardly date material dressed like that," he shrugged, "so what does it matter?" He too stared out of the window, his senses becoming finely tuned to every breath she took. What was it about this woman? The closeness of her thigh and her endless legs were almost suffocating him. I just need to fuck her and she'll be out of my system, then she can go back to her whoring ways.

***

Nerves was beginning to get the better of her, she felt sick. What did he mean they would go 'somewhere more fitting to your outfit', was he taking her somewhere for sex straight away? Oh God . . . what the hell have I done?

The journey was short and when the car came to a standstill, Ezzio guided her out and down some steps to a basement club. As her eyes became accustomed to the dark, she soon realised it was one hell of a seedy club, and gaped in awe at the topless pole dancers. She caught sight of one of the well-endowed females straddling a drunken man, and could almost believe he was frothing at the mouth.

There was an abundance of scantily clad women dressed in tarty outfits fawning over men, and the expression she'd heard before, 'a den of iniquity' sprung to mind; now she knew exactly what it meant.

Ezzio appeared totally unconcerned and guided her towards a dingy bar in the corner, "What can I get you to drink?" He motioned to the man behind the bar who was sporting a naked torso with a ridiculous black bow tie, and asked for a whisky. She felt absolutely trashy just being in the place, and more so especially dressed as she was. Her eyes strayed to the couples writhing intimately to the music close to the bar, which made her feel even more uncomfortable.

She was beyond angry, "I don't want a drink thank-you-very-much," she spat, "This place is absolutely disgusting, why the hell have you brought me here?"

With a passive expression on his face, he shrugged, "To be honest," he paused looking directly into her eyes, "I'd have preferred a civilised evening at a fine Michelin-starred restaurant, somehow though I don't think the maître d' or the diners would have been at all comfortable with my dinner guest's attire." His gaze went insolently from her head slowly down her body to her feet, and then back to her breasts where it remained fixed.

She was livid, he'd made his point. "Look, I've told you, I didn't want to have dinner or anything else with you, I just want to be left alone."

He took the drink from the barman, and held his glass up as if scrutinising the clarity of its content, "Well, you agreed to dinner?"

"That's because you blackmailed me," she scowled.

As he turned back to face her, his eyes widened in feigned surprise, "Tut tut tut, that really is a nasty word, I don't believe I did any such thing."

"Yes you did, and you know very well you did. You referred to me as Rebecca and I am not called that."

He took a gulp of his whisky, "You were, once upon a time."

"Well, I'm not now. I'm Kate so stop calling me Rebecca. Anyway, I've already had enough of you this evening, I'm going to go home now and I don't need you to take me."

He thwarted her attempt to leave by once again firmly grabbing her arm, "Stop behaving like a spoilt child, Rebecca. I'll take you home once I've finished my drink, believe me, I've had more than enough of your theatrics for one night."

She knew she was behaving petulantly but she couldn't help it. For some reason this man totally unnerved her, making her behave in the most inappropriate way. This whole charade was absurd, and her fury intensified as he leisurely sipped his drink. By the time he emptied his glass and placed it on the bar, she was seething. Then to add insult to injury, with a straight face he turned and asked, "Now are you sure you wouldn't like to dance before we go?"

He instilled such anger in her, that her hand itched to slap him across his smug face. Instead, and with as much hate as she could muster, she hissed, "Fuck you."

Ignoring her, he made a call on his mobile, and placed some money on the bar for his drink. With his hand on her arm, he led her outside. It was such a relief to get out of the place and it was pointless arguing with him about taking her home, she knew he wouldn't budge on it.

They stood in silence for a few seconds waiting presumably for Ezzio's driver. She felt cold in the short dress she was wearing and unintentionally shivered.

"Here, take my jacket." Ezzio was removing it but she stopped him, "No thank you, I'm fine."

He shrugged, pulling the sleeve back on, "Okay, freeze then."

The car arrived a few minutes later. Once seated inside Ezzio turned to her, "Where do you live?" He picked up on her hesitation, "Your real address. If you think I'm dropping you off at some fictitious house so you can walk the rest of the way in that slut's outfit, then you're somewhat mistaken."

She reluctantly gave him her address. He was right on that score, dressed as she was, she could quite well attract the wrong attention walking home alone.

Ezzio gave the driver directions and closed the partition, while she continued to stare out of the window rather than look at him. Just keep quiet and maybe he'll get fed up, he's clearly pissed. How wrong can you be?

"Now, if you would do me the courtesy of looking at me when I speak, Rebecca."

She turned her head towards him, and snapped, "I would if you called me by my proper name."

He ignored her and carried on, "As you've ruined this evening, we'll start again shall we? You heard me earlier at the Fountains Hotel book a table for dinner for tomorrow night, I'd like you to join me so that we can have a civilised dinner together." He stopped her interrupting, "You'll be picked up at seven and can I advise you, wear a sensible dress rather than this ludicrous get-up you're wearing tonight, goodness knows what you were thinking dressing up like this?" He looked genuinely puzzled as he waited expectantly for her to answer.

"I was thinking you'd asked a whore out to dinner, so I dressed to fit the bill."

"Really, so that's what this is all about?" He paused as if digesting what she'd told him, "Then, let me tell you this. When I first saw you walk into the hotel tonight, I nearly took you up to one of the rooms and fucked you like a whore, so be warned, if you turn up dressed like this again, I will do."

"Well, you might as well have done, you've treated me like one anyway, taking me to that disgusting seedy pit."

He laughed out loud, "You want to think yourself lucky, that was one of the better clubs I took you to. Don't push me, Rebecca," he warned, "tomorrow we'll have dinner together properly, just two people getting to know each other."

"And what about afterwards?"

"What would you like to do afterwards?" he asked innocently.

"Not sex with you that's for sure," she scowled aware of the car coming to a standstill. With a sense of relief and a desire to get away, she attempted to open her door but he put his hand on top of her arm. As she turned her head back towards him, his eyes held hers, "I think you're getting a little ahead of yourself," he raised an eyebrow, "Isn't it polite to be asked for sex first?"

How does he always manage to turn an insult round?

"I'd like to leave now if you'll let go of me." He released his grip, and she rushed to get out of the car only for him to exit his side and come round to hers. As she straightened up on the pavement, he stepped towards her leaving only inches separating them. He towered above her and his closeness stopped the breath in her throat.

"What, no goodnight kiss?" he asked mockingly.

Glaring at him, she hissed, "No chance. Not tonight . . . never with you." Standing so close to him, even her nostrils betrayed her as he smelled divine.

She needed to get away, but before she could, he cupped her chin firmly and almost in slow motion touched her lips briefly with his, "Until tomorrow then, Rebecca, sleep well."

Not bothering to respond, she dashed into her bedsit block and slammed the door shut. She brought her fingers to her lips, touching where he'd kissed her . . . were they actually tingling? The feeling of male lips on hers just for that brief second was so strange. Dashing to the window, she looked out into the street and breathed a sigh of relief, thankfully he'd gone. For the first time that evening, she could let her guard down. What now though, nothing had gone to plan tonight? Her keenness for him to see her for what she was had completely backfired on her. As if that wasn't enough, he wanted her to meet him tomorrow night. Darlene was away on business so she could do, but if she'd been around, there would be little chance of seeing anyone. Darlene was demanding exclusivity, and while she was paying so generously, she needed to oblige.

She considered her options, and knew she would have to see him the following evening to find out exactly what he wanted. Then she would need to make some decisions. If it turned out he did know something about her past, there would be little choice, she would have to move on. Logic told her though that he couldn't possibly know about her background, how could he? No, it was best to have dinner with him and see what his agenda was. As he hadn't demanded sex or anything tonight, maybe she shouldn't feel so threatened. Feeling much better, she decided to ring Emily.

"Hi sweetie, you're not settled down yet are you?"

"No, I've been playing Monopoly and I won."

"Oh, you clever thing, who were you playing with?"

"Jess and Ellie. I had loads of money left at the end and Jess said I was lucky and should buy a . . . er . . . a ticket from somewhere," she paused as if trying to remember the name, "where you can win lots of money."

"She means a lottery ticket, Em. People buy them and win millions of pounds."

"That's it," Emily jumped in, "Can I get one?"

"If you want to, but it's unlikely you'll win so don't go getting your hopes up."

It didn't sound as if Emily was listening at all as she continued, "If I win, we can buy a great big house for us . . . and we can have a dog."

If only life was that simple. "Well, make sure you only buy one, don't waste your pocket money on loads of tickets, will you?"

"I won't," she replied. Then, as only Emily would do once she had her answer, she moved quickly on, "Don't forget it's tomorrow that Mrs Coo is taking me and Jess to the theatre?"

"I know it is, that's why I rang. I bet you're looking forward to it, aren't you?"

She could hear the excitement in Emily's voice, "Yeah, we've been playing the CD, so we know all the songs. I'm wearing that blue dress you made me with mummy's locket, and Mrs Coo says we can get a burger afterwards."

"Oh, lucky you. You'll have a great time, I know you will."

Emily was quiet for a second, then she heard the sadness in her voice, "I wish you could come with us."

"I know you do, but I'm working so I can't. I'll be there on Saturday though to see you and you can tell me all about it." She wished she could go to the theatre with Emily, nothing would please her more than taking her sister out, but she couldn't afford for them to be seen together in public. As they were identical, they'd attract too much attention, so it just wasn't worth the risk. Also, refraining from outings was a sort of coping instinct. If she ever went to jail, she knew Emily would have to live without her, so she needed her to become as independent as possible.

Emily interrupted her thoughts, "Can you ring before then 'cause I don't want to wait that long to tell you all about it."

"Of course, I can. Now then, you have a lovely time and be good."

"I will. Mrs Coo says I'm always good."

"I know she does, she tells me that too."

Emily suddenly remembered, "What's that ticket called?"

She smiled, "A lottery ticket. Right, I'll ring Monday and you can tell me all about the theatre. All my love, darling, have a great time. Night, night, sleep tight, don't let the bed bugs bite."

Emily pleaded one more time, "Don't forget, will you?"

"I won't, sweetie, have fun." She cut the call and felt much better. The independent living accommodation for Emily was turning out so well. She was blossoming under the watchful eye of Janet Coo, so every penny was worth it. Her thoughts returned to Ezzio Marin, he was a complication she didn't need. Her priority was to keep earning the money, so she couldn't afford him exposing her in any way. She would have no choice but to comply with whatever he wanted; she'd promised her mum that she would look after Emily, and she wouldn't let her down.

CHAPTER 8

Promptly at seven the following evening, Kate heard the peep of a car horn and looked out of the window. In front of her bedsit block was a light blue Aston Martin and leant against it was Ezzio. The car looked ludicrously out of place in the downmarket estate. She grabbed her bag, and rushed to the door as quickly as she could, anticipating that if he had to wait too long, he would come and find her.

Dressed in an above-knee simple lemon dress with a short white jacket, she realised as she approached him that her ornate flat shoes gave her a disadvantage as she appeared almost petite beside him without heels. His smile appeared to be one of approval, but then again, she had to acknowledge that the tart's outfit she'd worn the previous evening, was pretty bad.

"Good evening, Rebecca, you look rather lovely this evening." As he bent and kissed her cheek, a sudden gush of shyness crept upon her, which was something she rarely experienced. As a prostitute servicing females, her demeanour had to be one of dominance.

"Can we stick to Kate please?"

He opened the car door for her and then made his way round to the driver's side. He fastened his seatbelt but delayed starting the engine. A serious look crossed his face as he looked directly into her eyes, "You'll never be Kate to me," and in an instant the charming smile was back, "remember first impressions count, and

I'm afraid the image of a sixteen year old girl called Rebecca on the brink of womanhood, is firmly imprinted on my mind."

"What, you knew then that I was only sixteen?"

"Not initially no, but when I did," he grinned, "I was quickly out of there, I can tell you."

Yes, didn't she know it? She remembered the utter despair she had felt that night, and the broken heart she nursed for so long afterwards.

"Well it's a pity whoever told you that, didn't tell you I was almost seventeen."

He shrugged, "Sixteen, seventeen, whatever, it didn't really matter," his eyes widened cheekily, "I'm afraid a girl of that age was not exactly what a rampant twenty three year old man was looking for."

What on earth was she supposed to say to that? She had no idea, so she secured her seatbelt, and quickly changed the subject, "No driver tonight?"

As he turned the ignition on, he smiled teasingly at her, "I thought you wanted your date to drive you?" he paused as the engine gave a powerful roar, "Last night I'd been drinking at my business meeting so I couldn't."

Who cares, I just want this evening over as quickly as possible.

He moved the gear select to drive, and the car pulled away slowly in the direction of the Fountains Hotel. In the confines of the car, he was too close, and a whiff of his masculine aftershave overwhelmed her senses making her feel odd. Did he have the car heater on high?

They continued the journey in silence, until they came to a halt at roadwork's, and the quietness between

For The Love Of Emily   Joy Wood

them felt uncomfortable forcing her to speak, "You seem to have several cars."

He kept his eyes on the road, and nodded in agreement, "Your point being?"

"Nothing, I was just saying that you have a lot. How many do you actually own?"

"A few," he turned his head toward her, "Does it matter?"

"No," she shrugged, "I just think it's extravagant. At the end of the day, you can only get from A to B in one car."

He laughed, "Well maybe it's the way I get from A to B that's important."

"I don't see what difference that makes?"

He rolled his eyes, "Only a woman could say that," he grinned, "Anyway, I'm surprised you haven't resorted to men and their cars being an extension of . . ." he didn't finish the sentence, just paused for a second and then added, "well, you know."

She had absolutely no idea what he was talking about. Growing up in a female household with just her, Emily and their mother, her dealings with the male species had been quite minimal. Until that is, their mother had brought the hateful Derek Clay into their lives.

On arrival at the hotel, the receptionist greeted them both politely as they walked past, "What, no wink tonight for the receptionist?" he asked sarcastically, which she ignored, and carried on walking with her head held high.

At the restaurant, they were taken to their table in a discrete alcove slightly away from the other diners. The maître d' greeted them both, and smiled welcomingly as he eased the chair out for her. As he slid the linen napkin on her lap, Ezzio requested two Kir Royales while they perused the menu. Surreptitiously she assessed him. He was perfectly proportioned, with a broad chest, wide shoulders and extremely long legs. There wasn't an ounce of fat on him, which indicated clearly that he was a man who took care of his body. He was wearing a lightweight taupe suit, and a polo shirt without a tie, which might look amiss on some men, but on Ezzio it looked somewhat stylish.

She tried to study the menu but her stomach was doing somersaults, and she felt almost breathless, which was so odd. Half of her wanted to run, and the other half willed her to stay. Covertly she glanced again at his incredible frame. Everything about him was pure masculine; there was no doubt about that. Her eyes were drawn to the fine dark hair on his enormous hands as he held onto the menu . . . I wonder what they would feel like.

Dark eyes looked up unexpectedly from the menu, "What would you like to eat, anything special?" Eat . . . was he really under the impression she could actually eat? She felt strange. Even though her heart rate indicated she had at least run a marathon, she needed to focus.

"Why don't you choose, I'm sure you have excellent taste?"

Ezzio ordered fish for them both and once the waiter had left them, he smiled teasingly, "If you keep looking at me as though I'm on the menu, we can forget dinner."

Bloody hell, he reads minds as well. "I don't know what you are talking about," she dismissed using the best schoolmarm stance she could muster, "You know I don't want dinner with you, or anything else that's on offer. Can you just cut to the chase and tell me why you are insisting you and I get together?"

Ezzio took a sip of his drink, savouring the flavour before answering, "Let's just enjoy a nice meal together then we can talk, mmmm?"

It was probably wise not to antagonise him, she didn't know him at all but she was fairly certain that he was a man used to getting his own way. The food was rather nice, and his conversation over dinner was polite. To onlookers, they must have appeared like an ordinary couple as they chatted courteously, but her heart plummeted when he asked, "Do you live alone or do you share?"

Why did he want to know that? "I live alone."

He raised his eyebrows, "What about family, do they live locally?"

She shook her head emphatically, "I haven't any family."

"I thought you had a sister?"

Had she told him that when she was sixteen, how had he remembered? She kept her voice steady, "She died."

"Oh, I am sorry, forgive me. I know how hard it is to lose a loved one." Momentarily, he looked sad himself. Hopefully she'd deflected any further questions about Emily, the last thing she needed was anyone to find out about her precious sister.

For dessert, he opted for cheese while she savoured a 'to die for' delicious chocolate concoction. Normally, she never ate dessert so the decadent gateau was such a delightful luxury for her, and as she slowly licked the thick whipped cream off the fork, she watched his dark gaze become even darker. Her eyes clashed with his, and she became conscious of a sexually charged atmosphere.

"Will you stop staring at me?" she challenged, feeling uncomfortable.

"Well, stop playing about with the fork," he answered thickly.

The waiter appeared, and Ezzio asked for a few minutes before they had coffee which clearly meant give us some privacy. As he collected their plates, she silently willed him to stay. Now it's the time of reckoning.

As she gulped a large mouthful of wine, Ezzio broke the silence, "The reason I asked you to dinner is because I wanted us to get to know each other a little better."

The intensity of his eyes held her attention, and she felt a flip somewhere deep inside her as he lowered his voice, "You are a beautiful woman and I find myself enormously attracted to you." He seductively gazed directly into her eyes, awaiting her response.

"Well, I'm not attracted to you," she snapped.

She watched his eyebrows raise in mocked surprise, "Is that right?"

"No, I'm not," she emphasised.

She felt the heat of his gaze on her face, "Your demeanour tells me otherwise. You're like a startled rabbit caught in the headlights around me, nervous, but your eyes tell a different story, they look longingly at me. I don't think you're sure what you want?"

Who the hell does he think he is? "I know exactly what I want, and it isn't you."

"Really . . . mmm? Shall I tell you what I want?"

She swallowed, and as much as she wanted to look away, his mesmerising eyes held her gaze.

"I would like to make love to you very much. I want to remove your clothes slowly and savour that exquisite body of yours; I'm hard now just thinking about it."

While he paused for her response, his eyes never left hers. Flustered by his graphic image, she had to force herself to breathe and focus. She shook her head firmly, "That isn't going to happen . . . ever. You must know I'm with Darlene and . . . er . . .what our relationship involves."

Why couldn't he leave her alone?

He drew in a slow, steady breath, "I don't care about that. I've wanted to make love to you since the first time I saw you, and I'm getting rather impatient now."

"Well, I don't want to make love with you, so are we done?" She made a half-hearted attempt to stand, but he halted her progress with a firm grip on her wrist, "Sit down," he advised ominously, "we're nowhere near done yet."

She sat down and he continued, "I want you in my bed willingly, but if not, we need to negotiate." Pausing, he took a sip of wine, and continued to watch her.

Did negotiate mean she had a choice? "And what is your idea of negotiating might I ask?"

"I'm guessing that you have worked exceptionally hard to build a new life for yourself here in London, to ensure that nobody finds out about your past life?"

Bastard! Uneasiness crept in, how much did he know; she needed to push him to find out what information he had. "So what? Lots of people move away and change their identities, there's no crime in that."

"No there isn't for most people, but you are a wanted woman, Rebecca." She felt a wave of nausea as she battled the despair deep within her. He knows.

"How come you know all of this?"

"Because I did my research. By knowing your birth name and date of birth, I can find out anything I want to know about you. When I want something, I work hard to get it, and I want you Rebecca," he paused, "badly."

Damn, she'd forgotten they shared the same birthday. She needed to establish if this sex would just be a one-off episode.

"Let me get this straight. You're not saying you are going to turn me in, then, you just want sex, is that it?"

He nodded, but she needed more assurance than that.

"How can I be sure that once we've had sex you won't renege and turn me in to the police?"

"Rebecca," he waited until she looked directly at his eyes, "I'm not interested in what happened when you were sixteen. For all I know, your father deserved what he got."

"My stepfather, he wasn't my father," she corrected him, "and yes, he deserved everything he got."

"Did he beat you, was that it?"

As if I'm going to tell you. "Yes, something like that."

He took a deep breath, "Look, I just want a night with the young Rebecca that I met all those years ago; it's as simple as that."

She needed time to think, so stalled him, "Where did you find out all of this information about me?"

"There are ways to find out about anybody if you really want to."

Her stomach churned. He had the ability to expose her new life which wasn't much of one admittedly, but he could undo everything. As if sensing her anguish, he touched her hand, "Come with me now," he urged, "just one night, that's all."

Her jaw tightened, "Are you so desperate for sex that you have to resort to someone who isn't interested in you? Why don't you find yourself someone that's turned on by your macho image?"

"I don't want someone, I want you."

"And if I say no, what then?"

His brow shot up, "The little secrets you're hiding may just slip out in conversation with Darlene."

She sucked in a breath, "What makes you think she'll be bothered? She's actually quite fond of me."

"Oh, yes I can quite believe that, but did you know her son Piers is coming over from the States this week. I'm quite sure he wouldn't want a murderer with his mother even if she is paying for you. Darlene might be a formidable businesswoman, but believe me, she's like putty in her son's hands."

With a heavy heart, she considered his scandalous proposal. Would he keep to his word, and was one night all it would take? Could she even tolerate penetrative sex? The very thought of it scared her, but she was a survivor; she hadn't come all of this way to have everything undone now.

She lowered her eyelids to the table, and focussed on the fine white wine. The significance of the amount in the crystal glass was not lost on her; was the measure half empty or half full? Raising the glass to her lips, she savoured the fruity bitterness on her palate . . . backed into a corner with no way out, it has to be a half full approach.

She lifted her chin, and looked indifferently at him, "Okay, sex it is then, but I'm not spending the night with you, once it's over, I'm going home." It was necessary that she kept some control.

One of his dark eyebrows lifted and he murmured seductively, "You might not want to dash home afterwards."

"Oh please," she rolled her eyes, "spare me the charm. Save it for someone who wants to screw you."

Ezzio impatiently took the wine glass from her hand, "Leave that now, if you want another drink, I'll get you one later."

"Well, make sure you do. In fact, get me a bottle. . . I'll need it to get through tonight."

Ignoring her, he beckoned the waiter over to inform him they wouldn't require coffee. The maître d' appeared and held her chair, smiling knowingly at Ezzio as if he understood the urgency for their leaving. She bit her lip, stifling an impulse to laugh as the whole situation was so bizarre, when in reality, it felt like she was being led to the gallows.

As they left the restaurant, Ezzio took her arm and guided her towards the lifts. For some reason, she thought they'd be going to his home . . . how stupid am

I, he wouldn't want sex with a prostitute in his own home now would he?

The lift doors opened and as they entered, the penny dropped, "What sort of a man are you? Were you that confident I'd have sex with you that you pre-booked a room?"

The bored expression that crossed his face reminded her how much she disliked his self-assurance, "I use a suite here when I have business in the city."

Oh, he just would have wouldn't he . . . so bloody typical. They travelled in silence in the lift and she daren't look directly at him because she was nervous, so her gaze travelled down to his expensive leather shoes. They were smooth and highly polished . . . just like the man himself. It won't be that bad, surely, he's really good-looking, with a bit of luck it will be over quickly and I can get home and forget all about him.

They entered the most beautiful suite at the top of the hotel, and Ezzio showed her the bathroom indicating she might want to freshen up while he fixed them drinks. Freshen up . . . what am I expected to do for Christ's sake, have a shower?

Grateful for a minute's reprieve from the intensity of him, she entered a huge contemporary bathroom which seemed larger than her entire bedsit. Approaching the mirror, she chastised herself for the high colour in her face as it wasn't a good look for her; she was more used to seeing that on the woman that paid for her services.

Silently, she prayed Ezzio wouldn't interpret her high colour as desire when in fact it was quite the opposite . . . wasn't it? Her heart was hammering in her chest as if to say let me out, and her hands trembled, signifying her nervousness. The endless mirrors adorning the stylish walls seemed to be mocking her from each angle, reminding her that she had nowhere to hide; she really needed to calm her nerves. Take some deep breaths. . . calm down . . . you've had sex lots of times with women. Just act it out and give him what he wants, or maybe just lie back, he'll soon get bored with a lack of response.

Splashing cold water on her face and neck, she urged herself on . . . right, you can do this girl . . . it's now or never.

She closed the bathroom door, and took another deep breath as she walked the few steps to the lounge area. Ezzio was sitting on the sofa with two glasses of wine perched on the coffee table waiting. Smiling at her, he patted the seat next to him, "Come and sit down, I've got you that drink you wanted."

She urged her trembling legs forward towards the sofa but remained standing. Bending to pick up her drink from the coffee table, she took a large gulp of the bitter wine for confidence, and then decided to come straight out with it, "Look, you don't have to play the role of seducer here, it's a done deal. Shall we just go to the bedroom and get on with it?"

If she was hoping to embarrass him in any way, she was disappointed; his expression never changed as he sipped his drink, "Who says we've got to make love in the bedroom?" How this man constantly surprised her, every time she tried to put him down, he bounced back . . . right, I've lost that one.

She reluctantly sat next to him on the sofa and their eyes locked causing an uncontrollable fluttering sensation deep inside her. Mutely she had to acknowledge that he was incredibly attractive, he was so male and big . . . was he like that all over?

He took a mouthful of his wine, and almost as if he sensed her anxiety, he asked, "Why are you so nervous around me? I'm not going to hurt you. I'm hoping tonight will be a pleasurable experience for us both."

She said nothing and continued staring downwards at her hands. He put his drink on the table, and moved toward her closing the gap between them. Without warning, his huge hands clasped her face and as if in slow motion, he brought his mouth unhurriedly down onto hers. The kiss was gentle at first, and as her lips opened to invite him inside, he deliberately deepened it. His lips were firm and the sensation felt really strange to her after years of kissing women with soft lips. Enjoying the pressure from his masculine lips, she found her own matching his as he slithered his tongue into her welcoming mouth demanding more from her. Their lips synchronised and moved smoothly creating a feeling inside her which was intensely pleasurable. Involuntarily, she placed her hands on his chest unaware she was giving a signal for more. Their lips seemed to fit perfectly together. The kiss dragged deep within her as her whole body contracted. Never had she experienced anything so sensual in her whole life, she felt in a daze, totally overwhelmed by his masculinity as his arms enveloped her, pulling her closer. As his lips left hers, she felt oddly deprived until he started to weave his magic down her neck as his warm breath and mouth worked its way along the sensitive space between her collar and shoulders, initiating sensations in her tummy that were completely new to her. For the first time in her life, she was aroused by a male, but then without warning, it stopped.

With his dark eyes glistening he whispered in a low husky voice, "I think we will take this to the bedroom after all, I need to see you naked."

He stood up, with his outstretched hand reaching for her. She placed her much smaller one into his, and silently matched his strides into the luxurious bedroom. As they approached the huge bed, he kissed her tenderly before easing them both down onto it, and he began the kissing assault again. It felt good. She really shouldn't like this.

Ezzio had managed somehow to undo her dress and was tugging at it to expose her breasts, while she was like a floppy puppet as he gently held each arm and slipped the dress down over them. Effortlessly, he eased her cream bra away from her breasts until she was topless in front of him, "I knew you'd be stunning," he breathed.

He eased her back onto the bed, and her eyes watched him bend his head and suck on her breasts. The feeling of him kissing her nipples was amazing, she'd done this to endless women before, and they to her, but she felt nothing, yet now for the first time, she knew the pleasure it could bring. Slow in his approach, she savoured the feeling of his hands on her breasts, teasing and caressing them. Just watching his mouth on her skin, caused a dragging sensation deep within her. Somehow, he'd eased her dress off until she was lying on the bed in only her cream thong.

***

He'd been wrong. There was no evidence of a surgical breast enhancement, she was all natural which for some absurd reason, pleased him. His eyes devoured the shape of her feminine core evident through the delicate silk fabric of her thong. Slowly he eased the tiny scrap of silk down her long legs, his gaze being drawn to her perfectly groomed pubic area, and it struck him that she truly was magnificent, like a Goddess.

"You're so lovely, Rebecca," he breathed.

He moved away from the bed to remove his clothes as quickly as he could, he didn't want to waste a minute now he'd got her gloriously naked in front of him. The slight tension in her face puzzled him, but he quickly dismissed it. Being a little nervous with a new sexual partner was perfectly normal. Either that or she's putting on some sort of virginal act?

It was amazingly erotic to finally have her lying naked in front of him, and so responsive. He kissed her hungrily. Touching the heart of her with his experienced fingers, he felt her slippery moisture and savoured the feel of her softness. She was writhing and breathing more heavily now, and it took all his restraint not to climb on top and thrust inside of her, so he could feel her taut muscles around his throbbing dick. Struggling to find the right words, between kisses he groaned, "God, I want you."

He watched her intently, appreciating how amazing she was in the throes of sex. Her nipples were erect making her perfectly round breasts even more desirable. Using two fingers, he smoothly circled her swollen clit with the intention of applying further pressure, but the slight touch on her core appeared to be more than enough. She thrust her pelvis upwards, and as he continued to rub, her guttural scream told him all he needed to know.

He was experienced enough to know it wasn't fake, but he was amazed how quickly she'd come. As he watched her eyes slowly open, it was obvious she was surprised herself, and her complete exposure and vulnerability thumped hard in his belly. He tenderly stroked her face, "Okay?" he asked gently.

***

What was she supposed to say, this was all completely new to her? She'd never experienced anything so breathtakingly beautiful, it was as if he'd taken off her armour and crushed the shield she'd built around herself.

As her body bathed in the aftershock of pleasure, he began kissing her again, and as if sensing her uncertainty of what to do next, he took her hand and placed it on his penis. Feeling his hardness, she moved her fingers slowly along the shaft, it felt good. Becoming bolder and more confident, she increased the pressure, up and down, up and down. She had nothing to compare him with, but he seemed awfully large to her, and she liked the sensation of touching him intimately. She became more assured, and moved her hand faster along the slippery organ until for some reason, he put his hand on top of hers indicating she was to stop.

"That's enough for now." he groaned.

Leaning towards the bedside table, he produced a condom, and without using any words, his eyes questioned if she wanted to apply it. She shook her head, and watched him tear open the packet and sheath himself slickly, knowing he'd have done that hundreds of times before.

He turned his attention again to her, and carefully straddled her, supporting his huge body with his fore arms. His eyes never left her face and he kissed her again, almost eating her up, and she felt his penis tormenting her vagina, fleetingly, before it was replaced by his hand intimately preparing her for him.

A wave of anxiety washed over her. He won't fit, I know he won't . . . he's too big . . . he'll hurt me.

"Are you alright?" he whispered as he continued with small fleeting kisses to her face, eyelids and lips.

She nodded yes, unable to utter a sound.

"Good because I can't wait any longer, I need to be inside you."

She braced herself for the pain. Her body had been ravaged before and she remembered every second of the acute torture on her young innocent body. And not just the physical pain, but even more lasting, was the utter humiliation of losing something so precious that she'd wanted to save for marriage.

***

Knowing he was large, Ezzio slowly tried to edge his penis inside her. She was moist enough he knew that, but she was so tight. What was it, she was no virgin yet she felt like one? His eyes were drawn to her face, probing . . . what's wrong? Her manic green eyes were darting about rapidly in absolute horror, she looked totally petrified. What the fuck's going on? The compliant female who had kissed him hungrily and only seconds ago, and came apart in his arms, had long gone and he was staring at one terrified lady.

Immediately, he turned away from her and stepped off the bed while she scrambled to pull some covers over her naked body. He pulled on his boxer shorts and stood by the bed towering over her.

Bewildered, furious and excruciatingly frustrated, he challenged, "What the Hell just happened? One minute you're with me, the next you're like a terrified virgin."

"How do you expect me to act," she snapped, "you know I didn't want to do this yet you still forced me?"

Rage boiled inside of him, "Well you put on a pretty good show for someone being forced to have sex." Grabbing the rest of his clothes, he walked towards the door and turned back to her, "Get dressed, I want some answers.

***

The door reverberated as it slammed behind him, and she slowly released the breath she'd subconsciously been holding. Hastily, she dressed, praying desperately he would take her home. *Why did I respond to him when I hate him so much? If I never saw him again, it would be a moment too soon.*

With her stomach in turmoil, she ventured back into the lounge area where he was stood, fully dressed with his back to her looking out of the panoramic window. He must have sensed her entrance, as he turned towards her with an interrogative look on his face. With anger still evident in his voice, he snarled, "I don't know what just happened in there," his eyes glanced towards the bedroom "but we definitely aren't finished yet."

She felt absolutely mortified and terribly embarrassed by it all, so didn't answer. *How on earth she could get away from this awful nightmare?*

Unrelenting, he continued, "Tell me what the problem is, you fuck with women for money don't you?"

You bastard, what do you know? "Oh, thank you for putting it so eloquently."

"It's hardly an eloquent occupation is it Rebecca?"

"Trust you to be so crude."

He paused, as if he was working something out in his mind, "Why just women, why don't you fuck men for money?"

She didn't answer. He was the enemy, so she didn't owe him an explanation.

"Well?" His voice was raised, as if totally fed up with her silence.

"I just don't that's why and I'm not answering any more of your stupid questions. You knew what I did when you started this fiasco. I want to go home now."

His eyes were like a hawk, watching her intently before breaking the silence between them, "I'm in England for one more week and then I leave for the States. While I'm here, I want you to spend the week with me." It wasn't an invite; it was more a fate accompli.

Is he for real? "I can't. Darlene will be back tomorrow."

"I don't care about Darlene; you'll be with me for the next week, not her."

"Well you might not care, but that's how I earn my living. When you clear off to the States, I won't have an income?"

"Tough. I'll pay you a severance package when we're finished."

She stiffened, "And if I turn down this wonderful opportunity you're offering me, what then?"

"You know the answer to that. Come on, my driver will be waiting, we need to go now."

Although curious as to why the driver was taking them home when they'd arrived in Ezzio's car, she didn't want to ask . . . maybe he's had too much to drink?

As she picked up her bag, he waited gesturing that she went to the door before him. Always the gentleman. If people only knew what a blackmailing monster he was.

They entered the lift together, and while it was only seconds until they reached the ground floor, it seemed like an eternity. He ushered her out of the lift and across the foyer to the front of the hotel where his driver was waiting. There was no need to give her address this time, the driver just said good evening and once they were strapped in the back of the car, they set off.

Ezzio curtly closed the privacy partition and turned to her, "Tomorrow my driver will pick you up at eleven and take you to my home in Surrey. Bring your personal belongings and you'll need some evening clothes. Don't bring any clothes Darlene has bought for you, I'll get you anything you need."

He can't be serious? "And what exactly do you expect me to say to Darlene tomorrow evening after her trip?"

He shrugged indifferently, "I couldn't care less, tell her you've decided you prefer men after all."

Hostility surged through her, "What a bastard you are. You steam roller yourself into my life despite me telling you I'm not interested, you have the audacity to force me to have sex with you, and then you intend to discard me once I have," she paused, and shook her head before adding in a contemptuous voice, "I wonder how you sleep at night."

"I sleep well enough, and you will too for the next seven nights I promise you."

The male smirk on his face irritated her, along with his inference that she would sleep better after sex with him.

"You really think your something, don't you? Well get this into your thick skull, I don't want you in any shape or form, I'm doing this under sufferance, I absolutely loath you."

His tone oozed cynicism, "Yeah, keep telling yourself that Rebecca, I saw how you loathed me tonight when you climaxed."

Furious with him to the point of wanting to physically hit him, with as much venom as she could muster she spat, "I hate you so much."

He raised his eyebrows, appearing totally unconcerned, "Well don't worry about that, you don't have to be in love for great sex. Now I've seen how responsive you are to foreplay, I can't wait to see what you're going to be like in the full throes."

The car came to a halt. Ezzio exited at the same time as her and he walked silently alongside her to the entrance of her bedsit. At the door, she glared at him with as much hate as she could muster. Willing him to go, she watched the pupils of his eyes darken with significance as he recapped, "I'll see you tomorrow night at my house and we can carry on where we left off tonight." There was no answer to that. Opening the door as wide as she could, she swung it hard and slammed it in his face. Oh, how she hated Ezzio Marin.

CHAPTER 9

Ezzio put the phone down to his housekeeper, Rebecca wasn't there. He was furious, and rang his driver George, "Why haven't you collected Miss Jones?"

As if prepared for his annoyance, George calmly replied, "She said I was to return at six for her as she had an appointment to attend to."

He was livid, it was a good job his driver wasn't in front of him right now, "I asked you to collect her at eleven."

"Yes I know, but I couldn't force her to get in the car, she was quite insistent that she had to attend her appointment."

He sighed. There wasn't any point in berating the driver when it was Rebecca he was angry with. "Well see that you are there to collect her at six, and any problems ring me straight away."

"Yes, I will do boss."

What was it about this woman that instilled such a rage in him? Was it because she was immune to his advances? He didn't have any problems getting women into his bed as they usually came quite willingly, but not the elusive Rebecca.

Recollecting their encounter the previous evening when she'd came apart in his arms, he'd spent the rest of the evening frustrated and trying to analyse what had happened to make her so fearful of full sex. She was an absolute delight quickly reaching orgasm with him just touching her. He thought of the lengths he had to go to with some women to make them climax, but not her. He just didn't get it. Even after yesterday's fiasco, he still wanted her, now more than ever.

He unlocked his desk drawer and retrieved the information he had on Rebecca which he'd been given by his investigator. She'd killed her stepfather when she was sixteen and had spent almost a year in a youth detention centre, but had escaped before her trial. The file mentioned her twin sister but that must be old information as she was dead now.

Frowning, he questioned what could have happened to make her stab a man; it must surely have been an accident? But if so, why did she run? It was a complete mystery, but one he didn't want to dwell on. The only thing he was interested in was shagging the woman senseless and getting her out of his system once and for all. Then he would fly back to the States and forget all about her. It was as basic as that he told himself as he put the file away.

During his afternoon meeting, Ezzio had been conscious of Darlene's eyes boring through him so he wasn't surprised when she asked at the end of the meeting if she could have a word in private. Refilling his coffee from the dispenser, he waited for the remaining staff to leave. Irritation gnawed at him as he didn't like to see anyone impromptu preferring an appointment to make sure he was prepared. He silently cursed the fact that Darlene had waylaid him guessing she must have spoken to Rebecca.

He would get rid of her quickly, the last thing he needed right now was to be reminded of Rebecca's sexual exploits with her. Once the others had left the boardroom, he took his seat again at the head of the table with Darlene to his left.

"How was your trip?" he inquired, politely taking an appreciative sip of his coffee.

"Fine. I sorted out what I needed to."

"Good. When is Piers arriving?"

"Tomorrow thank goodness. I need someone I can trust to scope the Milner side of things, and there's no-one better than my own son."

Her tone seemed almost as if she was trying to convince herself, and having only met him twice before, Ezzio couldn't stand the loathsome Piers Milner so wouldn't be at all surprised if, as his mother, she didn't have her own problems with him. He wasn't going to go there though.

"Yes, I'm sure he must be an asset to you. We'll need to set up some meetings, I'll instruct my secretary to get some dates in the diary for us all."

"That will be useful." Darlene answered politely, and then her expression became icy, "I've just come off the phone to Kate." He remained impassive as she carried on, "She's just informed me she can't see me currently as she is spending some time with you, is that correct?"

Darlene looked questioningly at him, as he answered casually, "Yes, it is she's staying with me for a week at my home in Surrey." Her piercing eyes glared into his indifferent ones, and her voice went up an octave, "What do you mean staying-with-you?"

"As my guest."

"What sort of guest?"

"That's none of your damn business," he glared, "As she's already told you, she's unavailable for the next week."

"And what about after that?"

"I'll be going back to the States, so she's all yours after that."

Darlene's eyes blazed and she shook her head "I don't understand Ezzio, Kate's a lesbian so she won't be interested in anything you have to offer."

He ignored the accusing glare she gave him, and stood up, "Well we shall see. Now if you'll excuse me I have to leave for another appointment." It was fictitious, but he needed to get rid of her quickly.

"Are you paying her?"

"Darlene, this conversation is over. As I've already said, my private life is none of your business and I'll thank you to remember that."

"I think I have a right to know. Kate was with me until you came on the scene, and she didn't sound too happy to be spending any time with you."

Ezzio gave no further response, and gathered his papers from the Boardroom table indicating the meeting between them was over. He was relieved when Darlene made her way towards the door, and then as if having second thoughts, she turned to face him with another question, "Why her, when you can have any woman you want?" A stony silence separated them. She shook her head, repeating again, "Why her Ezzio?"

It was more a statement than a question which he had no intention of answering. How could he when he didn't know the answer himself?

"Goodbye Darlene, I'll catch up with you tomorrow no doubt." He couldn't have been any clearer that he wanted rid of her. His dislike of the woman had intensified lately. As she closed the door behind her, he breathed a sigh of relief. *I don't want any other woman, that's the problem, I wish I did.*

***

Despite being dismissed, Darlene's mind was working overtime. She felt a tremor of anger bubbling and a gut wrenching jealous knot in the pit of her stomach. On the phone, Kate didn't sound ecstatic that she was spending any time with Ezzio, so why would she want to be with him . . . was he paying more?

She was in an inner rage particularly as Kate had agreed to the offer of more money for exclusivity with her. Jealousy wasn't an emotion she was used to, but she just couldn't bear the thought of Kate with a man at all, especially Ezzio Marin, a clone of her husband with his brains in his trousers. Kate was hers. Only Kate could satisfy her, even today flying back her thoughts had been to see her. Going two days without sex had been torture, so she wasn't giving up.

She returned home and headed straight for the bathroom cabinet. She poured a glass of water, and took a handful of her prescribed tablets which was more down to habit than anything else as they didn't appear to be lifting her mood at all. As well as being furious with Ezzio, she was sexually frustrated also. First of all, she wanted some relief, and then needed to plan how to get Kate away from him.

A warm bath calmed her and she felt some of the tension ebb as she eased her body into a laying position with a rubber pillow supporting her head. The warm water and bath oil she found comforting as she tried to relax her body from the tension she was experiencing.

Fucking Ezzio Marin, she never liked him. On the advice of her lawyers she'd agreed to the merger as Milner Enterprises was going through a difficult period with the recession. Part of the plan was for Ezzio to return to the States, so she was content in the knowledge he would eventually go but she needed a plan to get Kate away from him somehow, she couldn't bear the thought of him with her.

With the coarse brown sponge, she made a lather, and using gentle circular motions, she massaged her body concentrating on her breasts and nipples as they were tender and needy. Closing her eyes, she visualised Kate's beautiful naked body which she knew every inch of, and pictured Kate sucking her nipples which made her abdomen churn. Those pert breasts dangling in her face gave her so much pleasure, and even her mound was perfect, no sagging labia, just a taught ripe plum. How she loved to suck and lick her. Moving the sponge down to her own genitals, she caressed them slowly and pictured Kate's head in-between her legs and fantasised about how often Kate bathed her and made her wait for her orgasm. Using the sponge effectively she relished the sensation of the friction on her intimate core. Darlene would plead with her for release, but Kate would take her time helping her out of the bath and making her sit on the edge so she could dry her. The roughness of the towel would be so delightful on her turned on body and Kate would rub the towel down her sensitised skin slowly. Lifting each arm to dry underneath, she would rub the towel sensually around her neck and then the slow torture of her breasts would begin. Once the breasts were dry, Kate would kiss them gently and tug at the nipples to further excite her and then would dry from her feet and toes, moving up the legs towards the groin and vaginal area. When she eventually got to that area, Darlene would have her legs wide open silently pleading to be brought to fulfilment, but still Kate would make her wait. She would then watch the naked Kate fetch scented body lotion and the torture would begin again as she massaged it in slowly into every crevice of her body.

Beside herself just thinking of Kate bathing her, she exited the bath barely drying herself and headed for the bedroom with one thing on her mind.

She opened her bedside drawer and reached for her vibrator which she disliked using on herself, but she'd learnt a long time ago that her own fingers were never enough. Pushing the vibrator deep inside her moistness, she carefully positioned the pulsating clitoral stimulator in place, and switched it on. Slumped on the bed with her legs wide open, she watched herself in the mirror, and turned on by her own nakedness, she savoured the exquisite sensations the vibrator was giving her. Her mind drifted to licking Kate's beautiful body, and pushing her fingers deep inside her. An image of Ezzio fucking Kate's gorgeous body popped into her mind fleetingly, for a moment spoiling the delightful sensations, so she had to imagine Kate's sweet mouth delivering the pleasure instead of the artificial contraption. Remembering Kate nibbling her ear and whispering . . . come kitten, come for me, she grabbed her bulging nipple with one hand and increased the speed of the vibrations with the other. Desperate for release, she was rewarded by the pulsating contractions of her orgasm ferociously rippling down her body.

Languishing in the aftermath of her climax, she needed to think. Kate belonged to her and she was desperate to get her back. She would have speak to Piers tomorrow and ask for his help, even though she knew he would be angry with her for paying for sex. She had to acknowledge also, that nobody wanted to think of their mother having sex at all, let alone paying for it. However, Piers knew which way his bread was buttered, he knew she was gay and had accepted that a long time ago.

Pier's was a total disappointment to her, and she accepted some of the responsibility for that. He was a product of wealthy parents who sadly gave him little attention during his informative years sending him off to expensive boarding schools so that they could live the high life.

Darlene's thoughts drifted to her husband Edward Milner currently ensconced in a care home. He resembled little more than a vegetable requiring twenty four hour care, and on the occasions she visited him, he had no idea who she was. Marriage to Edward Milner had not been a match made in heaven, and Darlene knew early on in the marriage that it wasn't for her as she couldn't tolerate sex with a man.

As a sixteen year old girl, she'd had her first experience of female sex which unbeknown to her at the time, had shaped her sexual preference for life. As a teenager on a French holiday visiting a cousin of her mother, she'd enjoyed the company of the daughter and her friend who were both slightly older than her.

On a beautiful summers day, the girls took her on a picnic to an idyllic isolated lake and as they hadn't brought costumes, they decided they would have to go skinny dipping in the lake. Darlene could remember thinking how beautiful their naked bodies were as they lay on the grass drying themselves in the sunshine.

The older girl asked her if she had ever had sex and she admitted that she wasn't really wise to anything sexual because she hadn't been exposed to any more than biology at school. Sometimes she did feel a little funny inside her tummy, like when she stared at their beautiful naked bodies, but was unsure what it all meant. That afternoon, the girls introduced her to the pleasures of sex and orgasm.

She was exposed to the delights that could be given with touch and with the mouth. Not only did she receive sexual pleasure, but she was taught how to give it.

The girls were in a sexual frenzy all afternoon and Darlene thought she would burst with pleasure from one of the girls giving her oral sex, while the other one knelt over her head while she gave it to her. For some reason she found great excitement in giving oral sex as receiving it, to her it was such wonderful pleasure. Her body was in such a height of arousal with the newly found feelings she had, and the rest of the trip was spent with either touching herself, or the girls doing it for her. Every second of the trip was spent in a highly sexual state. She was in such a frenzy with it all, and her knickers were so wet with excitement, that she had to wash them by hand rather than put them in the laundry.

One evening, Darlene was told by the girls not to wear knickers for dinner, just a skirt. Unbeknown to the adults around the dining table, Darlene's sex was in an agitated state underneath it. Both girls would tease her terribly, touching her sexually beneath the table cloth. Quite how the adults didn't suspect what was going on, she had no idea. So turned on, Darlene would try and be involved in the table conversations with the adults, while small hands were working their magic around her. She would even wriggle to the edge of the chair to give them greater access.

One particular day, she couldn't hold back and climaxed while the parents moved away from the table to clear away the dishes. The girls seemed to enjoy getting each other aroused during meal times when adults were present, and would excuse themselves immediately after they'd eaten to use the bathroom. Darlene would lean against the bathroom wall while one of the girls knelt and pleasured her orally. Then she would do the same for each of them. When they all watched TV in the lounge at night, the girls would slip off their knickers so they were exposed under their skirts and would open and cross their legs so she could catch a glimpse of their pure feminine cores. Her clitoris bulged and ached from the constant arousal and attention it was given.

Late one afternoon when the parents had gone grocery shopping, the girls took Darlene into the parents' bedroom and found a box in the wardrobe. Darlene was unsure what the contraption was they took out, and was pleasantly nervous when they stripped her naked and used it on her. They sensation on her breasts as they moved the vibrator around her nipples was excruciatingly pleasurable and she remembers screaming out loud with delight. One of the girls laughed and she recalled her saying if you think that's good, wait until you feel the next bit, and oh how right she was. The vibrator was placed on her clitoris and the quickness and depth of her orgasm was absolutely sensational.

She was introduced to her husband by her wealthy parents and duly married him as expected. However, it wasn't long before he was looking elsewhere for his sexual pleasure as Darlene hated sex with him and wasn't at all receptive.

Nevertheless, he still demanded they had sex but it was always quite degrading. More than once he would hoist her over a chair or table so he could thrust away inside her for what seemed like hours, and he never prepared her for sex, just seemed to have the urge and then tell her to take her knickers off.

Sometimes he didn't even bother with the rest of her clothes, he just wanted access to her core. Apart from their wedding night, not once did they ever have conventional missionary position sex, it was always from behind. Even in the bath she had no privacy as he liked her body wet and soapy and would make her get on all fours and have sex from behind. As she bent over, he'd kneed her breasts until they hurt and relentlessly plunge in and out of her with what felt like an enormous penis.

Worse than that though was oral sex which she loathed, but he made her give it to him. Penetrative sex had to be better that, but he was a sexual man and often would tell her he needed 'his favourite'. That meant stripping off naked, kneeling in front of him and taking his filthy penis in her mouth. Balking as his excitement reached its pinnacle, he would plunge it deeper and deeper in her mouth, and when he was about to ejaculate, he wouldn't let her pull away, he would hold her head until she swallowed every last drop of his semen.

She knew it was abuse and that normal people don't make love that way, but she was young and had no experience with men, so would often escape in her mind to being sixteen with the lovely French girls.

On one occasion, she tried to talk to her own mother, but as usual she didn't give any support. Her mother spent the majority of her adult life in counselling and taking a cocktail of pills. Quite what was wrong with her, nobody was ever certain, but she did display shocking behaviours which indicated some sort of undiagnosed mental health condition. Her answer to Darlene's despair in relation to her husband's sexual needs was, what went on between a husband and wife in the bedroom, stayed between them in the bedroom.

She did meet a female and had one sexual relationship which was quite lovely, but most of the time in her marriage, she kept up the front of a normal husband and wife relationship and gave herself sexual pleasure with her vibrator. That all changed when her husband started with dementia and he was placed in a care home where his condition deteriorated rapidly. Finally, free of him, led to the discovery of a huge sexual appetite for women which probably stemmed from years of suppressing it.

Paying for sex suited her and she vowed that she would never tie herself down again, until she met Kate who fulfilled every fantasy she'd ever had, which meant that she was in a constant state of sexual arousal around her. The thought of her with Ezzio incensed her, was he making Kate have sex from behind . . . was he making her give him oral sex . . . was she letting him come in her mouth?

Anger overwhelmed her, she couldn't bear Kate being subjected to any of that. She had to get Piers to help her, quickly. Yes, he could be a bit of a loose cannon and Darlene knew some of his dealings were of the unscrupulous nature, but she needed him right now as she was no match for Ezzio Marin. Getting Kate back and out of his clutches was a priority and she would use her son to help her. Feeling more content, she poured herself a large gin and tonic, and decided that a couple of sleeping tablets wouldn't do any harm either.

CHAPTER 10

Kate walked from the train station to Hadleigh House as it was such a lovely day. The driver had arrived to take her to Ezzio's house, but she'd asked him to return for her at six. Guessing that he was concerned about the wrath of his boss, she told him she had an urgent appointment to attend, and he seemed to accept that. Nothing was going to get in the way of her visit to her sister.

After her stepfather's death, Emily had been taken into foster care, while she was held in a young offenders' detention centre. For endless hours she'd meticulously planned her escape, and eventually, when she did break free, she covertly observed Emily, and it had been a shock to see how her confidence and well-being had deteriorated. She made a vow that day; she would do everything in her power to ensure that Emily was put into an environment that would guarantee her happiness.

Luck had shined upon her when she'd first escaped from the detention centre. An elderly gentleman had advertised in a shop window for a female that could assist him with daily care and light housekeeping duties, and in return he would provide rent-free accommodation. As he didn't have any living relatives, her inability to provide references was of little concern to him, he needed somebody quickly, and it appeared she was the only applicant. Instantly it became clear that she needed him, just as much as he needed her.

Quickly recognising her value and honesty, he started to pay her small amounts of money. Then, as his health deteriorated and she began to attend to all of his needs, he gave her more money. He was astute enough to realise she was running away from something, and as a result, became more than generous towards her. She humoured him when he tentatively questioned about her past, and didn't disagree when he suggested that she had been in an abusive relationship. Theirs was a relationship based on deep friendship and nothing more, but unfortunately the money he paid was not enough to cover the cost of Emily moving out of foster care, so she needed to earn more.

Quite by chance, she came across an agency specialising in gay prostitution, and somehow, sex with a female seemed a realistic option for her. She joined the agency, and watched, learned and practiced her technique, until she perfected a performance that would appeal to any gay female. She had inherited her mother's looks, and had a body that was in great shape, so she used every asset she had to her advantage. If the client wanted kissing and caressing, that's what they got; if they wanted penetrative sex with a dildo, she gave it to them. Finally, Rebecca, the on-the-run criminal, became Kate, the willing-and-able prostitute.

The agency kept her busy with established clients, but as she became more popular, she did private sessions. Eventually, she'd amassed enough clients that paid well for her services, so she left the agency. It was amazing how many wealthy gay females would pay for sex, and as many of them relied on discretion, they paid her well. She only ever took cash, and charged high fees which they paid willingly, almost as if paying high, guaranteed receiving a better service.

One of her regular clients, Noy, sprang to mind. She was married to a wealthy banker, who couldn't manage sex, therefore he was happy to pay a female to satisfy his wife's needs. Each time she visited Noy's apartment, it was the same arrangement. Both her and Noy would take off their clothes, and they would sit around the elaborate dining table, enjoying several courses of gourmet food, which had been prepared earlier by Noy's chef. Noy would become more and more excited as their conversation and titillation gained momentum, and then, at the end of the meal, she would expect oral sex while seated at the table, with Kate on her knees. After that, she liked Kate to bathe her, and then massage her body all over, slowly, again bringing her to climax. Then she paid, and Kate could leave. It was as simple as that.

Yes, money was her goal, and she saved every penny. Once she'd secured herself a bedsit in London, she began researching independent living accommodation on the internet at the local library, for young people with learning disabilities. The initial places she visited weren't suitable, but eventually she stumbled upon Hadleigh House, and she knew immediately, it was a place where Emily would be happy.

She continued to service women sexually, but saved hard until she had enough for the initial monthly fees, and then took Emily away from her foster parents.

Emily thrived at Hadleigh House, and was extremely happy, so as far as she was concerned, all the breasts she had to suck, and all the clits she had to lick, were worth it. Her sister needed close supervision, and as she wasn't able to take care of her, she would meet the costs, she had no choice.

She removed the first part of their double-barrelled name, so instead of Price Jones, they became Jones, and she always paid the monthly fees for Hadleigh House in cash, to ensure that she wasn't traceable.

Emily simply blossomed as she loved living there, and taking part in all the activities. Seeing her beloved sister happy, was enough for Kate to know that every sacrifice she made in her life, was worth it.

As she approached Hadleigh House, she saw Emily in the window waving excitedly, and then seconds later, the front door opened and she rushed towards her. She wrapped her arms tightly around her, savouring her beloved sister. Emily, never staying still for long, pulled away smiling, "Hurray at last, Rebecca, you're here; I've been waiting ages."

Emily was the only person that called her Rebecca, apart from Ezzio and she deeply resented his intrusion. She lovingly chastised, "Darling you only saw me on Thursday, it hasn't been that long."

"Well it seems like months and months and months to me."

She knew how impatient Emily could be, that's what made her so adorable. "All right," she smiled, "I'm here now. How was the shopping trip with Mrs Coo?"

Emily leant forward and whispered in her ear, "I'll tell you later, let's go in the garden first, I've got something else to tell you."

She took Emily's outstretched hand, "Oh right, I can't wait to find out what it is."

They sat down on the garden bench, set back from the main house. The gardens were full of beautiful flowers and as she stared into the little fish pond, Rebecca's thoughts were that, as it was such a gorgeous sunny day, she was going to enjoy it. Squeezing Emily's leg playfully, she asked, "Come on then, what is it, I'm dying to know?"

As if she was some sort of spy on a mission, Emily looked over her shoulder making sure that nobody was around before she said anything, "Can you keep a secret?"

Rebecca was highly amused, "Yes of course I can, tell me." Imagining that Emily had probably bought something nice at the shopping centre, she was totally unprepared for her announcement.

"I've got a boyfriend," Emily declared proudly, looking very pleased with herself.

Rebecca felt uneasy, "Oh, that's . . . nice . . . who is it, do I know him?"

"Yes, it's Bradley; he lives here all the time now." Bradley had been there on her two previous visits so she knew him; he'd been one of the first male boarders that had been introduced as part of Hadleigh House's new, mixed sex approach. As Emily had not really been exposed to any males before, alarm bells were ringing in her ear. As lovely as it was to see her sister excited and happy, she was disturbed about the prospect of a boy/girl relationship, which she knew without any shadow of doubt, Emily hadn't had yet.

"How long have you been his girlfriend?" she asked hesitantly, fearing the worst.

"Since yesterday." Emily giggled and turned pink as she carried on, "We kissed for ages, and we moved our heads from side to side and opened our mouths like they do on the television . . . then he said I was his girlfriend."

Rebecca felt like she'd been punched in the stomach. She didn't want Emily to sense her apprehension, so she attempted to keep her face impassive, "Oh right, I see, do you really like him?"

"Yes. We are going to get our own house, and I'm going to have lots of babies."

Jesus Christ. Her heart plummeted, she needed to rein her in, "Well, you don't want a baby straight away, there's plenty of time for that."

A sad look crossed Emily's face, no doubt she'd been expecting a different response, "But I want one, and you can be its aunty."

While her innocence was endearing, Rebecca needed to be firm, but this was all so unexpected and she wasn't prepared at all. She swallowed, "That would be nice later on," she paused trying to find a way to stall her enthusiasm, "but you need to get to know Bradley first of all, and then if you love each other, you should get married before you have a baby."

"We do love each other," Emily answered indignantly, and then frowned, "he didn't say about getting married, though." She paused, thinking for a moment, "Shall we go and ask him?"

"No, Em, it's too soon, and anyway, girls don't ask boys to marry them, it's the other way round, boys ask the girls."

Her mind was racing ahead knowing that if Emily became pregnant, she wouldn't be able to remain at Hadleigh House. Equally as worrying, was the fact that Emily couldn't possibly manage a baby as she was no more than a child herself, therefore if she ever did give birth, then the baby most definitely would be taken into care. She couldn't afford anything like that to happen, so needed to act fast, but Emily was in a dreamlike state, "I liked him kissing me, it was nice. It felt funny in my tummy . . . do you like kissing?"

"Yes, it's nice when you're with someone special."

Although Emily had the mental age of a child, she had the body of a woman so it would be impossible to stop her having a sexual relationship if it was consensual, so clearly she would have to get her to a doctor and on some form of contraception. It would need to be something permanent as Emily could not be relied upon to take anything orally.

Emily stood up and impatiently asked, "Shall we go and find Bradley, then, he's in the house." Not wanting to spoil the excitement on her eager little face, she stood up, and linked her sister's arm, "Yes, let's do that," and as they walked towards the house, she playfully warned, "but don't be asking him about getting married just yet, okay?" Emily giggled and nodded, but Rebecca wasn't at all convinced she would comply with that request.

Once Rebecca had spoken to Bradley and observed Emily hanging onto his hand possessively, she went to the Matron's office to discuss her concerns. Janet Coo was in total agreement about the need for contraception. While she questioned Bradley's physical ability to have full sex, it couldn't be ruled out, especially with Emily being so eager to please him.

She scanned the telephone directory, until she found the number she wanted, and quickly made an appointment to visit a sexual health clinic with Emily.

Janet Coo assured her she would do her best to supervise Emily and Bradley until then, however, the house was run with the intention of allowing the young people their independence, so it was likely there could be a bit of sexual dabbling.

Dabbling . . . Bloody hell. She really didn't need this complication right now.

As she stared wearily out of the train window, she contemplated the new development of Bradley and Emily. Janet Coo's statement about it being, 'human nature' was not helpful at all. Financially she was just managing to keep Emily at Hadleigh House, so she didn't want any further complications, nor could she afford them.

Her thoughts inevitably led back to the insufferable Ezzio. The sooner he left for the States the better. Now, because of him, she would have to pursue some of her previous female clients, as well as trying to find new ones. Ideally, she'd like to rekindle her relationship with Darlene, but she had to be realistic and accept that she may not want her anymore. Darlene would hate the thought of her indulging in penetrative sex with a man, so it was highly unlikely she would want her after she'd been with Ezzio.

It was all so unfair. She felt bad about Darlene who had been more than generous with their arrangement. On the telephone, she'd skated around the issue as much as she was able, but Darlene had wanted answers. Why was she going to stay with Ezzio? Was she going to have sex with him? How much was he paying her? In the end, she had no option but to terminate the call, telling her to take it up with Ezzio. What could she possibly say - I've got to do as he says because he knows that I'm a convict on the run? No, she couldn't risk that. If she was taken back to prison, who would look after Emily? The only option she had was to carry on the fiasco with Ezzio, and pray he wouldn't turn her in at the end of it all.

At six o'clock, George the driver collected her as planned from her bedsit. Sitting at the huge bay window in the library at Ezzio's house, some of her tension ebbed away, as the gardens were truly stunning. She thought about her mother, who had loved gardening, and recalled the fun her and Emily had helping. As she sat appreciating the beautiful colours of the plants and flowers, she watched the spectacle of two blackbirds hovering around the gardener as he was digging the soil. Clearly, they were opportunists hungry for worms.

The view was interrupted by a sleek Jaguar car arriving and coming to a standstill. Ezzio exited the car, and the gardener moved towards him. They exchanged a few words, and then the gardener got into the driver's seat.

As she observed him covertly, Rebecca recognised what an impressive man he was, and each time she saw him, she was unprepared for the impact on her senses. Even his walk encapsulated grace and power, and, as he approached the entrance of the house, the sheer presence of the man was overwhelming. Perfectly proportioned with a broad chest, wide shoulders and extremely long legs, he was dressed in a dark suit, and she noted the impressive muscle definition of his abdomen visible beneath his white shirt. She swallowed, he looked extremely pleasing on the eye, and despite her dislike of him, she had to acknowledge that he definitely unsettled her equilibrium.

Straining her ears, she tried to listen as he spoke to the housekeeper in the hallway, who had introduced herself as Dorothy, when she'd arrived earlier.

Does he know I'm here? She'd wanted him to already be at the house when she'd arrived, so that he was kept waiting.

As he entered the library, hot on his heels was the housekeeper, fawning over him and offering to get them both some tea. Suppressing her anger, she sat quietly listening to the housekeeper while she went to great lengths, explaining the dinner she'd prepared for them both.

***

He responded to the housekeeper attentively, but in reality, he was only half listening. Out of the corner of his eye, he saw her, in the leather armchair, and if her expression was anything to go by, she was obviously seething about something.

She had removed her sandals and was barefoot, and his eyes were drawn to her feminine toes painted a delightful shade of pink, which somehow gave his manhood a jolt. As if the toes weren't enough, the tight black leggings she wore only strengthened his involuntary reaction. He'd never been a fan of leggings, his preference was for women to dress in a more flattering and sexy way, but on Rebecca he was easily converted. The tight-fitting material clung to her shape, emphasising her beautiful racehorse legs, which never failed to wake the maleness in him.

Keen to hide his impending desire, he sat himself down in the armchair adjacent to her, sensing that she was simmering for a fight.

Patiently she waited until Dorothy had left the room and then angrily burst out, "Your housekeeper says I can't have my own room," she glared at him, "even I can see you've dozens of rooms in this house, why on earth would she insist I share yours?"

He shrugged indifferently, "Because that was my instruction."

"Well you've no business telling her that, I want my own space while I'm here." Ignoring her request, he replied calmly, "You'll sleep with me while you're here, that's what we agreed, Rebecca."

"I didn't agree to any such thing, and stop calling me that. I'm Kate, Kate, Kate, Kate," she scowled, "why can't you get that?"

Ezzio saw that her amazing eyes had turned a deeper shade of green, and that her nostrils were almost flaring. She stood up with her fists clenched, as though she could take on the world, and he had to acknowledge that ordinarily she was gorgeous, but angry, she was simply amazing. Spirited as well as beautiful, what a combination. All he really wanted to do was pick her up, carry her to bed, and screw the life out her.

The sound of the door opening interrupted them, and his housekeeper brought in the tea and placed it on the oak coffee table. Ezzio gave her an appreciative smile, "Thank you, Dorothy. Oh, lovely, you've brought some of your delicious cakes. We'll try one, but no more than that, I want Rebecca to enjoy your lovely cooking tonight."

***

He's so bloody charming with women. She waited until the housekeeper closed the door, and swallowed,

"Look, you and I know why I'm here. Once we've . . . done it . . . had sex or whatever, then I want to sleep in my own room."

He reached for a plate, and raised his eyebrows questioningly, "Once we've done it, Rebecca, we may want to do it again during the night." He winked suggestively, sending a bolt of electricity straight through her abdomen. Furious, didn't come close as she watched him nonchalantly take one of the cakes.

"I'm pleased you find all of this so amusing, I feel sick at the thought of having to do this. I've had to call Darlene today, and she is not very happy at all."

Ignoring her, Ezzio took a bite of the delicacy, "Mmmm . . . these cakes are just wonderful, won't you try just one?"

Her temple throbbed, "No, I won't. I don't want a bloody cake, and I'm telling you now, if you don't sort out a room for me, then the deal is off."

Wiping his fingers on a serviette, she watched him rise from the chair and move to stand inches in front of her. Because she'd removed her shoes earlier, he towered above her, and if his intention was to intimidate her, then he was doing a pretty good job.

His piercing eyes looked directly into hers. "Here's the deal in this relationship. If you want something from me, ask nicely," his eyes glinted mischievously, "I have been known to be easily persuaded by a kiss if you want to throw one in."

His humour ignited her fury, "You must be joking. Forget it, I'll never kiss you willingly, I'd rather sleep on a bed of nails."

She glared defiantly at him, and he threw his head back and gave an almighty laugh, "Oh Rebecca, you really are such a tonic. I can see the next few days are going to be an absolute delight."

Rage bubbled inside her, and she hissed, "I'm pleased you're happy with all of this. Don't you have a girlfriend or someone who might want your attention?"

He shook his head from side to side, and grinned, "No girlfriend I'm afraid, just you and me."

She remembered when she'd first seen him at the Marin and Milner function, and recalled that he had a woman with him that night. Wanting to knock the supercilious smile off his face she asked, "You had one before, what happened to her? Don't tell me . . . your overbearing presence was just too much for her, and she dumped you?"

As he walked towards the door, he raised his eyebrow mockingly, "On the contrary, she couldn't get enough of me."

"Well she must have been desperate, that's all I can say. I can't imagine it was anything other than the size of your wallet that was the attraction."

He turned back, still with a ridiculous grin on his face, "Oh how you wound me, Rebecca. I tell you what, after dinner shall we see how attractive I can be?"

"No thank you, I'm tired and want an early night." Imagining what he would say to that, she quickly added, "In my own room."

"You're not reneging on our deal, already are you?" he asked.

"I'm here, aren't I?"

He grinned, "Yes you are most definitely, here. I'm just going for a shower before dinner. Would you like to come and wash my back, or would you prefer to fix us both a pre-dinner drink . . . mmmm?"

Rebecca wasn't amused and just for the hell of it would have liked to have knocked the smirk of his face and joined him in the shower.

With as much sarcasm as she could muster, she replied, "Oh, what choices I've got. I think I'll go for option two, the pre-dinner drink, as the first option leaves me somewhat cold."

"Tut tut tut . . . then we'll have to warm you up after dinner, won't we? Until then, it will have to be a cold shower for me."

If she could have, she would have thrown something at him . . . how does he always manage to have the last word? He really was just the most aggravating man she'd ever met.

CHAPTER 11

The succulent roast beef dinner that the housekeeper had prepared, was a gourmet delight. Conversation between the two of them was polite, as Dorothy, kept popping in and out. When she came to clear away the last course, Ezzio instructed, "Dorothy, would you be kind enough to move Rebecca's things into the Lavender room please, as she'll need her own space while she's here. It was insensitive of me to presume otherwise."

She couldn't believe he'd relented. For the first time that evening, she smiled genuinely at him, but he spoilt the moment by leaning towards her and whispering, "You can show your appreciation later."

After dinner, he indicated they leave the table, and she followed him to the subtly lit lounge. The delicious red wine had made her relax, and she felt oddly comfortable as she took her seat on the luxurious sofa. Would he be expecting sex tonight? If only she could slip away to her room and worry about that another night.

He took the top off the brandy decanter, and poured himself a generous amount, "Would you like a nightcap?"

"No, I've had quite enough already." She had consumed more alcohol than usual over dinner, and as she needed to retain a level of control around him, it was best not to drink any more.

He sat down next to her on the sofa, clutching a glass that was so large, it could have been a vase. As she watched him sipping his brandy; she could see the cogs turning over in his brain, before he spoke.

"Why didn't you come at eleven o'clock today when my driver arrived to collect you?" He stared directly at her, waiting for her response.

She'd never had to answer to anyone about her free time, so didn't like being questioned . . . what business was it of his anyway?

"I had things to do."

"What sort of things?"

"None-of-your-business sort of things."

He breathed in, "I'm just asking, that's all."

"Well don't. I wasn't aware the agreement meant you had to know my whereabouts twenty-four hours a day?"

The air was heavy with the silence between them. Despite not wanting to, her eyes, almost as if they had a will of their own, were drawn to his hands swishing the huge glass in circular motions. It appeared as if he was lost in thought, but from what little she already knew about him, he would most likely be planning his next move. As he raised the glass to his lips, and tipped his head back, her eyes were drawn to his huge Adam's apple. He was a startlingly attractive man, there was no question about that, and it was ironic that some women would kill to be in his company, with the likelihood of having sex with him. Well, she'd be more than happy to trade places right this minute . . . wouldn't she?

He placed the empty glass on the coffee table, and smiled at her, "Come up here," he patted the sofa gesturing that she should move towards him.

She wanted to say no, but knew it was pointless as he would only come to her, so shuffled towards him looking anywhere but into his piercing eyes.

He leant towards her, and tilted her chin, before gently placing his lips on hers. Although she'd been expecting all evening that his kiss would instigate sex, she was unprepared at that precise moment for it. It was a subtle kiss, but one with significance. Again, she savoured the pressure of male lips, this time tasting of brandy, and felt his hand move to her neck as he gently stroked it. It felt good. Although she knew what his intent was, she vowed to resist the hold this man had on her; he was after all, her enemy.

As he deepened the kiss, she pulled away, nervously trying to stall him, "Please don't, your housekeeper might come in."

He kissed her again, brushing her concerns away, "She won't. She'll be on her way home by now." He continued the onslaught down her neck.

"How can you be sure?"

"Because I employ her, and she knows better than to come into my lounge when I'm entertaining."

She pushed him away, creating a gap in-between them, "Please . . . I'm uncomfortable about all of this."

He gave a huge sigh, and went over to the door and locked it. As he returned to the sofa, he had a meaningful look in his eyes, and she knew . . . there was no way out now.

Silently, he eased her gently back onto the settee and started kissing her again, and she became lost in the magic of his wonderful firm lips. All sorts of sensations were taking place in her body, as her breasts began to ache and her tummy did summersaults. He kissed her with such an urgency and need, it felt like he genuinely wanted her. His mouth, nuzzling her neck with little pinches and sucks, felt quite heavenly, and she had to remind herself to resist him, she really must.

His lips moved onto her ears and she marvelled at the sensations he was creating inside her body; her sensible head was saying no, but her treacherous body was saying yes. Her blouse buttons seem to open of their own accord, and her bra, which had a front fastening, was removed by his dextrous fingers causing her excitement to intensify, as she watched his dark head covered in thick wavy hair, bend to nuzzle her breasts. Taking his time suckling each breast made her almost delirious, and she could feel the effect radiating from her core. Her nipples stood out, proudly erect, and he gave an appreciative sigh, "You're stunning, Rebecca," he whispered, as his mouth closed over one of them as if he was going to gobble it up. He continued to devour her breasts with his magic lips and tongue, and much as she really ought to, she didn't protest when he eased her top off.

He remained in his clothes, but she didn't want to say anything, as he would see it as an invite to take them off. Easily he removed her leggings and panties, as if he undressed women every day . . . he probably does.

Within seconds, she was blatantly exposed in front of him. She felt shy, which was an odd experience for her as she'd been naked so many times in front of women, but her shyness soon changed into excitement as she saw the burning need in his eyes, staring at her body in awe.

Moving his head down to her abdomen, he slipped his hands under her bottom and took her hips in his hands. The light sensation of his tender kisses on her tummy felt amazing, and lost in the sensuality of his lips kissing her so delicately, involuntarily, her legs opened. She tried to focus on thoughts of resisting him, but it was almost impossible . . . shouldn't I be undressing and caressing him?

His mouth was back on her breasts, and as he cupped them both again, the sight of them encased in his hands with the nipples jutting out, made her stomach do a somersault. Her eyes closed absorbing the pleasure of this sensational rollercoaster ride. She didn't like this man one bit, but oh what pleasure he could weave. Lifting his head back to her face, she felt him gently like a butterfly, kiss her closed eyelids.

"Look at me, Rebecca," he coaxed, bestowing tiny kisses all over her face.

Her eyes were closed for two reasons. The first because she was savouring the wonderful feelings she was experiencing with him, and the second was that she felt acutely embarrassed by it all. It was almost an out of body experience, as if she wasn't really taking part, but the crescendo inside assured her she most definitely was. She felt as if she was about to internally combust.

She opened them, her gaze sinking into his hot fiery eyes, as he breathed heavily, "I'm going to kiss you orally to make you come." He wasn't asking, he was telling, and she could only nod. She'd done this hundreds of times to females and they to her, but it didn't actually do much for her . . . will I like it with him?

The onslaught on her body continued with tiny kisses, beginning with her neck and then applying gentle pressure behind her ears. Oh, such ecstasy, she never knew she was so sensitive in this area. He moved back to her breasts, and once again began sucking her ripe nipples. Was that her womb contracting? Massaging her tummy, he kissed it moving his head lower and lower as his lips found her pubic area, and then he began the assault on the inside of her thighs, nibbling and kissing; who'd have thought they could be so sensitive? The feelings inside her surged, as he gently touched her genital area, with his long fingers. They felt so large and assured, as he moved them repeatedly along her moist lips, which she knew were engorged. Continually his fingers slid back and forth along the swollen labia, carefully avoiding the one spot which would guarantee her orgasm. Inside she was begging, until he inserted a long finger in her vagina and reflexively, her muscles tightened around it. She reacted by trying to close her legs but he eased them open again, and continued with his gentle probing and kissing, until she relaxed again and opened them invitingly to allow him space to kneel in-between, which he eagerly took.

His tongue moved smoothly along her labia, gently at first, then applying pressure as he licked and licked . . . who is that screaming? Something amazing was happening to her body as the pressure of his tongue circled, round and round on her ripeness, and then, the inferno burst and erupted, and she was coming and coming and coming. Screaming his name repeatedly, she had never known such an incredibly gratifying feeling . . . he was so bloody good, this man she hated.

Easing himself back onto the sofa, he lifted his head level with hers, and his black eyes seemed to pierce into her very soul. With the backs of his fingers, he stroked her face and kissed her tenderly, "You really are so receptive; I could come just watching you."

He'd removed his shirt displaying a fit honey-brown torso, and as he kissed her deeply, she kissed him back, tasting herself on his lips. He repositioned them both into a lying position on the sofa so she was encased in his arms, and his dark mesmerising eyes stared hungrily into hers, "I want you . . . badly, but I don't want you going all frightened again," he stroked her face, "I'm bulging, but if you don't want me inside you, then we will have to look at other ways."

She saw genuine tenderness in his eyes as he carried on, "I'm hungry for you since watching you come," he kissed her softly, "Say right now if you don't want this."

Although she felt awkward, for some peculiar reason, she trusted him not to hurt her, and whispered in his ear, "I'd like to try."

The assault began on her lips again, and slowly like a dance, their heads turned in unison, with their lips moving as if they were glued together. Somehow Ezzio had removed his trousers and boxers and she felt his erection on her thigh. Although nervous, she didn't feel quite so frightened this time. Breaking away to apply a condom, he was soon back with her, and he continued to kiss her and use his magical fingers to prepare her for him. Levering himself on top of her, she felt his penis nudging her moist entrance, as he supported himself on one arm, and stroked her face affectionately with his other hand. "Rebecca," he breathed. Lifting her eyes to meet his, she felt like she was drowning. How was it, this man had such power over her? She felt like a puppet in his arms. Through gritted teeth, he groaned, "I'm going to go slowly, just say if it hurts . . . ok?"

She nodded. His eyes, full of arousal, never left hers, as he rose over her with his athletic hips, and she felt the length of him at her core.

***

Their eyes mirrored each other as slowly he pushed forward, first the tip . . . pause . . . then the shaft . . . pause. Desperately eager to be inside her, he urged himself to hold back, vowing to take it slowly after the last time.

Each time pushing forward, he had to clench his teeth. His dick throbbed and his balls ached. What he really wanted, was to fuck her hard, but he knew that he needed to exercise a bit of restraint. God, she was tight. Slowly he moved, and gradually her inner sheath accepted him. It felt perfect, foreplay had made her ready. Feeling like a schoolboy shagging for the first time, he fought to control himself, he was so near to climax, yet he'd hardly moved. For a few seconds, he paused, savouring the feeling of being one with Rebecca. In a guttural voice he demanded, "Lift your legs around me."

***

As she wrapped her legs tightly around his hips and held him inside her, she experienced the most wonderful feeling of him filling her. Rhythmically he started to move and she was with him . . . it felt so right.

He produced a cushion from goodness knows where, and hoisted her up so the cushion was under her buttocks, and, as if things couldn't get any better, they just did. Deep inside, he filled her with exquisite sensations; it was as though they were making love in colours, bright flashing shades, one minute a kaleidoscope the next an exploding firework. She felt his warm breath in her ear, "I'd love to make you come again, but I'm too close."

His thrusts were gentle one moment, and pounding the next, plunging in hard, and withdrawing out slow. In and out, in and out.

She kissed the beads of sweat on his forehead, watching his obvious effort to hold back, and savoured the feeling of his pubic bone gyrating against her clit. Taking his handsome face in her hands, she kissed him deeply; boldly thrusting her tongue in his mouth. Being turned on by a man was totally new territory for her.

Breaking the kiss, she coyly invited, "Don't hold back, Ezzio."

***

It was all he needed. Whether it was because she was incredibly tight around him, or whether it was hearing her use his name, he wasn't sure, he just pushed harder and harder, higher and higher, and felt his control slipping away as his eyes devoured this incredible woman beneath him with her perfectly flat stomach, endless statuesque legs, and the most gorgeous breasts he'd ever seen. He inhaled her body scent, and with one last mammoth thrust, roared like a lion as he felt his release coming in powerful waves down his spent body. Never in his thirty-two years had he experienced a sexual experience like it, which completely blew his theory that if he screwed her once, he could get her out of his system.

CHAPTER 12

Rebecca woke sometime later in bed feeling disorientated, and her eyes focussed on Ezzio who was lying facing her. It took a few seconds for her to recall them both making their way to his room after they'd had sex in the lounge.

Completely naked beneath the sheets and feeling terribly embarrassed, her first thought was how on earth she could get out of the bed and into the so-called Lavender room, where she could be alone.

Ezzio, was watching her intensely, until he broke the silence, "Why don't you have sex with men?"

Oh, how wonderful, post-coital sex talk, just what she needed. She attempted to sit up, but he held her down and repeated, "Answer me . . . why not men?"

Here we go again. An awful sadness washed over her. He was spoiling something that for the first time in her life, had felt special.

"What is it with you? Do you get off talking to all your lovers about their previous sexual encounters?"

"No I don't," he scowled, "I just want to know about you."

"Well I'm not in the habit of discussing my whole sex life after one night with a man."

He pressed further, "I want to know, Rebecca, and I want you to tell me."

"Look, I'm not going to answer any of your stupid questions, not now, not tomorrow, not ever," she glared, "my life's my own, and one that I'll go back to when you go, which won't be a moment too soon for me. Now, I'd like to go to my room," her defiant eyes met his, "you said I could have my own space."

She clutched the sheets around herself, and waited. The silent tension stretched between them, until he nodded dismissively, "Okay, go to your room, then."

Although relieved, she hesitated, "Have you got a tee shirt or something I can cover myself with?"

"Why?" he asked tonelessly, "Are you worried the sight of your naked body will bring out the male in me and I'll ravish you again?" His eyes moved from her face to her body covered in the sheet, almost as if he had x-ray vision and could see her nakedness through it.

She felt her face flush, which was so ridiculous when he'd seen every inch of her body, and even her most intimate place, had been in his mouth. She needed to get a grip, "No, I'd just like to preserve some dignity, surely that's not too much to ask?"

He threw the sheets off himself, and her eyes were drawn to his groin. Surreptitiously she watched him confidently walking across the bedroom to his dresser and select one of his tee shirts. He was perfectly proportioned, with a broad chest and tight abdomen, but it was the size of his penis which had her full attention . . . had that really fitted inside her? Standing in front of the bed, he flung the tee shirt to her, not appearing at all embarrassed about his nakedness, or his large protruding appendage.

Uncomfortable didn't even come close to covering how she felt when he intimately asked, "Would you like a warm bath, you must feel a bit sore?"

God, this is so embarrassing. She swallowed, "Yes that would be nice," and then noticed a flicker in his eyes, so quickly added, "in my own room."

Quickly pulling the tee shirt over her head, she tried desperately hard not to expose herself, which judging by the look on his face, amused him. Once she was completely satisfied nothing was on show, she stepped out of bed and tried to pass him, but he caught her wrist, "I'm afraid there's only a shower in your room, and I'm sure a soak in the bath would be more helpful," his eyes scrutinised her face, "As I'd like a bath, how about we have one together?"

She was silent, so he continued, "And, gorgeous as you look in my tee shirt, making me want you all over again, I know it will be too soon, so, if I promise to be behave . . ." he left the sentence unfinished and looked questioningly at her. She hesitated, which he obviously took as a maybe, and coaxed further, "You run the bath and get in first. It's a big bath so I can sit up the other end if you would prefer. Or if you don't want me to join you, just say and I won't, how about that?"

Anxious to put some distance between them and gather her thoughts, she headed for his en suite bathroom and closed the door, as if that could shut him out. Why she'd agreed, she really didn't know. For some inexplicable reason, she wanted to bathe with him, which was completely ridiculous considering she didn't like the man.

Gazing around the masculine bathroom, she admired the contemporary design of the black and cream colours, but it was the size of the gigantic bath that was eye-opening. Darlene's penthouse apartment was luxurious, with a double-size bath, but this one of

Ezzio's was like a small swimming pool. It was perched on top of tiled steps, and would easily hold five or six people at the same time.

She turned on the ornate taps, and selected a bottle of luxury bath essence from the row of toiletries, lined up like an eye-catching display in a department store. Shaking some of the liquid into the running water, she inhaled the fragrant masculine aroma, which smelled of Ezzio . . . so typical, he even smells bloody gorgeous.

Once there was sufficient water at the right temperature, she eased herself into the bath, and left the taps running to deepen it. The warm water felt comforting, soothing the delicate internal muscles she'd used to accommodate Ezzio.

Due to the size of the bath, it was slow to fill, so she laid back on the head support and gathered her thoughts. He'd been unbelievably patient with her, and the sex had been amazing. I wonder how he feels about it all?

Almost as if he was aware she was thinking about him, Ezzio entered the bathroom. Fortunately, she was well covered with the water and bubbles, so she breathed a sigh of relief that nothing was exposed. As he stood at the edge of the bath, partially naked apart from the small towel covering his modesty, his eyes looked questioningly at her, "Am I okay to join you?"

His masculine physique almost took her breath away, and something else appealed. His brown torso was devoid of any unappealing tattoos which she disliked intensely. . . maybe subconsciously they reminded her of her stepfather?

Although she noticed that his erection appeared to have subsided, she warned, "If you want to, but please, no more . . ." she struggled to find the right words, "no more . . . funny business."

He threw back his head, he laughed out loud, before raising his hands and showing his palms as if to surrender, "Okay no funny business, I promise."

He cast aside the towel, and stepped into the bath at the opposite end to her, squatting to allow the hot water to cover him. Slowly he eased himself down further, allowing his body to gradually become accustomed to the hot water. Once settled, he smiled quite tenderly at her, and with his warm eyes, beckoned for her to join him at his end of the bath. "Come and sit up here," he coaxed, "I won't do anything which might lead to me having my evil way again, I promise." He was smiling his cheeky grin again . . . God he really was so handsome.

As if she was under some sort of spell, her treacherous body moved towards him, and he widened his legs to welcome her. She sat between his legs, and automatically turned to face the other way, so that her back was leant against his chest. Somehow, it just felt right.

Almost immediately she felt him becoming erect again and tried to move away, but he wouldn't let her, "It's okay," he reassured, seeming to sense her anxiousness, "you're tender, I know. I promise I won't do anything to add to that."

Relaxing again, she asked herself, was it relief she was feeling, or disappointment, she wasn't entirely sure?

She felt his hot breath on her ear, as his sexy voice continued, "You were incredible today. I'm only sorry I couldn't make you come again, but I just couldn't control myself." He nuzzled her neck, "I can't get over what you felt like, you were . . . lovely. I want to do it all again, it was so unbelievable."

Her insides clenched and the fiery sensation, low down inside, was back, sending her pulse rate dangerously high. She didn't object as his hand caressed her breast . . . here it goes, my shameful body betraying me again.

"You have the most beautiful breasts; do you know that? They are so round and perfect, and the nipples so proud. Next time, I'm going to suck them until you beg me to make love to you."

Enveloped in his arms, she lay back against his chest as his hands worked their magic again, tweaking her nipples, and his breath continued the onslaught down her neck. Her nipples puckered, almost painfully, and she silently acknowledged the marvellous feeling of actually being turned-on sexually, which was a completely new experience for her. So often she'd wondered if she might actually be frigid.

He huskily murmured, "When you were in my mouth today, with your legs wide open, and your nipples bulging, I was so bloody turned-on."

Her tummy summersaulted, and she groaned as his hand slipped between her legs stroking her labia very gently, "Bring your knees up," he coaxed.

She did so quickly, desperate to give him greater access. The feeling of his lips on her neck, and his dexterous fingers playing with her, transmitted a blazing sensation between her legs; it was incredible. She relished his sexy voice, "Due to my schoolboy haste, I couldn't make you come again, but I want to now," his teeth nibbled her earlobes; "let me, Rebecca?"

He must have taken her groan as a yes, as he carried on stroking her very gently, but she wanted more pressure and attempted to move against his fingers.

"You're beautiful when you come, you know," he whispered, "tomorrow I'm going to make love to you and watch you come, and then, I'm going to make you come again. I want to be inside you, filling you."

He increased the pressure of his fingers, moving them in circles, pressing hard, round and round, applying exquisite force on her ripe bud. Biting her neck, he muffled, "I'm going to be deep inside you, screwing you hard . . . and . . . fast." His magical fingers pressed more firmly, "Think about me fucking you hard, Rebecca, think of me making you come."

Her control deserted her, and she screamed as her orgasm gushed down her body, on and on, and on and on. It felt so wonderful in the warm water, only seconds of ecstasy, but deeply fulfilling. Lying back against his chest, with his huge arms wrapped around her, she slowed her breathing.

Breaking the silence, he softly whispered, "Are you okay?" He could be so bloody considerate, this man she hated.

"Yes, I'm fine." What was the protocol for a first orgasm in the bath with a man?

He bent his head and gently kissed her cheek, "You get out first and go to your room, you must be tired. Dorothy will have put all your belongings away. It's just along the corridor from here, on the left, there's a plaque on the door labelled, the Lavender room."

She hesitated, and wriggled around to face him, "What . . . what, about you?" Although she could feel his erection, it didn't mean she wanted to do anything about it. Hadn't she read somewhere before that happened to men all the time?

"I'm fine," he winked, "tomorrow might be good for me, if I'm lucky."

She needed no further persuasion, and jumped out of the bath, wrapping herself in the biggest bath towel she had ever used. Without a second glance, she grabbed his tee shirt that she'd discarded earlier, and hotfooted along the landing to her own room, eager to put some distance between them.

She opened the Lavender room door, and closed it firmly behind her as if she was shutting out what had just happened between them. As she entered the bathroom, and switched on the ornate brass light, her eyes soaked in the spacious luxury, with the large ornate wall and floor tiles, the decorative sink with the chrome taps, and the functional toilet with the hidden cistern. But it was the corner of the bathroom that grabbed her attention. Only a shower in her room, he'd told her. She physically stamped her foot with fury. "He's such a bloody liar," she spat out loud, staring at the huge enamel bath in the corner.

After a surprisingly good night's sleep, she awoke the following morning to a gentle tap and her bedroom door opening. Ezzio wandered in carrying a tray of coffee. As usual, he looked drop-dead gorgeous in his dark business suit, white shirt and snazzy tie, and her stomach did a cartwheel just looking at the way his dark hair, damp from the shower, curled slightly at the edges.

Easing herself up on the pillows, her eyes followed him as he placed the tray of coffee next to her. He turned towards her, smiling, "Good morning, did you sleep well?" as if he already knew that his efforts of the previous evening had ensured she had. He sat down on the bed next to her, and she wrapped the sheet across her top half, "Yes I did, thank you, did you?' It was a bit of a ludicrous conversation really, more of a smoke screen for, was it good for you?

"After adding cold water to the bath, I did," he grinned cheekily.

Trust him to make reference to the fact she'd left him with a powerful erection, "That would be the one exclusive bath that only you have in your ensuite would it?"

He laughed, "So I'm an opportunist, don't hold it against me, will you?"

He looked so God-damn sexy she wanted to laugh herself, but was distracted by him as he leant towards her, and touched her hair which she knew would look absolutely horrendous, as it did every morning until she sorted it out.

"I like your hair like that, it suits you."

Her naturally curly hair required endless hours of straightening to get it into some sort of order and incredibly, he liked it like that.

"You're the first person that does, my stepfather used to tell me I looked like a poodle." What on earth had made her mention her stepfather, she never spoke about him?

"Well I think you look rather cute, you should keep it like that." He let go of the tendril of hair in his hand, and asked, "Is that your mobile?" as he reached across and lifted her phone off the dresser. For a split second she panicked, which was unnecessary as she didn't have Emily's name stored as a contact, she used a pseudonym for her.

"Why do you want my mobile?" she asked guardedly, taking the phone out of his hand quickly.

As if it was the most natural thing in the world to do, he answered, "So that we can exchange numbers."

He reached inside his jacket pocket for his phone, and waited for her to open the flip case of hers. She hesitated, and asked, "Why do we need each other's numbers? You'll be gone soon, and I definitely don't intend keeping in touch."

Exaggeratedly, he shook his head from side to side, "Oh Rebecca, how cruel you can be to me," he was mocking her as usual, but then more seriously added, "I want to be able to contact you, so just give me your number and I'll be out of here so you can rest that gorgeous body of yours, and go back to sleep."

It was pointless arguing with him, especially as she needed something also. Leo was waiting for her to complete two dresses, so she had to get back to her sewing machine. As he seemed to be in an affable mood, asking was worth a try.

"I need to go back to my bedsit today; would your driver take me, do you think?"

He raised his eyebrows, and asked, "Is this a condition of me having your mobile number?"

"No, I'm just negotiating."

A suggestive light flashed in his eyes, "I told you last night how to negotiate with me."

"And I told you no to that."

"Okay," he smiled, as if admitting defeat, "I give in. I'll ask George to take you back to your flat, now give me your number; I have to leave for a business meeting."

As she opened the flip case, she silently predicted that he would scoff at the antiquated nature of her phone, and he didn't disappoint.

"Good God, how old is that phone, it's positively archaic. Tell me it isn't a pay as you go?" His look was so disparaging, almost as if he wanted to take it from her, and throw it into the nearest bin.

"Yes, it is and it works fine for me," she smiled sweetly, "some of us don't have the luxury of expensive singing and dancing contract phones like yours."

As she handed the phone to him, she carefully avoided their hands touching. It only took a second for him to add his number . . . as if I'm going to be ringing him.

After giving him her number, she watched his large fingers deftly entering it into his phone. Remembering what they had done to her the previous evening, she suddenly felt warm and sensed the emergence of an ache in her lower tummy as he handed the phone back to her.

"What are you going to your flat for?" he asked suspiciously.

"I don't think that's any of your business."

He let out a low breath of irritation, "It will be my business if you make contact with any of your clients. I'm warning you, Rebecca, not to do that while you are with me." His menacing stare spoke volumes, so, knowing it was foolish to antagonise him, she quickly changed the subject and flippantly asked, "Isn't your presence required to save the business world?"

He got to his feet, "Yes, I must go," and clearly not perturbed by her obvious dismissal of him, asked, "Have you got a warm kiss to send a hardworking man on his way?"

Pulling up the duvet, she scowled, "Not a chance," and turned onto her side away from him, hoping he'd take the hint and go.

She felt his body lean over hers, and his warm breath on her ear, "You turned your back on me, Rebecca, and I don't like that. Shame I haven't time to teach you a lesson, I think you'd enjoy it from behind."

There was a moment of silence, before she felt a playful smack on her snugly-covered bottom. Annoyed, she grabbed a pillow and threw it at him, but he effectively dodged it as he made his way towards the door. He chuckled, "You fancy it that much, do you?"

She didn't move, but he wasn't quite finished, "Oh, before I forget, we will be going out with some potential clients of mine tonight, so be ready for seven. It's a black tie event, so wear something demure and becoming, if you can do that, and," he paused as if he'd just thought of something, "leave your hair curly, I like it that way."

You can get knotted.

"Bye then. Don't forget your coffee, will you?"

As he exited the bedroom, she had no way of knowing if he heard her last words, "I never drink coffee."

CHAPTER 13

The restaurant Darlene chose to meet Piers at was often crowded, so she'd asked her assistant Henry to book them a discreet table so that she could have a conversation about Kate without being overheard.

She ordered a gin and tonic while she waited for her son. Theirs was not a loving mother and son relationship; Piers worked for the Milner company but wasn't a great asset, and he was a gambling man, which Darlene hated. There had been many occasions when she'd bailed him out, despite him receiving a generous salary from the company. Because of this, she made sure that he didn't have direct access to the company's funds. She employed an excellent accountant in New York to ensure Piers' spending, was reined in.

He was single again having recently divorced for the second time. He'd taken legal advice, and had prenuptial contracts for both marriages, nevertheless, the divorces were costly. Darlene always felt he was high maintenance, and knew some of his activities were underhand.

On one occasion, he had physically assaulted a girl, and the costs of defending him were extortionate. From an early age he'd shown aggressive tendencies. A neighbour's pet cat had its tail cut off, a local dog fed poison, and various other incidents she didn't have the proof of, but guessed he may have been responsible. She didn't like her son very much, but maybe on this occasion his misdemeanours would work to her advantage, and he would help her get Kate back. He had to, she was depending on it.

Over a fine lunch, Darlene explained about Kate to Piers, and her desperate yearning to get her back. She was fully prepared for his reticence, as he made no secret of his dislike about her gay lifestyle.

As expected, his disparaging voice spoke volumes, "Why can't you just wait until this fling with Ezzio is over? You say he's going back to the States next week, surely she will be running back to you then anyway?"

Darlene shook her head, "She might not, though. What if he wants her to go to the States with him?"

Piers laughed, "Mother, do you really think Ezzio Marin is going to make a high class whore his mistress? I don't think so. He's just having sex with her and no doubt paying for it," he paused, shaking his head, "To be honest, I can't understand why he's paying for sex anyway; he must be fed up with the usual models and actresses he favours."

"Look, I haven't asked you here to talk about Ezzio's exploits. I want you to help me get Kate back, and there doesn't appear to be a lot of time, so we need to move quickly."

"What the hell do you expect me to do?" he asked incredulously.

"Well, something other than criticising my choices would be helpful. Haven't you ever wanted anything so badly, that you'd do anything to get it?"

"No, I can't say I have," he shrugged dismissively, "and I wouldn't be wasting my energies on a whore, that's for sure. A woman with your money could have her pick," he took a sip of his drink; "it's just a shame you go for the wrong bloody gender all the time."

Irritated by her son's criticism, she abruptly asked, "Are you going to help me or not? I'm not interested in your opinions, Piers, I just want her back."

"And how am I supposed to do that, for Christ's sake, offer her more than Ezzio is paying, surely mother you can see she's not worth that?"

Darlene pondered, "If you have to do that, then yes, it's a start. Maybe if you arranged to meet with her, money is her driver, she'll do anything for money. Can't you try and entice her with some sort of package?"

He breathed in deeply, "Does she live in London, have you got her address?"

"No I haven't," she shook her head, "Kate is quite a private person and to be honest, I know very little about her."

"So, all the information you have about her is, that she's currently staying at Ezzio's house in Surrey?"

"Yes. Oh, and I've got her mobile number, but I'm not sure if you can do anything with that?"

Darlene could see by the look on his face that he really didn't want to help, yet she knew with absolute certainty that he would. Piers Milner knew which way his bread was buttered, so was unlikely to rock that particular boat.

With a resigned look on his face, he shrugged, "Okay, I'll do what I can, but don't blame me if it turns out she's married, with a couple of well-hidden kids."

"I doubt that very much," she snapped, and then paused, considering such a scenario, "I think I'd have an idea, if that was the case."

"Yeah right, sure you would. Give me her mobile number and Ezzio's address, and I'll do some digging, but I'm not promising anything."

For the first time since Kate left, Darlene felt her spirits rise, "Thank you, Piers, that's all I ask."

Darlene left the restaurant and returned to work. Sitting in her palatial office with spectacular views overlooking the Thames, she filled her glass from the jug of water on her desk, and swallowed a handful of her pills. She gagged as the tablets caught at the back of her throat causing a reflex cough, and she considered the irony, not only were they reluctant to go down, they didn't seem to be having any impact either. Maybe I need to stop taking them and throw the lot away?

As she gazed out of the window at the hustle and bustle going on beneath her, she tried to focus on her forthcoming meeting that afternoon, but the shrill of the telephone interrupted her thoughts.

Henry spoke, "Darlene, Dr Crawford's secretary has called, and said that your review is overdue. They've had a cancellation on Friday afternoon and your diary is free, shall I tell her you can attend?"

Blast, the last thing I need right now is a counselling session. "No, I need to visit Edward on Friday, make an appointment for next month, would you?"

"Okay, will do, thanks."

The call was cut. It was a lie, she didn't need to go and visit her husband who didn't know her from Adam, but anything was preferable to a session with Dr Crawford right now. What the hell was he actually doing for her anyway? Yes, he had a comfy counselling suite and a good ear, but all he would do was adjust her medication dependent upon anything she disclosed to him, and she didn't want that right now. She knew exactly what she needed and it didn't come in the shape of a pill in a bottle.

Kate was dominating her thoughts constantly, and she missed her desperately even though it had only been two days since she'd returned from Amsterdam. Sorting herself out sexually was not enough, and she would have to resort to the agency for someone if she didn't get Kate back soon.

The problem was, however frustrated she felt, she really didn't want anyone else. It was Kate she craved. Kate sucking her nipples, until they swelled into deliciously painful points. Kate fingering her . . . Kate rubbing her clit . . . Kate licking her . . . Kate's tongue making her come and come and come. Shit, why was she thinking of that now, she'd have to go to the ladies to relieve herself with her fingers.

CHAPTER 14

Rebecca stayed in her flat for most of the day finishing two dresses for Leo. She'd dismissed Ezzio's driver and asked him to return at four, and continued sewing, acknowledging to herself that she was at her happiest creating beautiful clothes. If only she could earn enough money to support her and Emily from sewing dresses, oh, what a perfect life that would be.

She recalled the previous evening with Ezzio, and considered how difficult it was going to be, going back to paid sex with female after having experienced such delightful sex with a male. Although she disliked Ezzio, she had to admit he really was a handsome man, and her cheeks flushed when she recalled the gentle way he had brought her to orgasm in the bath, it really was quite wonderful. As always seemed to be the case, he was right again when he had said she would have been too tender for any further penetrative sex, even today she was aware of internal muscles she didn't know she had.

Once the finished dresses were wrapped, she took them by bus to Leo's fashion outlet, and as usual insisted on cash. Leo underpaid her; she knew that however, she couldn't really negotiate as she had no way of running a legitimate business. Every outgoing she had, was paid by cash, even the rent on her sparse bedsit.

Her thoughts strayed from the dresses to Ezzio, and the fact that while she was with him, she wasn't earning any money. She had a little put by which would ensure she could manage, but she needed to go back to prostitution as soon as possible. When was Ezzio going back to the States? She needed to be free of him soon.

Tomorrow her plans were to visit Emily and take her to the clinic for contraception. She'd use a baseball cap to cover her head, as she knew that both her and Emily's thick hair, was their most startling feature, and gave them away as twins before anyone even looked at their faces. She'd wear sunglasses as well to disguise their likeness, as she just couldn't afford to attract any undue attention.

Was this all necessary? Would Emily actually want to have sex with Bradley? Her mind wondered back to a conversation years earlier, sitting at the dining table in the cosy family home, having dinner. Their mother had asked Emily, who attended a school for special educational needs, how the sex education lesson in class had gone that day, and did she understand how babies were made. Emily had shaken her head, and screwed her little face up, almost if she'd been force fed a wedge of lemon, and blatantly declared that she was never going to do that, and wasn't there something else you could do to get a baby. The same lovable Emily, who had announced after her first period, that it was 'disgusting', and that she 'wasn't going to have any more of them'.

Emily was a grown woman now, though, so perfectly capable of a physical relationship, and describing her obvious enjoyment of kissing Bradley, it was quite likely things might progress in that direction. Therefore, she had no choice but to get her on some form of contraception.

She'd read all the informative literature, and decided that the best option was an implant which would be inserted into Emily's arm, and would ensure three years of contraception. It was amazing that she wouldn't have to take tablets or visit the GP for repeat injections, and with the implant, there was a cast iron guarantee that she couldn't get pregnant.

It would be quite a challenge to get Emily to comply with the procedure, but she had a cunning plan. She would buy her some lottery tickets, as currently, winning millions of pounds seemed to be her greatest desire, and if self-belief had anything to do with it, Camelot would be knocking on her door any day soon.

George, the driver arrived promptly and took her back to Ezzio's Surrey mansion. During the drive he was very polite, talking about the weather and asking if she'd had a nice day. Chatting pleasantly with him, she avoided giving any details, as she was certain Ezzio would be informed of her every move.

Once back at the house, Dorothy had prepared her afternoon tea. She'd spent so long eating little to save money, she didn't have a huge appetite. Fortunately, she had been blessed with a nice figure which needed little maintenance, but she knew if she ate all the food offered to her for the next few days, she would gain weight and then where would she be? Clients craved her body, it was her money-earner, so she couldn't afford to disappoint.

If Dorothy was disgruntled about her not eating the sandwiches and scones, she was far too polite to show it. She busied herself with the tray and asked if she would like a tour of the house, which seemingly Ezzio had suggested.

The house was truly magnificent and smacked of wealth and opulence. The sheer splendour of the decor most probably was due to the skills of a gifted interior designer. Each room she was shown, ranged from comfortable and inviting, to elegant and sophisticated.

A huge spiral staircase dominated the hall, and although she knew nothing about art, she could see the pictures donning the walls were tasteful and more than likely, worth a fortune.

The indoor swimming pool area was stunning; a piece of heaven where you could escape, and attached was a state-of-the-art gym. According to Dorothy, Ezzio used the pool and gym early each morning before work. That's why he looks so toned.

She gratefully accepted the offer to use the gym, and enjoyed exerting herself with a strenuous workout. Later, in her room, relaxing in a steaming bubble bath, she imagined how wonderful life would be, surrounded each day by such luxury and wealth, and not have to paw over women for a living.

As she leisurely applied her makeup and reached for her dress, she heard Ezzio coming up the stairs, heading for his room, she guessed. Time was tight so no doubt he'd be rushing for the shower. The thought of him naked, with warm water cascading down his fit body sent her pulse racing. . . oh, stop it.

Once ready, she waited. Should she go and tap on his door, or would it be best to wait for him to knock for her? Her tummy was doing the usual summersaults at the thought of seeing him again, which was silly as she'd seen him that very morning.

Again, she checked herself in the huge mirror dominating one of the walls. The Cadbury blue cocktail dress she was wearing was new, and she loved the slight flair of the skirt. It was one of her own creations made out of some of the leftover material of two dresses she'd sold to Leo. She loved visiting market stalls and would lose herself in selecting textiles in vibrant colours, and visualising how she would turn them into dresses.

Thanks to her gifted mother, she had the ability to turn a basic fabric into something special. She was particularly pleased with her new dress which clung to her contours, not in a trashy way, more in a sophisticated way. The dress was strapless and relatively plain, and although it could be worn with a strapless bra, she felt it looked elegant enough without one, and fortunately her breasts were high and perky. The length of the dress she'd finished a little shorter than usual, just above her knee, as she liked to show off her long legs. The only thing missing was jewellery, but she had none at all. Any little bits she'd kept from her mother, she'd been forced to sell. In her position, sentiment was a luxury she couldn't afford.

She'd never bothered with a great deal of makeup, but liked experimenting with her eyes, and was pleased with the smoky look she'd managed to achieve. Ezzio had requested she wear her hair curly . . . oh sure, like I'm going to do anything to please him. Religiously each day she straightened it, and certainly wouldn't be changing now. She piled her thick hair up on the top of her head as normal, and secured it with pins. It suited her up, and the dress was shown to its advantage by exposing more of her neck.

Looking back at herself, she was satisfied with her appearance . . . will he think I look nice? Despite taking her mobile number that morning, he hadn't contacted her all day. Tonight felt like a first date and her palms were sweaty, confirming her anxiety. Fed up with pacing the floor waiting, she made her way towards his bedroom. As she stood outside, she took a deep breath trying to control her erratic heart rate. Tapping on his door, she looked down at her cleavage, are palpitations visible?

***

She stood in the doorway, looking like every schoolboy's fantasy. His hello greeting, momentarily dried on his lips, as he was overawed once again by her beauty. Every time he saw her, he appreciated her physical attributes, but her transformation this evening was nothing short of stunning. The dress cut high above her knee, gave him a glimpse of legs that went on forever, and which he now knew, coiled around him like a vine clinging to its host. The material displayed her figure impressively, emphasising her small waist, but it was her voluptuous breasts the dress clung to provocatively, that was incredibly arousing. Breasts, which were just as nature intended. Inwardly, he chastised himself for behaving once again, like an oversexed schoolboy. Without fail, every single time he'd been away from her, and saw her again, he wanted her.

He cleared his throat, "This is a first, a female ready on time."

She appeared slightly awkward, "Well, I have had all afternoon to get ready," her eyes looked enquiringly at him, "I wasn't sure what to do, whether I should wait downstairs?"

You should wait in here, naked in my bed. "Yes, please do. Dorothy will get you a drink while you're waiting, I'll only be five minutes."

"Okay," she nodded, "I'll go downstairs." She turned, and like a catwalk model, made her way towards the staircase, walking with such elegance and poise that his lustful gaze followed each step she took in her sexy silver heels. What legs! Why did he have a ridiculous urge to grab one of his overcoats and wrap her up tightly, so that nobody else could see that gorgeous body, except him?

Quite how he was going to keep his hands off her tonight was anyone's guess. Even now, looking back at himself in the mirror, he was making a real hash of tying his dickey bow despite having done so dozens of times before. He was all fingers and thumbs, almost as if he was a young boy tying it for the first time. An unexplainable kick jolted in his abdomen; every man in the room would want her tonight. Had she any idea how she looked . . . she must, surely?

***

Declining a pre-dinner drink, she waited in the library as Dorothy instructed, and rather than sitting and creasing her dress, she stood by the fireplace scrutinising the array of photographs lined up on the mantelpiece. As she examined each one closely, a voice interrupted her.

"Hi."

She turned, how could this man make a simple word like hi sound so sexy? Her heart did its usual flip flop at the sight of him, but as she looked at his face, something about the dark intensity of his gaze, worried her. Maybe he didn't like her looking at his photographs?

"Is something wrong?"

"No, not at all," he dismissed, "How was your day, did you get everything sorted at your apartment?"

She wanted to laugh, apartment indeed, he's so blinking rich he has no idea about the shoe box that she thought of as home.

"Yes, I did thank you." She didn't elaborate further as it would only mean making up lies.

His intense scrutiny made her feel uncomfortable as she couldn't read his thoughts, "Why are you staring at me as if I've grown an extra head or something, is my dress not appropriate?" she paused, "I can change if you want me to?" They faced each other with the expanse of the room between them, and his eyes darkened, "Did Darlene buy you the dress?"

The only clothes Darlene ever bought for her were the slutty sex outfits, nothing else, but she wasn't about to discuss that with him, "No she didn't."

Some of the tension in his face evaporated, "In that case your dress is fine, it's more you I'm concerned about." His eyes assessed her from head to toe before adding, "You look stunning, Rebecca, and so very sexy. Every man in the room is going to want to remove that dress from your gorgeous body tonight, including me."

Is that an insult or a compliment? She genuinely wasn't sure of his meaning; this heterosexual stuff was so new to her. "So, does that mean you want me to change the dress?"

He looked hungrily at her, "No it means if I had the time, I'd strip it off you now, but," he shook his head and smiled playfully, "I'll have to curb my carnal instincts and delight in savouring that thought all night."

Was he aware of the effect he had on her equilibrium, standing in front of her looking incredibly handsome in his dinner suit, making outrageous sexual suggestions?

As she gazed into his penetrating brown eyes, heat scurried through her and pooled between her legs, and she realised in that split second that she wanted him to strip the dress off her. Almost as if he could read her thoughts, he raised his eyebrows, "Save that look for later," . . . so he does know what I'm thinking, "we need to go now."

She picked up her wrap, and he led her out to the front of the house where his driver was waiting. Dorothy had told her earlier that her husband George was Ezzio's driver, and that while Ezzio actually preferred to drive himself, on social occasions alcohol prohibited him doing so.

During the car journey, Ezzio discussed the people they were going to be with that evening, and then surprised her by asking, "Why did you straighten your hair?"

She eased away so that his thigh wasn't quite so close to the top of her leg, "Because I don't like it curly."

"Does it remind you of your stepfather?" Bloody hell, what is he now, some sort of psychiatrist?

"Look, what business is it of yours? I told you, I never wear it curly, it looks a mess."

"Okay, okay, I get the message. Maybe one night while you're with me you might leave it curly, I like it."

Does he really think I care about what he wants? She took a deep breath, "Am I missing something here? I'm not some sort of regular girlfriend of yours wanting to please you. Have you forgotten that you are actually forcing me to be with you?"

The car came to a halt but before they got out Ezzio had the final word.

"Oh, Rebecca, I pride myself on not forgetting anything. In fact, I recollect last night in the bath watching you come, how keen you were for me to have some sexual satisfaction too, so when we get home tonight, I'll hold you to that."

He grinned sexily at her, and exited the car . . . he's just a bloody smiling assassin.

CHAPTER 15

The elaborate venue in the swanky hotel was simply spectacular. From the extravagant décor of the room and table decorations, to the beautiful young woman playing the harp, it smacked of wealth and affluence. The waiters circulated unobtrusively, refilling beautiful crystal glasses with the finest champagne and liquors.

Rebecca thought about her small bedsit, far away from all of the glamour and opulence, and found herself almost pining for it, which was completely ridiculous as it was just a sparse box room and not a place you could call home. Possibly it was more about what the bedsit represented. Not total freedom, she'd never have that, but certainly free from Ezzio Marin, and the constant fear of him exposing her.

A particularly enjoyable part of the evening was mixing with David Lock, Ezzio's lawyer, and his lovely wife Laura. She liked them both instantly, and, almost as if they sensed her discomfort, they kept her entertained with stories about their teenage daughter's exploits, while Ezzio mingled with the other guests.

Inevitably, she had to circumvent the social chit-chat questions about her occupation, which she was able to do by stating that she was simply a stay-at-home girl, knowing that people would draw their own conclusions that she was Ezzio's bit of eye candy.

The finger food on offer was a gourmet delight. She ate very little, not just as a way of controlling her weight, but more because she was on edge, making it impossible to enjoy the food.

In the cloakroom, she'd been complimented by two women about her dress, which amused her as clearly they assumed that it had a designer label attached to it. She'd have loved to be able to admit she'd made it with material bought from a market stall, just for the shock value, but that might lead to further questions, so she thanked them politely instead.

As she engaged in conversation with a pretty actress about a West End play she was starring in, out of the corner of her eye, she saw Ezzio approaching. Despite her animosity towards him, she had to admit that he looked extremely attractive. Evidently, she wasn't the only person that thought so either, judging by the amount of females that chatted to him during the course of the evening. It was like watching bees around a honey pot, and he seemed to lap it all up. An unfamiliar knot twisted deep within her which she didn't like one bit. Quickly she dismissed it . . . what do I care?

Ezzio greeted the actress with a kiss on her cheek, and enquired about the play, giving his assurance that he would make every effort to attend. After a respectable amount of time socially chatting, he politely excused them both and linking his arm in hers, led her away.

They'd only walked a few paces before he whispered, "Not long now and we can leave," which made her tension increase. He'll be expecting sex again.

"There's no rush is there? I'm enjoying myself here." She wasn't, but anything was preferable to leaving.

His eyes twinkled, "I'll make sure you enjoy yourself even more at home."

She knew his inference, why did all their interactions always have to involve sex? Because he doesn't have any respect for me, that's why. For some peculiar reason, that saddened her, but she wasn't sure why as she didn't give a jot about Ezzio Marin and his opinion of her.

Interrupting her thoughts, he gently probed, "What's the matter?"

She shook her head, "Nothing."

"Yes, there is, I can tell by the look on your face."

Should she tell him?

"I don't like the way you speak to me, that's all."

He drew his brows together, "And what way exactly do I speak to you?"

She lifted her chin, "With a lot of sexual innuendoes."

It was obvious by the expression on his face, he was angry, "What's wrong with saying that I want to make love to you?" he asked through gritted teeth.

"It's the way you say it, in a sort of . . . threatening way."

The tone of his voice rose slightly, indicating his displeasure, "Threatening," he pronounced stiffly, "You really need to grow up, Rebecca. We both know how you earn your living, so don't start becoming all prude and virginal with me." He continued to stare menacingly, and she watched his eyes darken with fury, "Plus, do you need reminding, that you are actually a criminal on the run."

She stared at him in absolute horror. What low life would mention that in the company of guests? What if someone had overheard, she could have been arrested on the spot? She felt the colour drain quickly from her face, which had happened before, usually prior to her fainting. He must have realised that he'd overstepped the mark, as he quickly grabbed her arm, and ushered her out of the function room to the front entrance of the hotel, at the same time, reaching into his pocket for his mobile phone.

He found a vacant chaise longue in the foyer, and eased her down onto it, explaining that George was on his way, and he would be back after he'd said goodnight to the guests.

She tried to rid herself of the unpleasant light headed feeling by breathing deeply, in and out. What if someone had informed the police about her and she was arrested, who would take care of Emily? A feeling of intense claustrophobia overcame her, pushing her towards the door for some fresh air.

Her legs seemed to have a will of their own, and she began walking, not entirely sure where she was heading, but anxious as everything seemed to be spiralling out of control. Before Ezzio had come into her life, she was doing okay. Yes, there was always a chance that one day she might be found and sent back to prison, but as each year passed, she became a little more confident that it wouldn't happen.

Ezzio had started to make her fearful again, and equally as disturbing, she was unsure how to deal with the feelings that she experienced when around him. She had to acknowledge that she wanted him, which was inexplicable, when really she hated him for forcing her to go through this charade. She continued walking, and as each step propelled her forward, her thoughts became utterly desperate. How she could find a way out of the awful mess she was in?

***

Ezzio looked around hopelessly, realising that she'd gone. He rushed outside to where his driver George was waiting for him.

"Have you see Rebecca?" he barked, "she was sitting right there," he nodded towards the foyer.

George shook his head, "No I haven't, but I've only just arrived. Maybe she's in the ladies?"

Ezzio, marched into the female powder room adjacent to the reception area, much to the surprise of a woman washing her hands. He couldn't care less, he needed to find her, quickly, but she wasn't there. He swiftly made his way back to the hotel entrance where George was waiting, and got into the front seat of the car.

"Drive along the road will you, she can't be that far," and almost under his breath, he muttered, "Stupid woman, she must have set off on her own."

He knew what George must be thinking, a woman on her own and all that, and normally George was too much of a good employee to question, but not this time, "Setting off on her own at this time of night, that's madness. Why on earth would she do that, anything could happen?"

Ezzio didn't answer, knowing full well it was because of him, "Just drive the bloody car will you," he chastised.

As he anticipated, it was only minutes before he spotted the lone figure, a few hundred yards from the hotel. For some reason, he felt a thump in his gut seeing her alone, she looked horribly vulnerable, and he had been far too direct with her. He was just so furious with her for calling him threatening. The car halted alongside her, and he opened the window.

"Get in the car, Rebecca," he demanded, indicating with his head that she sat in the back. Her green eyes stared, appearing almost to look through him, "please," he added, a little more gently this time, totally unaware that he was holding his breath.

She remained still. Impatiently, he got out of the car, and put his arm around her, guiding her towards the door, "Come on now, you're cold, let's get you home."

He assisted her into the back, and secured her seatbelt before fastening his own. A glance at her pale face, caused his insides to tighten. "We'll be home soon," he reassured her, before wrapping his arms tightly around her, like a small child that he cherished . . . only to keep her warm, though.

Ezzio nodded to George through the mirror, and the car pulled away.

The journey home was relatively short, maybe she'd dozed off, she wasn't entirely sure. She'd purposely closed her eyes to avoid having to speak to him.

Ezzio dismissed George for the night, and walking up to the front entrance of the house, with his arm around her, she felt overwhelmingly tired. As they entered the warm hallway, he removed the wrap from around her shoulders, and placed it on the chair.

"You go upstairs and get into bed, and I'll bring you a brandy."

She gave him a sideways look, "Which bed do I get in, mine or yours?"

He lifted a brow, "Whichever one you want, just get comfortable and I'll be there shortly."

Quickly putting on a vest top and pyjama bottoms, she got into her own bed before he returned. She was brushing her hair, when she heard a gentle tap on the door, and there was a pause before he came in. He was carrying two drinks on a tray, and smiled kindly at her, "This should warm you up." He'd taken off his jacket, and was barefoot, but just wearing a white dress shirt and black trousers, he still looked as gorgeous as he did in the full dinner suit, making her whole body feel weak. Placing the tray on the bedside table, he sat down on the bed, and the intensity of his eyes, made her feel nervous. The butterflies, which permanently lived inside her since she'd met him, fluttered, "Why are you staring at me?"

"Because, you look about sixteen years old," his mouth curved, "and that hair of yours, loose, looks amazing."

"Did you know I'd be in here, or did you try your own room first?" she asked, keen to change the subject.

He shook his head, "No, I knew you'd be in here."

Reaching for the crystal glasses, he handed one to her, and her eyes were drawn to his dextrous fingers as they clasped the brandy balloon. She watched as he gently swirled its contents around the bottom of the glass and lifted it towards his mouth, taking a moment to inhale its fragrant aroma, before slowly sipping the liquid. How does he manage to make drinking a glass of brandy so seductive?

Without the practised display, she raised her glass to her lips, and savoured the taste as she swallowed its warm contents. Her eyes looked directly into his, and she saw genuine regret.

"I'm sorry, I shouldn't have said those things in public," he said softly, "but I'm sure we weren't overheard."

She wasn't going to forgive him that easily, "No, you shouldn't have. You knew exactly what I did before you brought me here."

He had the grace to look remorseful, "Yes, I did."

"And I will be going back to it, when you leave for the States," she clarified.

"Yes, I know all of that," he took her hand, "Look, how about if I promise not to mention anything like that again while you're with me?"

Oh yeah, as if. "You can't do that," she lifted her chin, "you thrive on intimidating me."

Shaking his head, he refuted her words, "I don't think that's quite true," he stroked her face with the back of his hand, "I thrive on wanting you."

The tummy butterflies swooped again as his voice thickened, "Right now, what I'd really like to do is kiss and makeup."

His warm, seductive eyes gleamed at her, and instantly, her body started betraying her again. Feebly she replied, "Yes, and we both know what that will lead to." As she looked into his persuasive eyes, she knew the game was lost, she wanted him.

Taking the glass out of her unsteady hands, he rested it on the dresser, and leant forward, touching her lips very gently with his own, "Well, I'm hoping."

She didn't resist his lips. He cradled her head in his hands, deepening the kiss, and for a few moments, she savoured the continual assault on her mouth. Oh, how good he tasted.

Pausing, he eased the bottom of her vest up, and she assisted by lifting her arms, as he pulled it over her head. He eased her back onto the pillows, and eagerly took one of her nipples in his mouth, while his fingers continued to tease the other. She moaned with pleasure, it felt so lovely. He stepped away from her, and stood at the side of the bed, slowly undoing the buttons of his shirt, and then taking it off. He reached inside his trouser pocket, and produced a condom which he tossed onto the bed, and her excitement flared as she watched him remove his trousers and underwear. There was something very stirring about Ezzio stripping off in front of her, but what thrilled her most of all, was, during the whole time he undressed, he never took his eyes off her once.

She devoured his hard and lithe body, with a magnificently proportioned chest, covered in dark hair which her fingers itched to explore. The dark hair tapered down his flat stomach forming a dark thatch surrounding his manhood; he was truly amazing. Pulling the bedclothes back, his large hands eased her gently out of her pyjama bottoms, and his sexy eyes ravished her naked body, "God, you're so beautiful," he whispered huskily, before his lips consumed hers again, and he slid himself into the bed next to her. The feeling of his erection against her belly thrilled her, and she pushed her breasts against his taut chest, eager to feel all of his hard body against hers.

Practised fingers caressed her, slowly, which felt like heaven, and his hands were everywhere, stroking her, loving her, first gently and then firmly. Feeling his tender lips on her breasts was quite wonderful, and she felt the pull drawing deep inside her. How she wanted this man . . .did he know how much?

In between kisses, he groaned, "I want to be inside you when you come."

Overwhelmed with the sensations he was creating, she could only nod. Gently he turned her onto her left side facing away from him, and cradled her in his arms.

This was all so new to her, and she just loved the feeling of this huge man holding her tightly, and so intimately. Kissing her neck repeatedly, she felt his potent erection between her legs as he moved deliberately against her. He positioned his penis against her slippery, but accommodating labia, and it glided along teasingly, each time almost moving into her welcoming entrance, but stopping short of doing so. With one of his large hands cupping her breast, and his fingers circling her clitoris, she savoured his huge organ rubbing along her sensitive core, and for a spilt second she considered . . . when has anything ever felt this good?

She pushed her bottom against him wanting more, and felt his breath in her ear commanding, "Lift your knees up."

She did so, and from behind he eased himself inside her, slowly. The fact that he was deliberately taking his time so that she could get used to his size, caused her tummy to cartwheel.

Impatiently she pushed herself backwards, wanting him to fill her, and he obliged by pushing further, until she accepted all of him.

He moved gently at first, and then slowly increased the pace, "You fit me perfectly," he whispered in her ear.

The sensation of this man inside her with his hand cradling her breast, while the other continued to massage her hard nub in circles, was building unbearable pleasure. Wrapped in his arms she experienced something that she had not felt in her life for such a long time . . . she felt cherished.

She was lost in the rhythm of him filling her once, and then filling her again, and again. On and on, huge powerful thrusts and the thrill he was creating with his hands was almost intolerable.

Abruptly, when she was so close, he moved out of her and she felt bereft, until he lifted her by her waist onto all fours, and placed her facing the mirrored slide-robes, adjacent to the bed.

Kneeling behind her, he entered her again, not gentle and slowly this time, just one thrust, and he was deep inside her. Automatically, she closed her eyes to feel the sensations again.

Ezzio urged gutturally, "Open your eyes, watch us."

She did, and was even more excited to see how primitive they looked in the mirror, like animals mating. He was so huge behind her, cupping her breast again with his arm under her waist, while his other hand continued to thrill, stretching and stroking. It felt like she was a slave being screwed by her master, and oh how it excited her. In and out he plunged, in and out, in and out.

For The Love Of Emily

"Come," he urged in a husky voice that inflamed her, "I want to watch you in the mirror, when you come, baby."

It felt like she was about to combust. The sensations he was creating were excruciating, and suddenly, they reached a peak, and exhilarating hot pleasure gushed down her, like a fountain, cascading through her body as she called out his name, and fell down, and down, and down.

His own release came simultaneously, and she felt him thundering into her with a punishing force. It was unbelievable. Her legs were like jelly as he drew her down on the bed, and they lay for a second in silence, as if neither wanted to break the spell.

Slightly easing himself away from her, he turned her to face him, stroking her head and kissing her so very gently, "You really are exquisite, do you know that?"

He pulled her to him, and she fitted perfectly, resting her weary head on his shoulder. She stilled. How could this man she hated so much, complete her in every way possible?

***

Once it was evident she'd fallen asleep, he extracted himself to dispose of the condom in the bathroom, checking carefully to ensure it hadn't burst. If it had, he wouldn't have been surprised with the force of their lovemaking. He'd never experienced such powerful orgasms as he did with her, the sex was simply amazing.

He crept back into the bedroom and observed her sleeping, noting how angelic she looked, with her long lashes acting like curtains hiding her eyes. For the first time in his life, he had the urge to get back into bed following sex, but quickly reminded himself, it was best to avoid any post coital intimacy.

As he headed to his own room, he considered what it would be like for a woman to sleep next to him. It wasn't something he'd ever experienced as he'd suffered from insomnia all his adult life, so rarely fell asleep after sex. Once the deed had been done with whoever, he promptly left.

Tonight, he knew that she'd wake up and be embarrassed about what had happened between them, while he was already erect thinking about repeating the whole thing again. Rebecca really was an incredibly sexy woman, and despite his head telling him to keep her at a distance, his body hungered for her desperately, which was a first for him also.

Why did this particular woman have such a hold over him? It must just be the chase. Rejection from a woman was completely new territory for him, he just wasn't used to it. It wasn't conceit. From his experience of dating women, they usually welcomed his advances, and the challenge had always been to keep them at a distance. Now for the first time in his life, he'd met a woman that didn't want him, and he didn't like it one bit.

CHAPTER 16

Darlene was trying to absorb the information Piers had brought her.

"So, what if she has got a twin sister, how on earth is that going to bring her back?"

"Think about it, you'll be able to use it as a negotiating tool."

"What . . . look, Kate, I know you have a sister that's not all there and you keep hidden away, now I know all of this, you'll have to come back to me."

Piers sighed, "No, Mother, even you're not that stupid."

"Then how on earth is this going to work?" She was disappointed, she'd expected more from Piers.

"We can send the sister on a little holiday and bring her back once Kate returns to you. The sister is a retard, so it shouldn't be too difficult to entice her away from the nuthouse she lives in."

She interrupted, "You mean kidnap her?"

"Keep your voice down," Piers chastised, "who said anything about kidnapping, I'm talking about a holiday break, with supervision?"

She was dismayed, "And you think Kate will want anything to do with me after that?"

Piers sighed again, "She will because you aren't going to be involved, I'll see to it all. Once I have the sister, I'll see that Kate dumps Ezzio and returns to you. When she does, I'll bring the sister back and you won't have been involved at all."

His eyes scrutinised her face, making her feel uncomfortable. Leaning forward, he placed his folded arms on the table, and moving his face closer, he leered, "Yes, I can see why my mother is smitten; you're not bad looking for a whore."

With a look, as distasteful as she could muster, she hissed, "What are you talking about? I'm here to discuss my sister."

"And I'm here to discuss my mother," he paused, his eyes on her breasts, "with a proposition that will suit us both."

She shook her head, "Who the hell is your mother?"

He raised an eyebrow and smirked, "Darlene Milner."

It felt like someone had punched her in the stomach. Darlene had no knowledge of Emily, nobody had.

Disbelief flared inside her, "What has Darlene got to do with my sister?"

"Nothing. I don't suppose she even knows that you have a sister, and even if she did, she wouldn't care anyway."

If only she was a man, she'd knock the insolent look off his face. He carried on, "Family life isn't what you lot are interested in, is it?"

She didn't answer, her eyes drawn to his hands as he reached and fiddled with a sugar sachet as if they were two normal people out for coffee. His eyes met hers, "For some reason, my mother seems utterly besotted with you and wants you back in her life."

"I know all of that," she spat, "Look, where's my sister? Is it money you want?"

He threw his head back and laughed, "You couldn't afford to pay me, darling."

"Try me, I can get money."

"I'm not interested in your money."

"What do you want, then?"

"I want you to go back to my mother."

This was too ridiculous for words, how had he found Emily? She scowled, "What are you talking about?"

He waited until the approaching waitress put the coffees down and walked away, before continuing, "It's simple. You go back to my mother, and you can have your sister back."

Leaning backwards in his chair, he had a smug look on his face, while she struggled to comprehend exactly what was happening.

Her insides churned with fury, "I can't believe Darlene would resort to this."

His eyes looked menacing, "My mother hasn't resorted to anything. I told you, she knows nothing about this."

Rebecca shook her head disbelievingly, "Why would you do something like this?" She glared, hating him, "What sort of a person are you?"

"One that likes to keep my mother happy." He raised his eyebrows, "Personally I think your sort need a regular fucking to show you what you're missing," he leant in close, "I don't usually have time for dykes, but in your case, I could make an exception."

Sensing it wasn't wise to antagonise him, she needed to clarify exactly what he expected. "Let me get this straight," her voice was filled with contempt, "I return to Darlene, and you'll bring my sister back?"

Taking a slurp of his coffee, he wiped his mouth with a serviette and nodded smugly, "Yep, that's it, but," he warned, "you have to go back today."

Devastated, came nowhere close to describing her emotional state; she had to get Emily back, but by crossing Ezzio, he could turn her into the police.

A sudden thought entered her head, "You say Darlene doesn't know about this. What will she think if I just turn up? She's already asked me to go back and I've said no."

He shrugged, "Tell her you've changed your mind. I've told her I'll do my best to get you back for her, so say that I've paid you highly. After all, that's what floats the boat of a whore, isn't it . . . money?"

Ignoring his insult again, she clarified, "So, if I go back to Darlene now, right this minute, when will I see Emily?"

"When my mother tells me," he raised his eyebrows, "that you are fully back into her, if you get my drift."

She got it alright; she had to be with Darlene sexually.

He continued, "Then, I'll see that your sister is taken back to the nuthouse. They think she's gone on a little break and will be back in a day or two."

God, what an evil bastard. "How do I know you'll bring her back?"

His malicious little eyes met hers, "You don't. You'll just have to trust me."

Trust him, the man that had taken her sister in the first place? While she had little choice but to go along with his demands, before agreeing to anything, she needed to speak to Emily.

"Let me speak to her, and I'll go back to your mother's penthouse now."

The smirk he gave her spoke volumes, he'd known all along that she'd comply.

He took his phone out of his pocket and keyed in a number. She heard him initially speak in a hushed tone to whoever answered, and as he leant across to pass the phone to her, she snatched it out of his hand, "Em, is that you?"

Emily sounded breathless and excited, "Hiya Rebecca, when are you coming?"

"I can't," she exhaled a shaky breath of relief at hearing Emily's voice. "Are you alright?"

"'Course I am, it's fantastic here," Emily replied before her tone changed and she challenged, "Why aren't you coming?"

Not wanting to scare her, she kept an even tone to her voice, "I'm working, but you'll be back soon and I'll see you then."

She sensed Emily's mood change as it went quiet. Desperate for her to stay on the line, she demanded "Are you still there, Em?"

Emily's voice signalled her disappointment, "It's not fair. I want you to see the hotel and the beach, and . . ." the call was cut dead.

She glared at him, and he returned her stare. Like other men before him, she saw the glint of sexual desire in his eyes, but chose to ignore it. From her early teens, she'd been used to men seeing her as a sex object.

With as much hatred as she could throw in, she hissed, "You harm my sister in any way, and you'll be sorry."

"Oh, now I'm really quaking in my boots," he laughed, "having a slut like you threatening me. I've a good mind to teach you a lesson you won't forget before you go back to my mother."

Calling his bluff, she sneered, "And I'm sure your mother would be really pleased with you after that."

Fury registered on his ugly face, but she knew he couldn't argue with that. He shrugged indifferently, and as if to compensate for her cutting remark, replied, "Right, you run along now and play whatever games you cock-less lot get your kicks from, but remember, no police. If you involve them, you will be sorry."

After leaving the coffee shop, she headed straight for the pawnbrokers, and accepted the amount of money she was offered for Ezzio's watches. They must have been worth considerably more than she had been given, but she wasn't in a position to argue.

As she made her way on the tube to Darlene's penthouse, she thought about the disgusting level she'd sunk to, and a stab of self-revulsion hit her stomach. There was no way back now. As well as being a prostitute, she was a common thief. Although she would use the money from the watches to make sure Emily was moved to a new place out of harm's way, she was appalled with herself, and fearful about the ramifications of her actions. Ezzio would never forgive her, not that she deserved his forgiveness, but there was no point in worrying about that. What she needed to do now, was go and get her sister back.

CHAPTER 20

Piers had pulled it off. Darlene called ahead to the concierge to let Kate into her apartment, and drove home in a sexual frenzy with every bump in the road heightening her excitement. Parking the car in the basement, she raced to the private lift taking her closer to paradise. The doors opened directly into her penthouse apartment, and there she stood, with a drink in her outstretched hand, completely naked. She gave an appreciative look at Kate's beautiful rousing body with the pert breasts and neatly trimmed pubic hair, before walking towards her to take the drink out of her hand, even though alcohol was the last thing on her mind.

Nevertheless, she knocked back a huge gulp of the energising gin, before placing the crystal tumbler on the hall table, and reaching for her gorgeous face, she kissed her longingly, putting her heart and soul into their exchange, almost devouring her. She tasted so good, much better than she'd remembered, and she slowly but surely, thrust her tongue forward into her accepting mouth. The kiss was intentionally prolonged, so that she could savour the familiarity of her delicious lips.

Breaking away, Kate pushed her against the nearest wall, and her memorable green eyes, flashing their emerald brilliance, focussed directly upon her eyes, while her nimble fingers began blindly unbuttoning her jacket and blouse. Neither of them was speaking, which she found incredibly arousing, and as she concentrated on her beautiful face and luscious lips, her whole body quivered with anticipation.

Kate stood back, staring at her partially clothed body, and brazenly instructed, "Get rid of the rest." With an impatience charged with urgency, she started with her bra, and then swiftly removed her skirt, tights and knickers, desperate for those skilled hands on her sex-starved body. The whole process took less than a minute, with Kate watching intently, only moving once to reach for her own drink from the hall table, and downing it in one. It was a surprise to see her drink so much, as she never drank a great deal of alcohol in her company.

Once she'd removed her clothes and shoes, and stood completely naked, Kate stepped towards her, once again pushing her against the wall, and as she felt the coldness on her bare flesh, she pressed her hands against the partition to steady herself.

Reaching for her breasts, Kate first took one, and then the other into her mouth, biting, sucking, and teasing the tight buds. Heat expanded in the pit of Darlene's abdomen, and she twisted her hips restlessly from the intense pleasure causing a contraction deep within her. Internally, blood had to be gushing to her core, and she groaned out loud from the powerful sensations she was getting from Kate's exquisite hot mouth as it suckled, and continued to draw strongly on her ripe nipples.

Kate paused and urged, "Hold your tits." Darlene didn't hesitate, cupping her breasts and pushing them towards her, enthralled as Kate dipped her head, and with her long flexible tongue, graphically licked every inch of them. As she looked down at her nipples, she saw they were wet and tightening to hard peaks, begging provocatively for more. Their eyes clashed, and still holding her breasts expectantly, Kate's index finger began feeling for her throbbing clit hidden beneath its swollen protective hood, and as she stroked and lightly squeezed, she was seconds away, oh God . . . oh God, she writhed, but Kate stilled and with a slight smile playing at the corners of her mouth, she instructed, "Come into the bedroom, I've got a surprise for you."

Darlene, feeling slightly dazed, and more than a little bereft as she was so close, took her outstretched hand, and walked with her into the bedroom. Having no idea what to expect, but excited beyond words by the foreplay, she quickly did as instructed and lay down, moving towards the centre of the bed to allow Kate room to sit down on the edge next to her, the whole time, keeping her eyes firmly fixed on her glorious naked body.

Stroking her face, Kate purred, "I'm going to give you something special tonight," and Darlene nodded in breathless anticipation . . . get on with it, then, I need it now.

Kate leaned her head towards her and kissed her, thrusting her tongue inside her mouth, and the pleasure was simply wonderful. Breaking the kiss, she tilted her chin, "Have you been with anyone else since I've been away?"

"No," she shook her head truthfully.

Kate's mouth moved back to her wanting breast, and she watched as her open lips closed over one burning nipple, suckling hard, before she lifted her head to ask, "Then you must be really hungry . . . are you?"

"Yes," she nodded, savouring the delightful tingling sensation of her mouth on her breasts again, "I'm truly starving," and then breathed in deeply, "please, let's just get on with it."

Kate's mouth continued kissing and sucking, moving her head down her belly, and lower still until she licked, just above her burning clit, "We will do, in a minute . . . have you missed me?" The licking onslaught continued, dampening her pubic hair.

"Yes, I have," she moaned, "Look, we can play all the games you want later, but right now . . ."

Kate interrupted her, "We're going to do something a little different tonight, which I know you're going to love."

"Well let's do it, then, I can't wait much longer," she urged.

Kate's head became level with her own, "For my treat to work, you're going to have to be really wet," her tummy flipped, "Are you wet, kitten?"

"Yes," she groaned, "I'm soaking."

"Open your legs and let me feel."

She quickly opened them wide, and felt a gush of excitement deep within her as Kate's eyes stared at her most intimate area, before she placed two of her fingers in her juicy mouth, in and out, in and out, sucking them slowly, and when she eventually removed them, saliva dripped liberally down the back of her hand.

With her deliciously wet fingers, Kate wiped the moisture from her mouth along her slippery labia, unhurriedly, stroking and tormenting her core. She instinctively lifted her pelvis, desperate for clit stimulation, but Kate ignored her, graphically sucking her own fingers again until they were sopping wet. Then with practised precision, she pushed them high inside of her, causing a guttural moan to escape from deep within her; wanting more, desperately wanting so much more.

Kate's green eyes flashed directly into hers, "Oh yes, you're almost ready for what I have in mind for you." She trailed the dry fingers of her other hand around Darlene's engorged nipples in tiny circles, tormenting, and making them prickle, while she continued fingering her, "But I need you to be wetter than you are."

Moving away from her, she opened the bedside drawer and removed a tube of lubrication, and Darlene watched mesmerised, as Kate squeezed a generous amount on her fingers. Placing one hand on her tummy, she used the lubricated digits to reach deep inside her again, sliding her slick fingers around her spongy internal walls, causing ripples of excitement deep within her.

She removed her fingers, slowly, and continued to massage her labia with the slippery gel. It felt like it had gone from wet and hot, to sodden and burning, and she pleaded, "Please . . . please," as she became lost in the assault on her senses.

Kate's expression darkened, "Right, my hungry little kitten, I think you're ready for my surprise."

Her puzzlement as she watched her lean downwards and reach under the bed, quickly changed to wonder, when she saw her clutching a lightweight sexual harness, with a large dildo protruding out of the front. While she suspected that Kate did this with her other female clients, it wasn't something they'd ever done together. She met her eyes, and in them saw challenge; she wasn't asking if she could use it, she was telling her that she would.

"Yes, kitten," she nodded, "You're going to be fucked now."

While her own sexual preference had always been caressing and mouths with a partner, today, having Kate back, and already being incredibly turned on, she'd do anything for release. Her anticipation intensified watching Kate secure the harness around her hips, and once it was in place, she commanded, "Get on all fours and face the mirror."

Excited beyond words, she quickly obliged, leaning forward on her knees and supporting herself on her own forearms, with her arse in the air. Watching Kate, kneeling behind her in the mirror was a new experience for her, and when she felt her intensely pleasurable mouth biting and kissing the cheeks of her bottom, a sexual charge surged through her, as every erotic nerve ending pulsated and throbbed. An excited squeal escaped from her lips, as skilful fingers slid deep inside her, reaching high and filling her sensationally, before being withdrawn and replaced by the substitute penis tormenting her entrance. Frantically writhing, she raised her voice, "Please get on with it," and to reiterate, she asserted loudly, "I need it now." She was desperate, seeing Kate's beautiful naked torso, and feeling her sensual pubes pressed against her arse. She opened her legs wider, inaudibly begging, and was rewarded by the dildo being shoved deep inside her, hard and high, and she screamed at the sheer forcefulness of it.

Kate's voice was sharp, and commanding, "Hold it. Don't let it slip." She clenched her internal muscles tightly around the dildo, and held it firmly in place, suspecting by the tone of her voice, that if she did let it slip, she'd miss out.

Slowly, she felt the dildo moving. The regularity of Kate's hips touching her arse, and then moving away, touching, then moving away, as she plunged rhythmically with the substitute penis, was sensational. The internal friction was completely new to her, and hugely exhilarating, made more thrilling as she clamped her internal muscles tightly around the dildo, causing ripples of ecstasy to surge in her lower abdomen.

Kate's breasts were bouncing, and the dildo was filling her; it was all so basic and erotic, and as she felt Kate's hands cupping her engorged breasts, and demanding, "Does it feel good kitten?" she could only groan a response.

"Do you want it like this?" . . . she slowed the pace down . . . "Or do you want it like this?" . . . she speeded the pace up.

"Fast," she pleaded, "Please, hard and fast."

"Do…you…like…me…screwing…you…like…thi s?" Each word was accompanied by a deep thrust, and she whimpered in sheer ecstasy as her core pulsated.

"Yes!" she yelled, and then louder, "Yes!"

"Good, 'cause now I'm going to give you what you want."

Kate's fingertips were kneading, caressing and tweaking her nipples forcibly, and she gasped in delight as her fingers moved down and stroked her erect bud. She eased her legs wider, needed more, "Now," she pleaded, "please, now . . . don't stop."

The delightful fingers and thrusting dildo stilled, momentarily, as Kate ordered, "When you come, say my name," and then with greater emphasis, she growled, "Say it." The pressure continued, relentlessly, driving into her, faster and deeper.

The pleasure was rising, and then rising higher still. Expert fingers rolled her clit from side to side, and the dildo pushed deep inside her. Then taking her completely by surprise, Kate grasped a chunk of her hair and pulling hard, lifted her head, "Say it, Darlene," she urged, "say it while I'm fucking you."

She took one last look in the mirror, and couldn't contain herself for a second longer, as waves of pleasure engulfed her. She was coming and coming, and screaming and screaming, "Kate . . . oh Kate . . . Kate," she wailed loudly, as the tidal wave erupted down her body with an orgasm so powerful and explosive, she shuddered uncontrollably with the force it.

For a few seconds she stilled, and then while still on her knees, she turned and grasped Kate her in her arms and kissed every inch of her beautiful face over and over. . . my Kate, I'll never let you go again.

"Thank you my darling, thank you," Darlene sighed, "You are simply the most amazing woman that I've ever met. I needed you so much tonight, and that was so wonderful," she hugged her appreciatively. "Will you stay with me tonight?"

"Yes, if you want me to," Kate nodded.

Darlene waited until she'd removed the harness, and then eased them both down onto the bed, pulling the bed sheets over them. Yawning contentedly, she held onto Kate like she'd never let her go, "Let's just have a little sleep, and get a bite to eat, then we can chat."

Tiredness overcame her as she thought about her husband and how he made her perform on all fours. The penetrative sex had hurt her, but tonight's experience had been completely wonderful, and tomorrow night, she would take a turn at using the harness to fuck Kate. What a night, she was back, and all was well.

**

As Darlene slept, Kate stifled an urge to sob, but a silent tear escaped and rolled down her cheek as she pictured her sister in a dingy hotel room with a virtual stranger. The only comfort was that Emily had no idea what was going on, in fact, bless her, she even sounded happy on the phone.

Had she done enough with Darlene to get Emily back? What if tomorrow Piers said she had to do more? Was it true that Darlene had no idea about Emily being taken, maybe she was part of it, and this was all a charade? She chastised herself, there was no point in worrying about that now. She had to be positive, she'd done what was asked, so she could only hope that tomorrow Emily would return.

A shudder ran through her, and she felt revulsion at the sex she'd had to perform tonight. Inevitably, her mind drifted back to the wonderful sex she'd shared with Ezzio, but that only made her feel terribly lonely. That's in the past, she scolded herself, she must forget about it. Now, was about getting Emily back. She must erase Ezzio Marin from her mind, and pray that their paths never crossed again, because if they did, the consequences didn't bear thinking about.

**

The following morning Darlene showered and dressed for work. They hadn't discussed why Kate was back, somehow it wasn't necessary.

She was meticulous with her appearance, not for the sake of vanity; she'd never be one of those types, she just liked to look clean and tidy, wearing well-cut suits with tailored jackets, to disguise her middle-age spread.

Her hair was kept in a manageable bob by regular visits to a salon, and she used the minimum amount of make-up. No, beauty was never her top priority. As she was putting the final touches to her hair, she saw Kate hovering and looking absolutely scrumptious in a short silky robe tied loosely around her waist.

"Are you likely to see Piers at work this morning?" Kate asked.

"Yes," she nodded casually, careful not to give anything away to indicate she knew what Piers had done, "He's still working with me for a short while until he returns to the States."

Kate moved closer, "Will you tell him about us?"

Darlene smiled, "I could do, but to be honest, he's not that interested in my personal life."

She picked up her handbag, heading for the hallway to the lift, but paused as Kate rushed over, and gave her an unexpected kiss.

"Just before you go, I want to give you something to remind you of me today when you're working."

She wasn't sure what she meant until she sexily instructed, "Why don't you sit down," her eyes nodded towards the ornate hall chair, "And take your knickers off so I can kiss you goodbye properly."

As Darlene met her eyes, her lower abdomen tightened, and in almost slow motion, she dropped her handbag to the floor, and slipped her hands under her skirt, bending to ease her pants down to around her thighs, all the time keeping her eyes on Kate, as she cajoled, "Sit down and hitch your skirt up so I can see all of you." Darlene was hypnotised, and sat on the hallway chair, hoisting her skirt around her waist in anticipation of what was to come.

Before she could remove her knickers further, Kate knelt down in front of her and eased them down her legs and over each of her shoes, at the same time commanding, "Open your legs for me."

Her lower abdomen began performing summersaults sitting half clothed, in her shoes, with her femininity completely exposed. She gasped as Kate, kneeling at her feet, slowly removed the tiny robe she was wearing, displaying her sexy body, and as instructed, she eagerly opened her legs.

Her head fell back against the wall as she felt sensational fingers massage the insides of her thighs, with her thumbs caressing her pubic area. Kate lowered her head, and she felt a long, slow drawn-out lick along her labia. She looked up and met her eyes, as she sexily purred, "You're very dry after your shower." God, she's such a fucking turn on.

Firm hands clasped her hips, and as she dipped her head again, she felt the delicate sensation of her tongue licking fiercely to moisten her core. She closed her eyes . . . Jesus, Christ, this feels so good.

Kate carried on unremittingly, giving one drawn-out lick after another, "I want you begging for me, Darlene." This woman is just incredible.

With proficient fingers, she felt her labia being parted, and then the firmness of her tongue around her entrance, and she breathed deeply savouring the exquisite torture, "You want this, don't you, kitten?" Oh, do want it.

Another lick, pressing hard, and she felt the burning desire heat up between her legs, "Tell me, then."

"Yes, oh God, yes," she pleaded, "I want it." Don't you dare stop!

Another lick . . . God, my tits are tingling.

Another lick along her hot throbbing labia, "You taste so good, Darlene." For Christ's sake, my clit, you keep missing it.

She felt long fingers inside her hot and clenching channel, "You're really turned on now, Darlene, I'm going to make you come in my mouth." The fingers slipped out, and the licking assault started again, sending quivers of awareness to her core causing her inner folds to pump. I'm so close . . . Oh for fuck's sake . . . touch me where I need it.

"Is that what you want?"

"Yes, hurry now . . . please," she begged feeling the moisture dripping from her wet folds.

Kate paused again, her hot breath tormenting her core, "Tonight I'm going to fuck you again with the dildo and watch you come in the mirror."

Finally, she felt her tongue press on her engorged clit, and she reeled in ecstasy at the pressure, like a stiff rod moving round and round. She pushed on Kate's head as if it would give her a greater peak, and then screamed as the pleasure reached its pinnacle, and she began to climax, her whole body contracting with powerful sensations as wave after wave of undulating pleasure flowed over and over, before splintering into millions of tiny pieces. What an incredible orgasm from an amazing woman, she was simply magnificent.

***

Kate stared at her slumped in the chair, with her skirt around her waist exposing her core. In the aftermath of sex, she looked deeply fulfilled.

She stood and looked directly into her satisfied eyes, "Make sure you speak to Piers, won't you? Tell him you are happy to have me back."

Using the chair to steady herself, Darlene stood up and sighed deeply, "Of course I will darling. Look, I don't know how much Piers paid you, but I can assure you there will be a big bonus from me tonight, you've been absolutely sensational."

She watched Darlene put her knickers back on, and then step towards her smiling affectionately. Tilting her chin, Darlene kissed her briefly on the lips, "Thank you for coming back. We'll have so much more time to talk tonight, last night was a bit hectic."

Observing her smug face, Kate smiled at her submissively. You have no idea. Once I've got Emily back, you and your wretched son will never see me again, ever.

After assuring her she would leave the key with the concierge, she closed the door, and rushed into the bathroom. Kneeling down with her head over the toilet, she heaved and wretched, as if she would never stop.

CHAPTER 21

The Warden, Janet Coo could see the despair in Rebecca's eyes. Still stunned by the abduction of Emily, her thoughts were toward her own future. With absolute certainty, she knew that the Local Authority would suspend her, pending an enquiry as to the abduction of a young person whilst in her care.

What if she didn't come back? It just didn't bear thinking about. We should have called the police, but Rebecca said no as she was certain that her sister would be back today. Although it wasn't personally her fault that Emily had been taken, as manager of the accommodation for vulnerable adults, it had happened on her watch, so she knew she would lose her job, eventually. Then what?

According to Rebecca, Emily had been taken on a supposed trip. They quickly deduced it was the laundry lady Iris that had taken her, clearly having been paid by some unscrupulous individual to do so. It was apparent Rebecca had communicated with whoever had taken her sister, as she was convinced that she was on her way back. They both stood side by side, looking out of the bay window, almost as if by doing this, it would bring her back sooner.

"What time is it now?" Rebecca asked, which was a futile question, as it was only five minutes since she'd previously asked, "I can't stand much more of this," she muttered hopelessly, "When are they going to bring her back?"

Janet was trying to think further ahead, "What's going to happen when she does come back, are you going to take her away from here?"

Rebecca nodded, "I'll have to. I don't have any other option. I can't leave her here, not now."

"But where will you take her to? Emily's happy here and needs care and support, and you work, so can't be there for her twenty-four hours a day."

"I know. I'll have to think of something, she can't stay here after this, you do understand that don't you?" Rebecca's voice was trembling, and her eyes bright with unshed tears.

Janet felt an enormous amount of sympathy for Rebecca. What a terrible ordeal. You didn't need to be Einstein to work out something wasn't quite right. Insisting on paying cash all the time, and never taking Emily out, even for lunch or a trip to the seaside, was all so strange. But she didn't ask questions, as long as she paid the fees, then it was none of her business. Emily, who was usually so open about everything, said little about Rebecca's life, only to say that she worked really long days looking after a poorly old man who didn't have any family.

She touched Rebecca's arm reassuringly, "Of course I understand. I feel I've let you down so badly, if anything happens to . . ." she left the sentence unfinished.

Rebecca was emphatic, "It won't. Nothing is going to happen to her, she'll be back today, I know she will." Although she spoke with conviction, Janet felt it was more to reassure herself rather than being absolutely certain.

"And you haven't let anyone down, please don't think you have," she insisted, "Emily loves it here, you know that. I'm afraid it's me that has let everyone down, not you."

Janet shook her head, "I just don't understand it, why would anyone want to take her away, and what did they want for her return?" she demanded, "have you had to pay to get her back?"

Rebecca's face appeared almost trance-like, as she confessed, "Oh yes, I've had to pay alright . . . just not with money." She looked directly into her eyes, "The least you know, the better, we'll be out of here soon, I promise you."

Janet couldn't let it drop, "But they've broken the law, it's kidnapping and they need punishing," she insisted, "we really should call the police."

Rebecca's eyes blurred, "They'll just say Emily wanted to go away for a few days, and as no money has changed hands to get her back, there's been no kidnapping as such," her voice trembled, "and I'm sure Iris will be long gone after today with whatever money she'll have been paid."

She nodded in agreement, "Yes, you're probably right."

Janet's insides were in turmoil imagining the consequences of Emily not returning, it was unthinkable. She had to be positive, and watching Rebecca, glued to the window, she had a thought, "Could I make a suggestion which might help?"

Rebecca turned her head towards her, "Yes?"

"My sister and her husband own a farm in Sleaford, Lincolnshire. They have young people residing on the farm that help out with the animals and in return, receive a small wage. It's primarily for young people unable to get regular work, and they have been known to take on people in the past with learning difficulties. There's also purpose-built accommodation for them to stay in. It's nothing grand, but it might be a place where Emily could be happy, even if it's for a short time until you get sorted."

She suspected Rebecca didn't have an abundance of options on the table, and watched her face as she considered the suggestion. Shaking her head, and in a croaky voice, almost to herself she whispered, "I'd be terrified she might be taken away again . . . I don't think I could stand that."

It was clear that Rebecca was close to breaking point, so she put her arm around her, "She'd be safe, nobody but you and I would know where she was, and I'm not likely to tell anyone, am I?" She continued in a reassuring voice, "I could arrange for you both to go for a short while to see if you like it," she gave a little wry smile, "that's as long as you don't mind roughing it and sleeping with the others?" She carried on speaking although it was pointless as she wasn't really being heard, "Anyway don't worry about it for now, let's just get . . ." a car door banged, and their eyes were simultaneously drawn towards the window. There in the brilliant morning sunshine, directly in front of them, was the wonderful sight of Emily, sauntering nonchalantly up the drive, in a summer dress with a cute sun hat, and they watched her turn to wave to the car as it sped away.

***

Rebecca ran out of the house, flung her arms around her sister, and held her tightly. Emily wriggled, struggling for breath, "You're hurting me," she pulled away from her grasp looking puzzled, "Why are you crying?"

Through watery eyes, Rebecca smiled "I'm just pleased to see you, that's all. I've missed you so much."

Emily looked accusingly at her, "Why didn't you come to the seaside, then? I asked you to come, but you didn't."

Rebecca sniffed, stifling an overwhelming urge to sob, "I wish I had, Em, but I couldn't get away from work." She hated lying, but it was the only option. "Was that Iris from the laundry driving away, did she take you to the seaside?"

Emily nodded excitedly, "Yes, I like Iris. We played on the slot machines and paddled in the sea . . . and she bought me hot chocolate with marshmallows . . . and I had chips, and er . . . oh yes, I've got two lottery tickets."

Rebecca felt sick in the pit of her stomach, but couldn't let her know, "It sounds such fun, was anyone else there with you?"

"No just us. A friend of Iris's came one day, but he didn't stay very long though," and then her face lit up, as her mind quickly moved on, "I've got you a present, and one for Mrs Coo as well."

Bless her, she has no idea whatsoever exactly what had just happened.

"Come on, then, my darling, let's go inside and you can tell us all about it." With her eyes still moist, she squeezed Emily tight, and silently thanked God for bringing her back; the consequence of losing her beloved sister was unthinkable. Kissing her affectionately on her forehead, she smiled, "I love you so much, Em."

Emily rolled her eyes, "I know you do, I love you just the same."

CHAPTER 22

Ezzio was clearing his desk in preparation for flying to the States that evening, and it couldn't come soon enough. David Lock, his lawyer, would be overseeing his side of the Marin and Milner merger, with the assistance of Michael Golding, his newest protégée. He wouldn't be back, not for a while at least, England had lost its charm.

The telephone interrupted his thoughts, and his secretary announced that Piers Milner wanted a quick word with him, and could she send him in. Blast.

Seconds later, Piers sauntered into his office with a smirk on his face, "Morning Ezzio. I just thought I'd come to say goodbye."

Ezzio remained standing and saying nothing, hoping he would get the message that he wasn't welcome.

Piers seemed oblivious and carried on, "I won't keep you. I wanted a quick word to reassure you, that while I'm here in London for the next couple of weeks, I'll do everything in my power to support Michael, until he finds his feet, so to speak."

Ezzio supressed an urge to laugh out loud. Michael Golding, his newly appointed CEO, had previously been an assistant Chief Executive of a rival company, and he'd headhunted him because of his proven track record; he could eat men like Piers Milner for breakfast. Piers' assurances meant nothing; he barely tolerated the man. His goal was to gain full control of the Milner

Company, which now, was only a matter of time, and then Piers and Darlene Milner would be history.

"Thank you, I'm sure Michael will appreciate that. He exaggeratedly looked at his watch, "Is there anything else, as I have flight to catch?"

"Yes, of course, I must let you get on. Maybe we can catch up in the States, have dinner together perhaps, I'll be back there at the end of the month?"

Ezzio had absolutely no intention of catching up with him in the States or anywhere else. He needed rid of him, "Right, if that's all, then?"

Piers wasn't finished, "Oh, before I forget, I wanted to let you know that Kate, or whatever she calls herself, is back with my mother as of yesterday, I wasn't sure if you knew?"

It felt like he'd been thumped in the stomach. Although he knew she'd gone, and had stolen two of his Rolex watches, he wasn't interested in exactly where. She had betrayed him in the worst possible way, and nobody did that to Ezzio Marin.

"It's of little concern to me," he dismissed, closing his briefcase, and entering a security code.

Piers continued, "My mother seems happy now she's back. Personally, I can't stand the thought of her with that dyke, attractive as she is." He winked suggestively, and Ezzio hated his inference. So, the little thief had run back to Darlene Milner had she? Why wasn't he surprised, she had absolutely no morals.

Piers made his way to the door, and opening it, turned back towards him. With a slight smile playing at the corners of his mouth, he added, "Safe trip and all that. Hope to see you when I'm back in the States."

Ezzio was seething, and had an overwhelming urge to knock the smug look off his face, "Tell your mother to watch her back, she might not realise it yet, but she's screwing with a murderer."

***

It wasn't until five days later, that Piers Milner fully appreciated the information Ezzio had given him. He was simmering with his mother, who had invited him to her office, lulling him there under the premise of a business lunch. Unbeknown to him, she'd found out Ezzio Marin was buying up more stock from their holding in the company, which had weakened her own position. Henry Carr, her personal assistant had been investigating the extended family to ascertain who had been selling their stock, focussing initially on those with minimal shares. It didn't take Henry long to work out that it was him selling. Although he'd only sold three percent of his ten percent Milner shares, it was a significant blow to his mother. She had ranted and raved at him, as if he was some sort of teenager that had been caught stealing, not a mature man in his twenties. She had thrown the book at him, which he only half listened to, until he heard her say that she was reducing his income from the company.

He enjoyed a lavish lifestyle, which he wasn't prepared to compromise for anybody, why should he? The only consolation he had from having such dysfunctional parents, was the fact they were rich, as he'd received little in the way of love or affection from either of them. His father was now ensconced in the nut asylum they called a care home, and his mother was a raging dyke who owed him, and had a duty to, at the very least, support his lifestyle, not threaten to curtail it.

If he was totally honest, he knew he wasn't the greatest asset to the Milner Empire. Living off the profits gave him an unrestrained lifestyle, which he wanted to continue. There were concerns about the Milner Corporation losing money, but his mother had attracted investment from Ezzio Marin, and things had started to improve. Admittedly, he had an inkling that Marin was behind the purchase of his shares, but that was of little consequence to him as he needed to sell them regardless. A run of bad luck at the poker table meant he needed an influx of money to bail him out. As any gambler knows, if you play high stakes and lose, then you need to pay your debts. If you don't, then there are consequences. Not monetary ones, more the physical kind, and they were just too fearsome to think about.

An inner rage burned inside of him towards his mother, who had told him that she was cutting his income by a third, despite the fact that he'd managed to get that whore back for her. It wasn't his fault she'd run away when she got her sister back. That was half his mother's problem; she was totally fixated on that woman. Now it seems she'd engaged a private investigator to try and find her, which he smiled wryly about.

He wasn't particularly fond of his mother, and certainly never felt any love towards her. All his life, she'd never had any time for him. She was an odd woman prone to bizarre outbursts. Her mother, his late grandmother was admitted to a mental institution, and he always felt some of her idiosyncrasies had genetically passed onto his mother.

His mother's success was largely down to his father who was the brains behind the business. Working closely together for years, his parents successfully ran the company, but when his father's health had deteriorated, his mother had to take over. Her success had been largely due to Henry Carr his father's 'right hand man' who was completely devoted to her. He was an odd individual that lived and breathed the Milner Company, and he'd always suspected that Henry cared deeply for his mother, but even he must have realised long ago that he couldn't compete for his mother's affection, against her preference for the female of the species.

Although she was a shrewd businesswoman, there was a side to her that many outside the immediate family weren't aware of. Mentally, she was unstable and on occasions had been known to display odd and sometimes shocking behaviours, all of which were dependent upon prescribed medication keeping her on an even keel.

He thought back to his childhood and remembered clearly the time when his cat had kittens and his mother drowned each one of them in a bucket in the garden telling him that was nature. Aged only seven at the time, he couldn't understand why she did that in front of him. Surely if you were that way inclined, you'd do it out of sight of your child? It felt like he was being punished for the cat having kittens.

On a separate occasion, he recalled the meeting with Mrs Griggs, the Head Teacher at the public school he'd attended. The school had sent for his parents because of bullying issues. His father never came, of course, far too busy with the business, but his mother did. As he sat in the Head's office, he watched the interaction between Mrs Griggs and his mother, and still cringed when he remembered witnessing her assaulting the Head Teacher. It was no slap across her face either, it was a full blown physical attack, which was actually quite scary. As a result of the incident, the Head Teacher expelled him permanently, and sued his mother for assault, which she settled out of court to deflect publicity. At the time, he thought his mother behaved that way to protect him, but over the years, he came to realise, it was nothing of the sort. It was a massive inconvenience to her to have to find another school for him. So, the reason for the assault on the Head was simply frustration that her organised life was disrupted somewhat by her nuisance of a son.

Yes, he'd certainly witnessed strange behaviours on occasions from his mother that made him wary of her, but not fearful. The stupid cow had no right treating him like a naughty boy and cutting his salary, and she would pay for that where it would hurt her most of all.

His contact in the Metropolitan police had done some research, and quickly ascertained who Kate Jones really was. Ezzio Marin had sealed her fate by telling him she was a murderess; the rest was easy. Finding out Rebecca Price Jones was a wanted woman, was music to his ears. When trying to help his mother to get her back previously, his private detective had built up quite a dossier on her, including her routines around London, which he'd passed on to the police. She might be lying low now, but he was confident that she would be back, and when she did return to London, the police would pick her up and she'd be banged-up for God knows how many years. Yes, that will teach you, mother dearest . . . don't you fuck around with me.

PART TWO

Rebecca

CHAPTER 23

"I'm not coming back to England, David. Can you and Michael call a board meeting and I'll attend by video conference." Ezzio was on a call to London, he'd been back in the States for nine weeks, with no immediate plans to return anytime soon.

"Yes, of course we can, David answered, "but it would be better if you were here in person. The Milner stock that we were steadily acquiring has come to a standstill as Piers Milner has disappeared." He paused, breathing in, "Have you any idea where he is?"

"I haven't," Ezzio replied, "he's not someone I keep in touch with."

"No, nobody seems to know where he's gone. He seems to have vanished into thin air, and Darlene is behaving rather erratically about it all, so I think it might help if you were more visible."

"I hear what you're saying, but I'm confident in your ability to handle things. I really don't have the time to be coming to England at the moment, I'm at a crucial stage of negotiations with the Belpher buy-out here, and I may lose out if I leave now."

He heard David's sigh, "Okay then, we'll try and locate Piers, if not, we can put some feelers out with the other shareholders. Have you any idea when you're likely to be coming back?"

"No I haven't, but it won't be soon." He had no intention of being in the same country as Darlene

Milner and the scheming little bitch that had stolen his watches.

"Okay, but before you go, I just wanted to let you know that Rebecca Jones has been arrested."

He stiffened as David continued, "It seems she was on the run from prison . . . well, a detention centre really. Can you believe she was on remand for killing her stepfather?"

He kept his voice steady, he didn't want to divulge what he already knew, "I'm not at all surprised, to be honest, that girl is serious trouble."

A sinking feeling emerged in the pit of his stomach. Piers may have acted on the information he had inadvertently given him about Rebecca being a murderer. Although furious at the time about her going back to Darlene and stealing his watches, he'd been careless disclosing that to Piers, and deeply regretted it.

David continued, "I'm not telling you for any other reason than there's intense media speculation, and I think you might be named by the tabloids as one of her lovers."

"I hardly think the tabloids will be focusing on me," he quickly dismissed, "they'll be more interested in her colourful lifestyle, I would have thought." Used to intense press speculation for most of his adult life, it ceased to have any effect on him.

David spoke again, "Yes we've had all of that, the media have turned her into some sort of celebrity and are now focussing on who is the father of her baby."

Ezzio felt uneasy, and his palms were sweaty holding the telephone receiver, "Baby," he stalled, taking a few seconds for his brain to register what had just been said . . . Rebecca pregnant, surely not? He couldn't comprehend what he was hearing.

"Pregnant . . . are you sure?"

"Yes, it seems so. A prison guard has given an interview to one of the tabloids saying she's ten weeks pregnant. The media are having a field day painting her as a madam, with headlines such as Immaculate Conception, and Gay Sex Makes a Good Thing Conceivably Better . . . you can guess the sort of thing."

Ezzio was completely stunned. Maybe she'd got a taste for heterosexual sex since him, and been with another man? No, he didn't believe that for a minute. They'd had unprotected sex once, but she'd taken the morning after pill, which was supposed to take care of it, wasn't it? Hadn't the pill worked? The nurse's words echoed in his ears, 'no guarantees'. Had she conceived the night they'd had sex on his desk . . . please, no.

It took only seconds for him to register that the baby she carried, was his. The irony was, he'd spent all of his adult life making certain he wasn't trapped into fatherhood, and now his child, theirchild, was most likely to be born in a prison cell. What a pathetic start in life for one that might eventually inherit his fortune, his heir.

His brain went into overdrive, he didn't want a child of his being born in prison; he would have to get Rebecca out. The first thing he needed to do was to hire a barrister quickly, and he knew just the person. An elite female barrister, who had an enormous success rate with challenging legal cases. Returning to the telephone conversation, he instructed David, "Find Imogen Allen and engage her services, whatever the cost."

He heard the surprise in David's voice, "What, you want her to represent Rebecca?"

"Yes, she's one of the best criminal barristers in England."

"I know that Ezzio, but there might not be a trial. Rebecca most probably will plead guilty in exchange for a lesser sentence."

"Just do as I say," he snapped, "speak to Imogen, I need to get her out. I am not having any child of mine, born in prison."

David's voice sounded cautious as he posed the question, "What . . . you think the baby's yours?" he hesitated, "Can you be sure?"

Ezzio's voice was as firm, as it was angry, "It's mine." He was irritated that his friend would question him, "Now, do what I pay you for, and hire Imogen Allen. Fix up an initial meeting as soon as you can, I'll be in England tomorrow." He cut the call.

A telephone call to his secretary and he was booked on a flight the following day. Sitting in the window of his Manhattan apartment, he recalled how only ten weeks ago he'd personally burned all of Rebecca's clothes, and hurriedly left England vowing to erase the little thief from his mind . . . if only it had been that simple.

Each day he went through the same routine, from early morning until late at night, a punishing schedule of work, work and more work. Channelling all of his energies into business, his only reprieve was the gym where he pushed his shattered body relentlessly until he fell into bed exhausted each night. Still he didn't sleep, and when he did, images of Rebecca haunted his dreams.

Now he knew, with absolute conviction, that he would be seeing her again. What he wasn't entirely sure about was, did that make him angry, excited or just plain scared? The only certainty was, she had the power to upset his equilibrium and that truly did unnerve him. Silently he acknowledged that ordinarily Rebecca Price Jones was trouble with a capital T, but pregnant with his child, now that scared the shit out of him.

CHAPTER 24

Confined to bed rest in the medical centre of the prison for almost a week was driving Rebecca crazy. The vaginal bleeding had now stopped, but she wasn't allowed up. She was awaiting the arrival of the stenographer with the portable scanner which would tell if she still carried a baby.

The smart lawyer that visited, had said there would be one day in court for her to plead guilty to the manslaughter charge, and that she would be given a custodial sentence. The fact that she had absconded meant that she would receive a longer sentence, however due to her age at the time of the crime, they would request that the court show leniency.

Rebecca didn't like the lawyer, as he stared inappropriately at her. She knew exactly what he was thinking; that she was an attractive piece of meat to be screwed. If only there wasn't such a thing as sex, life would be so much simpler.

What if I am still pregnant, the baby will be born in prison and then taken away for adoption? Please God, don't make me pregnant. I can cope if I'm not having a baby . . . I already have Emily, she's my baby.

She thought about her sister, and a wave of despair washed over her, knowing that Emily would be pining for her, and it hurt deeply. God give me the strength to get through this . . . I must not think of her now, she's safe.

Dear Emily, who was so gullible, and had swallowed the tale of how she couldn't leave the elderly gentleman she looked after, as he was dying and didn't have any relatives to care for him. She hated lying, but it was best for the time being, the truth would come out soon enough.

Ezzio's Rolex watches had enabled her to place Emily at the farm in Sleaford where the evil Piers Milner would never find her, but the money wouldn't last forever, she knew that.

Piers Milner, her Achilles' heel. Once she had Emily back, she'd bolted out of London and headed to Sleaford. They both stayed on Janet Coo's, sister's farm, and Emily loved it, and in return, they loved her. Janet Coo had spoken to her sister, and it was reassuring to know they would keep a watchful eye on her. Emily's infectiousness often brought the best out in people, and she was confident that they would look after her beloved sister. It was as if Emily had finally found her niche, she was so happy with the animals, and not at all upset about Rebecca leaving. In recent years, she'd only ever known her 'working away', so as long as she visited, Emily was fine. She'd paid an advance for her lodgings, and left pocket money with Mrs Collins to allocate each week.

The break on the farm was just what she needed, and both her and Emily had enjoyed their time together. They'd mucked out the horses, fed the pigs, and even tried their hands at milking. Their antics made them laugh and fool around like children. It had been an unexpected holiday for both of them, and certainly a luxury she could never afford. It gave her chance to recuperate from the overwhelming tiredness she was feeling, which she'd thought was due to the stress of Emily's abduction, she certainly had never considered pregnancy.

With a heavy heart, she returned to London. Although she still had money left from the watches, she needed to pick up some of her old clients and earn more. One emphatic decision she had made, was that she would steer clear of Darlene Milner and that wretched son of hers.

When she left Sleaford, she was less anxious than she had been in weeks, completely unaware of the disaster awaiting her in London. Had she known, she would never have returned. Within days, she was arrested.

The nurse, Linda, appeared in the doorway accompanied by a well-dressed woman. Linda had been so lovely to her, and she wasn't used to kindness. People always wanted something from her, usually sex. She watched as they passed the two other occupied beds and stopped at hers.

Linda spoke directly to her, "Rebecca, this is Imogen Allen, a legal barrister," she turned to the well-groomed lady, "and this is Rebecca Price Jones."

She stared as the woman approached with her outstretched hand smiling at her, "Hello Rebecca, I'm pleased to meet you." She shook it, what was going on? What had happened to her lawyer, Mr I'd-like-to-see-you-naked-eyes?

Linda brought a chair to the bedside before excusing herself, and the lawyer sat down, explaining quickly, "I know you're about to have a scan, so we can't talk properly now. I just wanted to meet you to tell you my team are likely to be representing you from now on."

Judging by her chic appearance, this woman must be an expensive lawyer, and she certainly didn't have any money to pay her, "Where's my other lawyer gone to?" Rebecca asked wearily.

"He's no longer likely to be looking after your case," she explained, "I will need to speak with you privately to explain in more detail, so once you've had your scan, we can have some time together."

Rebecca was cautious, "Look I'm not being funny, but you look like an expensive legal package to me, and I don't have any money to pay you."

"Don't worry about that for now," she smiled sympathetically, "there won't be any contributions required from you."

God this is all I need, pregnant, locked up in jail, and now my fairy Godmother arrives. "What do you mean, are you part of my Legal Aid?" She didn't look anything like a Legal Aid lawyer.

"No, I didn't say that." As if on cue, Linda reappeared accompanied by the stenographer and the lawyer stood up, "I'll see you shortly once you've had your scan and we find out if there is a baby."

Rebecca's quizzical eyes were drawn to the lawyer's hands as she picked up her huge handbag. She'd had sex with enough rich women to recognise a designer handbag when she saw one, so quickly deduced that this particular lawyer would not come cheap.

Hang on a minute, what was she talking about . . . if there is a baby?

"What do you mean you need to find out if there is a baby, are you only offering your services if I'm pregnant?"

"We can discuss all of this later. I'll get out of the way for now and let you get sorted."

Rebecca watched her walk away. What on earth was that all about?

The gel was applied to her abdomen and she stared ahead. Whether she was pregnant or not, she wasn't going to look at the screen. Half the trouble was, she didn't feel pregnant, and had no idea at all that she was having a baby until the prison medical, when she gave a sample of urine. Her menstrual cycle had always been erratic, and she'd continued to have light bleeding, so how on earth could she be pregnant? Weren't you supposed to be sick or something if you were having a baby? No, it would all be a mistake, she was sure of it.

The stenographer pressed the probe down firmly. Linda was staring at the monitor with anticipation . . . what is it about babies that excites females so much? As if her world wasn't in disarray by being back in prison, the last thing she needed was a baby. She was facing Linda, who was staring at the monitor screen, and she watched her expression change from serious scrutiny, to one of sheer delight.

"Look Rebecca . . . look at the screen," Linda urged.

She didn't want to look. If there was a baby, she couldn't afford to become attached to it. Somehow though, as if she had no control over her head, it turned, and her eyes were drawn to the screen. Initially, she couldn't make anything out, but it didn't take long for her to see there was an actual baby.

The stenographer pointed out the heartbeat and it appeared as if the baby was no more than a blob. Measurements were taken, and the conclusion was that everything was progressing normally. Rebecca declined a print-out of the scan. What was the point? She might be carrying a child, but it would never be hers. What child would ever want a prostitute that had killed a man, for its mother?

Shortly after the scan, the prison doctor visited her and said she could start mobilising gently. He gave her the expected date of the baby's arrival, explaining how this was usually calculated from her last period, but due to the difficulties with her menstrual cycle, and her periods being irregular, the doctor was using the measurements of the foetus to ascertain the expected date.

Rebecca was silent, knowing that she could categorically state the date she'd conceived the baby. That night in Ezzio's study would be etched on her mind forever. But she must not think of him, not now, not ever.

She was tired. The doctor had said she was to remain in the hospital wing for observation, rather than going straight back into the main prison block. Once she was over twelve weeks pregnant, she would be moved.

Lying on the bed, she thought about her life which was now spiralling out of control. How had she ever allowed herself to be caught? And to compound that, she was having a baby. The future looked so bleak. She needed to sleep; the overwhelming fatigue was hard to cope with.

Later, she was taken by wheelchair to meet with Imogen Allen in a private room. She transferred herself to a chair opposite the lawyer, who was poised with a file on the desk. Prior to her escape from the Young Offenders Centre, a date had been set for her trial, so she was guessing that the documentation was the prosecution's case.

Imogen's whole persona was one of class. She appeared to be in her early thirties and was immaculately dressed, with flawless make-up and expensive jewellery. Her dark hair was tied back in an orderly bun at the nape of her neck; a power-dressing hairstyle if ever there was one.

Imogen cleared her throat, "I'm not sure if I should be congratulating you, or commiserating. How are you feeling?"

"I'm fine thank you," she sighed, "still very tired, but I'm told it will pass."

Imogen smiled sympathetically, "That's good. First things first, we need to get you out of here. Tomorrow I'll start preparing our defence case for consideration. Until the trial, I'll be proposing bail."

"Bail?" Rebecca raised her voice disbelievingly, "You have to be joking. How would I ever get bail, the court would never go for that, they'll think I'll abscond again?"

"No, they won't," she explained, "because you can't do that. The money they'll require to release you will be astronomical, so you can't possibly run away. It will mean you will be on sort of house arrest, but you'll be free from prison until the trial."

Imogen paused as if giving her time to digest everything, and then carried on, "I'm proposing this option as you're not a danger to the public, and due to your difficult pregnancy, the need to have you closely monitored medically."

Her head felt woozy, but she needed to be firm, "Yes, well, about the trial. I've had a lot of time to think, and I'm going to plead guilty to manslaughter. I'm no barrister, but I understand that I'll get a lesser sentence if I admit I'm guilty."

Imogen widened her eyes and sighed deeply, "You're quite right, you're not a barrister, I am, and my intention is to produce evidence which will secure your acquittal at a trial." The corners of her mouth twitched, as she confidently added, "So you won't end up going to prison at all."

Where on earth had this woman come from, was she totally mad?

"Look, I'm really grateful, but please, my minds made up. I don't want you to waste your time with all of this," she insisted, "I killed my stepfather, escaped from juvenile detention and now I'm back again, ready to go to jail and complete the sentence. Then hopefully be able to build a new life for myself." There, she'd said it out loud. The last few days in jail had afforded her thinking time, and now she had finally accepted her fate.

Imogen gave a dismissive sigh, "Rebecca, I know you aren't aware of my reputation, so, you'll have to trust me when I tell you that I am a good barrister surrounded by a great team," God, don't let modesty get in your way, will you? "I intend to go for a trial on the basis of not guilty, and while we await a date for that trial, I'm asking for you to be released on bail." She smiled sympathetically, "As I said, due to the complications of the pregnancy and your health, I'm sure I will be able to get that for you."

She couldn't believe what she was hearing and shook her head, "I don't want to take the risk, they'll find me guilty and I'll end up with a lengthy sentence. I did kill him," she confessed, "so I'm prepared to admit it, and hope that the court will be lenient with me."

Imogen was dismissive, "There's mitigating evidence as to why you killed him, which will gain you sympathy with the jury, and they hopefully, as a result of this, will find you not guilty."

"There is no mitigation," she blurted, "I killed him, and that's the end of it," she gave a weary sigh, "What could you possibly produce that would alter that?"

"I'll tell the court your stepfather was a bully that physically abused you."

"Who told you that?" Rebecca's heckles went up, nobody knew that, she'd never divulged it to a soul.

Imogen raised her brow, "I thought I'd read in somewhere in the statements."

"That's not true," she snapped, "you couldn't have done, as that has never been discussed."

"Well you can't deny that he was mentally abusive to you, surely?" Imogen insisted.

A feeling of tiredness overwhelmed her, and she shook her head in exasperation, "There's no proof of that, it would be my word and the court would hardly listen to me."

Imogen's tone became more sensitive, "The court needs to hear that account so they can understand exactly what happened."

Rebecca didn't like the way this was going as she'd more or less resigned herself to pleading guilty, "I'm just not sure I can relive it all," she paused, struggling for the right words to explain, "For years, I've blanked it out as if it didn't really happen, it would be terrible having to go through it all again."

"You won't have to, as you won't be required to give evidence," Imogen answered calmly, "I will present the information about the abuse, which will throw doubt on the prosecution's case."

She tried one last time to say no, "My other lawyer said it would only be a matter of months until the trial. Surely they will keep me in prison until then?"

"No, Imogen confidently dismissed her doubts, "due to your pregnancy requiring close medical monitoring, they will let you out on bail, but they'll just put a high price on the bond. You're right though," she acknowledged, "the trail will be expedited, so we won't have long to wait."

So, the fancy barrister had it all worked out. She let out a long sigh, "Look, I really do appreciate you trying to help, but I've made up my mind. I haven't got any money so there's no point in applying for bail, and even if I had, I haven't anywhere to live, I'm homeless," she paused, "and don't even go there about paying for your services, as that just isn't going to happen."

To her surprise, Imogen's face showed genuine compassion, "What if I told you someone is willing to take care of all of that?"

Rebecca stared suspiciously, who on earth would help her? This woman was not only mad, she was also a fantasist. "I'd say you were talking rubbish, there isn't anyone."

"Yes, there is," Imogen replied, "There's someone that wants you out of jail and has engaged my services to ensure this happens."

"Who?" She held her breath for no more than a second, and then the penny dropped, "Oh no, please tell me it isn't Darlene Milner?"

Imogen shook her head dismissively, "No, it's not her. It's Ezzio Marin, he's paying for your defence."

She lifted a hand to her mouth, and gulped in utter dismay, silently pleading she may have misheard, but knowing full well that she hadn't. Would she ever be free from this man that had caused such havoc in her life?

Her heartbeat slowed, and she felt light-headed. Her eyes kept involuntarily blinking. It was hot and she found it hard to breathe. She tried to focus on something, anything, but the tiles on the ground started to move towards her. Can you faint from a sitting position?

Imogen Allen's voice seemed to come from far away, "Are you alright, Rebecca, here, please take some water."

***

Imogen had absolutely no idea the impact Ezzio's name would have on Rebecca. What had brought this on?

"Take some deep breaths, Rebecca," she urged, and gently pushed her head forward. She felt clammy.

The prison officer came forward quickly, assessing the situation, "We need to get her back to the medical centre," she looked questioningly at Imogen.

"Yes, please do as quickly as possible, she needs to lie down."

The prison officer used her radio, and within seconds, health colleagues arrived and helped Rebecca transfer from her chair back into the wheelchair. Imogen was completely shocked to see the transformation, her eyes had gone hollow, and her skin drained of colour. She looked on as an oxygen mask was applied to her nose and mouth.

Rebecca had wanted to know the facts, so she'd told her. There was little point in representing her otherwise. She'd agreed to take the case, not only because Ezzio Marin was paying her an extortionate amount of money, but also because of her reputation. She rarely failed, only taking on cases she knew that she could win. They were usually controversial which suited her, she worked hard, and the fact that Rebecca's pregnancy had been confirmed was the deal breaker. No baby, no representation, she'd been clear with Ezzio.

As Rebecca was being wheeled out of the room, she turned and feebly asked, "Does he know I'm pregnant?" Imogen felt an enormous amount of sympathy for this woman who was clearly distressed, but trying desperately to hold on. There was no point in lying to her though, "Yes he does."

Growing paler by the second, Rebecca muttered perceptively, "That's why you're here today, isn't it, to see if there is a pregnancy?"

Imogen remained silent, what could she say . . . it was the truth.

Rebecca's voice trembled, "If I wasn't pregnant with his child, then there's no way he would engage your services," and in a barely audible whisper, she added, "no way at all."

CHAPTER 25

Imogen sat in Ezzio's study hoping for some answers, but he was evasive and had interrupted their meeting to take a telephone call. Waiting for him to finish, she covertly observed him, and quickly deduced how pleasing he was on the eye. He certainly coined the phrase, drop dead gorgeous, with bucket loads of sex appeal, and an innate charisma that oozed style, and exuded power. Clearly, he had his pick of willing females, judging by the frequency his photograph adorned the tabloid newspapers alongside his latest floozy.

During her marriage she'd met him socially, but he had been off limits then. Now, having been single for almost a year, he suddenly seemed extremely appealing. Although abstinence from sex wasn't usually a problem as she challenged her energies into work, today, watching him closely, she unexpectedly felt a rush of heat, pooling between her legs.

As he was such a tall man, she deduced that it was likely he would be big in areas that count, and her eyes were drawn to his hand clutching the telephone receiver. He had large hands, which she liked in a man as it signified power, and as she looked at his long fingers, she breathed in and shuffled her position in the chair. It was almost as if an internal switch had been turned on, and she realised that she was definitely up for intimacy, and scrutinising him as he ended his conversation, she silently wondered, was he?

He apologised, "Sorry about that, where were we?"

"We were discussing Rebecca," she replied. "Why was she so distressed when I told her you were paying for my services?"

She studied him closely, but his expression remained impassive, "I have no idea. I haven't seen her in months so I'm afraid I can't answer many of your questions."

"Can't answer, or won't?" she asked, his elusiveness annoying her, "You've been vague with me since I arrived. If you want me to defend Rebecca, I will need some answers."

His voice remained calm, but his eyes darkened giving a hint of irritation, "Imogen, I engaged you to defend Rebecca as I know you are one of the finest barristers in England. I am paying you a considerable amount of money, which I know you will earn," she tried to interrupt, "Let me finish. I am prepared to tell you that my brief relationship with Rebecca is well and truly over. It was a casual fling and no more than that," his brows lifted, "but out of that liaison, is a pregnancy and an innocent child, and I'm engaging your services to ensure this child is not born in a prison." He paused, shaking his head, "There is no more information to give you, and no more I wish to say relating to Rebecca and myself."

If he thought that was the end of it, he hadn't reckoned on dealing with a woman that earned her living questioning, "So, if she comes out on bail, and you've already agreed she can reside here until the court case, is it likely the relationship will resume?" She guessed he was holding something back as he hesitated before replying, "I'll answer that, but please don't ask me anything further about my personal life, it isn't up for discussion."

"Very well," her eyes met his as she waited for an answer.

"I will not be pursuing Rebecca if she gets out on bail. For reasons, I don't wish to discuss with you or anybody, I actually despise the woman. My concern is for the child and nothing more, so if you are able to channel your energies into securing her release, then I will be grateful."

How grateful? She liked his directness, but she needed to conclude once and for all. Her legal brain kicked in with another question, "While I respect there are aspects of your relationship you don't wish to discuss, is the reason for your . . . erm . . . dislike of Rebecca, likely to come up and bite us in court?"

"No," he answered emphatically.

He better not be lying. The reason she was successful as a barrister was her attention to detail, however small. It was her tenacity that defined what information was relevant and would be useful in court, and what could be discarded as no use at all.

She nodded, "Very well, then, I'll start preparing the bail application. I'm hoping we can get the hearing next week.

His gaze sharpened, "What are our chances, do you believe you'll get her out?"

"Yes," she answered positively," I'm confident I will. The prosecution will raise objections, but I'm prepared for that. As I've said before, the pregnancy goes in our favour, and greatly increases the chance of bail being granted."

"Let's hope so, then," he looked at her coolly, "judging by the way you say she is, the sooner she is out of there the better."

He stood up, indicating their conversation was over, which was fine for now. During the next few months she'd be working closely with him, and he'd offered her his hotel suite in the city while she prepared for the trial. This hopefully would mean visits from him and late night dinners. As she'd established that he wasn't currently attached, any extras that were on offer from him would be a welcoming bonus.

CHAPTER 26

As Imogen had predicted, the bail hearing was held the following week. Rebecca had been taken to court early that morning escorted by a security officer, and Imogen was already waiting for her. The navy suit and white blouse she was wearing, had been previously brought for her by Imogen specifically for the hearing. For the first time in weeks, she felt half decent. The prison clothes she'd been wearing were starchy from the prison laundry, and had irritated her skin.

Imogen had met with her on several occasions during the last few days, and while she couldn't warm to her, she didn't dislike her either. She was an extremely beautiful woman, as dark as she was fair, and Rebecca wondered if her and Ezzio were in a relationship, because if attractiveness was anything to go by, they would certainly make a striking couple.

Imogen smiled calmingly. "How are you today, nervous?"

"No," she answered truthfully, she wasn't. Despite all the groundwork that had been done, she was pretty certain that they wouldn't grant her bail. Why would they?

"Good, there's no need to be," she smiled, "We'll get you out of here by the end of the day and safely back to Ezzio's."

Now that did make her nervous. In a matter-of-fact voice, she asked, "Is Ezzio going to be here today?"

"Yes of course. He'll be putting up the bail bond so will need to complete all the necessary paperwork." Rebecca's stomach did a nervous summersault, how can one man have the power to make her feel like this?

Imogen patiently went over the formalities again before she left, and reminded her for the umpteenth time she was not to appear aloof, but not to smile either, and must not stare disparagingly at the judge.

Nerves did kick in as she was escorted into an almost empty courtroom, and allocated a seat alongside a security officer. Not daring to look around the court, she fixed her gaze straight ahead.

Ezzio would hate her; she knew that, so she willed herself not to look for him. How could she possibly explain why she'd stolen two of his Rolex watches? She couldn't just say that everything she'd done in her whole life was for her sister, when nobody knew she even existed. Her fear that someone would challenge the fact that Emily wasn't dead, never happened, so the story she perpetuated that she'd died from a drugs overdose, seemed to stick.

***

Ezzio's eyes were fixed on Rebecca as she entered the courtroom. Nothing had prepared him for the wrench in his gut, and he hated her that moment for having any influence over him.

She looked pale, and had lost weight, but to him, she was still the most beautiful woman he'd ever seen, and a visceral stab of desire hit him. The suit she was wearing was too dark for her skin and hung limply on her hidden alluring body. Her magnificent blonde hair was a curly mass cascading down her back . . . no time for hair straighteners in jail, then.

Not once did she look across at him, too ashamed after stealing his watches no doubt. Bitch, look at me, he willed, but she didn't. She just kept her treacherously innocent eyes staring straight ahead, looking proud but vulnerable, and held herself with the same grace and poise she'd always done.

Until this moment, he'd thought about her having a baby, but this was the first time he'd seen her pregnant with his child. His protective instincts kicked in and he felt a clench of possessiveness. Even at a distance, she had power over him, and he had an overwhelming desire to look after her despite her betrayal . . . she's a thief, don't forget that, he reminded himself. Why he hadn't divulged to Imogen that Rebecca had stolen his watches, he wasn't sure. The scheming bitch certainly didn't deserve his loyalty.

Dragging his thoughts away from Rebecca, he tried to concentrate on the proceedings, and his eyes were drawn to Imogen Allen. Now there was a woman he should be interested in. Since he'd first engaged her to represent Rebecca, she'd overtly been transmitting signals that she was ready to move in that direction, but his only focus had been getting Rebecca out. However, if it wasn't for the fact she was carrying his child, he wouldn't be wasting a second on her. He couldn't actually give a toss about the scheming cow.

The application for bail was presented by Imogen, who fluently gave a logical and structured application, pleading for bail on the grounds of Rebecca's complicated pregnancy and the need for close medical supervision, which was supported by a concise medical report. Succinctly, she articulated that Rebecca would be more able to withstand the pressures of the trial, thus reducing the threat of miscarriage, because she would be better able to continue resting in a home environment, rather than the overcrowded health centre in jail. Stressing again the threat of miscarriage, she concluded that Rebecca was no danger to the public and would obey any bail conditions set out by the court.

Lawyers acting for the prosecution protested, and gave a rigorous counter argument that a man had lost his life, and because of the seriousness of the case, requested that the accused was held in custody until the forthcoming trial. They cited that Rebecca had escaped from custody previously, and been on the run for eight years. While they couldn't dispute she was not a danger to the community, they maintained that she had been engaged in the illegal activity of prostitution, and concluded that she was a flight risk, placing excessive emphasis on the likelihood she would abscond at the earliest opportunity.

Imogen's response was that releasing the defendant on bail, would give her unlimited access to Rebecca in a neutral setting. She claimed that increased contact with her client would lead to greater knowledge about the facts of the case, and the defendant's circumstances as she had been a minor at the time of the offence. She argued there was no supporting evidence that her client had been engaged in prostitution, and no cautions or convictions relating to such activities.

The judge listened patiently to both side of the argument, and agreed to bail with a surety bond. The amount set was half a million pounds, which was to be deposited to the court clerk before release. Conditions were imposed about residency at a fixed address, and emphasis was placed upon forfeiting the bail bond should the defendant fail to appear in person for the trial.

Ezzio had David with him and completed the necessary documentation for Rebecca's release. Using his mobile phone, he then requested that George had his car brought to the front of the courthouse. The task ahead was getting Rebecca out of the court, past the crowd of waiting press and into the car. Imogen had insisted that they left the court by the front entrance. There would be gross speculation about his relationship with Rebecca, and Imogen wanted to use that to their advantage. It was to become known that he was the father of the child and would be supporting Rebecca throughout the trial. Any further conjecture would be capitalised upon, which Imogen hoped would influence the jury as everyone loved a good romance and baby story it seemed.

***

One the formalities were complete, Imogen visited her in the holding bay. Shock didn't begin to describe her emotion now that Imogen had pulled it all off, and Rebecca had to acknowledge that she certainly was a legal force to be reckoned with. It had been compelling watching her present the facts in a detached, but persuasive way.

Imogen was standing and loomed above her sitting position, "You need to listen very carefully to me now. There are an enormous amount of press and photographers at the front of the building, but we are purposely going out that way. Ezzio is going to be your escort to the car. You must not speak to anyone, or answer any questions that are thrown at you. You do understand, don't you? No one, you must not speak or answer any questions."

"I won't," she shook her head tensely, "I don't want to speak to anyone. Will you be coming with us?"

"Yes, but we have orchestrated this purposely. You are going to be reunited with Ezzio who has paid the bail bond and come to collect you. It will be newspaper headlines tomorrow. Remember, I'm just the legal help and have to be in the background."

Stunned by the events that had taken place, her voice sounded slightly hysterical, "Reunited with Ezzio! What are you talking about? I don't want to be reunited with Ezzio," she dismissed fervently, "he hates me, please can we stop all of this nonsense." She really couldn't face him, she just couldn't.

It was clear by the tone of her voice that Imogen was irritated, "Rebecca, I've worked my socks off to get you bail, and today, against all odds, I've got it, so can you please stop whining about Ezzio?" She scowled, "I'm not one bit interested in your previous relationship with him, I've been paid to do a job, and I'll do it, my way."

Rebecca was suitably chastised for behaving irrationally, but she couldn't help it. Now that bail had moved on from a discussion to reality, and being minutes away from seeing Ezzio again, was completely terrifying.

Imogen continued, "Look, I do understand that you must be really stressed after today, but for goodness' sake, you need to grow up quickly now." She took a deep breath in, "We have a long road ahead of us, and you have to understand that you and Ezzio are your defence. Everyone loves a romance and they'll soak up the fact he's put up the bail money for your release," she paused, "but you must allow me to lead on things and do as you are told. Do you understand?" Her eyes darkened as if to say, don't you dare argue with me.

With her heart thumping and her head pounding, she nodded her compliance.

"Good, now remember, don't speak to anyone."

Imogen picked up her briefcase and walked towards the door, leaving Rebecca no choice but to follow. They walked up the stairs and along the cold dismal corridor, and she had to remind herself to keep breathing. Her legs trembled, and her head felt like it was trapped in a vice that was tightening with every step she took. She forced herself to put one foot in front of the other, and as their heels clicked and echoed on the antiquated floor tiles, she silently wished that Imogen would slow down, to give her a few precious moments more before she had to face him again. It seemed such a long time ago since she'd last seen him, yet every contour of his handsome face was imprinted on her brain like an indelible tattoo.

Far too quickly, she saw him in her line of vision, leaning nonchalantly against a wall and fiddling with his phone. Her thumping heartbeat accelerated, and her palms began to sweat. The tightness in her head was replaced by a woozy feeling. How was she going to face the father of her child, the man she had stolen from? God, give me the strength to do this.

***

As he watched her approach, Ezzio was totally unprepared for the impact on his senses at being close to her again. Never normally a man to struggle for words, but what do you say to someone in circumstances such as these? Even after the trauma of being in prison and court, she looked stunning. For some obscure reason, he wanted to pull her into his arms and hold her, but common sense prevailed and he kept an even tone to his voice, "Hello, Rebecca." No more or no less. No pleasantries, just hello. His eyes met hers, and trying to interject some sympathy into his tone, he spoke gently, "It must have been a long day for you, so we just have this last bit to do then we are home and dry."

In a voice, no more than a croak she answered, "Yes, Imogen has explained, thank you."

They all made their way towards the impressive court doorway, and Imogen exited the building first, followed by the security team that he'd employed. The amount of flashbulbs was overpowering, and the press called out questions but Imogen just ploughed on ahead to the car not acknowledging or answering.

Then it was their turn. Ezzio put his arm around her and led her from the court, moving as swiftly as they were able. The flashes from the cameras were endless and the press called out randomly, "Is Ezzio Marin the father of your baby?" "Are you going to marry her, Mr Marin?" "Did you hate your stepfather, Rebecca?"

***

The journey to the car seemed to take forever and Ezzio's words echoed in her ear, home and dry. . . was he mad also? He's been spending far too much time with Imogen; the pair of them lived in some sort of fantasyland if they thought she was going to get away with killing a man.

After a mammoth physical effort, ably assisted by the burly security guards, they were safely inside the car and the doors were closed firmly on the reporters. Sitting side by side, her and Ezzio simultaneously fastened their seat belts. Imogen sat opposite, and Rebecca felt herself welling up at the familiar sight of George with his hands firmly clasped on the wheel. Smiling sympathetically at her through the mirror, he spoke kindly, "Welcome back, miss."

She gave a grateful nod of thanks; unable to speak because tears were starting to flow down her cheeks . . . it must be my wretched hormones again. She wasn't one bit emotional normally, but since being pregnant, she found herself tearful over the slightest thing, particularly if anyone showed her any kindness.

George pulled away slowly, using all his skills to navigate through the crowds, and Ezzio closed the partition before handing her his handkerchief, "Here, have this." Careful not to touch his hand, she took it from him and wiped her eyes.

Tension was high in the back of the car and Imogen broke the silence, "Well that's the worst part over with," she smiled encouragingly, "You'll be tired today so it's best you rest, but tomorrow we need to start going over your defence," turning to Ezzio, she asked, "Can we go through this at the house rather than the hotel?"

Rebecca watched as Imogen spoke to Ezzio. They were both physically attractive, their colouring was similar, and for some reason, watching their interaction closely, caused a knot deep within her belly.

"Yes," Ezzio answered, "but not until after we've seen the obstetrician. We have an appointment at Harley Street at ten thirty."

Hang on a minute. "What Obstetrician . . . what are you talking about?" Rebecca glared, "I've seen a doctor recently and had a scan, so I know how things are progressing."

He turned to her with the usual brown intimidating eyes that seemed to go darker when he was being forceful, "I'd like you to see an obstetrician of my choice, so that I can have some information about how things are progressing."

"Oh and let me guess what the first thing is you'll want your obstetrician to do. I'm not stupid Ezzio, you'll be requesting some sort of DNA test to see if the baby is yours." Her eyes glinted hatefully at him, for some reason wanting to rile him.

"Now why would you think that?" he asked drily, "Do I need a DNA test?"

His menacing look made her feel jittery and light-headed. Why was she arguing with him anyway, he only ever did things his way, so it wasn't worth it.

"Do what the hell you like, I really couldn't care less," she turned away from his face, anywhere so she didn't have to meet his piercing dark glare, but out of the corner of her eye, she saw him clench his fists tightly, further evidence that he was furious with her.

"Yes, well, maybe that's half your problem, Rebecca, you just don't care."

Angrily, she turned back to face him, "And you do?" she hissed, "You're only helping me because I'm pregnant."

"Well somebody has to try and make sure the baby isn't born in jail."

Typical, Mr bloody organiser. "Perhaps if you'd been more careful in the first place, then there might not be a baby." Why was she was persisting with this? She'd never won a sparring battle with him yet.

He stared threateningly at her, "Oh so it's all my fault, now is it?"

She raised her chin in defiance, "Well, you're hardly a stalwart for safe sex, are you?"

"What, and you are?" he spat back angrily.

What a complete bastard. She lashed out again, "Maybe if you'd kept your trousers on in the first place."

"Oh yeah, like you weren't up for it."

"Enough," Imogen interjected with such force, they both stopped in their tracks. Her voice dropped an octave, "Please, that's quite enough. If you don't mind, I'd rather not have to sit and listen to every single detail of your private lives."

It was a relief their bickering had stopped as it had made her feel shaky and her palms were sweating, but Ezzio had the last word, "For your information, I've been advised that any testing is best postponed until after the baby is born." He took his phone out of his pocket, giving a clear indication their conversation was over, and Rebecca turned to gaze out of the window. Whether that meant he was going to eventually have a DNA test, she wasn't sure, the only thing she did know was, how much she hated Ezzio Marin. If she hadn't met him, she'd never have been caught, and wouldn't be in the middle of this horrendous nightmare.

The car approached Ezzio's magnificent Surrey home, which never failed to impress. The days and nights she'd spent there were permanently etched on her mind, but it all seemed such a long time ago now.

The car slowly came to a halt in front of the imposing entrance, and George opened the car door for her. It was a welcome relief to be out of the confines of the car, any time spent in close proximity with Ezzio, was just too much to bear.

Straightening up she thanked George and asked, "How's Dorothy?"

"See for yourself," he grinned, "she's coming now."

Her eyes followed Ezzio's as they watched Dorothy approach from the side of the house. She flung her arms around Rebecca to give her a welcome hug and then stood back keeping her outstretched arms on her forearms visually examining her, "Welcome back, my dear, you must be exhausted. Isn't it just marvellous what Ezzio has done?" Rebecca just nodded, what could she say . . . I'd prefer prison to being anywhere near him?

Dorothy took her arm and looked for approval from Ezzio and Imogen before she escorted her into the house and up to her room. Rebecca was shown to the room she'd previously used, the Lavender room, and it somehow felt welcoming. When Dorothy finally left her after endless minutes of baby talk, she got undressed, and slipped into the luxurious soft bed and slept.

CHAPTER 27

It was dark when she woke, and it took her a few seconds to register that she was no longer in a hard prison bed. For a moment, she savoured the sheer luxury and comfort of Ezzio's house. The king-size bed with the crisp white bed linen seemed to be coaxing her to stay, but she was desperately thirsty.

She peered inside the wardrobe, amazed to see tops, jeans and leggings neatly positioned on hangers, all in a size ten, and she opened a drawer and found bras and panties to fit her also.

Selecting a pair of navy leggings and a striped top, she made her way downstairs. Even before she saw them, she could hear Imogen and Ezzio, and followed their voices. They were dining intimately together at the huge dining table just as she and Ezzio had done when he first brought her to the house. Seeing them both chatting warmly together made her feel somewhat resentful, which was absurd . . . it's not as if I want him.

As she moved closer, she heard Imogen accuse, "You implied a casual fling, which isn't strictly true, is it? As soon as I saw you two together today, it was obvious that beneath the tension, there's a powerful connection between the pair of you."

Inadvertently, she must have made a noise, as Ezzio turned his head towards her, "Ah, you're awake," he greeted courteously, "come and join us."

She didn't want to spoil their dinner together, so hesitated, "No, I'm fine thank you, I just need to get a glass of water. Please carry on with your meal, don't let me disturb you." She stood still, trying to hold her ground but Ezzio was having none of it, "Nonsense Rebecca, you have to eat, please, come and sit down."

It seemed silly continuing to protest, so she selected a chair next to Imogen's with Ezzio facing her, and sat down. Her eyes were fixed on his hands as he poured a glass of water from the jug, and handed it to her. For a brief second she remembered what it felt like to have those large hands on her body, it seemed such a long time ago now, and so much had happened since then. She took a gulp of the cold water, which quickly dismissed any further thoughts in that direction, she must forget about it now.

Imogen smiled warmly and asked, "How are you feeling after your rest, it's been quite a day for you, hasn't it?"

"I'm fine, thank you," she nodded, and then, seeing Imogen's eyes showing genuine concern, she added, "really I am." She needed to say more, but struggled to find the right words, "I'd like to thank you for your efforts today, Imogen," and her eyes were drawn to Ezzio, "and you too, thank you for putting up the bail money." What else could she say? She felt so awkward particularly as he didn't acknowledge her thanks.

"It's okay," Imogen smiled reassuringly, "I'm just doing my job, but remember, the hard work is still ahead of us," she cautioned, "anyway let's talk about you. Is your weight about right for the dates of the pregnancy? I'm sure the food they give you in the prison leaves a lot to be desired."

Discussing the merits of prison food, with the father of her baby and his latest woman, was just so ridiculous, she felt like laughing out loud, "It wasn't too bad. I lost a bit of weight initially but it's steady enough now."

The rest of the meal was spent talking about mundane things of little significance. Rebecca was content to listen to them both. It was all so false, as clearly Imogen and Ezzio wanted to be alone together. As soon as she was able, she was going to try and excuse herself, but Imogen beat her to it.

"If you both don't mind excusing me, it's been a long day and I'm well ready to go back to the hotel and get some sleep."

Hotel? . . . Doesn't she spend the nights here with Ezzio? Rebecca quickly stood also, "Please don't go on my account, as I'm going to my room now." The last thing she needed was to spend any time alone in Ezzio's company.

Imogen shook her head, "No, I need to go. I've got a lot of hard work ahead, and as I said earlier, I want to start to prepare for your defence. I'll need my wits about me as I'm up against the formidable Marcus Warr who will be the prosecuting barrister." Dropping her used napkin onto her plate, she moved around the chair and tucked it underneath the table, "I'll come and see you tomorrow afternoon for our meeting, after your appointment with the obstetrician." She turned to leave and then, as if she had a second thought, added reassuringly, "And please try not to worry too much, I can beat Marcus in the courtroom, I've done it several times before."

Ezzio walked with Imogen to the door before turning back towards her, "Could you wait a few moments please, I'll see Imogen off and be back shortly."

She nodded, oh great, waiting for him to return was like waiting for a firing squad. Why didn't he just produce his gun and get it over with?

The clocked ticked as the minutes dragged by, and she couldn't erase the image of them lingering over a goodnight kiss, and deduced that he probably visited Imogen later at the hotel, which seemed a bit of a farce when she could stay here at the house. Why doesn't she?

When Ezzio returned to the dining room, he made his way straight to the drinks cabinet to pour himself a large brandy. Dorothy knocked and came in to clear the plates from the table, but Ezzio stopped her, "Could you leave those for a moment please Dorothy while I speak to Rebecca. If you would be kind enough to make her some tea, I'm sure she would appreciate it." Dorothy scurried off, and Rebecca watched him take a sip of his brandy. He just would remember I only drank tea.

***

For a moment, he savoured the warmth of the brandy, recalling their journey home in the car. She became upset seeing George, his driver, and for some inexplicable reason, he'd been gut-wrenchingly disturbed by her tears . . . why was that when he couldn't stand the little thief? He needed to focus now, and conclude on the baby . . . the rest would be decided by a jury.

He stood by the fireplace, and thought how slight she looked sitting, "I'm sure you're tired, so I'll keep this brief. With Imogen's help, we hope you'll be acquitted. Although I'm optimistic, the outcome of the trial is actually out of my hands." He hesitated, conscious he needed to be sensitive with his choice of words, "However, if I am wrong and you do have to spend the next few years in prison," he paused again, trying to gauge her feelings about that scenario, but she was expressionless, so he continued, "I want you to give me full custody of the baby." There he'd said it. He'd laid his cards on the table, which is what he did best. Direct was always the best approach, there was no point in wasting time skirting around the issue. He watched her intently, but she didn't respond, she just stared back at him with those piercing green eyes.

The silence between them was broken by a knock on the door, and Dorothy entered with the tea. He found her clucky approach irritating, women had babies every day, there was nothing special about it. Dorothy seemed oblivious to his scorn and spoke to Rebecca, "Here you are my dear, weak tea just how you like it." She placed the tea tray on the table, "I'll clear the dishes when you're done," she smiled as she made a hasty retreat and closed the door, leaving them alone.

Rebecca poured her tea, and looked enquiringly at him, "Where did the clothes come from in my room?"

"Imogen selected them for you."

She nibbled on her lip, "I must thank her tomorrow. Are you two in a relationship?"

"No," he replied sharply, "I never mix business with pleasure."

"But you'd like to be?"

"That's none of your business," he snapped, but immediately regretted it when he witnessed her face colour with embarrassment as she replied, "I know it isn't. I only asked as I just feel awkward being here and . . . erm . . . having the baby and everything."

"Well don't be. You'll be here for a while and you must be comfortable, you'll need your strength for the months ahead."

She shot him a sideways look, "Oh please, save the bedside manner routine, we both know you can't stand me and aren't at all bothered about how I'm feeling."

He gritted his teeth, "That isn't quite true, is it? You're here in my home and not a prison cell, which is where you would have remained if I'd told them you'd stolen two of my Rolex watches." This time her face whitened, but he didn't give her chance to reply, "Anyway, you haven't answered my question, will you give me full custody?"

"Yes."

"Yes?" he repeated, questioningly. As she'd netted the greatest prize of all by carrying his heir, he thought she'd go for the jugular and demand money at least.

She didn't.

"You can provide a more prosperous upbringing than I can from a prison cell," she replied sarcastically, "so it's really a no brainer."

"No brainer?" he derided dryly, "Really Rebecca, I don't expect you to be overjoyed, but we are talking about a child here. A child we created together."

"Yes, with a punishment shag," she snapped.

She was right; there was no getting away from that, "Well, that's not the baby's fault, is it?"

She stood up, "Look I've agreed that you can have custody, end of, can I go now please?" She drew in a shuddering breath, "And one other thing, I didn't want to be in this position, I had a life, not much of one, but it was my life until you came along and caused chaos. So please, don't expect any grateful platitudes from me about the cost of my defence. I never asked for it, and I don't want it. I don't want this baby, and I certainly don't want to spend a second in a threesome with you and Imogen, do you understand?"

By the time she'd finished, she was shaking with anger, and he watched her clasping her hands together as if to control them. He too was ready to explode, and his jaw clenched as he hissed, "Yes I understand perfectly well. You're a thief, and an ungrateful little madam. Exactly how much did you get for my watches by the way?"

"Enough. Now can I go?"

"Yes, do. Get out of my sight before I do something I really regret."

She almost ran out of the room, which was a good thing because he could virtually strangle her for the way she'd behaved, the ungrateful bitch. How the hell had he ended up with his seed growing inside a thief and a murderer, with a side line in female prostitution? Jesus Christ, you couldn't bloody well make it up.

CHAPTER 28

A gentle tap on the door signalled it was morning and Rebecca opened her eyes to see Dorothy enter her room.

"I've brought you tea, dear," she said and placed a tray on the bedside table, "Ezzio wanted me to remind you that your appointment is for ten thirty this morning."

Rebecca glanced at the clock as Dorothy continued, "And he said he'd prefer you ate some breakfast before you leave." Trust him, it's not me he's concerned about, just the baby.

The thought of food made her feel queasy, but it was easier to comply, "I'll have a shower first, and then maybe just a small bowl of cereal."

As she concentrated on pouring her tea, Dorothy opened the drapes. The stunning view from her window of the landscaped gardens was beautiful, and she took a few moments to enjoy it. Having spent weeks ensconced in the hospital wing of the prison block, with the only scenery being the prisoner in the next bed, it was a delight to see such a sight.

She sipped her tea, enjoying the tranquillity of the moment until her pleasure was suddenly interrupted by the chattering of a magpie as he came into view and swooped across the lawn. As she watched the noisy black and white bird foraging, she recalled her mother's superstition, one for sorrow, that a single magpie signified death. A shudder went down her spine making her feel uneasy, and the tea she was drinking, suddenly tasted very bitter.

After a shower, she selected a dress from the wardrobe that wasn't exactly to her taste, but looked nice enough. Her insides were churning at the thought of facing Ezzio. Why did he have the ability to make her so nervous? Her tummy was in jitters. She'd been dreaming about him during the night, and while she couldn't recollect the exact details of the dream, she suspected that sex had been involved judging by the way she felt when she woke up. Why, when she hated him so much, did he still have the power to make her want him?

She walked downstairs, and as she entered the dining room, her eyes were drawn to him like a magnet. He was sitting with a newspaper in his hand and a half filled coffee cup in front of him. As always, in his business suit, he looked so handsome, and her heart quickened at the sight of him.

He rested the newspaper on the table and greeted her, "Good morning, did you sleep alright?"

"Yes, fine thank you." She tried to interject a little humour into their situation, and added, "Your bed certainly beats the prison one," but somehow it just ended up sounding flat.

***

He'd been harsh on her the previous evening, but those things needed to be said. Today, however, was a new day, and he'd promised himself he would go easy on her. As he watched her select some bran flakes and pour them into a dish, he was reminded by a kick in his groin that she really was quite beautiful. Despite everything, he had to acknowledge that he still wanted her in the most basic of ways . . . perhaps more now my seed is growing inside her.

There was no obvious evidence she was pregnant, in fact, she looked thinner than when he'd first met her. Her hair was tied up, as usual, this morning showing off her graceful neck, which in any other circumstances, he would like to explore, but he chastised himself. She might be a good-looking woman, but she was a devious one, he must remember that.

Stunned didn't come close to covering his reaction as he watched the scan of the baby. The tiny little thing they'd created was nothing short of a miracle. He wasn't a demonstrative man in any way, but seeing this tiny baby made him want to reach for Rebecca's hand, but he didn't.

For the first time in his adult life, he felt a degree of vulnerability himself. How was he supposed to react, what was he supposed to do? The emotions he was feeling were completely new to him. What was Rebecca feeling? Although she'd said she didn't want the baby, how could she possibly look at the screen and say that. A living thing growing inside her surely, she must want it, didn't all women want babies? One thing he did know was that he couldn't continue the animosity he felt towards her, they would need a truce. His focus had to be Rebecca keeping well physically and mentally, so that she could deliver a healthy baby.

Ezzio sat patiently with the eminent obstetrician, Charles Fields, while Rebecca dressed and joined them. As she took her seat next to him, he knew she resented the appointment, so he vowed to do his best to be supportive.

Mr Fields looked kindly at them both, "Everything looks to be progressing quite normally, and the size of the foetus is satisfactory for the weeks of pregnancy." He turned to Rebecca, "You mentioned during the scan that you'd had some vaginal bleeding, is that still happening?"

Discomfort was written all over her face, and she glanced Ezzio's way. He knew the look was a silent plea for him to leave, "I'm not going anywhere, Rebecca so you can stop looking at me like that."

She inhaled deeply, and turned back to the consultant, "I'm still having a bit of spotting, but nothing really significant."

Ezzio looked firstly at her, then at Mr Fields, "Why is she bleeding, what does that mean?"

"It could be a threatened miscarriage, but now Rebecca is over twelve weeks, things are looking more optimistic," the consultant reassured.

Ezzio felt uneasy, "Could she still lose the baby?"

"Yes, she could," he replied directly, "however, the baby's size looked healthy enough, and if Rebecca continues to rest and take care of herself, then I see no reason why the pregnancy shouldn't progress normally."

He watched the consultant smile comfortingly at Rebecca, but Ezzio needed to know more. He hadn't got where he was in life, without checking the finer details, "Is there anything else we can do to make sure the pregnancy carries on normally?" If he sounded like an anxious first-time father, then so what. Since seeing the scan, something had shifted inside him.

Mr Fields raised his brow and nodded, "Yes, you can keep Rebecca stress free. Of course, I know of the impending court case and the strain this will put upon her, but hopefully, she will be much further on into the pregnancy when this happens." He paused, writing something down in her notes, and then he looked up, "There is one other thing. It might be wise to abstain from penetrative sex for a few more weeks until the bleeding stops completely."

Clearly, the consultant thought they were sexually active, and why wouldn't he, they had actually conceived a baby together? Without looking directly at Rebecca, Ezzio sensed her discomfort as she fidgeted in the chair next to him. He cleared his throat, "Right, we do understand and that won't be a problem, but what about orgasm, should she refrain from that also?"

If the colour of Rebecca's face was anything to go by, embarrassment was radiating out of every pore of her body. She stood up, "Ezzio please, that's quite enough."

Mr Fields stood also with an apologetic look on his face, "I am sorry Rebecca. Would you like Mr Marin to wait outside so that you can speak with me privately?"

"No," she answered firmly, "There's no need for that. I'm pleased everything is fine, thank you very much for seeing me today," she picked up her handbag, and through clenched teeth spat at Ezzio, "I'll wait for you outside."

As the door closed behind her, he was pleased that she had refused the consultant's request. After paying out handsomely for his services, he wouldn't have been at all happy about her seeing him without being present, especially as it was his baby they were discussing.

Ezzio followed a few minutes later clutching print-outs of the baby's scan. They walked silently out of the clinic, and he took her arm firmly and guided her across the road to the car. Once inside, she turned on him furiously, "How dare you? You had absolutely no business discussing me like that," her voice was high and breathless, "What on earth gave you the idea I would be having any kind of sexual relationship with you?"

Remembering what the doctor had said about keeping her calm, he tried to look apologetic, "I read somewhere that pregnant woman craved sex," he leant in close, "something to do with their hormones, I think. I just thought if you felt that way inclined, I could help you."

"Help me!" she screeched moving her head away from his, "Have you gone stark raving mad? Why would I want you anywhere near me?" Fury shimmered in her eyes, "For your information, if I felt that way inclined, I can quite well see to myself. I'm hardly going to be running to you for sexual relief, now am I?"

"Why not? We were good together once, even you can't argue with that."

"That was a long time ago and certainly won't be happening again," she replied tartly.

"Fine," he shrugged, "but if you change your mind, you know where my room is."

She gave him a disapproving look, "I can assure you categorically that I won't be changing my mind."

The firmness of her voice was quickly dismissed by his new playful approach, "Well, I think you're sexually frustrated, that's what's wrong with you. I think you could have sex with me right now."

His grin took on a sexual persona which she seemed determined to dampen, "How on earth have you come to that conclusion?"

"I can see it in your eyes."

"That's wishful thinking on your part," she dismissed.

He laughed out loud, "I don't think so, Rebecca. I reckon with a little persuasion, I can have you in the palm of my hand in seconds, or better still in my mouth," his lips quirked into a mocking smile, "I seem to remember you liked that."

Colour rushed to her cheeks, "You're disgusting, do you know that?"

"Disgusting?" he said incredulously, "What's disgusting about sex? It's pleasurable and you know it."

"I said you're disgusting, and you shouldn't have been speaking to the consultant about me in that way."

"Why not, don't you think he has sex?"

Her retort stalled momentarily. The air between them suddenly seemed thick, and she looked tense at his close proximity.

"Can we please stop talking about sex? I really do not want to be having this conversation with you."

"The answer was yes anyway," he said with a lazy smile.

She scowled irritably as he started the engine, "What are you talking about now?" she snapped.

Checking the mirror, he looked over his shoulder and eased the car forward, keeping his eyes firmly fixed on the windscreen, "He said orgasms were okay, in fact, he said you need at least one a day to relax you."

Her head spun sideways, "You are such a liar, Ezzio Marin, no doctor would ever say anything like that, and you know it."

CHAPTER 29

The weeks dragged by. Dorothy became her constant companion, and she felt a real closeness to both her and George. It was almost as if she'd been released into their care.

Ezzio kept well away from her. Each morning when she got up, he'd used the gym and gone to work, and he never returned home in the evening until very late when she was in bed. Whatever the time, she rarely heard him. Dorothy prepared all her food, and while she had the use of the luxuries that the house provided such as the pool, the gardens and indoor cinema, it felt like she was on house arrest. She never went anywhere, even when Ezzio had to return to the States for a funeral, she was held in the house like a prisoner with Dorothy and George moving in to keep an eye on her, and Imogen visiting daily to go over her defence, which she hated. What more could she say? She explained over and over what had happened that night, but Imogen wanted to know every minute detail, did she like her stepfather, did he ever behave inappropriately towards her, was she frightened of him; the questioning was endless.

One Saturday morning, she was surprised to see Ezzio at the breakfast table. Guessing it was unlikely he would want to eat breakfast with her, she was unsure what to do. About to turn around, he surprised her by asking, "Come and have some breakfast, I want to talk to you." Her heart plummeted; she knew what his idea of talking would be, more than likely some sort of threat or intimidation.

He took a sip of his coffee, and asked, "Dorothy tells me you asked if George could take you to your flat?"

Blast, why had Dorothy told him that? It was evident now which side of the fence her and George was sitting on.

She tried to keep her voice even, "Yes, that's right. I wanted to collect some personal items."

"What personal items?" he gave her a considered look, "Tell me what you need and I'll get them for you."

The last thing she wanted was him anywhere near her bedsit, "I'd rather go myself," and before he could interject, she added, "it is my home after all."

He gave a dismissive shake of his head, "I have no intention of visiting your home, Rebecca, I meant I'll buy you what you need."

"I don't need you to buy me anything," her chin rose, "I just want some of my own things."

"Like what?"

"Clothing . . . cosmetics, things like that," she lied.

"I wouldn't have thought currently, you'd have any use for makeup, or those designer dresses of yours," he stated dryly. Their gazes met and held fleetingly, before he gave an abrupt nod, "Very well, I'll take you tomorrow morning, early. We don't want to give the press any photographs of you and I out and about.

Her tummy was in a turmoil travelling by car to her bedsit with him; he looked so big and imposing, behind the wheel. Classical music was playing on the CD, which she was grateful for so she didn't have to speak, preferring to surreptitiously watch him effortlessly manoeuvring the car around the streets of London. Her mind was occupied trying to think of a way to circumvent him coming into the bedsit. There was no way she could tell him that she wanted to retrieve the cash she'd hidden there.

As he pulled the car to a standstill and cut the engine, she didn't move. He turned towards her, "Well, do you want to go inside, or what?"

She gave him a hopeful smile, "Yes, but I'd like to go on my own if that's alright?"

"No, it's not alright, I'll come with you," he retorted, "the last thing I need right now is for you to do a runner, and it ends up costing me half a million and a whole load of bad press."

"I won't do a runner," she said, "why would I?"

He sighed deeply, "You'll have to make allowances for me not believing you. I'm afraid trusting your word is a weakness that I would never allow myself," he raised his brows, "so we either go in together or not at all, what will it be?"

I'll just have to play it by ear, "Okay," she conceded, "it looks like I don't have much of a choice." She exited the car, her mind racing ahead to how she was going to retrieve the money without him finding out.

He seemed so huge stood in her tiny bedsit, but there was nowhere for him to sit down, only the bed, and she wasn't going to offer him that, so she left him standing. The expression on his face as he looked around said everything about the way she lived. She removed two pillowcases off the bed.

"What are you doing with those?" he asked

"I'm going to put my belongings in them."

"Oh, for Christ's sake, don't you have a suitcase or holdall like a normal person?"

"No I haven't," she dismissed, "so what does that make me, abnormal?"

His tone was bored, "Your words Rebecca, not mine. Can you hurry up please, I've got work to do today."

She emptied some of the contents of her drawers, before opening her wardrobe door.

"You won't need any of those clothes," he snarled.

"I wasn't going to bring any of them," she said, "I'm just after a couple of sentimental bits."

"Good. And don't think about bringing anything that Darlene has bought for you," he added.

It was on the tip of her tongue to tell him that every item in her wardrobe she'd either bought, or made herself, but what was the point. He always thought the worst about her anyway. She retrieved a stool from against the wall and positioned it directly under the hatch of the false roof.

"What the hell do you think you're doing now?" he asked incredulously.

"I need something from out of the loft."

"What?" he queried with a puzzled expression on his face.

"A shoebox," she replied, but knew he'd want more than that, "it's full of keepsakes. I want them with me."

He took his hands out of his pockets, "Then you'd better let me, I hardly think standing on a stool is the most sensible thing for a pregnant woman to do." He stepped on the stool, and her breath caught in her throat as she watched him push up the loft hatch.

"It's to your left," she instructed, "you should be able to get it from there."

He reached in and lifted the shoebox out, passing it down to her, and she hastily took it from his hand. Lord knows what he would make of the hundreds of pounds neatly stashed inside, hidden under a couple of thin paperback novels.

As he stepped off the stool and placed it against the wall, his gaze lingered around the sparse bedsit, "Is there any rent due on this place?"

"No," she answered honestly, she always paid her rent well in advance.

"You'll have to let me know when it's due, and who to pay it to."

"That's hardly necessary," her voice wobbled, "I'd rather you didn't pay my rent for me." She hated that he could make her feel so vulnerable and a lump formed in her throat.

"Well, someone's got to pay it," he shrugged, "it's not as if you've got an abundance of other options to consider, is it?"

Bastard, as if she needed reminding there was nobody to help her.

He carried on, "Eventually I'll have to cancel the lease anyway, if you're acquitted, you can't continue to live here."

"Why not?" The lump in her throat was growing bigger, it wasn't much of a home, admittedly, but it was all she had.

"Because I most certainly am not having a child of mine spending any time in this," he looked disparagingly around the room, "hovel." He frowned, "Surely you earned enough money to live somewhere slightly more salubrious than this place?" To answer truthfully would mean incriminating herself, she could hardly say most of her money was spent on rent and Emily's keep. Ezzio Marin wouldn't have any idea what it felt like to struggle.

He sighed as he walked towards the door, and opened it. She looked around the meagre bedsit; he was right on that score, it wasn't at all suitable for a child. There was no point in worrying about that now, though; it was unlikely she would ever see this place again.

She took one last look around the room and her gaze was drawn to the plain table in the corner. It appeared just like a wooden occasional table, but cleverly disguised evidence of her precious sewing machine, in an inverted position underneath the lid. Staring longingly at it, she silently accepted that there'd be no place for that where she was going. To stifle her threatening tears, she took a deep breath, but it came out as more of a sob. Ezzio moved towards her, and with a rare glimpse of gentleness, he titled her chin and asked, "What is it, why are you crying?"

"Nothing," she stifled another sob but a single tear flowed down her cheek which he caught with his thumb. As if that wasn't bad enough, the normally aloof Ezzio, put his arms around her and pulled her closely towards his chest. His hold was tight as if he'd never let her go. This is all I need, him being nice to me, but she didn't break away. Instead, clutching the shoe box in one arm, she wrapped her spare arm around him, and with her head neatly ensconced underneath his chin, for a precious few minutes, she savoured the warmth of his huge arms, and the only noise audible in the tiny bedsit was the sound of her sobs against his chest.

CHAPTER 30

After weeks of preparation, finally, it was the day of the trial. As planned, her, Ezzio and Imogen travelled together to court. Imogen had staged-managed the whole operation, needing the media to believe that Rebecca and Ezzio were a love match, with their much wanted baby on the way.

Already the headlines were speculative, and Imogen's strategy was reliant upon that for the case, projecting Rebecca as more of a victim than a perpetrator, which hopefully would gain a degree of sympathy with the jury.

It took a huge effort pushing themselves forward through the waiting reporters, and the flash bulbs were overwhelming. Rebecca recalled warnings on TV about images containing flash photography, and thought wryly how bad those images were live.

As instructed she kept her head down, and allowed Ezzio to guide her. Once inside the impressive entrance and out of sight of the reporters, Imogen breathed a sigh of relief, "I'm not saying it's going to get easier each day, but you will get used to it. Are you alright, Rebecca?"

"Yes, I'm fine thank you." Imogen had briefed her on every aspect of the case so she knew exactly what would be happening during the next few days.

"Good, then it's time for us to go."

Imogen smiled warmly at Ezzio, "We'll see you later no doubt?"

"Yes of course." He smiled directly at Imogen, "Good luck, I know you'll do your very best." Rebecca noted the affection in his smile to Imogen, and then he turned to her, "And you also, Rebecca, I'm sure today being the first day will be particularly difficult." His smile was different for her, a sympathetic one, but not one of a suitor.

"Yes, I'm sure you're right," she agreed and turned towards Imogen, who smiled kindly and asked, "Are we ready then?" They left Ezzio, standing alone, and made their way to the waiting room.

***

Rebecca entered the courtroom, and her nervous stomach twitched as she was taken to a seat allocated for the defendant on trial. Surreptitiously she assessed the jury, trying not to focus on anyone in particular. As she counted their heads, she deduced there was an even number of each gender. Was that good or bad?

As she looked up at the public gallery, her eyes were drawn to Ezzio who was staring intensely at her, and sat next to him was David his lawyer, but perhaps the biggest surprise of all, was Darlene Milner seated well away from Ezzio, she certainly hadn't expected that. For a brief second their eyes met, and Darlene's smile was a sympathetic one, which hinted at more. Guilt, perhaps? She'd never been quite sure if Darlene had been involved in Emily's abduction, or if Piers had acted alone, and looking at her now, she recalled the times she'd spent with her and how generous financially this woman had actually been towards her. It was a time when she'd felt reasonably safe, before Ezzio had come into her life and spoilt everything. Her eyes moved on towards her stepfather's family, who were looking back at her with such disdain, that she quickly turned away.

Imogen looked immaculate in her brown suit and matching stiletto heels. There was no doubt about it, her 'can do' approach did instil a degree of confidence. However, that feeling never lasted long as Rebecca was certain she'd be found guilty, despite Imogen spending hours and hours going over events with her and focussing on the minutest detail.

She recalled a recent conversation she'd had with Imogen when she'd asked her if she was in love with Ezzio. Rebecca could see she was a little ruffled by the question, nevertheless, she answered honestly that she hoped, once the trial was over, she and Ezzio would pursue a permanent relationship. Seemingly Ezzio had indicated he felt the same way, but wanted the trial to be over first. What did her mother use to say, By all means ask a question, but you might not like the answer?

Imogen demonstrated her total commitment to her job by stating her only desire was Rebecca's acquittal, and quantified that she knew there was only the baby between her and Ezzio. She'd explained that was the only reason he was helping her, and even though she already knew this, for some reason, hearing his response vocalised, made her feel terribly sad.

The court usher requested they all stand for the Judge as he entered the courtroom. Rebecca looked at him and assessed he was about sixty years of age. Imogen had told her that Judge Quarmby, was a fair judge, and one that was known to be supportive of women.

As he sat down and they all took their seats, Rebecca felt a huge weight bearing down on her shoulders. Her head was telling her that she would be going back to prison, she was sure of that, so she just needed to get through the trial, she told herself. Imogen had reiterated that their aim was to cast doubt on the prosecution's case, that's all they needed to do. All. That didn't hold water with her, but she was grateful for not having to take the stand and give an account of that night, she just couldn't have done that.

Her eyes drifted around the courtroom once again, this time onto the prosecuting barrister Marcus Warr. He was easy to recognise from Imogen's disparaging description of him being vertically challenged. Imogen hadn't been complacent, though, reckoning that he might have 'little man's syndrome', but his standing was that of a Rottweiler in the courtroom.

Commencement of the proceedings was instigated by the judge as he invited Marcus Warr to put forward the case for the prosecution. Rebecca averted her eyes; she could barely listen as he cleared his throat to speak.

"Ladies and gentlemen of the jury, may I respectfully remind you all, that you are sitting here today tasked with ensuring that justice is done," he paused which she guessed was to ensure he had their complete attention, as if he wouldn't have. He continued, "A gentleman has lost his life. Derek Clay, a religious man who spent his life following the teachings of God. A family man, loved by many, and a law-abiding citizen who worked hard for a living. Through the church, he met a like-minded woman, whom he subsequently married and became the stepfather to two beautiful twin daughters, which he welcomed. His life was complete; he loved his family dearly and valued their home life together." He paused again, which Imogen had explained was all about impact, and was done to give the jury time to assimilate what was being said.

Marcus Warr continued, "Sadly, tragedy loomed. Just eight months into the marriage, his beloved wife, the love of his life, was diagnosed with pancreatic cancer. He nursed this woman until her demise, and on her deathbed, he promised to take care of her daughters who were only sixteen at the time. His beloved wife passed away before they had even celebrated their first wedding anniversary. He was a broken man."

Rebecca couldn't believe what she was hearing. *How long is this going to go on for? I could throw up it's so nauseating. I have never heard such rubbish in my life. I know you prepared me for the case, Imogen, but this is just a load of bullshit . . . Derek Clay was nothing like that.*

Marcus Warr had the jury's attention and was in full flow, "While Derek Clay was grieving for his beloved wife, he continued to support his two young stepdaughters, one of them with significant learning difficulties. His intention was to guide them both through life's trials and tribulations during this fundamental part of their young lives, as well as continuing to ensure food was on the table and the household bills were paid."

He took a sip of water, "Money was tight, and he didn't earn a substantial salary. The loss of his wife's income made things difficult, resulting in the need for efficiency savings to be made within the household. Not unreasonable to you and I, and the many others struggling each day on a tight budget. The thought of a person losing their life because of this is quite abhorrent to any of us here today, but I'm afraid that is what happened to Derek Clay."

He slowed his voice down, "Through no fault of his own, he had no option but to refuse his stepdaughter, Rebecca Price Jones a place on a school trip due to the costs, and for that, he paid with his life."

Melodramatically, he rested, which without legal training, she could see was a way to maximise the impact of his words. Imogen had explained that he would pause regularly, to allow enough time to pass so that the jury had time to absorb his opening statement. After a few seconds, he carried on, "During the course of the trial, the defence council will put forward many other explanations for Derek Clay's untimely death, which may, or may not, cast doubt on the evidence. I put it to you all that these blatant stories will be hollow attempts to discredit the prosecution's case."

Ladies and gentlemen of the jury, may I urge you all, during the course of this trial not to lose sight of Derek Clay, a true gentleman in the very sense of the word, who did his best to provide and take care of his family, and is sadly not here today. We owe it to him, indeed it is our duty to ensure that justice is carried out in this courtroom, on his behalf."

Marcus Warr sat down with confidence written all over his face. Imogen had described addressing the jury was part of the theatrics of the courtroom, and when Marcus Warr had finished, Rebecca was sure he would be content in the knowledge that his well-rehearsed opening statement would have given the jury focus.

The judge invited Imogen to respond on behalf of the defence, but she didn't stand immediately just as she had told Rebecca she wouldn't. She recalled Imogen telling her how the tactics and strategies of the courtroom always excited her, and it was a stage, where she was able to match her wits against others, and she loved the theatrics of it all.

Her approach would be slow and precise; she'd prepared thoroughly and planned the case meticulously, plotting her strategy.

Rebecca waited. Hurry up, please. All that nonsense was so damming and untrue. If only they knew. . . that bastard was nothing like the picture that had been painted.

Imogen stood, and facing each member of the jury, spoke slowly and confidently, "Ladies and gentlemen, a courtroom is a historical British institution charged with upholding the law. If we do not safeguard the law, then there would be consequences for each and every one of us here today," she moved her head from one jury member to another, as if addressing each one personally, "The law has remarkable powers, and in its wisdom, recognises that there are always two sides to every story. That is why we are all here today, to examine two different versions of a terrible tragedy, and then make a decision based on the evidence presented," she paused and moistened her lips, "During this trial, I aim to establish an alternative to Mr Warr's theory, and cast doubt on his assumptions."

Imogen paused, almost as if she was considering what to say next, and then adopting a sorrowful look on her face, continued, "Sadly a man has lost his life, and nobody is more distraught about that than the defendant. The young woman on trial today is not standing here satisfied that her stepfather has died, on the contrary, she has had to grieve for that loss and the part she played in it. Rebecca Price Jones did not plan to kill and certainly didn't intend to kill either. Derek Clay's tragic death was an accident; an immediate action of a young girl who momentarily lost control."

She waited, just as Marcus Warr had done to allow the jury time to take in her comments. When it appeared that enough time had passed, she continued, "It is my intention to produce evidence which will not only defend Rebecca Price Jones and her actions but also will cast doubt on the prosecution's theories. May I respectfully request that you consider all of the evidence presented before making your decision?"

Once the opening statements had been heard, Rebecca watched the prosecution begin with the death of her stepfather. They showed graphic photographs to the jury of him lying on the floor with the knife in his chest. A knife plunged into him by the defendant following an argument, they were quick to add.

No attempts were made to save him by calling the emergency services. There was a delay in calling the police following his death, and it was critically pointed out this was most likely due to Rebecca Price Jones thinking up a plausible story.

Explicitly, Marcus Warr described Rebecca as a dishonest young woman that had stabbed her stepfather, and while in custody awaiting trial, had escaped from a detention centre and reinvented herself as Kate.

In full swing, his emphasis was on her spending the next part of her life working as a high-class prostitute for her own financial gain. Imogen raised an objection about how Rebecca earned her living as that was not relevant to the case, or indeed proven evidence. It was upheld by the judge; however, the damage had been done and graphically illustrated to the jury, so they would no doubt form their opinions as to her character. He couldn't have been more damning if he'd tried.

Next it was the turn of the prosecution witnesses. The first two people to take the stand were her stepfather's relatives, both of whom gave exaggerated accounts of Derek Clay's 'loving personality' and 'caring disposition'. Imogen didn't cross-examine. Their defence was not to discredit her stepfather, rather than to display the trauma Rebecca was under when she stabbed him.

Rebecca watched the jury taking it all on board. She had to acknowledge it was reassuring to have a barrister who believed in her and was trying hard to get her acquitted, and she felt deep down that Imogen was also striving to prove her worth to Ezzio. While she understood that once she was out of the way, Imogen may possibly become a permanent fixture in his life, what she struggled with, was, the knot deep inside her, which tightened every time she thought about the two of them together.

CHAPTER 31

Judge Quarmby brought proceedings to a close on the first day. They all stood as he left the courtroom, and Imogen escorted Rebecca into the holding room. She gave Rebecca a compassionate look, and reassured her, "The first day was always going to be hard."

Rebecca nodded, "I know, it was no more than I expected, you really are exceptionally good at what you do." She sincerely meant it.

"That's because I care about justice. I know from what you have told me, you didn't intend to kill your stepfather, it was a terrible accident and I'm going to prove it."

Although appreciative of Imogen efforts, she was under no illusion, "I am grateful, really I am," she sighed, "but I'm fairly certain I'll be going back to prison. I did kill a man so it's right really."

"No, it isn't right," Imogen responded forcibly, "You were a young girl that had lost her mother; people have been acquitted and done much worse."

She watched Imogen as she filed papers into her briefcase. In another life, I could have liked you.

Imogen smiled and took her arm, "Come on, let's get back to Ezzio, he'll be waiting."

They made their way along the cold tiled corridor, and Rebecca's heart did the usual flip flop at the site of him, even though she'd seen him hours earlier.

He looked all male in his dark business suit and highly polished shoes. He exuded style and appeal, and the only word that sprung to mind to describe him was charismatic. She knew how busy his life was, yet he was willing to attend court each day. Imogen said it was so that people could see them as a couple, but she thought it must be to give Imogen support.

The journey home was a quiet one with Rebecca, Ezzio and Imogen each immersed in their own thoughts about the first day of the trial. Once back at the house, Rebecca made herself scarce imagining that Imogen and Ezzio would want to be alone.

In her room, she decided a bath was the best way to unwind, and she wanted to make the most of a luxurious soak as soon it would be all women together in the prison showers.

The warm bubbles she'd added to the bath water were relaxing and the floral smell was somehow comforting. Languishing in the warm water, she felt the baby kick and watched in awe as the movement inside her tummy was visible. It was becoming increasingly more difficult to remain detached from the baby, especially now it was moving and showing its presence each day.

The second scan had revealed the sex of the baby as being a boy. It would look like Ezzio she was sure of it, his dark gene must be much stronger than her fair one.

Contemplating what he would make of the baby's visible movements, as if on cue, she saw him through the crack of the bathroom door in her bedroom.

He called out, "Rebecca, are you okay, you've been gone a while and we were getting worried?"

"I'm fine, I'm just having a soak in the bath."

"I thought so; we are holding dinner for you."

"Please don't do that, I'll have something later."

"No, we can wait." His voice became louder as he approached the bathroom door, "Can I come in?"

"No Ezzio," she answered sharply, "I've got nothing on."

Ignoring her, he came in with a teasing smile on his face, "Yes I always find naked is the best way to have a bath."

Her eyes widened, "What are you doing?" she shrieked, covering her breasts, completely flustered as he was staring at her abdomen which no amount of bubble bath would be able to completely cover.

After a few seconds of staring at her tummy, he looked up at her face and she saw an expression that she didn't recognise in his eyes . . . astonishment and something else that she wasn't quite sure of.

No louder than a whisper, he murmured, "You're beautiful, Rebecca."

Their eyes locked, she'd never seen him so open and exposed. Hesitantly, almost as if he was afraid she would say no, he gently asked, "Can I feel the baby?" Hypnotised by this vulnerable side of him, there was no way she could refuse, "Yes, he's kicking at the moment, feel him."

***

As if in slow motion, with his eyes never leaving her abdomen, he knelt down at the side of the bath totally mesmerised by her moving tummy. Tentatively, he ran his hand along her protruding abdomen, and as if on cue the baby moved. Again, he pressed slightly and the baby responded by stirring. Astonished didn't come close to covering his reaction, he was overwhelmed that he and Rebecca had created a child, and his chest was bursting with elation and joy which were completely new emotions for him.

He continued with his hand to trace the baby's kicks on Rebecca's abdomen, and it was a few seconds before he understood exactly what he was feeling as he'd kept this particular emotion locked deep inside for many, many years. For the first time since his parents' death, he felt it like a wave running through his body, crushing his heart and touching his soul. It was love . . . love for this precious new life he'd created. Euphoria continued to move him as he moulded his hands around the baby's movements, but then something much more primal kicked in. His seed swelling her abdomen was as seductive as it was erotic.

***

Rebecca was completely overwhelmed by his caress, and tears pricked her eyes, there hadn't been much to feel good about for such a long time. As she watched him touching her tummy, she wasn't sure when the caressing became more intimate. His long fingers slowly moved lower and continued to stroke her abdomen, and she started to feel slightly breathless. She arched up to his caressing hand, and as if sensing her need, he moved his fingers lower and slowly began massaging her labia, ably assisted by the bath oil and bubbles. Her head seemed to fall back of its own accord, and she placed her arms on the edge of the bath, displaying her achingly aroused nipples. The damp heat of her swollen core throbbed. Through half closed eyelids, she watched him, but his eyes remained firmly fixed on her abdomen.

Welcoming his touch, her lids fluttered closed as she spread her legs, appreciating the heat of his hand as he cupped her sex tightly before inserting his fingers high inside her clenching channel. It felt good, and she groaned in appreciation, wanting more from him. He evidently understood, as he moved his finger to her swollen nub, and began to massage rhythmically. The pleasure was rising, and she became lost in the exquisite assault on her senses. She desperately wanted the delicate sensations to last, but was too turned on. Highly excited and overcome with the pleasurable feelings, she couldn't hold on, "Oh God, oh God," she groaned, quivering as the pleasure rapidly reached its pinnacle, and wave after rapturous wave of ecstasy advanced, taking her up high, before flowing down her entire body. He'd been right, pregnancy hormones had made her sensitive. Keeping her poised on the shuddering plateau of her release, still he pressed on her overstimulated clit over and over again, causing her to tremble uncontrollably with the intensity, until the crescendo built into a frenzy again, and she screamed his name as the powerful ripples radiated from her central core, as she shattered into a million pieces for the second time.

Acutely embarrassed, she opened her eyes, as he stood and reached for a towel to dry his hands. Casually, as if nothing had just passed between them, an easy smile curved his mouth, "We'll wait until you join us downstairs, don't be much longer though as the water's getting cold." And just like that, he was gone.

How the hell am I supposed to eat dinner with him and Imogen after that?

CHAPTER 32

The trial was not going well. As skilled as Imogen was, Rebecca knew that jail was beckoning. There was a dead man with a knife in his chest, so they'd find her guilty she was sure of it.

Each day followed the same pattern. Ezzio and Imogen would travel with her to court, and they'd travel back to Ezzio's house at the end of the day. Without fail, they were beseeched by the press.

What difference did it make about the outfit she was wearing or the colour of her eye make-up? They speculated daily about how Ezzio Marin would bring up the baby, how the baby would be heir to a million pound fortune, and how he was going to marry her in jail. On and on the inference went and not one denial.

They would dine together each evening after a day in court, and Imogen would then return to the hotel. At the end of each delicious meal prepared by Dorothy, Ezzio would escort Imogen to her car, and Rebecca would make a swift dash to her room so she didn't have to face him alone when he came back. It wasn't that she was scared of him; it was more that she was scared of her feelings for him. He'd been right, she was aroused around him.

Tonight after dinner, unlike the other nights, he'd taken Imogen back to the hotel, and her mind was working overtime thinking about them together. Knowing Ezzio's appetite for sex, she was sure he must be satisfying his sexual urges with her.

She made her way downstairs to the lounge area with the beautiful view of the garden through the French windows. It was a warm night, so she discarded her robe feeling more comfortable in her loose pyjama bottoms, and vest top.

Sitting on the huge comfy sofa, she contemplated her future behind bars. Resigned that there wasn't an alternative, she vowed that once she'd served her sentence she would start a new life, and work hard to make a home for herself and Emily. She missed her sister desperately, having to make do with telephone calls currently, which were as frustrating for her, as they were for Emily, who complained bitterly that she hadn't seen her for such a long time.

It was astonishing that no one had investigated where Emily was. Having maintained the story that she had died from a drugs overdose, it was surprising that nobody seemed to investigate further, not that she wanted her sister around while the trial was going on. Dear sweet Emily was an innocent who only ever told the truth, and didn't have a deceitful bone in her body. Unlike her, who had lied, cheated and stolen.

***

Ezzio arrived home and was on his way to bed when he saw Rebecca sleeping peacefully on the settee. He was loathed to disturb her, and stood for a moment looking at her angelic face. Although he couldn't be certain, he wondered if she'd been crying, as her cheeks appeared puffy. His eyes were drawn to her well rounded stomach accentuated by the tightness of her vest, and his new found feeling of love kicked in, for his son growing strong inside of her.

He had a desperate urge to make love to her, but he knew that to do so, would be his undoing. For a reason which he couldn't fathom, she had an almighty hold over him; he had never experienced the feelings he had for her, with any other woman. Pensively, he considered how the tables had turned on him. Extremely rich, he could have his pick of so many women to have his child, yet against all odds it was her that carried his seed, and his child would most likely be born in prison. You didn't need to be an expert in law to know that the trial wasn't going well, and Rebecca wasn't helping at all with her defeatist attitude.

The sound of him securing the patio door must have disturbed her, as she stirred. Although half asleep, she opened her eyes, and her drowsy pupils met his.

"Hi," she mumbled easing herself into a sitting position.

As if some sort of alien force had taken hold of him, he moved towards her and sat down on the settee, lifting her outstretched legs, and placing them across his own. Touching Rebecca always aroused him, and unable to deny his hunger any longer, he wrapped his arms around her expanding waist, easing her onto his lap, and almost in slow motion, as if a magnet was in control, his lips claimed hers.

Kissing her had tormented his dreams for so long, and the reality of it, was pure heaven. Remarkably, she was kissing him back with a passion that matched his own. As he savoured her luscious lips moving in sync with his own, he silently acknowledged that he never wanted to stop kissing her.

His hand found her braless breast, and stroked her taught nipple which was completely receptive to his touch. She kissed him hungrily as his hand moved down her abdomen and caressed her belly carrying his child. Her throaty moans drove him on, and as he moved his hand down inside her pyjama bottoms, her legs flopped open to give him greater access.

He touched her moisture, and for once she became bold, placing her hand over the top of his, urging him towards her sensitive bud. He pressed firmly, eager to pleasure her, while her hands travelled to his zip to undo his trousers, but he brushed them away, "No," he exhaled, "we can't."

Breathlessly, she kissed him again, "We can, I'm over the bleeding now, it'll be okay."

Much as his body was crying out for fulfilment, he knew that being inside Rebecca would be his downfall, and he couldn't allow that, he needed to be in control.

Sensing her confusion regarding his restraint, he lifted her vest top over her head, and gazed at her amazing breasts. They were larger now due to the pregnancy, and protruded superbly. He eased her down, and she lifted her bottom to allow him to strip off her pyjama bottoms. As she lay, gloriously naked in front of him, he was in awe at the sight of her enlarged breasts and swollen belly. His lips were drawn to her bulging abdomen and he bent forward and kissed it gently. Do all men feel like this about pregnant women?

The increased size of her breasts turned him on incredibly, and he eagerly took each one in turn into his mouth, and sucked hard on the tempting nipples, with the sound of her throaty moans spurring him on.

***

Desire ripped through her as his sensational mouth began sucking her receptive breasts. Cupping them, he rubbed his fingers back and forth across her sensitised nipples, making them tingle wonderfully. He aroused such a level of need within her, and the pulse between her legs throbbed relentlessly. She tried to sit up to remove his clothes, but as her clumsy fingers reached forward to unbutton his shirt, for some reason, he moved them aside.

Her body ached for him, and she wanted him to come inside her with all of his semen, as they didn't need protection now. Why wasn't he getting undressed . . . how could she free his penis? His head moved lower, and his rough stubble on her abdomen, thrilled her, and erased any further thoughts. The sight of his head disappearing in-between her legs was graphic and sexy, but nothing could have prepared her for his delightful tongue licking her moisture.

As she looked down at herself completely naked, with her erect nipples taut from his sucking, she realised she was enjoying her own naked body. She opened her legs wide to give him greater access, and was in awe of this gorgeous man pleasuring her in such a sensitive way. He licked and paused, licked and paused. The sensations were unbearable, "Please Ezzio," she begged.

Changing the movement of his tongue, instead of delicate licks, he applied relentless pressure on her clit. Round and round his tongue pressed. Taking a final look at his dark hair between her knees, and his strong hands on her hips, she succumbed to the delightful sensations deep within her and cried out as pleasure shuddered through her, on and on, and on and on.

As she came down to earth, she opened her eyes to see him getting to his feet. The expression on his face was almost as if he was repulsed. What's wrong with him?

He towered above her lying position on the sofa as he picked up her pyjamas, and handed them to her. There was something quite bizarre about him helping to dress her, but she felt less vulnerable covered, even if it was skimpy bed attire.

Facing him, she somehow felt fragile and exposed, "Why wouldn't you make love to me?" she confronted, "it's a bit one-sided if I'm getting all the satisfaction."

His expression was pained, "Sorry, I couldn't, I'm concerned about the baby." He looks more embarrassed than worried. Tears threatened, but she held them back, she'd desperately wanted him to make love to her.

Barely whispering, she challenged, "Is that all you think about?" she tried to catch his evasive eyes, "there was a you and me before the baby."

Although he responded by looking directly at her face, it was almost as if he was staring straight through her, and when he did speak, it was in a hushed tone, as if he was saying the words to himself, "There was never a you and me."

No longer meeting her eyes, she realised there was no more to be said. With as much dignity as she could muster, she walked away. Tomorrow she would need to face him, but no more tonight.

***

Ezzio watched her go. How he'd held back from making love to her he didn't know, he was still hard, but that was nothing new. He was used to being in a constant state of arousal around her, he'd lost count of the cold showers and do-it-yourself jobs he'd had to do, and he hated it. Never in his adult life had he resorted to self sex, he'd always been able to find willing bed mates.

He was a generous lover, he knew that, and in return he got what he wanted, but with Rebecca it was different. Her response to his touch blew him away, just pleasuring her meant so much to him, and he was overawed watching her climax tonight, but there was a side of Rebecca he hated. It wasn't so much the prostitution; he just couldn't come to terms with her stealing from him. He'd lived a life based on honesty and integrity, so could never forgive the fact she left him for Darlene, and had taken two of his watches. So many times he'd asked himself, why she'd done that, but the question that caused him the most anguish, and preoccupied his masculine pride was, did she actually prefer Darlene Milner to him?

He thought about her returning to prison, and it made his gut ache, but that was purely because she was pregnant . . . wasn't it? If the baby didn't exist then he wouldn't waste a minute on her. No, he needed to concentrate on Imogen, she was much more to his taste, and each time they were alone, her whole persona indicated she wanted him.

But as tonight had proven, there was only one woman he wanted to make love to, and he definitely wasn't going to go there. He had to distance himself from Rebecca, which was easier said than done, when he thought back to tonight and how responsive she'd been to him. He could still taste her. The ease in which she'd come tonight, made him feel masculine and powerful. Her orgasm, actually gave him pleasure, and recalling her sexy scream in the throes of it all, he could almost climax himself, he was so turned on.

Touching his hardness, he needed release. In the quietness of his room he conjured up images of Rebecca, naked with her legs wide open, and him kissing her intimately, smelling and tasting as only she could. Lying gloriously naked with her taut nipples and enlarged abdomen, he pulled her to the edge of the sofa and knelt before her. As she opened her legs to accommodate him, he entered her quickly with little finesse, and each thrust went deeper and deeper as he fucked her hard. His hands cupped her engorged breasts, which were so teasingly inviting, that he bent his head and sucked on her protruding nipples. Filling her, he pushed until he was ready to burst. The last thing he heard was her screaming his name, and with the final deep thrust, he felt his release coming, and waves of pleasure pumped through his body and into the palm of his hand.

CHAPTER 33

The ringing of his mobile phone interrupted his sleep, "Hello Imogen," his digital clock read 01.10hrs, "What is it?"

"Hi Ezzio, I'm sorry to disturb you at this time of night, but there's been a development which I think's important."

He switched on his bedside light and sat on the edge of his bed, "Go ahead, what is it?"

"I've met with Darlene Milner tonight at the hotel, and she's given me some interesting information."

Irritated by the sheer mention of her name, he sighed heavily, "I wouldn't put a lot of store by anything she has to say, she hates me so will be out to cause trouble."

"It isn't about you, Ezzio, it's about Rebecca," she paused, "well, she calls her Kate, but she really does want to help her."

"Yeah, course she does," he rubbed his eye with the inside of his wrist, "You don't know her, she's a middle-aged dyke with a fixation on Rebecca."

"Yes, she does seem fond of her, but the information she has given me is significant, I only wish I'd had it sooner as it may have helped."

He really wasn't interested in anything Darlene had to say, it was bad enough being in business with her, which the way things were going, wouldn't be for much longer, thank God.

"Go on, then," he answered sceptically, "what vital information has she given you?"

"She says Rebecca's twin sister is still alive."

"What?" suddenly, he was more alert, "she can't be serious. Rebecca told me herself she died from a drugs overdose."

"Yes, that's what she told me," she agreed, "but I've been looking on the internet, and can't find any evidence she is actually dead."

His head was hammering in disbelief, "If this is true, why would Rebecca lie about such a thing?"

"I really don't know, I'm as puzzled as you are. Apparently, though, the twin is mentally subnormal, so maybe she has her reasons."

"What difference does it make anyway if the sister's alive?" he asked, "She wasn't there the night of the stabbing, was she?"

"No, she was at a sleepover at a friend's house. I was thinking more along the lines that perhaps, with her help, we could have painted a picture of how bad the stepfather was, you know the sort of thing, treating both girls badly, a strict disciplinarian, and Rebecca trying to protect her sister. I've always felt sure that Derek Clay was a violent man."

Ezzio's mind was working overtime, it felt like a carrot had been dangled in front of him. "Can we find her . . . is it too late to bring her to court?"

"Yes," she answered in a defeated tone, "much too late I'm afraid, the judge would never allow it."

"Does Darlene have any idea where the sister lives?"

"No, that's the problem, nobody does, only Rebecca."

"Right," he replied assertively, "I'll go and wake her."

Imogen stopped him, "No, don't do that. Think about it, she's never mentioned the sister before, in fact, she's done a great job of concealing her. I don't think she's going to open up to us now at this late stage, do you?"

He inhaled, stifling a yawn, "I don't understand what the hell is going on here, why would she hide her sister?"

"I really don't know. We need to find her, though, as she might have information we could use."

"Are you sure Darlene doesn't have any idea of where this sister might be?"

"No, only that she's aware of her existence."

Jealousy reared its ugly head and he felt a thick tightening across his chest, "Did Rebecca tell Darlene she had a sister?"

"She says not, but won't say how she found out."

"You said nothing's coming up online?" he asked.

"That's right. We'll be able to find out more tomorrow. I'll get someone onto it first thing," there was a pause, as if she was thinking; "I just cannot understand why Rebecca is hiding her, and even worse, making up such a terrible story about her being dead?"

He didn't know either, but with conviction, he spoke about what he did know, "Don't worry, I'll find her, you can be sure of that."

"Please don't say anything to Rebecca; we need to make sure she knows nothing about this."

"I won't," he said, and cut the call. His wide-awake brain kicked in, he had to find the sister, not doing so wasn't an option. He never failed at anything, that's why he was so exasperated with the court process which he couldn't influence or control.

He remained on his bed thinking. Rebecca had said that her sister was dead. Why? He contemplated whether Dorothy and George knew anything as they'd been 'looking after' her while he was in the States. He needed to find out if she'd confided in either of them. Over the last few weeks, he'd watched his housekeeper interact with Rebecca, and it was obvious they'd developed quite a bond.

The following morning, Ezzio waited for Dorothy in the kitchen. Both her and George had worked for him for six years, and were excellent employees. He allowed them to live rent free in a cottage in the grounds, and paid them a generous salary. All he'd ever asked from them was loyalty, with no discussions about his lifestyle to outsiders, which they faithfully complied with.

A man of routine, normally at this time of the morning, he would be using the shower after his gym workout, and Dorothy would arrive to make his breakfast. He looked out of the window, and as if on cue, she entered the kitchen. If she was surprised to be met by him, she didn't show it, "Good morning," she smiled brightly.

His normal pleasantries were cast aside, "Do you know if Rebecca has any relatives?"

"I've no idea," she considered for a moment, "I don't think so, though, if she had, wouldn't they be supporting her now?"

She was right, but that was no help, "I know you've become quite close to her," he paused quickly adding, "and that isn't a problem, it's just that something has come up and I believe there's a relative that might be able to help."

Dorothy shook her head, "I'm sorry, Ezzio, she hasn't confided in me. You're right, though, I have become close to her, but she doesn't discuss anything personal with me." Tentatively she queried, "Wouldn't she tell you herself if you asked her?"

"No, she wouldn't," he switched the tone of his voice to authoritative, "and I must ask that what we've discussed, remains between us."

"Of course." She removed her cardigan and placed it over the chair, "I'm praying she gets acquitted, Rebecca isn't a bad girl, I'm sure they've all got her wrong, she really is a special person." Dorothy looked hesitant, almost as if she wasn't sure whether to continue, but she did anyway, "Both George and I have become really fond of her, can you believe she's made me a beautiful outfit for my nephew's wedding?"

He must have looked puzzled, as she continued, "She's a seamstress, you know, I've never seen anyone as clever as Rebecca at making clothes."

"When did she do this?" he asked sceptically.

"While you were in the States for that funeral, she made a dress for David's wife also. Laura called, and it seems they got talking and Rebecca offered to make her a dress. Laura bought the material, and it only took her a day or two to make. You should have seen what she created, it was fantastic. Ask Laura, she was thrilled to bits with it."

Sewing clothes? He couldn't quite believe it. Bloody hell, a regular Cinderella in his own house, and he had no idea. Bemused, he considered how little he really did know about her, until Dorothy interrupted his train of thought, "I'm not that good at sewing really, my limit is shortening curtains, that sort of thing, but Rebecca, now she makes the sewing machine sing." Seemingly eager to fill him in on information he didn't have, she carried on, "When she first came here, she'd made all the beautiful dresses in her wardrobe, herself. Can you believe that? They were gorgeous, I honestly thought they were all designer dresses, but no, she'd made them all."

Dorothy was on a roll, "And do you know what else she does?" he shook his head, "she stitches the letter E into each garment she makes.

He had no idea what that implied, and wasn't really that interested, but asked the question anyway, "And the significance of that is . . .?"

"Laura and I asked her that," she answered enthusiastically, "and she says the E stands for elegant, as she likes to think that each garment she makes is exactly that," Dorothy smiled fondly, "Isn't that just so lovely?"

His mind conjured up images of Rebecca sitting at a sewing machine, creating beautiful clothes. He'd also believed her stylish dresses had a designer label attached to them, and his overactive imagination had concluded that Darlene had bought them all. His heart felt heavy when he remembered the dresses she'd left behind, and how he'd coldheartedly burned them in the garden incinerator.

He thought back to the first time he'd seen her in the black dress that clung to her body like it had been painted on, and how fantastic she'd looked in the stunning backless number. Had Rebecca made them herself? He couldn't quite believe it. Very little surprised him, but in the space of a few hours, he'd found out two important sides to her . . . now he needed to find that sister.

At the dining table, Rebecca's awkwardness was evident by her silence as she sat alongside him eating breakfast. On a normal day, he'd be in his study by now until they had to leave for court, so she would eat alone, but speaking to Dorothy had altered his usual routine. His eyes were drawn to Rebecca's hands as she buttered her toast, even those long piano fingers were appealing, but then again, everything about her was tempting to him. He disliked the fitted jacket she was wearing, though, simply because it covered her snug camisole, and anything hiding her magnificent breasts, was an encumbrance as far as he was concerned. She was so close that he could almost reach across with one hand and slide his fingers under the cream satin covering. He imagined caressing her smooth, high breast, and if he pushed his fingers further under the thin lacy covering of her bra, he knew he would find a hard, erect nipple.

She caught him staring, "What is it, have I got butter around my mouth or something?" He clawed his way mentally out of his lustful hunger, "No nothing like that. I was wondering, how do you feel the trial is going?" Memories of the paleness of her breasts against his hands, and the rosy peaks that had tasted so sweet caused him to harden.

Her voice didn't waiver, "I think the same as I've always thought, it will be a guilty verdict and I'm going back to prison."

"You say that as if you aren't bothered, yet I'm sure deep down you must be frightened?"

She swallowed a mouthful of toast, "I try really hard not to feel. I committed a crime, and will have to pay the price, I know that."

"I wouldn't underestimate Imogen," he reassured her, "she's a fine barrister, if anyone can get an acquittal, then she can." He inwardly chastised himself for his erection, he really needed to get himself under control.

A resigned look crossed her face, "I'm pleased you have so much faith," she shook her head, "I'm afraid I don't share it though."

Sensing she was resolute, he swiftly changed the subject, "The newspapers are full of you and I, it's like the romance of the century."

"Yes, and I am sorry about that," her face coloured slightly which only heightened his desire for her, "but none of it is my doing. Imogen propagated this, I've never felt comfortable about us being portrayed as a couple."

"What bothers you so much," he asked, "We make an attractive couple, don't we?" He watched as she lifted the delicate china cup to her lips, taking a mouthful of the warm tea before she answered, and he remembered her delicious mouth sucking him hard. What he would give for that hot breath on his throbbing dick, right now.

"It's not about looks though is it," she dismissed placing the cup back on the saucer, "anyone in their right mind would know you wouldn't be with me out of choice."

Hopelessly aroused, he tried to focus on her perfectly sculptured face, "Why ever not? You're a beautiful young woman," he raised a lazy eyebrow, "and one I understand that has hidden talents." He was referring to the sewing, however the double entendre had his imagination working overtime, and produced a graphic image of her naked, with that gorgeous thick curly hair splayed all over his thighs. God, she's such a fucking turn-on. He shifted his position on the chair, and asked, "I've been told you make your own clothes."

***

Dorothy must have told him about her sewing, "I did, but not anymore. Imogen chooses my outfits for court. Apparently, I'm to appear feminine so that the male jurors don't see me as a tough lesbian, but not too womanly which may provoke the envy of the female jurors." Deep in thought for a second, the penny suddenly dropped, "I'm sorry, I guess you have to pick up the clothes bills?"

There was a pause before he answered, and she watched him shuffle in his chair, with an odd expression on his face, almost as if he was in pain. He cleared his throat before delivering his own apology, "When you left me for Darlene, I'm afraid that I destroyed all of your clothes. I'm sorry."

She nodded, "I thought you would."

His probing eyes were fixed on her, and in them she saw something she couldn't fathom, which made her uneasy, but it was his question that gave her nowhere to hide.

"Why did you leave in such a hurry that day, you took nothing of your own with you?"

Footsteps stalled their conversation, and they both turned towards the door to see Imogen approaching. Never had Rebecca been so relieved. Despite guilt flooding through her for stealing his watches, an explanation was impossible. How could she tell him? . . . I left in a rush that day because my sister had been abducted, and to get her back, I had to return to Darlene?

CHAPTER 34

Day four of the trial was not going well. Rebecca's previous Headteacher, Mrs Ross, took the stand and gave a lengthy account about how her school work had deteriorated following the death of her mother. Imogen had explained to Rebecca that she wanted to convey to the jury, how all aspects of her young life had been turned upside down by the trauma.

Imogen cajoled Mrs Ross into stating that in her opinion, the death of Rebecca's mother attributed to the decline in her education. It sounded convincing that she suffered greatly following her mother's death until the Headteacher was cross examined. Marcus Warr made mincemeat of her evidence, discrediting her testimony, and informing the jury this was all based on opinion only.

Fluently, he managed to convey that any child suffering bereavement might have a temporary lapse in their ability to study, but overall that would rectify itself, and out of all such children, none would go onto killing someone.

The next witness to take the stand was the family GP Doctor Beedham, who had been kind to her mother during her final few weeks, visiting the house often. He also gave an expressive account of the trauma Rebecca suffered, and also discussed Emily, stating she experienced developmental delay and didn't grieve in quite the same way as her twin sister.

He described Emily as being 'childlike', with 'a brain entombed in childhood', so didn't fully understand the ramifications of death. Tears threatened at the mention of Emily's name, and she breathed in deeply to stem the flow. Thank goodness, they all think she's dead.

Dr Beedham was coaxed by Imogen to discuss Rebecca's monthly menstrual cycle, and the medication she was prescribed to regulate it. He gave an explanation about pre-menstrual tension and the mood swings that can result due to the fluctuating hormone levels.

As expected, he was cross examined by Marcus Warr, and although not discredited in quite the same way as the Head teacher, the jury heard his explanation that as this particular disorder affects countless females, it was a poor excuse put forward by the defence for stabbing an innocent man.

After a break for lunch, Imogen called her expert witness, Hugh Cordy, an eminent psychologist, to the stand. Following his sworn declaration to the court, she interjected compassion into her voice, and asked, "Mr Cordy, could you explain to the court the medical condition of post-traumatic stress disorder, and how this . . . . ." she paused, emphasising her next word, "illness, can manifest itself?"

"Yes of course," he confidently replied, "Post-traumatic stress disorder is a condition of persistent and emotional stress occurring as a result of injury or severe psychological shock, typically involving a constant and vivid recall of the experience which may manifest itself in unpredictable responses to others, and the outside world."

"Thank you," Imogen nodded, "Could you outline, common symptoms of post-traumatic stress disorder?"

"I can, although the indicators differ with each individual dependent upon their coping mechanisms. Symptoms may include flashbacks, nightmares and severe anxiety, as well as uncontrollable thoughts about a specific event."

Imogen smiled encouragingly, "I'm sure that was helpful to the jury. May I ask Mr Cordy, would losing a parent be a psychological component of post-traumatic stress?"

"Absolutely," he agreed, "The trauma of nursing a beloved parent at such a young age can have a significant impact and detrimental effect on a person's mental health. For example, one could blame oneself for not saving that loved one. Maybe the care hadn't been good enough, or the late person could have confided their fears of death. The carer could feel guilty, because they were unable to prevent such suffering."

He paused momentarily, "Death and the grieving process can distort the mind, and it can take several months, even years for a person's mental health, and self-esteem to return to some sort of normality. The impact on an individual following the death of a much loved parent is difficult to measure, as each of us will deal with grief in a different way."

After a short pause, which appeared to allow the jury time to absorb the information, Imogen continued, "I know that the court has testimonies written by you in relation to the interviews you had with Rebecca Price Jones following the death of her stepfather. Can you give the court your expert opinion Mr Cordy, following your assessments, as to whether or not the defendant was suffering from post-traumatic stress at the time she killed her stepfather?"

Hugh Cordy nodded assertively, "It has always been my belief that Rebecca suffered greatly from the loss of her mother, and I do believe she was suffering from post-traumatic stress at the time she stabbed her stepfather."

"Thank you, Mr Cordy, no further questions."

Marcus Warr gave the expert witness a derisive smile. "I'm sure your explanation about post-traumatic stress disorder, has been helpful to the court," he acknowledged, "however, to ensure that the jury is absolutely clear on your expert opinion," he stroked his chin, "utilising your vast experience of mental health issues in young people, how many cases have you dealt with, where an individual suffering from post-traumatic stress, has thrust a knife into another person causing instant death from puncturing the aorta?"

"Objection." Imogen was on her feet.

"Sustained." Judge Quarmby indignantly peered over his spectacles, "Mr Warr, you know very well that is a totally unacceptable way to ask a question. Could you rephrase it please?" he raised his bushy eyebrows, "and be reminded that any further questions posed in such a way, will result in seeing me in my chambers."

Marcus Warr bowed his head looking suitably chastised, but it was too late. Rebecca knew, as Imogen would, that the damage had been done by the graphic description of how Derek Clay had met his death, and the visual reminder in the most explicit way, of her doing it.

Marcus Warr answered contritely, "Yes, of course, your Honour," but Rebecca was certain that he wasn't concerned about the rebuff as he'd been able to make his point valiantly.

He continued, "With your vast experience in the field of mental health, could you tell the jury how many under eighteens you have dealt with that have killed while suffering from the diagnosed condition of post-traumatic stress?"

Hugh Cordy shuffled his position, "There is a plethora of internationally published evidence available regarding killing while suffering from this disorder. I have written papers myself . . ."

Marcus Warr interrupted him, "In your capacity as an expert witness, Mr Cordy, could you please be more specific, so that the jury are clear." He glanced momentarily down at his notes before looking up again, "In your professional experience, how many . . ." there was a pause, and then he emphasised his next two words, ". . . under eighteens, while suffering from the diagnosed condition of post-traumatic stress, following the death of a beloved parent, have killed an adult?"

Hugh Cordy hesitated for a second, much to Marcus Warr's satisfaction by the expression on his face, "Let me try and help you. Would it be fewer than ten, over twenty, or even thirty, please could you tell the court?"

He was quicker this time, "Although infrequent, a situation can occur when a young person . . ."

"I must stop you there. You have been invited here today to give an expert opinion, so could you answer the precise question that I have asked. In your distinguished career as a specialist psychologist, exactly how many under-eighteens, have you dealt with, that have a clinical diagnosis of post-traumatic stress disorder," he took a breath in, "following the death of a parent, have actually gone on to kill an adult?"

"Five."

Marcus Warr widened his eyes, "I don't think the jury heard you, Mr Cordy, can you repeat that please?"

He cleared his throat, "Five."

"Only five?" Marcus Warr questioned, feigning surprise, but Rebecca knew it was all play acting.

Hugh Cordy nodded, "Yes."

Marcus Warr exaggeratedly raised his perfectly groomed eyebrows, and turning towards the jury, his final statement added another nail to her coffin, "Not that many to enable you to draw a definitive conclusion I would have thought. Thank you, Mr Cordy, no further questions."

CHAPTER 35

George cleared his throat conspicuously, until Ezzio noticed and abruptly asked, "What is it, George?"

"Well, sir, I hope I'm not talking out of turn," he hesitated as if he wasn't entirely sure what he was going to say, "You know that you asked my wife if Rebecca had any relatives?"

"Yes," he admitted. "why, do you know if she has?"

"Well here's the thing. Rebecca has given Dorothy two letters to post if she is found guilty, one of them is to you, and the other one is to an Emily Jones."

Halleluiah, this was just the break he needed. His pulse quickened, the same way it did when he successfully negotiated a business deal, "Where is it addressed to," he asked sharply, before quickly adding, "the one to Emily Jones?"

"Sleaford in Lincolnshire," George answered sheepishly.

There must be more, "Anything else?" Ezzio encouraged.

"Rebecca asked me to take her to the post office a couple of times, so I'm guessing she might have been sending mail to Sleaford."

"Bloody hell, George," he spat furiously, "anyone could have spotted her, you know how important it is that she's not seen out and about."

"I know that," his cheeks flushed slightly, "but she was very persuasive, and she was well covered with a baseball hat and scarf; she knew it was important that she wasn't recognised."

Ezzio couldn't believe it, he'd got everyone looking for the whereabouts of the sister, and the break he needed, was here right under his nose. The first thing he'd done was check his phone records, but Rebecca hadn't contacted anyone from the house.

George looked uncomfortable, "I'm really sorry . . . it's just that it seemed awfully unfair to say no when she just wanted to visit the post office."

He was such an exemplary employee, so there was nothing to be gained by chastising him now, especially as he needed his help, "Can you get me the letters?" It was more a demand than a request.

"Yes, I can sir, but there might be repercussions. Dorothy has been trusted with them, so she'll want to do what Rebecca has asked."

"George," he tried to keep his voice calm, "I'm desperately trying to find a way to get Rebecca acquitted, and I think finding this sister might help," he decided to go for his jugular, "surely you don't want her to go to prison?"

"No, of course I don't, I'm fond of the lass," he admitted, "I'll get you the letters. Dorothy has put them away in her hideout for safe keeping, so won't miss them if I take them."

"Thank you, can you get them now, this really is important."

Ezzio stared at the address on the standard envelope to Emily Jones. He didn't open her letter, only the heavy brown one addressed to him.

Hall Farm
Great Barr
Keddington
Sleaford
NG34 0AG

Dear Ezzio

If you are reading this letter, then I've been found guilty and will be in prison for the next few years. As you requested, when the baby is born, I will sign over full custody to you. I know you were surprised when I quickly made the decision and demanded nothing in return, and that still stands, but I do have a request for your help.

My twin sister Emily is not dead; she is alive and living in Sleaford Lincolnshire at the address at the top of the page. We are identical, but the difference is, Emily is mentally subnormal and is like a child. Currently, she is living on a farm working with horses, and the people that run the farm, Ann and Steven Collins, have been so good to her, and she is happy living there. I have written to her explaining I will be away for the next few years, which she will be absolutely devastated about, I know.

I pay £500 per month for her to stay there, and send her pocket money also. In my absence, would you consider paying these fees? I know it's an enormous ask, but I'm afraid I do not have anyone else that can help me. As soon as I get out of prison, I will work out a way to pay you back, I promise.

I also need to apologise for taking your watches. I cannot emphasise how sorry I am about that. Piers

Milner had taken Emily from the previous secure house she was living in, and at the time I thought he wanted money for her safe return hence taking your watches, but it turned out the price I had to pay was to go back to Darlene.

I have enclosed the pawn ticket and the remaining money I got for the watches, the money I've already spent, has gone on Emily's keep.

Take good care of our son, I know you will be a good father to him. I won't see you again, but once I'm out of prison I'll be in touch regarding any monies that I owe you.

Rage boiled inside of him. Piers Milner, the dirty fucking bastard. How dare he blackmail Rebecca into returning to Darlene Milner? His anger was so physical and violent, that he wanted to strangle the cunt.

Images sprang to his mind of his fury at her for taking his watches. How he'd berated her for stealing from him now seemed utterly pathetic. His gut ached thinking about how frightened she must have been when her sister was taken away. He needed to keep his composure, so breathed in deeply. All his adult life, his astute mind kept him one step ahead of any competition or adversary, and winning was the only approach he had in his armoury. So he was clear in his mind, the first path he now had to travel was to Sleaford in Lincolnshire, to speak to the sister, and while the second one might take him a longer, it had a guaranteed outcome. Piers Milner and his precious mother Darlene would pay dearly for what they'd done . . . he'd make sure of it.

***

Rebecca was in the pool swimming lengths when she saw Ezzio approach. It was like déjà vu, as she recalled the time when he'd come to the pool, pulled her out, and made love to her on the lounger. This time though, it was clear by the expression on his face, that he had something to say to her, so she swam towards the shallow end where he was waiting. Squatting down on his haunches at the side of the pool, he was apologetic, "I'm afraid I've got to go away for the weekend, but George and Dorothy are here if there are any problems."

She wiped the water from her face, and nodded, "That's fine, you don't need to babysit me, just go and enjoy yourself."

"It's business, not a pleasure trip," he explained, "I could be back tomorrow but most probably it will be Sunday. I am sorry, I know it's the last weekend before the summing up and verdict."

"Please don't worry," she reassured him, "it's not as if I'm allowed to go out socialising is it?"

"No, but Imogen has her reasons, you know that. It would hardly be appropriate for you to be seen out and about on the town. The papers would have a field day painting you as a woman without a care in the world razzle dazzling, it would play right into the prosecution's hands."

She pulled her hair into a ponytail to squeeze the excess water away, and agreed, "I know that, it isn't a problem honestly, I'll be fine while you're away." She couldn't resist asking, "Is Imogen going with you?" For a moment she held her breath, chastising herself for probing because she knew his answer would eat her up inside.

"Yes, she'll be coming with me."

Yeah, I bet she will. The thought of the two of them together, was like razor wire twisting deep inside her, but she kept her voice light, "Well, you both enjoy yourselves, Imogen deserves a break."

"Imogen and I are not in a relationship," he snapped in an irritated voice, "I keep telling you that."

She widened her eyes, "It's really none of my business, is it? I'll see you when you get back." She turned away and continued swimming. When she reached the wall of the deep end and looked back, he'd gone.

CHAPTER 36

Ezzio and Imogen set off by car late afternoon, heading for the farm in Lincolnshire. He'd instructed his secretary to book them in at a local hotel for the night.

As each day passed, it was becoming more likely that the outcome of the trial would be guilty, which most definitely would result in a custodial sentence for Rebecca. Ezzio was beginning to see some of Imogen's professional confidence eroding, and almost as if she could read his mind, she spoke, "Even if this sister has some information, I'm fairly certain we wouldn't be able to bring it to court at this stage of the trial. If the judge did consider it, Marcus Warr would object strongly."

He knew she was right, her knowledge of the law was infinitely superior to his, but can't wasn't a word in his vocabulary. Keeping his eyes on the road, he touched her thigh in a comforting way, "Let's see what the sister has to say hmm? I'm like you, not certain she'll have anything to contribute, but we have to give it a try. If she does have information that we feel is vital to the case, then we have to think of a way to bring it to the trial."

***

The feeling of Ezzio's hand on her thigh sent a fluttering wave of excitement running through Imogen. She'd anticipated that they'd be sharing a room tonight, and had prepared accordingly with every unwelcome hair shaved, and each limb moisturised. Winning the case would bring him to her, but the prosecution case was strong, so she prayed that finding the sister would produce the break she needed. Quite how, she hadn't yet worked out, as the prosecution would want to know why the sister had been hidden, which was an integral part of the jigsaw that baffled them all.

As Ezzio concentrated on the road, her eyes studied him, and she thought how incredibly handsome he looked in his black polo shirt and light khaki trousers. Dressed casually, he was so pleasing on the eye, and smiling to herself she recognised that Ezzio Marin could make a boiler suit look good.

She glanced down at his taut thigh, and her eyes measured his enormous femur bone stretching from his hip to his knee. He must have his trousers made for him as his legs are so long. He really was a magnificent specimen of a man, attractively large, and extremely well-toned. Everything about him oozed masculine supremacy, and his persona exuded power; it almost felt that, if Ezzio was on the case, then all would be well.

Recalling the dinner conversation with her and Rebecca, when she pressed him about his success in the early years, he had smiled that wonderful sexy grin of his, and said his motto had always been, 'The answer's yes, what is the question'.

Yes, in any field, Ezzio Marin would be a formidable opponent she was sure of that, and invincible was a word that sprung to mind.

As they arrived at the farm, they were greeted by Mrs Collins, the owner, who Ezzio had already spoken to on the telephone so was expecting them. She escorted them into the library, and asked them to wait while she brought Emily to them.

Ezzio gazed approvingly around the room, while her eyes were admiring him. Hopefully tonight she would make some headway, surely the two of them in the hotel together enjoying a leisurely dinner and fine wine, would lead to sharing a bed?

***

Ezzio looked round the old room with the high ceilings and ornate picture rail, eager for the sister to arrive. After several minutes, the door opened, and his eyes were drawn to Mrs Collins who entered first, but he was totally unprepared for the shock of the female that followed her, who he could only describe as an exact replica of Rebecca. He gawped in absolute amazement, absorbing her beautiful figure neatly encased in tight fitted jeans and a tee shirt, and the blonde untameable hair escaping from its clasp exactly as Rebecca's did. He was stunned. The likeness between the two sisters was astonishing; there was no other word for it.

Emerald eyes, as green as a lagoon, darted warily between him and Imogen, before Mrs Collins broke the silence, "Emily, this is the lady and gentleman that have come to speak with you, would you like me to stay?"

Emily viewed them both cautiously, and nodded to her, "Yes please."

It was mesmerising, even her voice was a complete duplication of Rebecca's. Ezzio smiled at Mrs Collins, indicating that it was fine for her to stay. He needed to be careful as he wasn't sure how much she knew about her sister. Although used to negotiating, he knew this was going to be the hardest deal he would ever strike.

Mrs Collins gestured to them all to sit down, and Ezzio chose the sofa next to Emily. He gave her what he hoped was one of his friendly smiles, "Hello Emily." He sensed her nervousness, and was keen to remove her anxious look, "Thank you for seeing us today, I'm Ezzio and this is Imogen, we're Rebecca's friends."

Emily stared at them cautiously and was quick enough to think something might be wrong, and asked nervously, "Is Rebecca hurt?"

Apprehension was evident in her eyes, as well as fear. Recalling Rebecca's letter explaining that Emily was childlike, Ezzio was quick to reassure her, "She's fine; we've just come to see if you can help us with a problem we have."

She looked questioningly at him, "Have you come from Wales?"

His face must have expressed his puzzlement as she continued, "Where Rebecca lives, Wales, she's looking after a poorly man," her expression was gut-wrenchingly sad, "that's why she can't come and see me at the moment, 'cause he's dying and she can't leave him."

The penny dropped instantly, that must be how Rebecca explained her long absences. He didn't want to condone her untruths, but he didn't want to upset Emily either, "We haven't come from Wales today, no, but we have been there before."

She gazed warily at them both, and he could sense her fear, "When I said nothing is wrong, that is true, Rebecca is fine, but there is a problem that we are trying to help her with, and we are hoping that you can help too."

Emily stared back at him with beautiful replica eyes which he'd lost himself in so many times. Directness was the only approach he had as they didn't have much time.

"Rebecca is," he hesitated, selecting his words carefully, "helping the police. It's all to do with your stepfather, you can remember him, can't you?"

She quickly shook her head from side to side, indicating no. Ezzio noticed she turned a shade paler, and her eyes became somewhat agitated.

With a quivering lip, she turned to Mrs Collins, and in a childlike pleading voice asked, "Could I ring Rebecca please, if I give you some money?"

Those few words made his heart almost combust, and the temptation to walk away rather than cause her any more anxiety was overwhelming, but he couldn't.

"We can't talk to her at the moment, Emily, as she's with the police. I need you to help me, though, so that I can speak to the police about Rebecca and try to help her, you do want to help your sister, don't you?"

She nodded yes, but was silent for a second as if thinking of what to say next, then she added, "But I'm not allowed to talk about my stepfather ever. Rebecca made me promise."

Tears threatened, and instinctively Ezzio took her hand, "Normally I would say it's wrong to break a promise, but in this case if you are helping your sister, I think that's okay."

The unshed tears seemed to have turned her eyes a deeper shade of green, and observing her, he recognised that she might only have the mind of a ten year old, but it was obvious she was fiercely loyal to Rebecca.

Emily shook her head more forcibly, almost as if she was shaking images of the stepfather away, "I don't want to talk about him; Rebecca said I haven't got to ever."

As she continued to shake her head, the heavens opened, and the tears she'd held back, started to flow down her cheeks.

Imogen quickly intervened and moved forward squatting down in front of her, "I'm trying to help Rebecca also, and I think the three of us need to help each other so that she doesn't get in any more trouble with the police." She paused giving Emily time to digest what she'd said, and then carried on, "Do you think you could try and answer a couple of questions either yes or no, that way you wouldn't be breaking your promise really as you haven't been talking about your stepfather, it would be us talking about him."

Emily looked unsure, and turned to Ezzio, "I don't want Rebecca to be in trouble with the police." He felt her despair in his gut, and tapped her hand reassuringly, "No, we don't either, and we're going to help her," he added, "but we need your help also." Imogen moved away, which he took as a silent cue she was leaving the rest to him.

Emily's eyes widened through her tears, "Can we tell the police that she's having a baby and then they'll let her go?" she sniffed.

So, she knew about the baby. It warmed him somehow that Rebecca had discussed the baby, because as far as he could ascertain from her behaviour, she'd detached herself totally from it.

Gently, he probed, "Did Rebeca tell you that she was having a baby?"

She nodded, "Yes, but I already knew. We have special powers, 'cause we're twins; we know how the other one is feeling."

Emily looked really pleased with herself, and as he needed her, he gently reassured her, "That's why we're doing our best to help Rebecca, so that we can look after her and the baby."

Emily sat silently for a minute, and then asked, "Can I come with you to see her?" and as if remembering her manners would get her what she wanted, she added, "please."

Ezzio thought his heart would burst. Never in his thirty-two years had he come across such vulnerability, and at that moment, it seemed just right to put his arm around her comfortingly, "I will take you to see her I promise, but we must try and help her first, you want to do that, don't you?"

She nodded and cuddled up closer to him. With his hand, he tilted her chin up so he could look directly into her eyes and softly encouraged, "Right then, blow your nose and I'll tell you what we are going to do." He passed her a handkerchief from his pocket, and she blew her nose loudly, smiling childishly at him through watery eyes at the noise she'd made. Ezzio smiled back kindly, before continuing, "I'm the daddy of Rebecca's baby, and I want to help her. Do you understand what a court is?" Emily shook her head, clearly not knowing.

"Well, a court is where Rebecca is going to be, and the police will say she killed your stepfather, and we want to try and explain why that happened," he looked at her fondly and urged, "Okay?" He took her half smile as a yes, and carried on, "That's where you can help. I know you promised you wouldn't ever talk about it, but do you think you could just answer one question that might help Rebecca?"

She nodded keenly.

"Good girl, now here's the question. Think back to when you lived at home with your stepfather after your mummy died, did you ever see your stepfather hitting Rebecca," he paused as a sudden thought jumped into his mind, "or did he hurt you in any way?"

Imogen and Ezzio both involuntarily held their breaths; the answer could be the difference between guilty or not guilty for Rebecca.

She broke away from his arms and stood, vigorously shaking her head from side to side, but not speaking, and then, almost as if she remembered that she only had to say yes or no, she answered, "No." It was as firm, as it was emphatic.

Imogen and Ezzio's eyes locked together in a defeated glance. Apart from the clock on the mantelpiece, the room was silent. Their visit had been in vain, she couldn't help them. Neither spoke, each immersed in their own thoughts. Seconds passed, and still the clock ticked, until the potent quietness was broken by Emily's barely audible voice as she whispered, "He did hurt Rebecca once, though."

It was her soft low voice that gave Ezzio a glimmer of hope, "How did he hurt her," he pressed gently, watching Emily's manic eyes appearing darker than ever, evidence that she was anxious about saying anything more.

He went to her and gently brought her back to the sofa next to him, and holding her hand again, he urged her on, "It's really important if he hurt her, that we tell the police."

Her eyes became glazed, and he deduced that she was conjuring up images that she'd long ago erased from her mind, so he pushed further, "Please tell us what he did."

Ezzio squeezed her hand, offering what he hoped was reassurance that it was okay for her to speak about the stepfather hurting her sister. By now he was certain that he'd physically abused Rebecca, and was quietly confident that Emily's account would shed more light on this, however, nothing prepared him for her shocking disclosure. Staring downwards at the old patterned carpet, in a voice hardly more than a whisper, she revealed, "He was on top of her, and I could see his bottom," she hiccupped, "and he was hurting her 'cause Rebecca was screaming, "no, no, NO.""

CHAPTER 37

Ezzio paced the hotel room floor, "Right, you're the QC, how do we get this fresh evidence into court?"

"We can't." Imogen answered resolutely, "The prosecution would never allow it at this stage, nor will the judge."

"They'll have to, that dirty bastard raped Rebecca," he paused, his chest constricted imagining what she'd been through, "no wonder she shoved a knife into him; there must be a way, they have to know the truth."

Imogen took a deep breath in, "It's not as simple as that, think about it. Rebecca has never once in any statement mentioned being raped, so did it really happen?"

"Of course, it happened," he snapped, "you heard the way Emily described it. Thank Christ she didn't understand fully what was going on."

"But did it happen that way?" she shook her head, "If it did, why would Rebecca conceal this, surely she would have used this to make sure she was acquitted?"

He was as bewildered as she was, "I don't bloody well know, I haven't got the answers, but what I do know is that Emily is coming on Monday and telling the court this happened."

Imogen was uncompromising, "Even if we could, what impact do you think this is going to have on Rebecca who has kept Emily out of this for years?" Her voice rose up an octave, "For goodness' sake, she'd told everyone she's dead, can you imagine her face if Emily appears in court, she would never forgive you, ever."

"I don't give a toss, if it gets her off, then it's a means to an end."

"But what about her health, and the baby, you know the pregnancy hasn't been straight forward, what if she loses the baby through shock? It's your son, Ezzio, your flesh and blood, do you want that on your conscience?"

His heart clenched, of course he didn't want that, "Let me worry about the baby, I'm paying you an enormous amount of money, so start earning it. I want Emily to take the stand and tell the court what happened."

"It's not that easy. Emily is like a juvenile, she would need support to give evidence."

Irritated by her stumbling blocks, his voice was firm, "Then get her the support she needs and more. I'm telling you, I want her to give evidence on Monday and I'm expecting you to make it happen."

Imogen removed her glasses, "Have you thought about the consequences of cross examination?"

"Yes of course," he hadn't thought that far ahead really, "but Emily is like a child and will only tell the truth. I'm not worried about cross examination; I just want the jury to know that Rebecca was raped by that bastard of a stepfather."

***

Although the development added a new dimension to the case, Imogen was gutted. So much for a night with Ezzio, when in the adjoining room, Emily was sleeping. They'd had a devil of a job persuading Mrs Collins to allow Emily to go with them. Naturally she'd wanted to speak to Rebecca, but they couldn't allow that.

Mrs Collins had made a phone call to her sister Janet Coo, who apparently managed a home where Emily had previously resided. Ezzio had spoken to this other lady, and given his reassurance that she would come to no harm with him and Imogen.

It was evident that Emily trusted Ezzio, and even though they'd just met, there a natural affinity between the two of them, and in the end, it was Emily's insistence that persuaded Mrs Collins to relent.

She resigned herself that Ezzio would not be making love to her tonight. Instead, she would be researching to find a precedence she could use, in which another witness was introduced at such a late stage of a trial.

"Fair enough, I'll do my best, but just remember even if the judge does allow her to give evidence, it won't guarantee an acquittal. Things are weighted heavily against Rebecca currently. Maybe if she appeared more positive herself, but she doesn't, she sits there looking guilty almost as if she wants them to send her back to prison. Has she ever discussed privately with you anything further I could use in my summing up, that might sway the jury?"

"No, we don't really have conversations," he admitted with a self-deprecating smile, "she spends most of her time avoiding me." His admission was a reminder of how much they disliked each other, which secretly pleased her. The thought of the two of them as a couple would completely destroy her hopes for the future.

She continued, "That's what I've found so odd about the case. And now this discovery of a sister, why would she hide her? It just doesn't make sense?"

Ezzio shrugged, "We can't worry about that now. I'm relying on you to get Emily on the stand on Monday."

Imogen's eyes lingered on Ezzio. Never had he looked more handsome as he did right now. His dark growth made him look so masculine, and her whole body hummed at the thought of his rough stubble leaving its mark on her thighs.

In for a penny, in for a pound, "If I pull this off, do I get a bonus?" She stared directly into his eyes, so that with absolute certainty, he understood her demand.

He did. "If you get her acquitted, then you can have anything you want."

She pushed further, "Anything?"

"Yes, anything," he nodded.

She wanted more. "Does that mean our friendship will definitely progress?"

He lifted his brow, "I'm not into marriage if that's what you're implying, but if it's sex you want, then you can have as much as you like."

His response was a little disappointing as she did fantasise about being married to him, but that may come later. Right now, she'd settle for anything to fulfil the desperate need she had for this man, but would he definitely deliver?

"And you won't renege on this promise?"

"No I won't, now if you'll excuse me." He left her room to go into the adjoining one, where Emily slept.

***

Sleep would be a long time coming, and when it did, he would take the sofa, but at the moment he needed to think and plan. He thought about Monday's court appearance, and the ordeal it was going to be, but not once did he question whether he was doing the right thing. He was a skilled tactician, so gambled that the jury would view the case very differently once they realised that Rebecca had been raped.

He recalled Imogen's question, if Rebecca had said anything to him that could perhaps help her during the summing up. When did he and Rebecca have any sort of conversation . . . never. He could barely look at her, except in the most basic of ways. All he ever wanted to do was screw her senseless, never more so than since she became pregnant.

Urging himself to forget about her, his thoughts turned to Emily. What was he going to do with her until then? His eyes drifted towards where she lay, it could almost be Rebecca in the bed. Sleeping, there wasn't a chance of telling them apart. What a sweet, lovely girl Emily was. Why did Rebecca keep her hidden? He just didn't get it.

He took his mobile phone into the bathroom, and called Dorothy, his loyal housekeeper, who he knew, would be willing to help. As he outlined the Emily development, she cautiously asked, "How did you find out that Rebecca had a sister?"

"The internet," he lied, "there weren't any records of the sister's death, that story was something that Rebecca perpetuated."

"Well she must have a good reason for doing that, surely?"

He was dismissive, "Who knows? The main thing is, I've found her sister now, and I need her to give evidence as she has vital information that can help the case. That's where you come in, I really need your help."

**

Dorothy listened while Ezzio outlined his instructions. She agreed that George would bring her the following morning with her overnight bag. Ezzio explained Emily's learning disability, and why he wanted her to look after Emily until the trial on Monday. Imogen was going to work with her on Sunday to go over the court process, explaining what she would be required to do. Fortunately, Imogen knew a court advocate personally, and was confident she would help on a Sunday by getting to know Emily. Ezzio would then return to the house on Sunday morning, and Emily would be in a nearby hotel with her until the Monday morning.

She was more than willing to help. Not only because Ezzio paid her wages, but more because both her and George were of the opinion that the killing must have been a catastrophic accident; Rebecca was no cold-blooded killer.

She had become particularly fond of her, and had promised faithfully that she would post a letter for her if she was convicted, and give a second letter to Ezzio. She'd been entrusted with the letters, and sworn to secrecy, so had hidden them well. What she now realised was, the letter addressed to a Miss Emily Jones, must be for this elusive sister.

Once Ezzio terminated the call, she felt uneasy, and headed for the spare bedroom to locate her secret box. When her and George first moved into the cottage, quite by accident when cleaning, she was trying to flatten the carpet that had lifted in the walk-in wardrobe, when she discovered a loose floorboard. On close inspection, she realised it was purposely unfastened, as she could easily lift it. Underneath the floorboard, was a small area that must have been used for storage at some stage? She had utilised the space previously for some personal items, and decided to store the two letters Rebecca had entrusted her with, for safe-keeping.

Reaching for them both, she took them out and sat on the bed to examine them closely. The seals were intact, so they hadn't been tampered with, and her eyes scrutinised the addresses written in black capital letters, were they from the same hand? It was hard to tell. She pondered momentarily, then placed them carefully back in the box and chastised herself for being silly. How could Ezzio possibly have access to letters hidden in her house, when even George was unaware of her secret place?

***

Ezzio took a small bottle of whisky from the minibar, with his mind on Rebecca. If he was totally honest, his thoughts were never far away from her. What an ordeal she must have suffered, it certainly explained why she didn't have sex with men.

His thoughts drifted back to the first time he'd tried to make love to her. He recalled her responsiveness, and the way she'd climaxed from him touching her, but when he was about to penetrate her, she'd coiled up. He could still remember the terrified look etched on her face. Then, the first time he did actually have penetrative sex with her, he had to take it slowly as she was so tight. No bloody wonder.

A wave of warmth spread through him as he remembered how she had managed to overcome the discomfort, and the subsequent times they'd made love, she'd been so receptive to him.

Taking another swig of the whisky, he chastised himself. He was just feeling protective because of the baby; it was nothing more than that; his future certainly wasn't with her.

No, he'd be much better with someone like Imogen. It amused him that the reward she'd wanted for winning the case, wasn't a monetary one. He liked sexual confidence in a woman, and would be more than happy to pay that debt once the trial was over. Resisting her for the length of time he had, was purely due to the fact her didn't want to mix business with pleasure, which reminded him, Rebecca was business, nothing more, she might be carrying his son but that was the end of it.

CHAPTER 38

Ezzio returned home late on Sunday to the house in darkness. He went straight to Rebecca's room. Tapping on her bedroom door, he heard a muffled call to come in, and his abdomen clenched seeing her propped up in bed, clearly unwell. If the scrunched up tissues and the watery eyes were anything to go by, she had a stinking cold. Her hair was a curly mess, and her nose bright red, but he still couldn't help but react to her astonishing beauty. As he walked towards the bed, she just managed to say hi before being overcome by a coughing fit.

"Oh dear, you aren't well."

Inhaling, she tried to smile, "How perceptive of you."

"Can I get you anything?"

"A nose transplant would be good."

"I'm fresh out of those I'm afraid," he answered with a shrug, "anyway I like the one you've got. It's a beautiful nose and it suits you."

He saw the heat begin to work its way from her throat to her forehead, and watched her effort to deflect from it with a witty response, "If it's money you're after, I haven't got any."

His lips twitched at the corners enjoying their banter. A conversation was something they didn't normally indulge in, "No it's not money I'm after, but I have got a request."

"Okay, go ahead," she sniffed, "I'm weak at the moment, what is it?"

"I'll make you some warm tea first I think," he grinned, "to soften you up."

"That would be lovely; I must say I'm pretty fed up with plain water," she grimaced, "By the way, Dorothy's been called away, family problems I think. She was a bit vague about it all really, did she manage to contact you?"

"Yes, she did."

"What is it?" she asked, "Is everything alright?"

Don't let her get suspicious, "She didn't go into detail, just that she needed the weekend off, and would be back on Monday."

"Oh, I hope there's nothing wrong," she said, clearly concerned, "Will you ask George when you see him?"

"Yes, I can do, but it's unlikely I'll see him as he's off this afternoon," he shrugged, "I'll drive myself if I need to go out later."

. He walked towards the door, "I'll get you that tea. Do you want some aspirin or anything?"

"Better not," she replied, shaking her head, "I'm not sure how safe they are for pregnant women, I'll just have to put up with it I'm afraid."

"Okay." Ezzio turned as he reached the door, "Just let me know if you need anything else," mischievously adding, "you know, Vick rubbing on your chest or anything like that."

She rolled her eyes, and the lovely grin she gave him, stuck in his craw. He swiftly turned away, keen to put some distance between them, because after tomorrow, she wouldn't be looking at him in quite the same way, that was for sure.

***

Ezzio appeared sometime later with a pot of tea and some biscuits, which he placed on the bedside table, and sat down on the bed next to her. There were two cups on the tray, and she watched him fill them both from the decorative teapot. Shuffling the pillows into a sitting position, she asked, "I didn't know you drank tea?"

"I don't usually," he agreed, "but as you're so fond of it, I thought I'd give it a try."

Passing her a cup and saucer, she watched him take a gulp from his own china cup, and the distasteful look on his face made her snigger, "I take it from that face you don't like it?"

"It's like dishwater," he scowled. How could weak tea possibly compete with the strong black coffee he favoured? As he placed the tea cup down on the tray, for a fleeting moment, she glimpsed compassion in his eyes, which really unsettled her. She watched his chest rise as he took a deep breath in, "Anyway, I said I had a request . . ."

"It's not about the trial, is it?" she interrupted.

"No."

She breathed a sigh of relief, "That's good because I couldn't face that right now."

"No this is a bit more personal," he reached forward and grasped one of her curls, and twisted it around his finger. To say she was flummoxed was an understatement . . . why was he being like this?

"You have beautiful hair, do you know that?" His warm eyes looked intensely into hers, almost as if he could see right into her very soul. He let the curl go, "I wondered if I could sleep with you tonight?"

Crikey, I didn't see that coming! She shook her head, "I really don't think I'm up for sex tonight, I feel pretty lousy to be honest."

"It's not for sex," he dismissed, looking faintly embarrassed, "I'd like to feel the baby moving through the night."

Of course, back to the baby . . . that's all he's ever interested in. He'll have had plenty of sex with Imogen during their weekend away. The last thing she wanted though, was him in bed with her, "I'll keep you awake, and you'll probably end up catching my cold."

"I don't get colds," he pointed out, "and don't sleep well anyway."

No, I don't suppose Ezzio Marin would succumb to the common cold like the rest of us mortals. She couldn't resist asking, "What about Imogen?"

"What about Imogen?" he repeated looking genuinely puzzled.

"How would she feel if she thought you and I were sharing a bed?"

"I wouldn't have thought she'd think anything, as her and I aren't in a relationship. I keep telling you that, but for some reason you don't believe me."

Widening her eyes, she looked directly into his, "Handsome virile man, attractive woman, both single and going away for a weekend . . . what do you expect me to think?"

"I expect you to believe me," he answered firmly, "I've never lied to you. There's nothing going on sexually between Imogen and myself."

The thought of them together, ate away at her, and even though it wasn't any of her business, she wanted to believe him. Best to quit now, in a couple of days this would all be over, and she'd be back in prison. Why not let him spend the night with her? It was his baby after all and despite everything, he had been good to her letting her stay at his house, and going along with the ridiculous pretence of them being a couple.

"Okay then, but when you're coughing and spluttering in a couple of days, don't say I didn't warn you."

Was that tenderness in his eyes? If so, it would be a first.

"Right that's settled, then," he stood up, "I've got some work to do so I'll leave you to have a sleep, and come back to see if you want anything later."

"Yes, I do feel tired. For some reason this baby sleeps all day and kicks all night," she sniggered, "I'm beginning to think I'm carrying an owl or something."

An hour or so later, he returned with a tray and some chicken soup. Rebecca found this caring side of him touching, and it actually brought tears to her eyes, which she quickly blinked away. What's changed, why is he being so nice all of a sudden?

"I don't think I can manage to eat, Ezzio."

"Try it," he urged, "I'm thinking about food for the baby."

Yes, I know it's all you ever think about.

"I'm sure the baby will be alright, I believe it takes all the nutrients it needs from the mother."

"All the more reason to have the soup, then," he coaxed.

He handed her a serviette, and then carefully passed her a large mug. Rebecca realised it was pointless arguing with him, and took it from him while he pulled up a chair to sit beside the bed. As he watched her tasting the soup, she became unsettled by the silence between them, "Will you hire a nanny, or get married so the baby has a mother?"

He raised his eyebrows, "Well, I can't just pluck a female out of thin air to be my wife, so I guess I will have to hire a nanny."

For a moment, neither spoke. She continued sipping the soup, not sure why that pleased her, until he interrupted her thoughts, "It isn't a done deal, you haven't been convicted yet. I've every confidence in Imogen."

Resigned to her fate, she took a deep breath in, "I need to go to prison. I did something terrible. Think about it, how you would feel if your father was murdered, you'd want someone to pay for that wouldn't you?"

He didn't answer her question, "It's all really emotive, and must be daunting for you, but I'm putting my trust in the jury."

She shrugged, "I can see what their verdict will be, even if you can't. Every day I watch them looking at me, and can tell what they're thinking. As sure as eggs are eggs, they'll find me guilty, I know they will."

"We'll just have to wait and see what the summing up brings. Imogen is a fine barrister, the best there is."

She felt a knot in her stomach . . . he's in love with her. What did he say, 'can't pluck a wife out of thin air', he doesn't need to when he's got a potential one right under his nose.

"I have to go out for a while; will you be okay on your own until I get back? he asked.

"Of course." She knew where he was going. He'd be off to see Imogen at the hotel.

Amazingly, he leant forward and tenderly kissed the top of her head, and she felt almost bereft as he walked to the door. She hadn't been prepared for that at all, and asked herself again, why was he being so nice to her? She just didn't get it.

CHAPTER 39

Rebecca must have dozed, and the shrill of a bell woke her. Drowsily, she deduced it was coming from the front door. Who on earth could it be? There was security at the gate to the house, so the only people actually reaching the front door had to be been given access through the main gate by telephone.

Grabbing her wrap, she slipped on some mules, and headed down the huge staircase; her head was throbbing and she felt cold.

As she looked at the security monitor in the hall, she was absolutely astonished to see Darlene. She pressed her face close to the locked front door, and raised her voice so that she could be heard, "Darlene, what on earth do you want? Ezzio will go mad if he finds you here."

"I'm not intending to stay, Kate; I just need to speak to you for a moment."

It felt so odd being called Kate again after all this time, "I've nothing to say to you, please go, now, before Ezzio comes back."

"I will once you've heard what I have to say. Ezzio's at the hotel with the lawyer, so I wouldn't have thought he'd be back for a while yet." Darlene's sarcastic tone didn't escape her, she knew what the inference was, but how did she know Ezzio's whereabouts?

Darlene persisted, "Please, I only want five minutes, the sooner you let me in, then the sooner I'll leave. What I have to say won't take long."

Should she listen and get rid of her, surely that was better than Ezzio returning and finding her on the doorstep? She opened the door.

It struck her as odd that Darlene's immaculate hairstyle was completely dishevelled as she entered the hall; she was normally so fastidious about her appearance.

"Right, you've got five minutes," Rebecca said.

Darlene's gaze fixed firmly on her swollen abdomen, before locking with hers, "I've missed you so much, my darling." Darlene moved towards her but she reeled back, "Stop it, say what you've got to say, and then you must leave."

A wounded look crossed Darlene's face, which surprised her, but she dismissed it quickly, more concerned about the consequences of her being there.

"I'm sorry, but we can't see each other, ever. I thought that would have been clear to you when I left."

"Kate, you have to understand, I need you in my life . . . badly. Nothing is the same without you." A shadow passed over her face as if she was struggling to find the right words.

She needed rid of her, fast, "That part of my life is over. I'm Rebecca now, and about to go to jail, but when I come out, I'll be a different person and will be able to make other choices." She spoke with conviction, possibly emphasising the statement more for her own benefit.

"What other choices?" Darlene's mouth twisted, "surely you're not stupid enough to think that Ezzio the gigolo will be waiting for you when you get out?"

"No, of course not."

"Good because he's cosying up to that lawyer right now, and by the time you come out, they'll be married with a couple of kids."

Why did that hurt so much? "Don't you think I don't know that? Look you really have to leave."

"I will, but let me say what I came for."

Rebecca glared at her. I'll let her say what she wants and then hopefully she'll go. She daren't think of Ezzio coming back, thank goodness Dorothy was away.

"Okay, say whatever it is, but please be quick."

Darlene gave a wry smile, "Well, I didn't expect to be declaring my intentions in the hallway of Ezzio Marin's house, but it looks like a candlelit dinner is out of the question."

Bewildered, she watched Darlene's face take on almost a loving persona, what the hell was coming next? "Please get on with it."

"I care for you, Kate, you must know that," she smiled affectionately, "and I want us to be together."

Never in a million years had she expected this. She was stunned, and raised her hand to stop her, "That's enough," she snapped, "you paid me for sex and that's all it ever was between us. I'm sorry if you think it was anything more than that, but it wasn't."

Darlene was not giving up, "I know that, but somewhere along the way, everything changed. Now I want a relationship with you."

"Stop it . . ."

"Just listen will you," Darlene interrupted, "I've thought about it carefully, maybe we could get married when anything happens to Edward," her eyes were searching, "if that's what you want?"

"Married!" she screeched, "have you gone completely mad?"

"Well alright, a civil partnership, then."

It was laughable if it wasn't so serious, "I'm going to prison, for Christ's sake, you really must stop all of this nonsense."

"So," Darlene scoffed, "I'll wait for you. It's taken me a while to realise that I want us to be together, for the rest of our lives."

Rebecca shook her head, "This is just ridiculous."

Darlene's eyes flashed, "Why is it ridiculous? You can have the baby with us if you want, we can hire a nanny for it, so that we can spend our time together."

She couldn't believe she was hearing this, the woman was insane.

"This is Ezzio Marin's baby," she pointed to her tummy, "do you honestly think he's going to stand by and let me take his son to live with you? My God, you must be crazy to even think that, it just wouldn't happen."

Darlene shrugged indifferently, "I can make it happen; I'm not scared of Ezzio. I'm a wealthy woman and if necessary, I'll fight him in the courts."

She'd heard enough, "You really must go . . . please I'm begging you."

"Think about it, Kate. We can be together, no more running and hiding. I'll give you my protection always, you'll have my name."

She felt terribly uneasy. Darlene was crazy, she must be, coming here like this. How on earth had she got it into her head I would even consider this?

Rebecca raised both of her hands upwards as if this would highlight her next point, "Look, I was a prostitute to earn money; it was no more than that. I don't even like sex with females, it was all an act. Your memories are being clouded by sex, you are no more in love with me, than I with you. Now please, you have to leave, I should never have let you in."

She was curious to know how she had got through the security gates and was tempted to ask, but she didn't want to carry on the conversation.

Darlene's expression softened, but it only made her look even more peculiar, "Okay, I'll go now, but be sure that we will be together soon. Once this court case is over, we can plan for our future, together, just you and I," her eyes drifted to Rebecca's abdomen, "and the baby if you want. Even if you go to prison, I'll be there waiting when you come out."

If she didn't know better, she would think Darlene was on something. She didn't look herself at all, her eyes were vibrant and alive, but almost abnormally alive, and saliva was forming at the corners of her mouth when she was speaking. No, it definitely wasn't the Darlene Milner of old.

She opened the door, hoping it was a visible indication that their conversation was over. Darlene took a step towards her, and standing only centimetres from her face, made her feel almost defenceless, which was odd considering that during their sexual encounters, she was mainly the dominant one. Yet at that precise moment, she felt uneasy as Darlene reached for her chin, and clasped it firmly with her fingertips. Almost menacingly, she added, "I'll see you in court, Kate. Remember whatever the verdict, I'm there because I care for you deeply, it doesn't matter how long it takes, you and I will be together." Darlene leant forward to kiss her, but she pulled away, and their eyes locked for a moment, before she turned and walked out of the house. Rebecca shut the door behind her quickly, and leant against it, her whole body trembling. The woman was stark raving mad, surely.

She studied the security screen, and watched Darlene walk down the drive in her casual trousers and anorak which was in complete contrast to her usual power-dressing style. Her thoughts quickly moved on to how she'd managed to get through the security around the gate to the house, and more importantly, would there be any video evidence that she'd been? Please no. She could face the wrath of the court, but not that of Ezzio Marin.

CHAPTER 40

Everything was set for the following day. Imogen was to meet with the judge and the prosecution barrister first thing, and would request that Emily be allowed to give evidence. Although uncommon when deliberations were due, precedence had been set on occasions where further evidence had been introduced late on in a trial, so Imogen was going to use this to try and persuade the judge and prosecution to allow Emily's testimony.

Imogen was becoming more assured about introducing Emily, and her account of Rebecca being raped, due to the endless practice sessions she'd done with her.

She had acted as the opposition to show to Emily that they would try to discredit her in court, and encouraged her to use her own words to describe the attack on her sister, as they were simple but conveyed so much. Although confident that the jury would believe her account, it was the prosecution's counter attack that she was uneasy about. Marcus would discredit Emily's evidence, bringing up more questions than answers, so introducing her was really a double-edged sword, but she needed to win this case for her standing as one of the great city defence barristers, although it wasn't just that at stake, she wanted Ezzio more than winning. Losing wasn't an option . . . she was too close now.

Up until this juncture in her life, she'd always put work first, which had contributed to her marriage breaking down, but that was then. Now she wasn't about to lose Ezzio. Her whole body hummed with desire for him since he'd promised her more, so the whole case was riding on an acquittal as far as she was concerned. For the first time in her adult life, work was no longer her main driver. It had been nudged into second place by Ezzio Marin, who was now in pole position.

***

Ezzio felt warm inside thinking about how the lovable Emily seemed to have taken to him. Her little face lit up this evening when he appeared, and she innocently held his hand as she told him about the horses on the farm that she loved to ride.

She had no idea of her loveliness, all she was interested in was seeing Rebecca. Her purity was wonderful to see; she thought that once she'd spoken about their evil stepfather, then Rebecca would be free.

Imogen and he had agreed that they still needed to prepare her for the worst outcome, so he sat Emily down on the luxurious leather sofa in the hotel suite, and began the difficult conversation.

"You know tomorrow is going to be a really tough day for everyone, don't you?"

She nodded, "People think I'm not very clever 'cause I don't always understand things, but I do. I'm going to see Rebecca and make everything alright again, like she always does for me."

He smiled inwardly at her naivety, "I know you'll do your best so that we can bring her home with us, but we need to be prepared in case that doesn't happen. If the men and woman called the jury find her guilty, that means she will go to prison and we have to accept that."

Emily thought for a second, "Will the prison be in Wales?"

"No it will be in England, so you'll be able to visit her until she comes home again."

"But how will I get there?" she looked unsure, "I'm not allowed to leave the farm."

"I'll take you to see her, I can promise you that if nothing else."

She looked pleased, but just like a child, her inquisitive brain had more questions, "Will she have the baby in prison?"

"If she goes to prison, then yes she will," he admitted, "but when the baby is born, I will take care of it. I've got a big house, with a lovely garden for the baby to grow up in."

"But if you take the baby from Rebecca, who will be its mummy?" Her eyes moved towards Imogen almost as if she was giving her an opportunity to say it would be her. He quickly quashed that, "No, Imogen won't be its mummy. One day when I meet someone special, she will be its mummy."

Emily's eyes looked sad, as she probed further, "Won't Rebecca be its mummy anymore, then?"

His lips twitched at her innocence, "She will always be the baby's mummy, and you will be its aunty, so you can help me if Rebecca is away for a while."

"Can I?" her face lit up, "I love babies so much," she confessed, "and horses, I love them as well."

"I know you do," he agreed smiling fondly at her, "Let's just hope we can bring Rebecca home with us."

Emily chewed on her lip, "Harry at the stables says that if you want something ever so much, you have to sleep with your fingers and toes crossed all night. I'm going to do that because Harry is ever so clever, he knows everything."

Ezzio laughed, "Well, if Harry says it will work, then we better all try and keep our fingers and toes crossed."

He smiled tenderly at her, and kissed her gently on her forehead, exactly as he'd done with Rebecca an hour earlier. Emily smiled at him with the carbon-copy green eyes of her sister, "Shall we, Ezzio, I know it will work, and Rebecca will come home with us."

***

Dorothy watched their interaction closely. It was obvious that Ezzio had developed a real fondness for Emily in the short space of time he'd known her. She knew without any shadow of doubt that he would stick to his word and involve Emily in the baby's upbringing.

The trial was not going well and she prayed Emily could shed some light on why Rebecca would stab her stepfather. Her instincts told her that she was no cold-blooded killer.

Emily was like a breath of fresh air, and Dorothy really enjoyed the time she'd spent with her. Sadly, her and George had not been able to have children. It had hurt them both in the early years of their marriage, but they'd immersed themselves in managing estates over the years, and had enjoyed watching the children of each family growing up.

Ezzio was the first single man whose estate they'd managed, and he was an exemplary employer. Dorothy had always thought he should have a wife and children, but she knew her place and valued her position, so would never venture an opinion. He occupied her thoughts often though, particularly when he was in a relationship. It was almost as if he chose artificial beauties with no brains, so that he wouldn't ever fall for them. She could even foresee when he began to tire of each one, because his choices were totally unsuitable, and he became easily bored.

Until Rebecca that is. Dorothy knew despite her background, that Ezzio was smitten with her. He hid it well, and she wasn't entirely sure if he was aware how deep his feelings were for her, but she knew he was capable of loving, just watching him with Emily melted her.

Emily was childlike and had a vulnerability about her which brought out Ezzio's protective instincts. Yet she was sure he fought his attraction to Rebecca, and she to him, if the truth be known.

Watching Ezzio orchestrate the court day, confirmed to Dorothy why he was so successful in business. He covered every single detail, and while Imogen was the barrister, Ezzio was the strategist. Introducing Emily was a huge gamble, but he was going ahead and had arranged a doctor to be on standby in the court, as he was concerned about Rebecca's reaction to seeing her sister.

She was to stay with Emily that night, and be with her at the court until they called for her to take the stand. Emily would be assisted inside by the advocate Imogen had engaged, and she would be able to watch from the gallery.

Yes, everything was planned meticulously. Dorothy was fairly certain that if Rebecca went to prison, Imogen would be around to pick up the pieces. She wasn't sure if they were already in a relationship, but it was quite apparent to her that Imogen wanted Ezzio. You'd have to be blind not to see the desire in her eyes. If he was aware, he didn't show it, treating her just as his lawyer, but Dorothy predicted that Imogen would be around long after the court case was finished, if Rebecca was found guilty, or not as the case might be.

***

Ezzio returned home, and finding Rebecca asleep in his bed, and not in her own room, caused his chest to tighten. He hadn't been certain whether she would be in his bed, even though she'd agreed he could sleep with her. Their musical bed situation had never been fully resolved, and despite having sex in his bed, they'd only actually slept together once on the night when she'd been to the hospital for emergency contraception.

Images of her tortured face when the nurse told her there were no guarantees, flashed before him, and looking at her beautiful angelic face as she lay sleeping, he had to admit that she had an intrinsic vulnerability that made him want to look after her. He thought about the hardships she'd endured, and as if being forced down the hellish road of prostitution wasn't enough, he felt a sense of loathing with himself. He'd given her no real option but to have sex with him, and had added to her already troubled life, by getting her pregnant.

Yet despite all the hardship she'd endured, she still hadn't disclosed her sister, even though that very person could be her salvation. Why was that?

He pulled back the crisp cotton sheets, and slipped into bed beside her. She was facing him, so he lay on his side and pushed his back against her abdomen hoping to feel his son moving. Sleep would be a long time coming as his mind was working overtime about the pending day.

Lying next to Rebecca with evidence of his own virility growing inside her, caused a stirring in his groin, and he had a desperate urge to make love to her. He willed himself to think of anything but sex, and savoured the tiny baby movements he could feel in his back.

He learned a long time ago that each problem that kept him from sleep needed to be dealt with, and a vision of his dear father sprung to his mind, possibly because he was about to become a father himself. He recalled his dad sitting on his bed when he was a youngster, and telling him that sleep was the most important thing in life, so the next day you were alert to face the challenges ahead. His dad explained the technique to use that would rid him of his night-time demons. It was to have an imaginary notepad in his head, and to tick off each issue once he'd dealt with it in his mind, and then sleep would come.

Presently, at the top of his imaginary notepad, was Rebecca. Now he'd found Emily, he anticipated her evidence would dispel the theory that the stepfather was some sort of saint, and as a consequence, he hoped the jury would acquit her. Yes, he could tick that one off.

The baby kicked again. Rebecca was right, it seemed to move continually. The fact that she was sleeping through it amazed him. She turned over, and he moved with her, until they were like spoons huddled together. He wrapped his arms around her tummy, enjoying the anticipation like any normal father-to-be, knowing that he might not get the opportunity again. That was certainly another tick.

The next issue was not so easy to address as his erection throbbed. His body wanted her, but his brain said no. A hand job was out of the question with her right next to him, so he'd just have to try and think of something dull and boring until his erection lessened. Problem three, a definite big bloody cross.

Finally, after wrestling until dawn with his imaginary notepad, his thoughts drifted back to Rebecca, and he savoured lying next to the most beautiful woman he had ever met, pregnant with his son, and thinking this was probably the last time he would hold her this way. For once in his life, he welcomed insomnia so that he could cherish his son moving. Tomorrow was another day, but even the prepared and composed Ezzio Marin could not predict exactly what it would bring.

CHAPTER 41

Something was wrong. Rebecca sensed it the minute she awoke alone but was unable to put her finger on it.

It had been such a lovely night with Ezzio cuddling her. She'd tried to stay awake, to savour the warm and contented feeling, but sleep overcame her. Maybe her head cold had something to do with that.

Ezzio was charming and polite this morning . . . too polite really. Was she just fearing the worst, and looking for something that wasn't there? Why for the first time ever, was Imogen meeting them at court and not travelling with them?

In the car, she sneakily watched Ezzio as he flicked through some paperwork, and noticed a slight twitch just underneath his left eye. Maybe he's admitting defeat and realising he can't win this war.

Their arrival at court was the same as every other day with dozens of camera lenses focussed upon them both. As usual, Ezzio offered the protection of his arm, and she huddled in closely as he led her into the court foyer. Once inside he dropped his arm, and seeing Imogen walking towards them, smiling her usual 'let's get down to business smile', she understood why he'd done so.

"Good morning," she greeted them, "I'm afraid there's going to be a slight delay to this morning's proceedings; seemingly the judge wants to see Marcus Warr and myself in his chambers."

Ezzio spoke up quickly, "Will Rebecca have to go through to the holding area, or can she stay here for a while?"

"No, she needs to go straight through until she has to go into court. I'm hoping it's just a technicality and it won't take too long."

Rebecca looked at them both and the sense of foreboding was back stronger than ever, "Can you hazard a guess as to why the judge wants to see you?" she asked.

Imogen shook her head dismissively, "I can't I'm afraid. Probably something has been said that may have undue influence on the jury and he wants it retracting. It's quite common, so I'm not concerned," she smiled reassuringly, "and you shouldn't be either." She turned to Ezzio, "Right, we better get a move on."

As she did each morning, she followed Imogen's lead, and was aware as always, of Ezzio's penetrating eyes as they walked along the corridor to the waiting area. A female security officer met her, usually the same one who accompanied her into court each day, and once seated, Imogen excused herself and made her way to the judge's chambers. Rebecca sat and pondered . . . what was going on?

***

In the austere surroundings of the Judge's chambers, Marcus Warr QC, listened silently to Imogen Allen's request for the new witness to give her evidence. He was irritated, as he'd almost got the case sewn up, so could do without this complication muddying the water and giving the jury far more thinking time than was necessary.

He had been quietly confident that Judge Quarmby wouldn't allow this sister to take the stand because she hadn't given a police statement, and as the prosecuting barrister, he had no preparation time to cross examine. However, Imogen Allen was a fine QC, and if Judge Quarmby's face was anything to go by, her approach was becoming extremely persuasive.

He needed to nip it in the bud, "Your honour, may I repeat that this request is highly irregular. My understanding is that the defendant's sister is dead. How can we be sure this woman is indeed the sister, and that her evidence is credible."

Imogen quickly clarified, "You only have to look at her to see she is the defendant's sister, they are identical twins, the only difference being this one has learning difficulties."

Adopting a persuasive stance, she pleaded, "Your honour, she has vital information which supports the defence case and has only just come to light. I'm requesting that her evidence is allowed to be heard by the jury." It appeared that she'd finished speaking, but then as if to give her request more credence, she added, "I acknowledge that it is late evidence, but we have literally only found out about her existence this weekend."

Marcus Warr was thoughtful. If the Judge does allow it; I will quickly be able to discredit her if she has learning difficulties.

Judge Quarmby asked, "You say she has learning difficulties, have you secured an advocate to support her?"

"Yes your Honour, a court advocate is with her now."

Imogen turned directly to him, rather than Judge Quarmby, "Marcus, you know that I can quote verbatim cases where precedent has been set, and a witness has been introduced at a late stage in a trail."

"I can appreciate that," he replied sharply, "but I am still objecting on the grounds I have already stated, and hope that Judge Quarmby will support that."

Marcus Warr didn't like Judge Quarmby, who in his opinion always favoured female barristers, so he was resigned to thinking he might indeed support Imogen's request. He silently observed the Judge looking over the top of his steel rimmed glasses at Imogen, and from the look on his face, he deduced cynically that he either fancied her or at the very least, she was his illegitimate daughter.

Judge Quarmby addressed them both, "Mr Warr, I have duly noted your objection," he paused, "however on this occasion, I am prepared to allow the sister to give her evidence. If I refuse and the defendant is found guilty by the jury, there will be an appeal on the grounds that the sister did have vital information and wasn't called."

***

Fifty minutes later, Rebecca was escorted into court and took her seat. As usual, the courtroom was packed and the public gallery full to capacity.

She looked up to the public gallery and saw an expressionless Ezzio in his usual seat, and as far away from him as possible, sat Darlene, with an absurd puppy-dog expression on her face, she's really lost the plot - bigtime.

Her stomach churned as she contemplated the next few years behind bars. The pregnancy was an added complication; however, one thing she was absolutely sure about, was that Ezzio would give the child a wonderful home and upbringing. He would be a good father, and she had an inkling exactly who the mother might turn out to be. The odds must be stacked in favour of the woman defending her.

Rebecca thought about the two letters she'd written and entrusted with Dorothy. She'd obtained her sworn promise that they would be sent if she went back to prison. It tore her apart thinking about how much Emily would miss her, and she her also, but was confident that Ezzio would help with the costs of keeping her on the farm until she was released. He'd do that in exchange for the baby, she was sure.

Judge Quarmby entered, and the court usher asked them all to stand. It was the same ritual each day. Proceedings were commenced only after he'd seated himself.

He addressed Imogen, "If you'd like to continue, Ms Allen."

Imogen stood and faced the jury, "I'd like to call my next witness, Miss Emily Price Jones."

What! Rebecca's eyes widened in sheer horror.

In a split second, she grasped what was happening, and the whole court and jury witnessed the sudden unexpected metamorphosis in the so far unspoken Rebecca. She let out the most piercing, gut-wrenching scream, "NOOOOOOOOOOOOO," she jumped up to a standing position, "STOP THIS. YOU MUST STOP THIS," there was an uncontrollable wildness about her as she shrieked, "STOP-THIS-NOW."

The judge vigorously banged the gavel against a sound block to silence the court, who were by now, joining in with shocked exclamations.

"Order, order, please, order in the court. Sit down, Miss Price Jones," he commanded, before turning to Imogen, "Ms Allen you really must control your client, the court will not tolerate outbursts of this sort."

A man rushed forward up the three steps to Rebecca's side, announcing he was a doctor, but she pushed him away forcibly with both hands yelling at him, "Get away from me." She spun her head back in the direction of the Judge pleading, "Please, I don't want her to give evidence . . . she's not part of my defence . . . don't bring her in here . . . please, I'm begging you."

The look on Judge Quarmby's face could only be described as one of horror at the disruption, and something else also, anger.

She looked at his distorted expression, but didn't care, "Can't you stop this? I'm telling you, I don't want her here."

Imogen intervened forcibly, "Sit down, Rebecca, and please don't say anymore."

Her heart was racing frantically, and her eyes darted around looking everywhere for Emily, even though she knew she hadn't actually entered the courtroom. She hissed at the judge, "This is my trial surely?"

Judge Quarmby, clearly beyond fury, addressed Imogen in a curt tone, "Ms Allen, may I strongly suggest that you have a short recess with your client?"

Imogen, answered apologetically, "I am sorry, your Honour. Yes, it would be helpful if I could have some time alone with my client."

"We will adjourn for thirty minutes," the judge directed, before warning, "any further outbursts such as the sort we have just witnessed, I'll be forced to clear the court," he stared menacingly at her, "and that includes the defendant also."

They all stood as he left the courtroom, and Rebecca was led away by the doctor and Imogen. She turned to the public gallery looking for Ezzio, the enemy.

***

His eyes had not once strayed from her since she entered court that morning, and despite what he'd done, he felt her agony in every pore of his body. How was it that this particular woman, had been able to smash so effortlessly through his defences?

Her manic green eyes fired venom as they locked with his, but he remained impassive . . . if looks could kill, I'd be a dead man.

***

Once inside the holding room, Imogen dismissed the security guard leaving the two of them alone. Rebecca stood against the wall clearly furious, and as Imogen approached her, she felt a degree of sympathy remembering the utter shock and despair on her face in the courtroom.

Nevertheless, she needed to be clear, "You can't stop this. Emily is already outside, so you can either stay in court while she gives evidence, or you can be removed. Either way, she will be giving evidence."

"How could you do this," Rebecca spat, "did Ezzio put you up to it?"

"Yes," she nodded, "he found Emily."

"I don't want her to give evidence . . . she doesn't understand . . . she'll be frightened."

"I know that, but she's been prepared," Imogen reassured, "she'll be fine, and she wants to help, so you must let her."

Rebecca raised her voice, "What do you mean she's been prepared," her eyes flashed contempt, "What the hell are you hoping she's going to say?"

"That your stepfather was a brute that hit you."

"Well she'd be lying because he didn't," she snapped.

"Why would she lie?" Imogen stiffened, "What is it with you Rebecca, why don't you want help? We're all trying our best for you, yet you are hampering us every step of the way."

"Because I killed him and I'm ready to take the punishment."

"But Emily's evidence may lead to your acquittal; surely it's worth a try?"

"No, it isn't and I'm telling you, I don't want her to take the stand. You must stop this now," she took a step towards Imogen, and reached for her arm, pleading, "please help me, I'm desperate, don't let her give evidence."

Imogen shook her head, "The judge knows that Emily has further evidence that the jury must hear. I'm sorry, but It's going to happen whether you want it to or not."

The crushed expression on Rebecca's face as she sat down was painful to see, and although she momentarily felt sorry for her anguish, her legal mind was on winning the case. She wanted Rebecca's acquittal and Ezzio's heart.

Imogen opened the door and asked the prison officer for the doctor be brought in. The silence between the two of them was awkward as they waited for him.

The doctor took her pulse and blood pressure, and spoke gently to Rebecca who answered each of his questions in one syllable answers. Once his examination was complete, he indicated to Imogen that he was satisfied and she could return to the courtroom.

CHAPTER 42

Thirty minutes later, they were back in court. As she sat, Rebecca vowed not to look at Ezzio, hating him more now than ever. She should have known he would find Emily, when did Ezzio Marin ever fail at anything?

How sad that her precious sister had been dragged into all of this. Every decision she'd ever made had been about protecting her, and the final irony was that Emily was now here trying to protect her. Apart from their mother's death, there was only one other time in her life that she'd felt such utter despair, and that particular occasion was likely to be replayed graphically to the court right now, and she had absolutely no control over it whatsoever.

Imogen called for the next witness, and Rebecca listened as Emily's name reverberated outside the courtroom. She kept her eyes firmly fixed on the courtroom door, and her stomach plummeted as the door opened.

A middle-aged woman entered first, with Emily tentatively following behind her. Gasps were heard from the public gallery as she was escorted into the courtroom. Their resemblance always caused the same reaction; nobody could tell them apart, until Emily spoke, and it was only then, that the difference between the two of them became apparent.

It took minutes for Emily to be taken to the witness stand, and her nervous eyes flicked around the courtroom until they locked with hers. Emily's green eyes, literally mirrored her own, the difference being Emily's were glinting with fear, while hers, she knew, would be sorrowful and resigned.

An enormous rush of love hit her hard in her abdomen as she looked at her beloved sister proudly standing in the brightly coloured blue dress she'd made for her. She was wearing their adored mother's locket around her neck, which contained tiny photographs of her and their mum that Emily cherished above anything. It suddenly came to her why she felt odd that morning, as a twin, she had sensed her sister's distress. Her heart was almost combusting, as she silently urged, don't tell them anything, sweetheart.

***

Emily looked across at the sister that had always taken care of her, and she could feel her fear shaking within her own body, but she needed to help Rebecca, just as Ezzio had asked her to.

She wished that she could go over so that Rebecca could put her arms around her, and tell her she would be alright. She took a deep breath in, remembering Imogen's words that if she got frightened, it would help, and then gave her sister one of her best smiles, before a hand distracted her.

The advocate lady wanted to go through the map that Imogen had drawn, so that she could see who every person was in the courtroom, and where they all were sitting. She listened carefully as each person was pointed out, but her eyes drifted around the court, until she found who she was looking for. Ezzio was sitting in what was called a public gallery. He was smiling kindly at her which made her feel brave. She liked Ezzio, he was a nice man.

She was given a bible to hold, and had to read from a card which the advocate lady held for her. She only made two mistakes, and that was because everyone was looking at her, and she didn't want to be in trouble for keeping them waiting. *I wish we could go home, I don't want to be here.*

She remained standing but her legs were shaking. She wanted to sit down, but wasn't sure if she was allowed.

Ezzio's friend, Imogen, smiled nicely at her as she stood up to speak, "Emily, you have been asked to attend today so that you can help the court to decide about your stepfather's death, do you understand that is why you are here?"

"Yes," she stated. *You've told me that already, why do you have to say it in front of all these people?*

"And you do understand the importance of answering questions that you are asked truthfully?"

"Yes." *I always tell the truth, Mummy said never to tell lies.*

"Good, because the court is hoping that you will tell us about your stepfather, Derek Clay.

I wish I didn't have to talk about him.

The court was quiet, until Imogen spoke again, "Did you like your stepfather?" She nodded. *She did like him a bit until . . .*

"You have to answer the questions out loud please, Emily, so that you can be heard by the court."

"Yes," she thought for a moment, "sometimes." *Not when he hurt Rebecca, though.*

"Only sometimes, why not all the time?"

Should she say? I don't like everyone looking at me.

"Sometimes he wasn't very nice." Rebecca said it was all the booze he drank.

Imogen urged her on, "Can you tell the court about a time you saw him when he wasn't very nice."

"I saw him smack my mummy's face one day." I didn't like him hurting Mummy, it made me cry.

"Did Rebecca see him hit your mummy?"

"No, she wasn't there." Rebecca's looking really cross with me.

"Did you tell her when she came home?"

"Mummy did 'cause her eye was bruised, but she said we were not to worry about it." Mummy was ever so brave, Rebecca said, 'cause her head would really hurt.

A man quickly stood up, was he the one Imogen talked about?

"Objection your Honour, "Where is this line of questioning going? Do we have to blacken the character of a man by discussing a marital dispute, which has nothing to do with today's case?"

Imogen spoke too, "Your Honour, I'm trying to establish the behaviour of the deceased, and the effect on two young girls."

The judge nodded his head, "Overruled. Proceed with your line of questioning, Ms Allen."

"Thank you, your Honour."

"You say you saw your stepfather hit your mummy. Did your stepfather ever hit you, either before or after your mummy died?"

She shook her head from side to side at first, but then remembered she had to speak her answers, "No." He never did; he was always nice to me.

"What about your sister, did he ever hit her?" She glanced across at Rebecca, she doesn't want me to say, I can tell.

"You must not keep looking at your sister before you speak. I'll repeat the question, Did you ever see your stepfather hit your sister Rebecca?"

Should she say? Ezzio said she had to speak the truth to help Rebecca.

"Once he did." I don't want to think about it.

"Can you think when that was?"

She couldn't, so shook her head.

"Remember to speak out loud your reply to the question," Imogen reminded her.

"No, I can't remember." My head hurts.

"Was it some months before he died, or close to the time he died?"

"Erm . . . just before, I think," she didn't like the questions, her tummy felt funny, and she needed the toilet, "I can't remember."

"That's quite alright. Think back to the time you saw your stepfather hurt your sister. Tell us, in your own words, what happened."

I'm going to tell them about him hurting you, Rebecca, "I was in my bedroom playing with my dolls, and Derek came in and told me to stay in my room until he came for me. He told me to pack some things in my rucksack, as I was going for a sleepover at Amy's house."

Rebecca's crying . . . she will be so cross with me, I know she will.

"Tell the court what happened next?"

"I waited for a long time, and then I thought I heard someone screaming, so I went to Rebecca's bedroom to see if she heard it too." I don't want to say the next bit.

"And did you go inside Rebecca's bedroom?"

"Yes."

"Where was Rebecca when you opened her bedroom door?"

"On the bed."

"Was she asleep?"

"No."

"So, she was awake. Was she on her own in the bedroom?"

"No, Derek was there." Should she say, she knew it was wrong?

"Did your stepfather often visit Rebecca's bedroom?"

"I don't know," she shook her head, "I don't think so."

"Had you ever seen him in her bedroom before?"

She thought for a moment, "Not really."

"Where was he in the bedroom, sat on a chair?"

"No, he was on the bed."

"And was Rebecca on the bed also?"

"Yes."

"Can you tell the court what you saw that night in the bedroom?"

"He was hurting Rebecca."

"By he, you mean your stepfather, Derek Clay?"

She nodded, "Yes."

"Was he hitting her?"

She didn't answer.

"Can you tell the court what he was doing to her?"

She didn't like speaking it in front of everyone, but she knew she had to say so that she could help her sister, "He was lying on top of her, squashing her, and she was screaming for him to stop."

Loud noises were coming from the public gallery. Why was the judge banging his hammer, and shouting silence, silence in the court?

After a short while, the noise stopped, and Imogen started speaking again, "Was your stepfather wearing any clothes? Please tell the court what you saw."

"I think he had a top on . . . but his trousers were pulled down, and I could see his bottom," she could feel her face going red, "he was hurting Rebecca because she was crying."

"Did you know what Derek was doing to Rebecca?"

Yes, she knew. Nodding her head, she felt silly saying it, but they were waiting, "It was sex." I saw his big fat bum moving up and down.

"How did Derek know you were there?"

"Rebecca saw me, and screamed at me to run to Amy's house."

"And did you run to Amy's house?"

"Not straight away."

"What did you do?"

"I ran away from the bedroom."

"Was that the only time you ever saw your stepfather hurting Rebecca?"

"Er . . . I think so." I don't want to say about him hitting her.

"After seeing that scene in the bedroom, did you ever see your stepfather hurting your sister again?"

". . . erm . . . no, I don't think so." My head hurts worse now.

"Thank you, Emily. You have been really helpful coming here today and telling the court about this. Mr Warr is going to ask you some questions now."

She nodded, knowing that next, a man was going to question her, and Imogen had said he would try and catch her out, but she just needed to be honest. I want to go home, I don't like it here.

***

Imogen sat down satisfied that Emily's evidence had been compelling. Years of experience studying individual jury members gave her an indication of their thinking, and watching them now, she knew that Emily's disclosure had added a whole new dimension to the case.

The next few minutes would not only be make or break for Rebecca, but for her also. This was a high profile case, and trials were not always won on the balance of truth. She'd unpicked every legal aspect of the case, and stage-managed the whole process by successfully playing the media. They had become willing pawns by building the case up into a romantic storm. The introduction of Emily was almost the icing on the cake. Now, there were two beautiful young victims, one of them carrying Ezzio Marin's child, and the other one, no more than a child herself. She was confident the two of them together, would instil sympathy from the jury, and if Rebecca was acquitted, then she would have her man. However, if she was found guilty, the happy ending would be in doubt, which was something she couldn't contemplate. She wanted Ezzio desperately, so failing wasn't an option.

Marcus Warr cleared his throat, and Imogen knew that this was the moment of reckoning. His job now would be to discredit Emily's evidence, which he was more than capable of doing. She waited with bated breath, willing Emily to win the jury over with her honesty and innocence.

Despite all the preparation she'd done, she could see that Emily was frightened and silently willed, remember, just tell the truth.

CHAPTER 43

The same man that had spoken earlier stood up, and Emily knew then who he was. She remembered Imogen saying he would be out to trick her, and although she mustn't say it out loud, she was to think of him as a sort of grizzly bear in a story. She liked Imogen, she was funny and would talk in a gruff voice, like a bear, when she was pretending to be him at their practice sessions. He looks silly with that curly thing on his head, Imogen was wearing one too.

"Thank you, Miss Price Jones for coming today to help the court decide what happened to your stepfather," he smiled, but she knew it was a pretend smile, "Firstly, it appears to us all that you love your sister very much, is that correct?"

She nodded, "Yes." I love her more than anyone.

"And does your sister pay for your living expenses."

Does he mean to stay on the farm? "Yes."

"So, it's fair to say that as your sister looks after you, you would always try your best to look after her also, is that correct?"

"Yes." Why is he asking this?

"That leaves the court wondering how far you would go to help your sister, for example, what would you do to prevent your sister going to prison?"

Her tummy was making a noise, and she felt sick which often happened when she got frightened, "I don't want her to go to prison," she blurted out.

"No, I'm sure you don't," he replied, and stopped for a minute. I thought he was going to ask me about Derek hitting Rebecca.

"Tell the court, Miss Price Jones, can you read?"

"Yes," 'course I can, I learned that at school.

"What sort of things do you like to read?"

"Animal books, about horses and dogs . . . and cats," she tried to think, had she said them all, Imogen had said she must remember everything, "and rabbits . . . oh and I like elephants . . ."

He stopped her, "Yes I think that's clear enough, thank you. Do you like television?"

"Yes."

"What are your favourite television programmes," he stopped for a minute, "could you perhaps name three?"

"Animal programmes and I like Emmerdale, EastEnders and . . . erm, Neighbours."

"Oh, you like EastEnders do you?"

Was she supposed to answer, he was looking so she'd better, "Yes I watch it with my friends, Hannah and Ruth."

"I see. Do you think some of the storylines on EastEnders can be a bit violent?"

I don't know what he means?

"For example, there's lots of arguing and fighting, people falling out all the time, don't you agree?"

She nodded her head, "Sometimes." Why's he's asking about EastEnders, Imogen never said he would talk about that?

"I'm just wondering if perhaps you are confusing television with real life, and you are here today making up a story to try and save your sister. Could that be the case?"

"No," she shook her head, "I'm not."

"Then let's go back to the time you say you saw your stepfather hurting your sister. You said you saw him having sex with her on the bed, is that correct?"

She nodded, I did see that.

"You have to answer the question."

"Yes."

"Prior . . . just before you went into your sister's bedroom, could you have been asleep do you think?"

She couldn't remember, "I don't think so."

"Well let's just pretend for a minute that you had been asleep. You could have dreamt that your stepfather was hurting your sister and that it didn't actually happen in real life?" He was staring at her, waiting.

"It did happen." I saw him hurting her.

"How can the court be so sure that you are telling the truth?"

". . . 'cause I saw him hurting her, and she was screaming for him to stop."

"But you've already told the court that you can't recall when this happened? Why should we believe you?"

This must be one of the tricks, well, I can remember when it was, "It was the night he died."

She watched his eyes widen, "Oh I see. This all happened the night he died. I think we are getting the picture now. You are telling us that you were there the night your stepfather died, despite police reports stating that you weren't."

She stared at him, not sure if she should be saying anything. He was speaking again, "I put it to you, Miss Price Jones, that this is all a figment of your imagination. Too many books, and too many soap operas. I don't think Mr Derek Clay, your stepfather, hurt your sister at all. I think you are telling lies."

He scared her, but Ezzio had said that it was, 'really important' to say what happened.

She didn't meet his eyes, and looked across at Imogen, "I'm not telling lies, he was hurting Rebecca, and then turned her head towards the judge, "I saw him and I ran away at first, but then I went back into the bedroom, and Derek was hitting her hard, and punching her hard in her tummy. . ." she took another one of the deep breaths that was supposed to help, "and she had her hands over her face, but he kept hitting her harder and harder. He was hurting her, I know he was," she blurted, "she was screaming at him to stop."

She was trying not to cry, but she didn't like the way grizzly bear kept widening his eyes as if he didn't believe her.

"If your story was indeed true, and you expect the court to believe this, why didn't you dial 999 for the police? You know how to use a telephone don't you?"

She didn't know what to say, and didn't like him shaking his head from side to side. His voice went soft, "You didn't see your stepfather hurting your sister at all, did you? This is all a made up story." He stopped talking and the room was quiet, waiting, and then he spoke again, "I think the jury has heard enough of your attempts to try and save your sister with these blatant lies."

He's horrible. Shall I say it, Rebecca, I know you'll be cross with me, but I don't want you to go to prison, "It's not made up . . . it happened." Her mouth felt dry, but she carried on, "All of a sudden, he stopped hitting Rebecca and just fell back onto the bed . . . and he was bleeding." She pointed to her own chest, showing where her stepfather was bleeding from.

Grizzly bear took a big breath in, "So you have no idea when this alleged attack took place, and police records tell us that you weren't at home on the night of your stepfather's death," he looked down reading something, and then carried on, "Are you now stating under oath that you witnessed your sister stabbing your stepfather in the bedroom, when in fact, the incident occurred in the kitchen where the body was recovered?"

His eyes went small, as if he could hardly see her, "I put it to you, Miss Price Jones, that your account of events is a complete fantasy in an attempt to save your sister. He turned towards the judge, "Your Honour, due to this witness's mental capacity, can I request that her evidence is disregarded by the jury? Clearly, these lies are a desperate attempt to save her sister."

Emily shook her head from side to side, and raised her voice, "I-am-not-telling-lies," and her voice became louder, "You're all telling lies."

Her advocate lady stood up, and Imogen did at the same time, speaking to the judge, "Your Honour, may we have a short recess, please? The witness has been giving evidence long enough now and is clearly becoming distressed."

Her eyes found her sister, "Tell them, Rebecca; tell them I'm not telling lies." In those brief seconds,

unspoken between them was the night she'd erased
from her mind such a long time ago.

All eyes in the courtroom were suddenly on her.
Rebecca had said it was all a nasty dream and she must
forget that night, but she knew it wasn't a dream. It
really happened.

Tears were rolling down Rebecca's cheeks, and she
was moving her head slowly from side to side, which
she knew meant don't say anything else. But she was
going to be brave. Her mummy always said there
wasn't a braver little girl than Emily.

Blinded by her own tears, she tried to speak but
struggled as the words she wanted to say, were there,
but she couldn't get them out. She swallowed, to clear
the lump in her throat, and looked directly at the judge.
In a barely audible voice, she whispered, "It was me, I
did it." Subconsciously she gestured a stabbing action
to her own chest with her hand, "I pushed the knife as
hard as I could," she sobbed, "to stop him hurting my
sister," her breath caught in her throat, "I'm not telling
lies," she turned towards her twin, "am I Rebecca? . . .
tell them."

CHAPTER 44

The judge stopped Emily giving any further evidence, and cleared the courtroom. He explained to Rebecca that she would return to the court for the case to be formally dismissed if the police and Crown Prosecution service accepted Emily's confession, and then he discharged the jury.

Emily was escorted by two female officers to the police station, with Ezzio accompanying them as her guardian.

In the waiting area, Imogen stared at Rebecca's zombie-like state, "We'd better go, Dorothy and George are waiting, they'll take you home."

Rebecca's bleak eyes stared back, almost looking through her, "Will she be held in custody?"

"No that's unlikely," she reassured, "she'll be allowed home until the Crown Prosecution makes a decision. I'd say, in light of her mental capacity and the provocation, she most probably will end up with a suspended sentence if it actually goes to court."

"Right," Rebecca answered, looking utterly defeated, and Imogen could understand why. This brave woman, who had done her utmost to protect her sibling, had failed. As an experienced defence barrister, she knew the trial was almost lost and that a custodial sentence was staring Rebecca in the face. Yet the truth had prevailed, which strengthened her belief in the fundamental principles of law which she upheld.

"Just be aware that you may be charged with perverting the course of justice, but again I think it's unlikely the CPS will pursue that. If they did, in light of Emily's evidence, you'd get away with a suspended sentence."

Rebecca moved towards the door, and Imogen put a reassuring arm around her, "Try not to worry. I've got an experienced colleague of mine to support Emily; he's on his way to the station as we speak."

***

It was over. She left the courtroom with George and Dorothy, relieved to have the security team escorting her to the car. She tried to close her ears to the shouts from the press, "Are you going to marry Ezzio now you're free?"

The journey home was mostly silent, with Dorothy interjecting the occasional pleasantries. Once she arrived at Ezzio's, she refused Dorothy's offer of tea, and headed straight for her bedroom, mentally exhausted. Her mind whirled with explanations, how on earth had Ezzio found Emily?

Her whole purpose in life had been to protect her sister, and that was all that mattered. She'd often considered whether Emily would have been spared a custodial sentence due to her mental capacity, but at the time of the stabbing, she couldn't risk it. The traumatic situation made it impossible to think clearly, so she instantly made the decision that she would take the punishment and let Emily continue with her beautiful life of innocence.

Rebecca had long ago erased the evil images of her stepfather attacking her, and as well as emphasising to

Emily she must forget that terrible night, she'd tried to blot it out too. Her thoughts drifted back to that fateful night and the torture of being raped, compounded by the horrendous stabbing.

She'd had to act quickly, sitting Emily down and telling her graphically about the consequences of what would happen if it came out exactly how Derek Clay had died. She hated frightening her, but she needed to make sure she wouldn't speak about it ever. The ramifications were terrifying.

She forced her to repeat over and over again that she was at Amy's all evening, and then sent an anxious Emily with her overnight things to her friend's house. It was only a short walk, which she was used to, and they were expecting her. Just before she left the house, Rebecca gave her two sleeping pills, hoping she'd be so drowsy that Amy's mum would put her to bed early. Amy had special needs like Emily, so her mum was well used to the challenges such a child can bring. It wouldn't be at all unusual if Emily was tired and needed an early night.

Taking care of her stepfather's body was the next daunting task. Adrenaline gave her the strength to drag his heavy corpse into the kitchen. She placed him in a position that she hoped would convince the police he'd died.

She hastily put the bed linen into the washer to clear up any evidence of him from her bedroom, and quickly remade the bed. Finally, she showered to remove all traces of him from her body. Only then did she call the police and admit to the killing, making up the story that they'd rowed, and in a fit of rage, she'd stabbed him with a kitchen knife.

She was held in a Youth Detention Centre awaiting the court case, and was advised to plead not guilty to the manslaughter of her stepfather. The police and psychiatrists all believed her tearful explanation of an argument about wanting to go on a school trip, and him refusing to let her.

Emily was taken into foster care. Whether it was the effect of the sleeping pills she'd given her that night, or the trauma of the stabbing she wasn't sure, but it became apparent over the subsequent years that Emily had completely blocked the memory of the incident out of her mind. Neither of them ever discussed it.

While awaiting the trial she quickly deduced that if she was convicted, she'd be transferred to an adult prison when she was eighteen, where escape would be virtually impossible. So, from the moment she was locked up in the Youth Offenders Detention Centre, she plotted her escape, and when the time came, it had been relatively easy.

Allocated to work in the kitchen, she gained the trust of the wardens who gave her a degree of supervised independence. Diligently, she responded to every task asked of her, and worked hard daily ensuring that the kitchen became the cleanest and most efficient part of the building.

It took a few weeks of biding her time until she spotted an opportunity to escape. Her probing eyes watched and timed the driver from the local waste company who attended monthly to take away the female sanitary bins. She recognised that he offered her a way out.

The main driver, Tony, was particularly flirtatious, and the female wardens seemed to enjoy his cheeky banter. Rebecca quickly made herself known to him. At first it was a subtle smile, which then progressed to a hello, and before long he started to look for her and they chatted each time he came.

She stroked his ego by appearing pleased to see him and waving goodbye, reckoning that the hardest part would be escaping from the building and getting into his van. If she achieved this, then she didn't want him turning her in.

Rebecca timed his shift and quickly established that he collected every fourth Friday, usually late in the afternoon. A plan to abscond was hatched, with a date set firmly in her mind.

On the actual escape day, she told the wardens she wasn't feeling well but suggested that she'd like to try and work it off. She worked quietly all day hardly conversing to give the impression she was ill, and as she heard the van arrive, she asked if she could go to her room to lie down. The warden gave permission, so she quickly left the kitchen area as if she was heading to her room, but diverted to the utility area adjacent to the kitchen. She hid inside the broom cupboard and held her breath, certain that someone would discover her, but nobody came. When the time was right, she opened the hatch to the dirty laundry chute, and crawled along until she reached the end. Outside of the chute, she crouched behind the bales of dirty linen lined up ready for collection.

Tony was always escorted around the building and collected the first of the sanitary disposable units placing them at the back door as usual. Prior to going to the west end of the building to collect the others, it was usual for him to be given a cup of tea, and the door was opened so he could go outside for a cigarette, often accompanied by one of the wardens going for a crafty smoke.

As usual, the door was opened for him, and he stepped outside just at the precise moment that one of the girls that she'd given money to, created a diversion by screaming out as someone had fainted. The warden quickly closed the door omitting to lock it and dashed forward to help, with Tony quickly following. During the disturbance, she swiftly crept out of the building and jumped into the back of the van. Within minutes, the warden reappeared to secure the door, and she heard her tell Tony to knock when he'd finished his cigarette.

For the next thirty minutes inside the van, Rebecca waited with a pounding heart. Even though she wasn't visible behind the stacked sanitary bins from his previous stops, she was terrified someone in the building would notice she was gone and raise the alarm.

As Tony loaded the last bins, she was hardly breathing, terrified that he would hear her. He climbed in the front of the van, started the engine, and they were away. She crossed her fingers and as expected, after a short drive, the van came to a halt. Her friend, as well as staging the fainting diversion, had slipped diuretics into Tony's tea, so Rebecca knew it likely he would need to stop to relieve himself. She heard him leave the van, but couldn't see him, so could only surmise he'd disappeared behind a tree.

She took her only chance, and slipped out of the back of the van, and crouched behind it. For several minutes, she waited until eventually, the door opened and slammed closed. Tony put the van into gear, and slowly pulled away . . . she was free. She turned and ran, and ran, and kept on running for eight years until Ezzio Marin entered her life and caused an almighty earthquake.

She must have drifted off to sleep as the next minute she woke in complete darkness. Groggily she got out of bed and headed downstairs, stunned to see Ezzio and Emily sat at the dining table chatting to each other like they were soulmates.

Never had she seen such a beautiful sight as her beloved sister filling her little face with cupcakes. Emily turned her head towards her, and ran from the table when she spotted her in the doorway. Rebecca wrapped her arms around her as if she'd never let her go. They were both crying, and laughing at the same time, and Rebecca went along with Emily's jumping up and down until they were both panting, "Oh, Em, stop, let me get my breath," she laughed, easing herself away from her.

Ezzio stood up, making his presence known. Still holding Emily's hand, Rebecca turned to look at him, wanting to speak, but the words wouldn't come . . . what do I say to him? He'd brought such despair to her life, yet may have actually saved it. Their eyes locked for what seemed like an eternity, until he broke the silence, "Emily has to reside at this house while the police prepare the case for the CPS, so for the next few months, you'll both be staying here, at least until the baby's born."

Back to the baby, always the baby, but she was so elated to have Emily with her, and far too exhausted to argue with him. That would come later she was sure.

He shuffled his feet in an impatient way, "I have to go to the hotel to see Imogen," he said, and then, almost like a warning, added, "we can talk when I get back."

It was the usual Ezzio command, no negotiation. What will happen now with him and Imogen . . . would they marry? Her and Emily would have to leave then. There was no way she could stay in a house with the two of them living together as a couple. She looked questioningly into his eyes, but his expression was veiled. What was going on inside that head of his?

Emily interrupted her thoughts, "Can I tell her about the surprise now, Ezzio?" she asked eagerly. His loving smile towards Emily as he nodded yes, caused her insides to constrict.

"What surprise?" she'd had enough of those today to last her a lifetime.

Emily pointed to the wall behind her, "Look."

Her eyes followed where she was pointing, and Emily happily exclaimed, "Ezzio bought it for you as a surprise." She gazed in amazement at her precious sewing machine standing against the wall, and tried to stifle the threatening tears behind her eyelids.

Ezzio cut in, "No, I told you Emily, I didn't buy it. I brought it from your sister's flat."

Emily seemed too excited to care, "I know. Rebecca will be able to make some dresses now 'cause she's ever so clever at sewing," she turned towards her, "aren't you? Tell Ezzio." Bless her. How could she say that he wouldn't be remotely interested in any sewing that she could do.

As if he read her mind, he said, "I've had the rest of your belongings from your flat put into storage."

That would be the settee, dressing table and wardrobe, then, there wasn't anything else. She wanted to thank him, but nodded her gratitude instead. Speech wouldn't come, due to the huge lump stuck in the back of her throat at seeing her much loved sewing machine. It certainly had been quite a day.

Ezzio walked towards the door without a backward glance, but it was clear Emily didn't want him to go. She rushed over to him, throwing her arms around his waist, "Hurry back, Ezzio won't you?"

Rebecca watched him wrap Emily in his huge arms, and hug her tightly as if he welcomed her embrace, "I will do," he promised, "Now you look after your sister for me, won't you?" As he kissed Emily's forehead gently, for a fleeting moment, his eyes locked with hers.

CHAPTER 45

Ezzio was on his way and Imogen was ready. The champagne was in the ice bucket chilling, with two crystal flutes alongside. She had bathed herself in sensual bath oil, and applied moisturiser to every crevice of her body, which had only heightened her arousal. Finally, he was going to make love to her.

As she stared at her naked body through the elegant bathroom mirror, she decided that at thirty-two, she still looked good. Her small waist and flat stomach were due to a sustained effort of regular workouts, and guaranteed the slim-line skirts and tapered blouses that she favoured, always looked stylish and chic.

Her breasts were the one part of her body that she disliked as they were small. The negativity about this part of her body had been compounded further by her ex-husband's preference for big-breasted women. The totty he eventually left her for had huge breasts which had severely dented her self-esteem at the time. Still, she'd had a sexual experience since the divorce and he hadn't complained.

She reached for her new full length designer wrap and secured it with the shoestring tie around her waist. The ivory silk and lace felt warm and sensual on her naked skin. As she left the bathroom, she caught sight of herself in the full-length wall mirror and smiled inwardly; she looked hot . . . and felt hot too.

Sitting on the hotel balcony, she watched the city lights and waited. In her vast experience of witnessing endless twists and turns in the courtroom, nothing could have prepared her for the sequence of today's events. Yes, it was abundantly clear now how Emily had stabbed their stepfather, and Rebecca had shielded her by taking the blame, however, nobody could have predicted that when Emily took the stand.

Ezzio's brief had been Rebecca's acquittal, and technically, she'd got that. When he'd looked decisively into her eyes after the trial and told her he would come to her this evening, she understood his meaning. The anticipation of him finally making love to her was thrilling.

His knock came sooner than she had anticipated, and she eagerly opened the door to him, "Hi, come in."

He looked even more attractive if that was possible. In a suit, he looked handsome, but tonight dressed casually in denim jeans and a crisp white shirt, he really was drop dead gorgeous.

As she watched him remove his jacket, and discard it on the chair, she felt slightly lightheaded at the thought of being intimate with him.

I need a drink. "Would you like a glass of champagne?"

She felt nervous, which was ridiculous considering she'd been waiting for this moment for what like seemed forever.

"Yes, that would be nice."

Grateful to have something to do with her hands, she poured the sparkling wine into the crystal glasses. Was he watching her? Could she see the outline of her body through the flimsy fabric?

She handed him the flute, and taking a sip of her drink, asked, "How are Rebecca and Emily?"

"They seem fine," he smiled, "Rebecca looks tired and strained, still worrying about Emily, of course. Emily . . . well, she's just happy being with Rebecca, and Dorothy is busy fussing round with endless cupcakes."

She smiled thinking what a sweetie Emily was. You just couldn't help but love her. Taking another sip of champagne, she asked, "Do you want to talk about the case?" He shook his head, and looked searchingly into her eyes, before seductively asking, "Shall we take our drinks into the bedroom?"

Not wanting to delay things a moment longer, she nodded and led the way. Excitement oozed through her and she clenched her core as it quivered in anticipation.

She walked around the side of the huge decorative king size bed and placed her drink on the bedside table, uncertain what the next move was.

He remained standing at the foot of the bed with half a glass of champagne still in his hand, and with a slight movement of his head, beckoned her towards him, "Come here."

The guttural tone of his voice churned deep within her tummy, and her eyes didn't leave his as she walked forward to stand in front of him so that their bodies were not quite touching, but thrillingly close. With his free hand, he reached for the tie around her waist and loosened the wrap exposing her naked front.

"Take it off," he demanded huskily.

She slipped the wrap over her shoulders slowly, enjoying the visual foreplay. It dropped to the floor, and unclothed in front of him, she watched his eyes fire as he soaked up her nakedness.

Due to his enormous height, she hadn't noticed he'd removed his shoes until she watched his foot kick her wrap away from them. Almost in slow motion, he lifted his half-filled flute and poured a small amount of the sparkling liquid slowly down the front of her naked breasts. The sensation of the ice-cold fluid on her skin momentarily took her breath away, and to see the desire in his eyes as he watched her nipples harden was thrilling.

The champagne cascaded down her stomach and over her pubic area eventually pooling at her feet. He leant sideways to place his glass on the dresser table, and then with his huge arms on hers, he eased her into a sitting position on the bed, before smoothly laying her down.

Nothing could have prepared her for the sensation of Ezzio licking the bubbly off her body. Never had she experienced anything so sensual. He took a champagne-soaked nipple into his mouth and sucked deeply, and her insides contracted as he moved to her other breast, giving it the same tortuous pleasure. He traced the liquid along her abdomen with his delightful tongue licking everywhere, until there was only one crevice left untouched. The anticipation was electrifying. He gently parted her thighs to follow the watery trail, and as his head moved to her needy area, she was in complete ecstasy. Her labia throbbed, and desperate for more, she thrust herself at him, but he continued to toy with her which only heightened her need.

She groaned noisily . . . begging, until his large hands slid under her bottom and lifted her towards him. This incredible man, who she'd dreamed about for so long, didn't disappoint. His tongue was like a rod pushing hard on her throbbing clit and the sensation was so exhilarating, she just couldn't hold on and exploded in an orgasm so intense, she shook and gripped the bed as she plummeted down and down, and down.

While she lay basking in fulfilment, he stood and removed his clothes. Just as she had suspected, he was big. Clearly comfortable with his nakedness, he took a condom out of his trouser pocket and placed it on the bed as he lay down beside her. I wish he would say something.

He leant towards her, and for the first time, kissed her. She wanted him to know how much she desired him, and put her heart and soul into the kiss. The oral sex had been brilliant, but she wanted this incredible man inside her. His sensuous lips moved in sync with hers and she wrapped her arms around his neck, he was here, and that's what mattered. Finally, he was hers.

She was overwhelmed not only by their naked bodies fitting together so effortlessly, but also by the intense feelings she had for him, and was desperate for him to make love to her. Although enjoying kissing him passionately, she pulled her lips away from his mouth and moved them down his neck kissing him hard, wanting to leave her mark on him. She kissed his nipples and gripped his erection in her hand. He felt good. Holding him firmly, she moved his foreskin up and down, eager to give him pleasure. Should I take him in my mouth?

He pulled away from her, and glancing at the condom, he urged, "Put it on."

She opened the packet carefully, and rolled it smoothly down his shaft, eagerly anticipating the feel of him inside her.

His powerful erection is all for me.

"Turn over," he whispered, and eased her smoothly onto her tummy. He reached for two pillows from the top of the bed and gently lifted her up, and placed the pillows under her abdomen. Momentarily, it felt undignified lying with her bottom in the air, as she would have preferred facing him when he entered her, but the anticipation of this huge man inside her was sending her wild. He eased himself onto her back, and the maleness of him, caused a twisting deep inside her which was enhanced as he swept her hair to the other side of her head to expose her neck, and with that gorgeous mouth of his, began nibbling and kissing it. The sensation was simply wonderful, and the feel of his huge erection poised between her legs made her breathless with excitement.

She wanted it inside her . . . quickly. His fingers glided along her moist core, so slippery from oral sex, and he breathed heavily in her ear, "Tell me what you want?"

". . . you to make love to me."

He nibbled her neck with his teeth, and huskily whispered, "You can do better than that."

"I want you inside me."

His fingers massaging her clitoris were amazing.

"Then say it properly."

"I want you to fuck me."

His breath felt hot on her ear, "Hard?"

"Yes," she panted, "fuck me hard."

He didn't disappoint. With one push and no finesse, he entered her, filling her massively. He felt so big, and every push was magnificent, in and out, in and out. Each time he withdrew his thrust, she thought he might slip away, but not once did he lose momentum.

Subconsciously she widened her legs, silently urging him to fill her more if it was possible, savouring every single inch of him. The pull on her labia from his massive penis was sensational, and her pleasure was heightened by his huge fingers kneading her clit. Pushing the bud harder than she'd had before, she loved the pressure and thought she would explode from such intensity.

Rising above her, he pushed himself into her again and again, again, and again. She couldn't control her second orgasm, nor did she want to, "Oh yes, yes, harder, harder . . . I'm going to come again, EZZIO. . ."

Another powerful explosion started in her chest and crashed down to her toes. He was incredible. Moments later, she came back to earth and rolled onto her side to face him. She'd wanted him for such a long time, and the intenseness of him loving her was as magnificent as she'd expected.

So grateful for the pleasure he'd given her, she stroked his face, "That was just so wonderful." She kissed him gently, unsure why his eyes looked tormented. Doubt crept in, "Did you come?"

He shook his head.

Maybe he wants me to go down on him now? She attempted to move her head down his body, but he held onto her, "Please, I want to?"

It was evident by the gentle kiss to her forehead that he didn't want her to. He eased himself away from her, and stepped off the bed, and her uncertain eyes followed him as he moved purposefully towards the bathroom, taking his clothes from the chair. She covered herself quickly, and sat up against the pillows. What's wrong with him?

A minute later, he was back, fully clothed. Anxiously, she watched him approach her side of the bed, and as he sat next to her, anguish was written all over his face. With the back of his fingers, he reached forward and stroked her cheek, still not speaking, as if he was preparing the words he was going say to her. Although eager for him to say something, she waited patiently. Not once had she ever seen Ezzio Marin struggle for words, it was so unlike him.

As he took her hand in his, and kissed her fingers, she watched the darkness of his eyes deepen. The endless fantasies of this great man loving her, and her future hopes of becoming Mrs Marin, imploded in front of her as he broke his silence, "I'm sorry, it isn't going to work between the two of us."

The first sensation to emerge was a brutal thump in her gut, and the second, a desperate ache deep within her. Devastation didn't come close to covering her emotional state, she had to hang onto him. "It could, Ezzio . . . no, please hear me out. Look, the trial has been a massive rollercoaster, and today especially has been fraught. We just need time now to step back and assess what we both want. Maybe have a holiday to try and sort out our future?"

"It won't do any good," he answered dismissively, "there isn't going to be a future for you and I . . . not together anyway. I'm really sorry, but that's the way it is."

Why, oh why, had he made love to her and given her a glimpse of such ecstasy? She shook her head in exasperation, "Why did you come to me tonight if you didn't want this?"

"I hoped that maybe I'd feel differently once we'd made love," he admitted with anguish etched all over his face, "you're an attractive woman, and my logical head tells me that you and I should be together, but," he paused taking a deep breath in, and she cut in quickly, "It's Rebecca, isn't it?"

She watched him wrestle with his reply, almost as if it was the first time he'd admitted it, "Yes," he nodded.

His tortured expression told her everything she needed to know, he would never truly be hers. She wasn't a member of the Queen's Council for nothing, she'd been beaten and the rejection hurt terribly.

"Does she know?"

He shook his head and raised his eyebrows, "No, she thinks I'm having a relationship with you."

A significant wave of pain replaced the earlier pleasure in her abdomen . . . if only.

"Then you'd better tell her that your future isn't with me, and it's her that you want."

He let out a long sigh, "I'm not sure how that would go down," a dry smile briefly moulded his lips, "I've never been her favourite person."

For some reason, seeing this vulnerable side of him, made her want to help, which was completely bizarre considering the last few months she'd been planning a future for herself with him, "Well you have to at least try," she thought for a second, "or do you think it's Darlene she actually wants?"

"No," he shook his head, "Rebecca's no more gay than you or I. She just went down that road to make money for herself and Emily."

"Has she told you that?" Even before she'd finished speaking, she knew what a stupid question that was. Rebecca would have responded to him sexually, much the same way as she just had, and the look in his eyes confirmed exactly that.

"Then it's simple," she said pragmatically, "you need to tell her how you feel, and don't take no for an answer." She tried to smile, even though she was hurting, "If that fails, then you'll have to get Emily to pitch for you."

That made him laugh, and an image sprung into her mind of dear sweet Emily trying to persuade Rebecca to take him on.

"Just do it, she can only say no," she paused considering something else, "if she does say no, have you got a plan B?"

"No," he admitted, "I've only just acknowledged to myself that I want her. If, as I already suspect, she doesn't want me, then I'll buy her a house so she can live with Emily and the baby, and that way, I'll get to see my son growing up."

"That sounds like a sensible plan B to me."

He lifted the hand he was holding to his lips, and kissed her fingers again, "Imogen Allen, how did you get to be such a wise owl?"

Even though her heart had been torn in two, she managed to smile back at him, "Me . . . I've always been one, although maybe not that wise where you are concerned."

He shook his head, and smiled affectionately at her, "I am sorry Imogen, really I am . . ."

"Don't," she interrupted, "We need to forget this ever happened between us," and as if to reinforce to herself also, she emphasised, "there's no need for Rebecca to find out."

He nodded in agreement, "You really are a special woman, you know that, don't you? If there's anything you ever need in the future, however small, please come to me, I definitely owe you."

"You don't owe me anything," she dismissed, "you've paid me well. Now," she smiled affectionately at him, "go and get the woman you want and live happily ever after."

As he stood, she saw genuine affection in his eyes. If only it had been more. He bent and kissed her on the lips softly, "I'll try, but she might not want me."

"Oh, I'm quite sure she will, but if not," she winked, "come back and we can commiserate lost love together."

He hugged her affectionately before making his way to the bedroom door. He wouldn't be back, she knew that. She took a deep breath in, and muttered under her breath, "What a lucky woman you are, Rebecca."

CHAPTER 46

Rebecca needed to concentrate on Emily. Apart from limited visits, and the days on the farm, this was the first time they'd been together since the death of their stepfather.

Dorothy opened the door, "There's a call for you Rebecca, it's Darlene Milner, she's quite insistent she speaks to you."

Rebecca hesitated, should she take it? The telephone would be a good way to make it clear she didn't want to see her again, ever.

She left Emily with Dorothy, and took the call in Ezzio's study. As she lifted the receiver to her ear, her eyes glanced at his huge desk, and she remembered that fateful night when he'd been so furious with her, they'd had sex on top of it, and their baby had been conceived.

"Hello, Darlene."

"Hello, Kate, it's so wonderful to hear your voice."

"It's Rebecca now, Kate's long gone."

"Well my darling, you'll always be Kate to me. I can't tell you what a relief it is to know that you won't be spending the next ten years behind bars."

Before she could interject Darlene added softly, "When can I see you?"

"You won't be seeing me again," she emphasised, "I thought I made it clear to you last time we spoke, that that part of my life is over."

"Kate . . . I mean Rebecca. I know what you said but as I explained last time, I want us to be together permanently. No more paying for sex, we can be a couple."

She was exasperated that Darlene didn't get it, "We'll never be a couple. I've moved on with my life now, and I won't be having sex with women anymore; I only did it for the money. I told you that."

"Please my darling, don't say that. I want you . . . I care about you. Spend some time with me and let me show you just how much I love you."

"Don't be ridiculous," she snapped, "you know full well there was never anything between us. I'm really sorry, but that's the way it is. Now I really must go, Ezzio's waiting."

"No, he isn't," Darlene snarled down the line, "do you think I'm totally stupid? He's here at the hotel, fucking Imogen Allen as we speak. Why you waste your time on him Lord only knows, he's a serial philanderer, with a dick for a brain, and he'll never settle for just you, baby or no baby."

God, why did that hurt so much? "I don't want him to settle for me, and I'm not going to stay on the line discussing him as he has nothing to do with my decision not to pursue a relationship with you."

"Well, I think you're holding some sort of torch for him. We were good together Kate, and we can be again if you'll just give us a chance. I really miss you so much."

"That is never going to happen," Rebecca hissed, "now please, just leave me alone."

"Right then, you're forcing my hand. Listen to this recording from Imogen's suite at the hotel."

She should have put the phone down, but for some obscure reason, stayed on the line, totally unprepared for what came next. A female's heavy breathing accelerated, and she sensed almost immediately she was listening to someone in the throes of sex. Please god, not Ezzio and Imogen?

"Oh yes, yes, harder, harder . . . I'm going to come again, EZZIO . . ."

Rebecca slammed down the phone with such force, it shattered the casing. An enormous pain exploded in the pit of her stomach, and she felt physically sick. Images of Ezzio and Imogen making love had saturated her imagination daily, so to actually hear the physical evidence of it, ripped her insides apart.

Aside from the internal ache, she questioned how Darlene had obtained the recording? She must have paid someone to bug the room. What a dangerous woman she was.

Rebecca felt nauseous, completely unable to remove the image of the two of them from her mind. They must be celebrating.

To calm herself, she took a few deep breaths. There was nothing she could do, and it was no more than she suspected anyway. It had always been obvious they'd end up together. She needed to concentrate on Emily now, and build a life for them both with no more hiding.

She used the downstairs cloakroom to splash cold water on her face, and headed back to the kitchen. Dorothy was chopping up vegetables, and she smiled kindly at the housekeeper, "Would you mind not accepting any further calls to the house for me please?"

"Of course, I won't," Dorothy agreed, "What about Darlene Milner, though?"

Rebecca met her eyes, "Especially her."

"Who's Darlene Milner?" Emily asked, blowing bubbles with a straw in a glass of milk.

"Nobody Em," she dismissed, "just someone that works with Ezzio." She would have to tell him about the call as he needed to know about Darlene's malicious vendetta against him.

Rebecca and Emily swam together in Ezzio's pool. Emily was in her element, and it was a delight to see her so happy. They were sat on the lower steps immersed in the water, when Emily curiously asked, "Why aren't you married to Ezzio?"

Gosh, where had that come from? "What's made you ask that?"

"'Cause you said you have to be married to have a baby."

"Did I?" she stalled, remembering saying exactly that, "I can't remember."

"You did say it when Bradley was my boyfriend and I wanted a baby. You said that I had to get married first."

"Ah yes, I remember," she admitted, "but I also said that you had to wait to be asked, and Ezzio hasn't asked me."

Emily thought for a while, "Bradley didn't ask me," she shrugged, "anyway, I don't like him anymore, 'cause he liked Molly Gibson better than me."

While they were getting dried Emily asked, "I love this pool, can we live here forever?" Bless her innocence, she didn't want to raise her hopes too much, but Ezzio had said they could stay until after the baby was born.

"We'll have to see, Em. It's been a long day and I need to speak to Ezzio and see what he says. Emily grinned knowingly, "He wants us to stay here with him."

"What makes you think that?" she asked towelling Emily's hair.

"'Cause he wants me to help look after the baby."

That didn't sound like Ezzio at all, "Did he say that?"

"Yes," she nodded, "he came to the farm to see me and said if you went to prison, I could help look after the baby."

"Oh, did he now . . . did he promise you anything else?"

"Erm . . . oh, he said he was going to take me to see you if you went to prison."

Had he really promised that?

Dorothy had made one of her home-cooked meals which Emily relished and Rebecca picked at. Neither spoke about the court case, that would come later. For now, they just enjoyed being together, and Emily's incessant chatter whiled away the time.

Rebecca collected some nightclothes from her room for Emily, and took her into the Rose bedroom next to hers, which Dorothy had prepared for her. Emily was excited to have such a lovely room, and gazed around in amazement, "Why is it called the Rose room?"

"Because all the bedrooms are named after flowers."

"What's Ezzio's called?"

"Do you know, I'm not really sure, he doesn't have a plaque on his door." Emily bounced her bottom on the luxury bed, and flung herself backwards, staring at the ceiling, until curiosity got the better of her, and she asked, "Did Ezzio win the lottery?"

The penny dropped and Rebecca smiled, "No he didn't, Em. He's worked really hard and earned lots of money, that's why he has such a lovely house."

Emily moved on, "I love it here, and I love Ezzio too," Rebecca knew what was coming next, "do you love him?"

She needed to be cautious, particularly now as it looked like his future was with Imogen. She reached for a hair brush from the dressing table, and sat behind Emily on the bed, facing the ornate dressing table mirror. As she started brushing her hair, she recalled how their mother used to spend hours doing the same to each of them in turn. It seemed such a long time ago now as so much had happened since then.

Keen not to raise her hopes, she cautiously replied, "I like him, but I need to speak to him when he gets back tonight. For all we know, he might want to make a life with Imogen."

"No, he doesn't," Emily shook her head from side to side, "he loves you."

She pulled a funny face in the mirror, "What makes you think that?"

Emily giggled, ". . . 'cause I know something."

She smiled lovingly at her dear sister and widened her eyes at her in the mirror, "And what something do you know?"

"That Imogen isn't going to be the baby's mummy."

She couldn't resist asking, "Did Ezzio say that to you?"

Emily nodded, suddenly bored with the conversation, "Can we have cupcakes again tomorrow?"

CHAPTER 47

Rebecca must have fallen asleep on the sofa because when she opened her eyes, Ezzio was sat on the sofa looking at her.

She felt groggy, "What time is it?"

"11.30."

As she struggled into a sitting position her eyes warily met his, "Did you have a nice time?" Why was she asking that?

He ignored the question, "I had some things to go through with Imogen, she'll be checking out of the hotel in the next day or so."

"Oh." Is she moving in here? "What happens now, then?"

"She'll liaise with the new solicitor that will represent Emily, although she feels it won't ever get to court," he paused, as if giving her time to digest what he'd said, "and then she'll move onto her next case, no doubt."

Was she being professional and distancing herself from the legal side of things, so she was free to pursue a relationship with Ezzio? However much it hurt, she needed to know, "What about the two of you, are you together?"

"No," irritation slipped into his voice, "why do you insist on rehashing this all of the time?" He stood up and walked towards the fireplace, as if needing to put some distance between them.

"Because I know, Ezzio."

His expression was confused, "Know what?"

"That you've been at the hotel, today . . . sleeping with her."

A silence developed between them which he didn't try to fill, almost as if he was stalling for time. Eventually, he asked, "What makes you think that?"

"Darlene rang me."

He rolled his eyes angrily, "Surely you don't believe a word she says?"

"Well, as she's got a recording of the two of you having sex, then yes, I do believe her. She must have had the hotel room bugged or something."

Ezzio looked stunned. Knowing how much he hated Darlene, she knew he'd be furious. Tension gripped his frame, "She actually told you all of this?"

"Yes, and then she played me the tape of you both."

"Jesus Christ," he cursed.

***

Ezzio was dumbfounded. Always one step ahead of the opposition, but this time, he'd been outmanoeuvred. Still standing, he furiously shoved his hands in his pockets and turned towards the mantelpiece. A framed photograph of his parents stared back at him, almost as if they were silently urging him on. He recalled fondly the years they'd lived together as a family unit, and how he'd witnessed their love for each other on a daily basis, they simply adored each other. If he was to ever have any sort of relationship akin to that, then he needed to fight for Rebecca. The thought of her leaving was like an elastic band tightening around his heart. He had to somehow persuade her to stay, but because of

Darlene's disclosure, all avenues were now closed, so truth was the only option he had.

He eased himself into a sitting position on the large marble coffee table directly in front of her on the sofa. Backed into a corner, he knew that the next few minutes were crucial if he had any hope of a future with her. He took a deep breath, "Ok, yes, I did have sex with Imogen today, but that's all it was," his eyes focussed intensely upon hers, "she made it clear all the way through the trial that she wanted me, but I never lied to you, nothing happened between us until today."

"Oh, well, as long as you didn't lie," she flung at him.

He understood her sarcasm and the necessity to lash out, "Please, just listen to me, will you? I promised Imogen that if she secured your acquittal, she could have anything she wanted. I gave her cash but she . . . desired more." He emphasised the last two words before continuing, "You can guess the rest. I paid up in full today, and now it's over between us. She knows there's no future for her and I, which is what she really wants."

***

She was staggered by his dismissive attitude, "Let me get this straight, you had sex with Imogen as a payment for services rendered," she scowled disbelievingly, "what do you think that makes you?"

Despite her obvious fury, he just shrugged his shoulders, "It meant nothing to me."

"That's alright, then, is it . . . if it meant nothing to you," she jeered, utterly exasperated, "what sort of man are you?"

"An honourable one," he snapped, "I gave her what she wanted, end of. It doesn't have to affect us."

"An honourable man," she shrieked "have you heard yourself? Honourable, you're no more than a . . a. . . male prostitute."

"So what," his eyes flashed fire, "you earned your money that way for long enough, so now we're equal."

God that really hurt. She swallowed, "We could never be equal," her voice dropped an octave, "Look, what you did with Imogen is your business, there is no us. I know we have to plan for the baby, but as for you and me, it was over before it even began. Without the baby, we would never have even seen each other again."

He exhaled impatiently, "Yes but we are where we are . . . no, hear me out. I admit it started out as a physical attraction; I wanted you and was prepared to do anything to get you. And yes, initially it was just sex," he paused as if searching for the right words, "but somewhere along the way things changed. I have feelings for you, and I've fought your corner every step of the way with everything I have." His eyes were growing darker and he pleaded in a weary voice, "You're a free woman now, please stay and let me look after you, and the baby . . . and Emily. At least give it some consideration."

She shook her head, "I can't. All I can see when I close my eyes is you making love to Imogen. All I can hear in my head is the two of you together and her screaming for you to fuck her harder. Have you any idea how difficult that would be to erase?"

His nod signalled his agreement, and she glimpsed his anguish as he briefly closed his eyes and pinched the bridge of his nose with his thumb and forefinger before taking her hand in his.

"I'm not trying to minimise that, but in time it will fade. Just remember I wasn't sleeping with you when I had sex with her."

"You were," she contradicted, "you have been intimate with me."

His jaw tightened, "Yes but I've held back from full sex with you, haven't I? You begged me for it, and I didn't."

She pulled her hand free from his, "So what is it you're asking, that I welcome you with open arms and to erase the fact that this afternoon, you've been in bed with a woman, while the one you supposedly want to be with is at home carrying your baby?" Refusing to give him a chance to speak, she carried on, "Every time you leave the house, I'd be wondering who you were with and if you were having sex with them."

"I've never had two women at the same time," he angrily bit back, "I would never let you down, I promise you. I never wanted Imogen, she wanted me. It's you I want . . . you have to believe that." His eyes scrutinised her intensely, almost as if he was assessing her response before continuing, "I want a life with you in it. You have no idea how hard it's been for me wanting you and holding back. Even when I was satisfying you and was frustrated myself, I didn't fall into Imogen's arms. I just had to deal with things myself like a schoolboy," he paused for a second and his expression seemed tortured, something she hadn't seen in him before, "All my life I've been self-reliant and independent, and yes, some would say, extremely selfish. I admit that, but suddenly it's all changed; I swear to you, I've never met a woman that makes me feel like you do."

He placed his hands on her knees, and his gaze softened, "I'm in awe of your courage. The way you were prepared to take the punishment to protect Emily, with little thought for your own needs all of these years," he swallowed, "it makes me feel humbled, and I want to take care of you and our son."

As if that wasn't enough to melt her heart, his voice cracking with emotion, finished her off completely, "I'm already fond of Emily . . . don't take her away now . . . please don't. Can't you just give us a chance?"

Could she . . . should she? Despite being the enemy, somewhere along the way, she'd fallen for him, but hated the thought of him with Imogen. Would she be able to move on and put that behind her?

"Okay, if you are being totally honest about this forced sex you had to perform today, how many times did Imogen climax."

"Once."

"You're lying, I heard the tape."

"For fuck's sake, Rebecca, once twice, who the hell cares, you have to let this go. It meant nothing to me, it was just sex. While you're so pissed off with me, did you bother to listen to the tape and hear that I didn't come?"

He can't be serious.

He raised his voice, "Well did you?"

"I didn't listen that long, but what the hell difference does that make anyway?"

"Quite a lot in my eyes," he said heavily, "the sex felt wrong, but I was just satisfying her. In my own naïve way, I was holding myself back for you."

She was completely thrown, "So you're trying to tell me that you didn't climax during sex?"

"That's exactly what I'm telling you."

"And you expect me to believe that?"

"It's the truth for Christ's sake."

A thought suddenly struck about the consequences if he wasn't telling the truth.

"Did you use a condom?"

"Yes, I always do." He sighed deeply and reached for her hand again, clasping it in both of his. His control was slipping, and sweat beads were forming on his forehead.

"Please . . . I'm begging now, don't go. I've never asked a woman to stay before because I've never wanted to, but with you it's different. I want to build a life with you. I want to get to know all of you and find out about Rebecca Price Jones. I want to wake up with you each day, come home to you at night, and prepare together for the baby . . . I want us to have a normal relationship. When you think about it, I've only ever taken you out to dinner once," his lips twitched a tender smile, "and that was more a getting-in-your-knickers kind of dinner rather than a getting to know you one."

She grimaced inwardly at his crudeness as he moved next to her on the sofa.

"I've always been a loner since my parents died, but everything has changed. I want to build a home together and be a family. We can wipe the slate clean now. I can't get over what that bastard of a stepfather did to you and Emily. I want to take care of you both, and our baby. Please, come to bed with me now and let this be a new beginning and the first time for both of us."

It was tempting . . . but hang on, "First time for both of us," she scorned, "I hardly think so. In case you hadn't noticed, I've got evidence we've had sex before growing inside me, and as you have been having sex with someone else all afternoon, how is it going to be a first for either of us?"

"Because," he paused, his eyes looking searchingly into hers, "you'll be making love for the first time with your fiancé, and as far as I know you haven't done that before." The tremor of his hand as he smoothed her hair from her face brought a lump to her throat.

Fiancé, who said anything about getting married? A warm feeling enveloped her whole body, and was that her heart that just missed a beat? While she could agree with the sentiment of his words, she was still puzzled, "Okay, then, yes I guess that would be a first, but try as I might, I'm struggling how you making love could ever be classed as a first considering the amount of women you've been with."

Judging by the glimmer in his eye, he seemed prepared for her disparaging remarks, and quickly added, "Ah, well, here's the thing. I've only ever had sex before. Admittedly, there's been rather a lot of it, but that's all it's ever been. That's really all I know," his gaze softened, "but tonight I want to truly make love to you, so it's a new beginning for both of us."

Considering he'd spent the afternoon satisfying Imogen, could she erase that from her mind? He must have had great restraint holding himself back in the throes of her ecstasy. The way he said he was holding back for her made her feel special, which was completely inexplicable.

"And if I agree to this 'first time for both of us' fantasy, aren't you too tired?"

Hope flickered in his eyes as he shook his head, "Never."

"And are you likely to climax with me?"

Tenderly, he tipped her chin, "You know I will."

She was captivated by his hypnotic brown eyes, and any composure she had, started to crumble as he smiled so lovingly at her. Didn't she owe it to her unborn baby to at least try to build a life with this man? He'd come into her life like a tornado, waking something in her that she couldn't explain, and it was because of him that she was here now, a free woman.

Was he serious about wanting to marry her? A flame of hope blazed within her, and she widened her eyes in feigned surprise, "Well I must say, when I woke up this morning, the last thing I expected to get was a marriage proposal."

Quickly, his large hands grasped her head, and as he eased her face gently towards his own, his eyes twinkled playfully, "Say yes and that's not all you're going to get today."

She smiled at his cheek, "Only Ezzio Marin would try to win a woman's heart with a promise of great sex."

"I don't know what your brazen mind is thinking about, Miss Jones," he grinned, "but I'm talking about an engagement ring."

"Yeah, sure you are," she laughed, as his lips came down on hers in a kiss full of promise of their future.

CHAPTER 48

Darlene sat in her car and the view through her binoculars made it clear that Kate had ignored the tape of Ezzio in the throes of sex. She could see them both embracing in the bedroom window. Why, when he was such a dick-brained womanising bastard, did she want to be with him?

Henry, her trusted friend, had initially been reluctant to have the hotel room bugged, but as always, he did as she requested, and even extracted from the complete tape, the part she needed which proved beyond doubt Ezzio having sex with the slut lawyer.

But what good had the tape done when she was still with him? This extraordinary woman was far too lovely to be touched by any man intimately, and the thought of a penis penetrating her beautiful body was totally abhorrent to her. Kate was hers, and she'd be damned if anyone else was going to have her, especially smooth talking Ezzio Marin who was no more than a wolf in sheep's clothing.

Minutes ticked by as she tried to plan, but she must have dozed off because when she looked again through the binoculars, the curtains had been closed at the bedroom window. The two of them sharing a bed tore her insides apart, and she squeezed her eyes tightly shut to try and clear her head . . . it's all those bloody tablets.

Her hip flask, disappointingly, was almost empty, so she drained the last dregs of gin, and tossed it on the floor. She opened the glove box and retrieved the small calibre handgun, which had been a total surprise when her husband had given it to her years earlier, 'to protect herself'. As she placed it in her bag, the tight band of heaviness around her head worsened, but she quickly dismissed it knowing that she needed to do this once and for all.

She draped her handbag across her body like a satchel, and exited the car, heading straight for the cottage at the side of the house. It was a relief that she'd worn trousers as the hedge shrubs persistently attacked her legs. Confidently, she approached the loose fence panel, remembering the night she'd got in the grounds previously to see Kate and tell her how much she cared, but Kate had been dismissive that night and wouldn't listen. Well, she'll listen tonight.

Thankfully, her previous effort to disguise the slack panel had paid off; it hadn't been repaired. Just a slight wrench to pull the panel off and she had access to the grounds behind what once must have been a gamekeeper's lodge. She climbed over the wall, and tiptoed past the cottage which she deduced must now be the home of a staff member, as it looked lived in with pretty curtains adorning the windows. A sudden illumination from an outside security light halted her progress briefly, but nobody came. Purposefully, she edged along the brick wall to the main house. Her head was throbbing and she was perspiring heavily, but she had nothing to lose now.

The voice in her head was becoming more frequent, urging her on, do it . . . do it . . . do it. She shook her head from side to side, as if that would take the acute pain away. Her thoughts had taken her no further than knocking on the front door as she knew

Ezzio would have security equipment, so getting into the house would be almost impossible.

But tonight luck was on her side. As it was such a warm and balmy night, the patio door downstairs was slightly ajar which indicated the house hadn't been secured for the night. Just shows his brain is in his trousers . . . fucking stupid Ezzio Marin with his mind on sex, had forgotten to lock up properly.

With a clammy hand, she pressed the patio door handle down half expecting the alarm sensors to register her presence and go off, but they didn't. All was quiet.

As she entered the house, she paused to allow her eyes to become accustomed to the dark, and inhaled deeply. Kate had been in the room recently, she could smell her perfume. It spurred her on, and she purposefully made her way into the hallway and stared tensely at the huge dominant spiral staircase. Surefooted and slowly, she mounted the steps, one-by-one, taking her time to make sure nothing creaked. As she tiptoed up to the top, the ever present voice in her head reminded her, do it . . . do it . . . do it.

The room they were in was located at the back of the house, which she'd scrutinised earlier through the binoculars, praying then that Kate would leave. Yet once again she'd been brainwashed by his charm, and despite his philandering ways, she'd chosen cock over her.

As she faced the enormous bedroom door, she paused and wiped her sweaty palms down the front of her trousers. The pain in her head was becoming unbearable, and she shook it rigorously as if it would miraculously erase the intolerable throbbing. It didn't.

Her hand delved inside her leather bag, and she felt for the small handgun. Once she'd located it, and positioned it securely in her right hand, she took another deep breath. Almost in slow motion, she reached forward and grasped the ornate knob with her other hand, and turned it slowly anti clockwise, to ease the door open.

Although heavy drapes covered the bay window, the room was bathed in moonlight from a roof window, and directly facing the door in a huge lavish double bed lay Ezzio and Kate, entwined together in a sleeping position. Both moved simultaneously at the sound of the door opening.

With the flick of her wrist, Darlene raised the gun, and aimed at her target . . . do it . . . kill.

"What the . . ."

Her finger squeezed the trigger once . . . then pulled it again. She stood motionless watching, as deep red blood oozed from the naked flesh, before placing the gun to her temple, and firing a third time.

EPILOGUE

Rebecca stared at Ezzio whose skin appeared a darker shade of brown as he lay against the crisp white hospital sheets. The medical team had spent the last twenty-four hours withdrawing the ventilator which had been breathing for him.

Due to the endless hours she'd spent urging Ezzio to keep strong and not leave her, and observing the medical staff and their interventions, she was now familiar with the purpose of the ventilator. Until this tragedy, she'd only known a ventilator as a life support machine, although she preferred to still think of it that way as she knew without doubt that without it, Ezzio wouldn't be alive.

As she watched the doctor withdraw a tube from his mouth, Ezzio spluttered, but still, he didn't wake. The doctors told her it could take hours for him to regain consciousness, if at all, so she was prepared to sit and wait.

The monitoring equipment seemed to be attached to every part of his body. The constant beep, beep, beeping of his heart would be indelibly inked on her brain, and even though the sound was reassuring and meant he was alive, it was incessant and telling on her frayed nerves.

Taking his warm hand in hers, she held it against her cheek willing him to live and give them the future he'd promised with their baby. She thought back to the shooting; was it only three short nights ago that he'd had placed his hand protectively on her tummy promising to cherish them both forever? That same night when they'd truly made love for the first time and she'd witnessed a tender, loving side of Ezzio Marin. Gone was the driven businessman, the clever strategist and the ruthless victor, and in his place was a caring man, loving her with complete sensitivity and adoration. He was hers, and she knew beyond any doubt that she loved him. Please God, I beg you, don't take him from me now.

Four hours later Rebecca was pleased by the interruption of her sister arriving. Rebecca smiled to herself knowing it was unlikely Emily would keep away for long, she was far too curious.

"Where's Dorothy?" she whispered quietly.

"In the waiting room next door, the nurses have given her a cup of tea."

Emily peered at the sleeping Ezzio from the foot of the bed, "I wish he'd wake up. I want to know what his bedroom's called. I've asked Dorothy," she paused as if recalling Dorothy's exact words, "but she says she hasn't got a clue."

Rebecca smiled at her beautiful innocence that she loved so much, "Come and sit down with me for a while," she urged. Emily did so, and placed her hand on top of hers holding onto Ezzio's. Impatient as ever, she was clearly fed up with waiting, and muttered encouragingly, "You're supposed to be awake now Ezzio, wake up."

"Shush. I know it's hard waiting, but he'll wake up when he's ready."

Emily looked thoughtful, "But what if he doesn't and stays asleep . . . you know, like sleeping beauty, she slept for hundreds of years." Deep in thought about the implications of her statement, she asked, "Would we still be able to live at his house?' Rebecca had a sudden urge to laugh out loud . . . out of the mouths of babes, her mother would say.

Interrupting her thoughts, Rebecca felt a slight movement of Ezzio's hand in hers. She watched as his eyelids twitch slightly, and as he coughed, his eyes continued to flicker. The changing tone of the monitor must have alerted the nurses' station, as a nurse came rushing in. She opened his eyelid and shone a small torch in his eyes.

"He's waking up. I'll get the doctor," she told them. Rebecca and Emily sat, still clutching his hand, willing him to wake up as his eyes fluttered open and closed. Within seconds, he attempted to speak. His voice was barely audible as he whispered, "Tell me I'm not dreaming and I made it?"

Rebecca's eyes brimmed with tears . . . he was alive. Lovingly she stroked the side of his face as he struggled to focus, "Yes, you definitely made it. Don't try to speak though; you're dosed up to the eyeballs with morphine.

Ezzio took a breath in and croaked, "Ah, that explains why I'm seeing double, then."

Emily giggled, "No, Ezzio, that's 'cause me and Rebecca are here and we both look the same." She turned curiously to Rebecca, and asked, "He's not going to die anymore, is he?"

Ezzio's lips twitched at her innocent directness, "No," he murmured hoarsely, "I'm not going to die, I promise you."

Emily looked pleased and stood up, "That's good, then. Can I go find Dorothy now, she said she would take me shopping?" Rebecca let out a deep sigh, only Emily could talk about dying and shopping in the same sentence.

"Of course you can, be good for her. . . ."

The doctor arrived and Emily hesitated, clearly wanting to stay in case she missed something. The doctor proceeded to check the monitor and then asked Ezzio if he knew his date of birth, the name of the Prime Minister, and which year it currently was, all of which he was able to croak an answer.

Once the doctor had finished examining him, and there was nothing more to see, Emily decided once again, it was time to go. Rebecca's heart melted watching her gently kissing Ezzio's cheek and stroking his forehead, "I'll come and see you tomorrow, and make you some cupcakes with Dorothy now you've woken up."

He managed a smile and a nod.

As Emily headed towards the door, a sudden thought struck Rebecca, "Oh, Em, no more lottery tickets eh?" Her eyes drifted lovingly towards the bed, "I think Lady Luck has already paid us a visit."

Emily screwed her face up, "Who's she?"

Joy Wood

As a working nurse, I've been creating stories in my head for years, but have never found the time, or had the confidence to do anything with them.

In 2014, I attended an 'Author Day' in my home town, and was inspired by local writers who gave me the encouragement to put one of my stories onto paper.

For the Love of Emily is my first attempt at a novel, and I sincerely hope you enjoyed it. Any feedback would be greatly appreciated, so please get in touch, I'd love to hear from you.

joymarywood@yahoo.co.uk

Lightning Source UK Ltd.
Milton Keynes UK
UKHW03f0004170418
321166UK00001B/23/P

9 781785 108860